ROYAL FLUSH

Also by Margaret Irwin
in Hamlyn Paperbacks

THE BRIDE
*the story of Louise
and Montrose*

ROYAL FLUSH

Margaret Irwin

St. Martin's Press
New York

Library of Congress Cataloging in Publication Data

Irwin, Margaret.

    Royal flush.
    1. Orléans, Henriette-Anne, duchesse d', 1644-1670
—Fiction.   I. Title.
PR6017.R84R6   1983   823'.912   83-2985
ISBN 0-312-69471-7

First U.S. Edition

10 9 8 7 6 5 4 3 2 1

First published in Great Britain by Chatto & Windus Ltd.

CONTENTS

•

To J. R. Monsell

NOTE
**None of the characters
in this book is imaginary**

BOOK I

COLD DAWN

CHAPTER ONE

She lay in bed, hugging her shoulders, her knees drawn up to her thin chest, her toes cramped close together with the cold. Sometimes she stretched down her hands to rub them and then she could feel her knees jerking against her ribs. She was small for her age, and if she did not lie stretched out in bed she would never grow up to be tall and straight as a princess should be. She was not quite straight; one shoulder was a little higher than the other (but only a very little, she was told).

But she could not stretch out in this cold. The single thin blanket had been folded four times to cover her and if she kicked or turned there would be a fresh draught at some corner. So she lay still except for rubbing her feet, and kept her nose just under the blanket in spite of its tickling, and peeped out over the edge of it to see the hard grey snow that had been encrusted for so many days now against the window-pane; to see her mother, in her shabby old green dress, stoop over the fireplace from time to time and poke and turn over the single lump of dull red coal and feed it with little bits of sticks, then kneel down and blow upon it till a few sparks shot up and a lively crackling noise told that one of the sticks had caught a flame. Her mother held out her hands to it, thin ringless hands that were blue at the tips, then straightened her back with a little sigh, rose and went back to the table where she sat writing, writing, till the child in the bed had long since ceased to count the number of times she dipped her quill into the ink-horn. The flame died down. The white quill was now the only thing that moved in the darkening room, its faint scratching the only sound. A little time ago the clock in the courtyard had struck three, and

1

yet it was growing dark, the days were in such a hurry to end.

At last the figure at the table rose, came over to the child in the bed, and tucked the folded blanket more closely round her. She moved quickly and with a pounce, like a cat that has never quite ceased to be a kitten. She was a very small woman, her face a pale oval, with dark hollows under the eyes, which were large and of a shining, mournful beauty. Her teeth spoiled her looks, for they stuck out. Wisps of black-grey hair, that should have been curled, fell over her forehead as she stooped down to the bed.

She said anxiously, 'You are warm now, Minette?'

'Yes, Mamma, quite warm.'

The Queen of England put a hand in under the blanket and felt the small sharp shoulder. The child curled up under the touch with a cooing sound of pleasure. She thought that Mamma was going to play with her. But the Queen's voice sounded anxious and distraite as ever.

'You do not feel very warm. I wonder if I could get a brick heated to put to your feet.'

'Oh, let me get up, please, and jump about.'

'No, child, not yet. Your vest is not yet dry.'

'What a vest! It has been by the fire all day.'

'But by what a fire!' said Queen Henrietta and actually smiled. Minette laughed, and at once the Queen began to cry.

'Oh, Mamma, I am so sorry.'

She ought not to have laughed, for her father was in prison and his cruel enemies would not let her mother go and see him, however many letters she wrote. But she had never known her father, and her family were always in prison. A brother and sister of hers were in prison with him, and it was difficult to go on being sorry for them all. She tried now to look sorry.

'No, no, child. Laugh whenever you can.'

'But indeed I won't, if it makes you cry.'

And she tucked her head under the blanket and burrowed right down under it. When she had first seen her mother cry it had given Minette a shock of disgust that her face should look so red and ugly, above all, so different. She was ashamed of having felt this, she hated to remember it, and always did.

It was scratchy down under the blanket. They had parted with their sheets long ago. 'Now I'm a rabbit,' she thought,

2

and felt snug and safe. Nobody could find her in her burrow underground.

There were scratching, fumbling sounds in the room and then the darkness under the blanket glowed very faintly, for the Queen had lit a small lamp from a taper thrust into the fire; Minette, pretending a necessity for caution, put up her head to see her mother tugging at the heavy shutters, covering up those grey frozen lumps of snow on the window-pane.

That was better. The room now looked warmer, though it did not feel it. But now there was no further change to look forward to until their supper, and perhaps even that would not come. This morning there had only been a very small piece of bread between them, and because her mother had said she was not hungry Minette had felt obliged to say so too, and they had had to persuade each other to swallow each crumb. She was now so hungry that she no longer felt it, only odd and light as though she might float away from herself.

Her very nose did not feel part of her; it was so cold it might have been a button that a malicious fairy had planted in the middle of her face. However hard she sniffed and rubbed it on the back of her hand it went on being damp at the tip. Why should she have a nose like that; why should she be here in this big hard bed with only one blanket on it; and why had her father's enemies threatened to cut off his head? It could never happen, they said, for such a thing had never happened to any king before. But strange things did happen. All their servants had left them and here they were shut up all alone in this vast empty dusty place, which she had been told was the Palace of the Louvre. They could not go out because of the fighting in the streets outside and the unpleasant sight of dead bodies. Sometimes the cannon made a dreadful noise, and then her mother told her that she had been born during a siege and must not mind.

Only now, on this everlasting dark silent day when she had had to stay in bed and no one had been to see them, did she suddenly realize for herself that here she was, Henriette, to call herself by her real name, youngest daughter of the King of England, that she had nothing else to put on while her vest was being washed, she, Henriette, and nobody else, chosen out of all the little girls that had ever lived or ever would live, to be lying in bed at just this moment of a January day and wonder what was going to happen next.

3

What happened next was a knock on the door. It would be Father Cyprian. No, it was the new English abbé, Mr Walter Montagu, for she knew the elegant and way he blew his nose, which he had to do in the very middle of his greeting to her mother. It sounded as though he had a bad cold, and she heard him breathing heavily, as though he had been running. There was a rustling sound as the Queen pounced forward and asked what news, and then came a great sigh. Mr Montagu's voice began in horror at the fire, and the Queen's joined in in duet. There was no more coal or wood. There was no more money to buy any. There was nothing left to pawn. 'Nothing is left to us, nothing, nothing,' said the Queen's voice over and over again in Minette's memory; for that was what her mother had said when she had pawned the little gold cup that Minette had loved. Its ghost danced just in front of her cold nose in the woolly scratchy darkness under the blanket. It had been made by somebody in a strange country where little boys had tails and horns and goats' legs, for there they had been dancing round the edge of the cup in and out of a maze of vine-leaves. She tried to pretend she was playing with them in a country where everything was made of gold and grapes fell into their mouths. The voices at the end of the room were like a dog and cat talking – Mr Montagu's gruff with his cold, reading aloud the Queen's letter, advising, correcting, bow wow *wow*. ('It's not a big dog – it's a soft silky one, a spaniel,' thought Minette.) Her mother's voice was the purring one that shot up into little hissing sighs, and once into a shrill spurt of laughter, answered after a pause by a rather sharp astonished bark; it asked small sad questions, not of Mr Montagu, but of Heaven, for whom, however, Mr Montagu would answer comfortingly and assuringly with no need to pause and growl as when he spoke of the Pope or the King of Spain and the likelihood of their assistance.

She fell asleep to the sound of the voices, and woke to hear silence. She peeped out of her blanket and saw her mother's grey head on the table, fallen on her clenched hands. Mr Montagu was standing beside her, he put his hand on her shoulder. She made no movement. He said, 'Madam, I beg of you – do not despair – God is with you.'

She answered, 'There is no God.'

'There are your sons. There is your child here the Princess Henriette.'

4

At the sound of her name, Minette knew that she was awake; she shrieked out 'Mamma!' and her mother sprang up; her face though wild was recognizable; she ran over to the bed, holding out her arms, and Minette threw herself into them and would not let go, so that her mother had to lift her and carry her over to the fireplace, gently scolding and soothing her, telling her there was nothing to be frightened of. Had she had a bad dream? Here was kind Mr Montagu to take care of her.

But Minette would not look at the new Englishman. She hated him for being there while her mother had put her head on the table. And her mother, who made her say her prayers so often, had said there was no God. She stared up at her mother's face. Every line in it was as she had always known it.

But grey, dishevelled, abandoned, her mother's head would lie on the table ever after, in a picture buried deep at the back of her mind. Not only did she never forget it, but she found afterwards it was the first thing that she could remember; all that had happened to her before was lost in the oblivion of her unconscious infancy; while that icy and terrible day in bed sprang clear and full-formed in her memory, so that it seemed to her that she had been born on that day when she had discovered herself, Minette, rubbing a nose as cold as a damp button under the blanket.

CHAPTER TWO

A wonderful present arrived the next day. It was an enormously fat piece of mutton, and when Queen Henrietta went to carve it open there was a bag of two thousand crowns concealed in its belly. This delicate tribute from an old admirer made her shed tears of joy. They were saved from starvation. Firewood followed, and food and a subsidy of money from the French Parliament. Old friends arrived again from the scattered court of English exiles, telling each other the adventures they had had in the warlike streets outside; and a new-comer, a tall fair boy who was Minette's brother, James. Best of all her governess, her dear Morton, was with her again and petting her even more than usual; though that, perversely, made her uneasy. But everybody seemed uneasy. They rattled here and there, moving and smiling unnecessarily,

5

talking a great deal, as though they did not dare leave a pause in which to hear of any fresh calamity.

Yet they did not talk so much of England as usual, but of this war in Paris of the Fronde, a war of schoolboys and their catapults that had given it that name; of court ladies and gallants in feathers and silk stockings who asked the ladies to dinner after a battle. But it was serious enough to have sent the French royal family packing to the safer air of the palace at Saint Germain. Minette and her mother might go there too, or else they might go and live among the naked savages in Ireland. Or to the Hague and join her eldest brother, Charles, and her eldest sister who was married to the Dutch prince, and her Aunt Elizabeth.

James had just come from the Hague and could talk of nothing but this English aunt, Elizabeth of Bohemia, who was as good a sportswoman as any man, and yet was called the Queen of Hearts – and the Winter Queen too – she had all sorts of nicknames – and when she wasn't hunting she wouldn't get up in the morning but lie in bed for hours, playing with all her pet dogs. And all her children (dozens of them there seemed to be) did nothing but laugh and squabble and tease each other from morning to night. He said they too were exiles and as poor as church mice, but he had never had such a jolly Christmas. When their cousin Sophie and Charles were together it was as good as a play, and he described Sophie's imitation of herself as a shivering little girl, reciting her task from Pebrac's *Precepts and Practice* on a winter's morning under the eye of the old governess who was cleaning her teeth with horrible grimaces.

'Oh, why do we not go to the Hague?' cried Minette. 'Mam, do let us all go to the Hague.'

And Mam, with a rather sad look, at which Minette at once felt guilty though she did not know of what, said, 'Why, Minette, do you want so to see your aunt?'

'Yes, Mam, I want to see why she is called the Queen of Hearts.'

'She is called it because many people think her a very charming woman,' said the Queen, and Minette wondered how she had displeased her. She rubbed her head against her sleeve and said, 'Then don't they call you the Queen of Hearts?' But Mam did not laugh at her and call her a shocking little courtier; she stroked her head and told her solemnly that charm was a dangerous gift unless it were used only for

6

God's service, and Minette said, 'Yes, Mam,' equally solemnly, and played with the cross on her mother's chain, and wished more than ever they would go to the Hague.

Messengers had been dispatched to Saint Germain for news, but none came. Then James offered to go; and his mother begged him to stay, and at the same time said she could live no longer without news.

'I shall stifle if I stay here,' said James, and went. But he sent back no messenger; and the little circle from the English court seemed as much cut off as if they were on a desert island. Nothing came through from outside but secret scurrying whispers. Wherever Minette went she came on people sitting in twos and threes in corners, talking very low, and they stopped as soon as they saw her, and smiled very hard and asked what she would like to play at now.

'Let us play at running away,' she said to Lady Morton, and then in a burst of audacity, 'Let us really run away.' They had done so once, disguised as beggars, and had got through a siege held by Cromwell's soldiers and slept under a hedge. But Minette had been only two and a half then, and did not remember it. 'I should like to run away with you again now, dear, dear Morton.'

'And leave your dear Mamma, who has only got you with her now?'

'Oh – oh *no*,' and Minette was abashed. Nevertheless, she was afraid to stay with her dear Mamma these days; the Queen was often as merry with her as ever, and always as tender, and yet there was something fierce and strained about her; she would clutch the child so violently to her that Minette could scarcely breathe, and in the literal fashion of her age supposed that that was why her brother James had complained of stifling here.

The Queen had ceased to write petitions to the English Parliament; she had heard they were not even opened. But one answer came to all the letters that begged leave to go and see her husband once more before he died.

By her own act, wrote Cromwell, she had refused to be crowned as Queen Consort of England, and had therefore forfeited her rights as wife as well as Queen. After that, she wrote only to her husband.

A messenger came at last from Saint Germain, but he did not see the Queen.

She now stood a little apart from all the rest, but she did

7

not know it. Those who spoke to her did so with difficulty, and the delicate hand of her secretary, Mr Cowley, trembled as it translated her loving messages to King Charles into his cipher.

Once he went on writing after the Queen had finished dictating and had left the room, and Minette pulled at his elbow and asked him to tell her what he had added to the letter.

'Nothing,' he said. 'What I wrote afterwards, Princess, has nothing to do with the letter.'

But she with childish obstinacy insisted that he should tell her what it was, and he read out in his precise, elegant voice the words that he had scribbled on another sheet of paper:

> *'And on my soul hung the dull weight*
> *Of some intolerable fate.'*

'Is that a poem, then? It is too short.'

'Much too short, Princess. Some day I may add to it.'

It was well on in February now. A peasant girl had given a bunch of snowdrops to the Palace guard 'for the poor Queen of England'. A servant brought them in with the message to where the Queen sat by the fire talking to Madame de Motteville, and the company looked at them nervously, and Minette heard one complain of the servant's stupidity. Suddenly she burst out crying. Everyone crowded round her, and told her that she was tired or that she had a pain or that princesses did not cry; they seemed quite glad to go on talking about her crying.

Yet for once her mother did not pay any attention to it. She stood up and said in a loud voice, 'Is there no one will go to Saint Germain and bring me news from England?'

Nobody answered, nor approached her. She stood there alone, and all the rest stood close together. There was a sob, but it did not come from Minette and she did not see who was crying. Her own tears had stopped. At last Lord Jermyn came forward and stood beside the Queen; he took her hand and looked down into her face, and began, 'Madame—' and then stopped, and then again, 'Madame, my Lord the King – Madame, it is of no use now for anyone to go to Saint Germain.'

She still stood there, looking up at him in question, with that trustful air she always wore when with Lord Jermyn.

8

'They would never dare,' she began. 'You said they would never dare.'

He was so spruce and curled and scented, he might have been a great wax doll standing there, until one saw his eyes. Agony was in them, and terror, and not for himself. His curved lips moved beneath his soft fair moustache and could bring out no sound at first. At last he said it:

'He has been foully murdered.'

Still she stood there, and neither spoke nor moved. They clustered round her now, weeping and kneeling to her, kissing her hand and the hem of her dress. She stood quite alone in the midst of them, noticing none of them.

'The shock has turned her reason,' said Madame de Motteville to Lady Morton, who had taken Minette up in her arms. The child clung to her convulsively. Lady Morton carried her out of the room.

'Where are we going?' asked Minette in a high infantile treble. 'Shall we go and see the girl who brought the snowdrops?'

'No, but we will find the kitten, shall we?'

Minette played diligently with the kitten, and when anyone came and talked to Lady Morton, appeared absorbed in her game. But she heard them say that the Queen had not yet spoken nor given any sign of life, that the shock was too great, that not all they had said could prepare her, for like all of them she had refused to believe this terrible news was even possible.

Minette had her dinner and cut a castle out of her piece of bread, showing it to her governess in confidence that this time she would not be reproved for playing with her food. Then she gave the kitten some milk in a saucer, and then climbed on to her governess's lap and said, 'Now tell me how you dressed me up in rags and called me Pierre, and I was angry and told everybody, "No, I'm not Pierre, I'm the Princess." '

And Lady Morton began to tell it all again for the hundredth time, but this time she stopped in the middle and said, 'Ah, Princess, you have lost the tenderest father that any child could have, and you have never known him; and now God knows what will happen to us all.'

Minette saw that the tears were running down her cheeks, so she looked down again quickly and occupied herself very busily with Lady Morton's silver chatelaine while she asked:

'Where was I before I was born?'

9

'I don't know,' said Lady Morton.

'Does God know?'

'Surely yes. – Dear changeling,' said the governess, gazing at the child's elfin face. When only a fortnight old, an infant with peaked ears and pointed chin, a creature so tiny and fragile that it seemed to have been made out of a white rose petal, she had been placed in Morton's sole charge while the Queen escaped to France. After two years the governess had followed with the baby princess, who had stolen all her care and attention and even her heart from Morton's own children to be devoted to herself. And there she was, perched on her knee, clamouring cuckoo-like for any crumbs that would distract attention from the sorrow that hemmed them round. Morton dimly perceived her unconscious purpose, struggled to comply with it, and found she did not know what they were talking of.

'Could I see what happened before I was born?' pleaded the insistent chirp.

'No, Princess, for you were still in your royal mother's womb.'

'Please go on.'

'The King your father was in the midst of battles and many troubles at the time. He wrote the doctor a letter all in one line, and I saw it. "Mayerne, for love of me, go to my wife, Charles R".' She flung back her head to choke down a fresh burst of tears.

Minette wriggled down from the lap. 'I think I had better see what the kitten is doing,' she said.

Soon after that Madame de Motteville and another lady came in and talked for a long time with Lady Morton, and then Lady Morton came over to the child, and asked if she would not like to come now and see her dear mother. Minette said yes, if she could take the kitten. They smiled sadly at her and told her she had better leave it; so she seized instead a Punchinello doll that her mother had made for her out of coloured rags, and declared that she could not be parted from her poor Tom, 'Mamma's poor Tom.'

Still clutching it, she was brought to where the Queen sat and looked at nothing. Minette ran to her, and began a long rambling story of poor Tom and the kitten. All the ladies round were watching, but still Mamma did not look at her, and to make her do so she thrust the doll into her arms and said, 'Look, Mam, poor Tom's a-cold.' She had been chatter-

10

ing in French as always with her mother, though Lady Morton talked English with her, but said the last words in English as her mother had often said them, laughing; and so hoped now to make her laugh. They were the words in an English play of a poor faithful fool who had been driven out with the old King his master to die upon the heath. The Queen had found something to amuse her in the gaping, shivering creature in motley, and used to repeat his words in idle mimicry to her husband when she coaxed him. 'Poor Tom's a-cold. What will you give him?' and the answer was a kiss.

Minette had succeeded. Her mother had noticed her, was in fact holding her to her breast in an almost frantic clasp; she was pouring tears and words over her head, calling her her poor fatherless child. Minette began to cry loudly.

'Poor child,' said one of the ladies, 'at last she has understood.'

'Poor Tom,' wailed Minette, 'I have dropped poor Tom,' and with a force almost equal to her mother's, she scrambled down from her knees to where the doll had fallen in a fantastic and abandoned attitude upon the floor.

The Queen said later that it was her little daughter's unconscious prattle that saved her reason in this dreadful hour. All her ladies said the same. But Lady Morton, who knew the Princess best, observed that she had been rather more childish than usual, and wondered for a moment if the prattle had really been unconscious. But such speculation was outside her range. The Princess prattled, and was therefore unconscious. But it is certain that her experience far outran her years, that she heard all that the Queen was saying, and buried it in a deep dark hole at the bottom of her mind, or so it seemed to her afterwards when, in answer to some sympathetic question, fragments that she had thought were long forgotten came floating up from that abyss.

'And you can remember how the news came of the King's murder?'

'Ah no, I was such a child then, more concerned with my doll than my unknown father. I remember crying because I had dropped it as I sat on my mother's knee, when she, poor thing, was weeping for his death.'

But, even as she says it, and remembers sitting on the floor with the doll, she hears deep in her heart her mother's voice crying, 'I have helped to kill him. I did not know. Why did no one tell me?' – and then a babble and confusion of protesting voices, and then that one voice again, alone among all the rest, speaking in a calm more dreadful than her cry had been, 'Madame de Motteville, go to your mistress; tell the Queen Regent of France that my lord the King of England has lost his life because he was never allowed to know the truth. Tell her this, before it is too late, to listen to those who would tell her the truth.'

CHAPTER THREE

One day in late summer Minette sat in a coach beside her mother, very hot in her black clothes, with her Punchinello doll clutched stickily in her hands. She saw through the window a horse's brown belly go swinging forward in its slow movement beside the coach. She saw the rider's black knee, and the long black calf of his boot, and now and then his hand, long, lean and brown, would rest on their coach door. This was her brother Charles, a very tall young man in deep black, grave and dark, who was King of England and had no money and had lately come to stay with them. They clattered through the narrow smelly streets of Paris where horrid faces gaped at them from black doorways that were like the mouths of goblins' caves. The faces multiplied as in a bad dream, they came thick all round them, twisting themselves and shouting things at them, a stone came thump against the coach and a handful of mud was spattered over the window. Then it was that Charles rested his hand on the coach door, and Minette, peering up through the window, saw his face very set and fixed, while the yells of derision swept upwards at him.

'Call yourselves Kings and Queens!'

'Keep your head on your shoulders, it's all you've got.'

'There goes the Queen who can't pay her debts.'

'Why are they angry with us?' sobbed Minette. 'Why don't we go faster?'

But her mother, who sat very erect with white pressed lips and blazing eyes, said, 'Because we will not let the rabble think we are afraid of them,' and Minette stopped crying, and tried to look just like her.

They left that macabre throng behind; they drove through a forest; they drove by a river; they came to a palace full of

12

people who swept up and down in bows and curtseys while their voices swept up and down in sad sighing tones of sympathy and commiseration. In the midst of them all a stout lady in black caressed Minette with soft white hands, and moaned over her, telling her she had been but a baby when she had seen her last, and now she was a little fairy, an infant angel, and had her father's eyes.

This, she was reminded, was her kind Aunt Anne, Queen Regent of France. The two widowed queens embraced each other again and again, wept, and talked so fast it was impossible they should hear what the other was saying. They looked like two black crows nodding and pecking at each other, thought Minette in the sudden disgust of weariness. She had not remembered that the Queen of France was like that; and where were her cousins, the young King of France and his little brother, with whom she was to play?

But suddenly she felt happy, for two greyhounds came circling round each other and the room; they rolled against her, nearly knocking her over, and laughed into her face with foolish lolling wet-licking tongues; they jumped up against the two queens' knees and pawed their skirts, and were scolded and slapped by the Queen of France and caressed by the Queen of England. In the middle of this whirlpool a tall flashing creature strode up to them, curtseyed to her mother, pulled Minette's ear, and told her she did not remember her (which she did not), tossed her head at King Charles, asked if he had learnt to talk French any better yet, and actually cut across Queen Anne's long explanatory speech about her distress at not being able to help her dear sister-in-law more during this past dreadful winter, but that neither she nor her son the King of France had known where to obtain either a dinner or a gown.

'True, my dear Aunt, I assure you,' called out that strange girl to Queen Henrietta, whistling the greyhounds to her, and patting and pushing them about as she talked, 'all the Court were in the same plight. Those who had beds had no hangings, and those who had hangings had no clothes.'

'They had hung their petticoats on the beds for decency, I suppose?' Charles inquired thoughtfully.

Queen Anne, who had looked annoyed at the loud tone in which the girl had taken the lead, remarked in a slightly acid voice that 'our clever niece had met her match.'

'Not yet, Aunt, I beg of you,' she replied, flinging up her

13

head so that you expected to hear the bells of her harness jangle. One of Lady Morton's songs began to jig up and down in Minette's head:

> *'Rings on her fingers and bells on her toes,*
> *She shall have music wherever she goes.'*

She was fascinated by her beautiful dogs, and her bold talk at her brother Charles when two black queens were moaning at each other, her many jewels and her lovely red and white and black dress.

'Why do you stare so, little cousin?' asked the magnificent creature, her attention swooping from King Charles on to the little black figure that had unconsciously drawn nearer and nearer to her side.

'Because you are such a fine lady,' said Minette, still thinking of the song. She drew back to her mother, abashed at the laughter, but Mademoiselle, as they all called her, smiled upon her in a very kindly fashion.

'The innocent!' she said. 'I adore children; if only I have not to bear them.'

And she told Minette what a scamp she had been as a child, and how she had once locked her governess into her room for sending her to bed with a cold. Queen Henrietta did not care for the possible effect of this story on Minette. With a caressing little pat or two in different directions she made her way into the conversation, and managed to include her son again as well. 'Do you remember, Charles, how you did not want to take your medicine, and wrote to your tutor when you were only eight years old ('such a lively little black-eyed brat he was then,' she assured her niece, 'with his hair in a straight fringe') and you told him, "My lord, I hope you will not have to take medicine as I am sure it will make you ill, as it always makes me." Something like that,' she added vaguely, seeing the blank look on the face of Mademoiselle, who thought this a very poor effort compared with her own spirited performance. She opened her mouth in an unabashed yawn, and Minette was astonished that she did not even put up her hand to hide it.

Mercifully at this moment two little boys came into the room, and everyone got up and swept down to the ground again in bows and curtseys. King Louis XIV, attended by his younger brother, had come to offer welcome and condolences

14

to his aunt of England. He was not yet twelve years old; he was rather pale, and his stiffness betrayed his shyness. When he spoke it was evident that he had just been learning by heart what he had to say. He declared that his heart bled for his aunt's bereavement; he rejoiced with her on the safe arrival of her gallant son, his brother monarch of England, lost a few words, turned red, but went valiantly on to tell them that they were to consider themselves as the guests of the French Court. He even made a separate speech to the Princess Henrietta, telling her that her infantile charms had already won all hearts in his capital and left an indelible impression on his own memory.

Minette at once became backward and mumbling; she knew well that her mother was longing to slap her for it, but she could not get out one word, nor even look at King Louis.

'The poor child is quite overcome by the magnanimity and tenderness of the King's sentiments,' murmured her mother to his in her most purring accents.

'I hope they will all be great friends,' said Queen Anne, and then, as a look of incredulity amounting to disgust flickered across the face of the boy king, she added, 'the dear child is too young a companion for them as yet, but then I always say girls grow up so much quicker than boys.'

Queen Henrietta always said so too.

King Louis' little brother, Philippe, was here called forward, told to amuse his cousin, and reminded that she was also his foster-sister.

'Do you know what that is?' he asked her importantly, and she noticed that a little boy was talking to her whose hands flew about like small yellow birds. 'We have all been fed at the same breast, and have the same milk in us, only it isn't milk now, it is blood.'

Queen Anne, who heard only the last word, called out to him not to be nasty, or try and frighten his little guest. 'He is going through rather a difficult stage,' she confided in low tones to her sister-in-law; 'the other day I had to have him beaten for lifting the petticoats of one of the maids of honour and making some odd remarks. He has been left too much with footmen and chambermaids, but then the difficulty I have had in bringing them up at all! It is worse to be royal these days than to be a cobbler's wife. What can have happened to the world?'

They shook their heads over the world. It was the same

15

everywhere. The thrones of England were tottering. Heresy and schism were the cause of it all. Once people fell away from the true Church and thought they could believe what they liked, then it was the end of society. And the French Queen turned with a majestic movement of her stout black body that somehow reminded Minette of the slow swaying of the horse's belly she had seen outside the coach window that morning, and asked King Charles his opinion of his prospects in England, and his plans there for the future. He was at the moment showing interest and even animation in conversation with his young cousin, for Louis was talking eagerly to him of his pack of English hounds and of the sport he could show him in the surrounding forest. But at his aunt's questions Charles' face shut down again, he answered unwillingly, and did not seem to know the French for the simplest words.

'Your Majesty does not take much interest in the affairs of your kingdom,' Mademoiselle said to him in a hard snapping voice. She had for some time been pawing the ground as though she would stamp and swear outright if someone did not soon pay her attention.

He glanced at her under his down-dropped eyes, and said, 'What are the names of your dogs?'

'This one is Madame Mouse, and that one the Queen,' and in a fast whisper, approaching her lips to his ear, she added, 'it is the nearest I can get to calling my kind aunt a bitch.'

He did not catch her meaning, and both annoyance and a thin rag of discretion prevented her repeating it. It was impossible to converse with anyone so dull of wit as not to speak French properly.

In the hot overcrowded over-perfumed room a lassitude had settled on him that was partly despair, partly weariness, and partly natural indolence, aggravated to some pride in itself in contrast with all these busy chatterers. His aunt and cousin must be fools to imagine he would discuss his plans with them.

Mademoiselle had to fall back on admiring the points of her dogs. Her father always asked first for news of them, she said, before even the King or Queen; and once from her window at midnight she had seen him standing in the dunghill in the middle of the lower court to see how Madame Mouse was getting on after some accident.

At the mention of her father the rather harsh beauty of

16

her face looked both tender and excited. She spoke of him as Monsieur, and little Philippe nudged Minette furiously, as he led her up to his doll's house, a beautiful Chinese cabinet at the end of the room. 'You hear that?' he said, 'she is calling my Uncle Gaston Monsieur, but it is *I* who am the real Monsieur, I am brother to the King, I am the first gentleman in France, and he is only brother to the old King who is dead.'

His voice rose into a shrill squeak. Minette stared at him, and thought how odd it was for boys to be French. She had played chiefly with the children of English exiled nobles; she had met several French children on polite and distant terms, but none so French as he. He was charming to look at, very small and lively; his dark eyes glanced here and there, brilliant with mischief and interest. With his head thrust into the cabinet, looking round at her, he made her think of the imps in Morton's stories, but a very pretty imp. He showed her tiny and brittle treasures of blown glass from Venice, of porcelain or jade from China.

'How old are you?' he said, 'you are very little. You must be several inches shorter than I.'

He was accustomed to be the smallest person in any company, and was inclined to be jealous of this prerogative. But it began to be agreeable to have someone so much smaller than himself to patronize, someone moreover so delicate and fair, that even he might break her with a rough or careless movement. He showed her this and that, their heads close together, pushed inside the cabinet; and she uttered little soft cries of delight, musically shrill, like the toy peal of bells that had been given him by a German prince. He felt as though he had added a living speciment to his hoard.

'Now come and see my dolls,' he said, and took her hand to lead her through the open doors into other rooms. He could put his hand right round her fingers and her tiny braceleted wrist; it gave him an odd sensation, the most nearly masculine he had ever known.

'Why do you wear all black? It is very ugly.'

'For my father,' she said, flushing; and he stared at the colour that flooded into her pale, peaked little face, making it suddenly pretty.

'Can I do that?' he asked, and dashed to a mirror to see; but was disappointed, and said maliciously, 'Your father was a stupid man, wasn't he? Louis says only stupid Kings would let themselves be beheaded.'

17

'My father was a holy martyr – much better than your father.'

Even her neck was pink now, and her hands were crumpled up into minute round fists. He told her not to be cross, he hadn't meant it; and very affably he showed her his dolls, their wax faces and glass eyes and long fair hair, which he said was real. She was glad she had left Poor Tom behind in the big room, for he might have felt out of it in such splendid company.

Philippe suggested running a race back to the others. He stopped in the middle of it to tell her that he and Louis had spent one whole day last winter running up and down through these rooms to try and get warm – 'and they were all empty; no furniture, no fires, nothing but empty rooms one after the other; and our boots – for we had no shoes either – clattered and clacked and then we started calling to each other, and it sounded like an army, there were so many echoes.'

'Why were they all empty?'

'I tell you they were. Ask Louis if you don't believe me. We didn't think we could go to bed at all that night. We had nothing until Mademoiselle's wagons came through from Paris, and then how she pranced about, just like a peacock!'

How confusing it all was, how fast he talked!

She was back in the big room again. A sunbeam stretched across the room, making some faces look yellow with nasty red patches on them, and others just beyond it look blue. It was funny to think of that room with nothing in it, and nothing in the rooms beyond too, nothing but two little boys chasing and calling to each other, and the painted and gilded figures on the ceiling looking down on them. And this had happened while she lay in bed one dreadful day when it was too cold for her to get up, long, long ago, as long ago as last winter.

The sunbeam was full of whirling specks; when she shut her eyes a gold cup came spinning down it, and round its surface little boys with horns and goats' legs chased each other and called and waved to her. It had come true then, they were here to play with her.

'Wake up, cousin, you must not fall asleep in company,' said a squeaky voice. She opened her eyes, to see Philippe examining the clothes of her Punchinello.

CHAPTER FOUR

King Louis had been promised to Mademoiselle in marriage when he was in his cradle, and she a noisy rumbustious girl of eleven. Since she was a child, therefore, she had thought of herself as potential Queen of France. Her father, Gaston d'Orléans, was brother to the late King Louis XIII, and heir to the throne for the greater part of his reign. Her mother had died at her birth, bequeathing her the largest fortune in Europe, her bright fair hair, and nothing of her gentle and feminine disposition. Mademoiselle did not even care to recall their connexion; as a child she used snobbishly to refer to her maternal grandmother as 'my more distant grandmamma, not my grandmamma the Queen'. But the rest of the family had kept as distant as possible from Marie de Medici, widow of Henry of Navarre, and Queen Dowager of France; even her dutiful daughter, Queen Henrietta, had been glad when the English Parliament paid her mother ten thousand pounds to go away.

But to Mademoiselle, the more royal the relative, the closer. Even her fascinating father used to be superseded by her uncle, King Louis XIII, whom she had called her little Papa. He had been very fond of her, and so had his wife, Anne of Austria. As a child, Mademoiselle had been a convenient chaperon to both. Louis XIII had pretended to give picnics for her which were really for a young lady he called his Angel; Queen Anne had discussed her difficulties and dangers in front of her when the terrible Cardinal Richelieu was trying to catch her out in infidelity or intrigue. Mademoiselle had repaid their trust in honourable fashion, for she listened as little as she could to what was said, so that there should be the less chance of her inadvertently betraying any secret.

But she had had shocking manners. She and her chief little girl friend kept the Court in terror of their practical jokes and rude remarks; they made fun of everybody; and elderly courtiers who longed to slap them had to make stiff and formal efforts to chaff them, since compliments were only received with giggles. She was sent away to a convent to learn better behaviour, but only for a few months. Soon after she came back her aunt, Queen Anne, after twenty-three barren years of matrimony, was with child. The most good-natured and simple joy in this belated birth of a dauphin was shown by Mademoiselle, innocently regardless of the fact that it would destroy her importance as daughter to the heir of the throne. Queen Anne was touched by such candour, and with mistaken generosity she promised her the baby and his throne in reward.

The child was called Louis, the Gift of God, though some ribald spirits suggested other names for the possible donor. Mademoiselle came every day to see her little husband, and as she tossed him in her arms, sang the nursery song:

> 'Mon père ma'a donné un mari,
> Mon Dieu! quel homme, quel petit homme!
> Mon père m'a donné un mari,
> Mon Dieu! quel homme, qu'il est petit!'

Cardinal Richelieu with his grim nose and cold grey eyes scolded her for her unbecoming behaviour, and the spoilt little girl retaliated by floods of stormy tears at his injustice. But Cardinal Richelieu did not last very much longer. He got more and more ill, he went away very slowly in a red and gold litter so large that walls had to be knocked down to let it pass; and he never came back. His faithful servant, King Louis XIII, died within a few weeks of him; Queen Anne was appointed Regent for her little son, now five years old, and the new Cardinal, the Italian Mazarin, ruled both.

> 'Le chat l'a pris pour un souris,
> Mon Dieu! quel homme, quel petit homme!'

The cat who ran off with Mademoiselle's little husband was Cardinal Mazarin, soft-footed, powerful, yet servile.

When the wars of the Fronde broke out in Paris each party in turn declared that it was fighting only against Mazarin, and never for one moment against the boy king. Mazarin had sucked all the wealth of the country to amass his vast fortune. Mazarin was the Queen's lover, her husband it was even said (for though a Cardinal, he had never actually taken vows), and he bullied her as only an Italian can bully his wife. Mazarin went covered with jewels himself, and kept the King in rags. Mazarin had forty little fishes on his plate while the King had only two.

And Mazarin would not provide a husband for that fine girl Mademoiselle, the granddaughter of France's hero, Henry of Navarre. She was of France, she would not take pampered foreigners to her bosom as Queen Anne had done. She was now in her early twenties, she had grown very tall, haughty, magnificent, and looked really beautiful on horseback, where her big nose did not show up and her complexion did; it was dazzling with youth and health and the pride of life, for no one in France had better birth or brighter hopes of the future. Even the King of France was not worthy now to be the summit of her ambition; she had her eye on the Emperor.

The Frondeurs raised barricades in the streets of Paris against the Queen and the Court, but when Mademoiselle with her usual courage rode out to see what they were doing, they rushed to raise the chains and let her pass, they kissed her skirt and stirrup and acclaimed her as the true Queen of France. Mademoiselle rode on, not deigning to look at them, and they worshipped her more than ever. The pale frightened faces of the Queen and courtiers delighted her; she felt how far she was above them – battle, conflict, tumult, these were her natural elements. She gave a ball at the Tuileries and danced all night to the music of the guns. There was an exaltation about her, she carried her head so high that her bright and unobservant eyes never saw the ordinary mortals who walked this earth. 'I take my own road,' she said. 'I was born to take no other.'

The royal family had to fly in the night to Saint Germain; the people of Paris kept back their wagons so that they were destitute until Mademoiselle came to their rescue with her baggage. It was a freezing January night, she had a sore throat, and had to share a narrow bed on the floor with her little stepsister, 'Mop', in a room that had no glass in its windows; the child with her tossed and tumbled about so all night that she had to sing to her to get her to sleep, but she was so happy that she was glad to sing, for she was of such importance that now even her aunt was forced to recognize it. A certain annoyance at having to share this importance was mingled with the shock of hearing that, at almost the same time as their flight to Saint Germain, King Charles of England had been executed by his rebellious subjects.

And now here was his widow and his orphaned children with them at Saint Germain, and they had all to be kind to them, which was trying.

21

'Happy' was the word of the moment; it was the Cardinal Mazarin's; he judged everybody by their likelihood of luck and had long ago pronounced the Stuart family deficient in that respect. He did not think that the new King Charles would ever recover his throne; people therefore took but little notice of him, and then, if kindly, as a great silent sad-eyed youth; if unkindly, as a stupid lout who showed no interest in politics, spoke little, ate enormously, and moped about the Palace with a vacant lost look when he was not trying to do what his mother told him, viz. pay court to his cousin Mademoiselle.

In spite of her good looks and her conquering air, Charles found this uphill work. He always managed to talk worse French with her than with anyone else. Last time he was in Paris his cousin from the Palatine, Prince Rupert, had had to act as interpreter, this time it was Lord Jermyn who made pretty speeches for him. 'What sort of a wooing do you call that?' she demanded.

'I cannot help it,' said Charles to his mother's expostulations, 'her nose is so big.'

It was big enough to form an effectual barrier between the families; for Mademoiselle, suspecting that he did not admire her, voted him a hobbledehoy. Heaven! how dull he had been in answering Queen Anne's questions about his affairs!

She was genuinely sorry for 'that poor lady' his mother, who was not even able to put her footmen into mourning for the death of the King her husband, nor herself into the regulation mantle of violet velvet, trailing five yards upon the floor.

But she realized that Queen Anne had forgotten her promises to her, and that in spite of occasional scratches she was bosom friends with this other aunt, who was for ever trying to foist her gawky useless son on her. Queen Anne snubbed her while Queen Henrietta flattered her, but they would both now side together against her. Aunts she decided were antiquated, cautious, corrupt. Queen Henrietta evaded taking any side in these exciting quarrels of the Fronde; she preached that tame and ignoble virtue, moderation, with so many examples of the 'As I have learnt to my cost' variety, that Queen Anne was driven to say in front of both the Courts, 'My sister, do you wish to be Queen of France as well as of England?'

22

To which Queen Henrietta meekly replied, 'I am nothing. Do you be something.'

'My aunt,' declared Mademoiselle, 'now behaves like a poor person.'

The admiration of her little cousin Henriette for herself she found really very touching. But this good effect was counteracted by an obscure jealousy; it annoyed her to see the undemonstrative Charles playing with his sister as though she were a kitten or a puppy. He actually prophesied the insignificant little thing would be a beauty. And it was he who had given her her pet name, Minette, as he had given his mother that vulgarly maternal title 'Mam'.

So Mademoiselle observed that even so young a child could give example of the degrading effects of poverty, for when she offered to give her a new wax doll to replace the deplorable Punchinello, the Princess Henriette asked for the money instead.

'Is that what you care for most?' asked the richest heiress in Europe, her lip curling; and the child, frightened and perplexed by her disdain, still haunted by that hostile crowd in Paris, led by their debtors, answered only, 'Yes.'

'The English are all tradesmen at heart,' said Mademoiselle, 'it comes of mingling their noble and even royal blood with that of their City merchants.'

She said it to Philippe, who nodded wisely; he was so much more precocious than her elder brother that she could thoroughly enjoy gossiping with him about their poor relations. He was never shy, never diffident of expressing any opinion, however ridiculous or contrary to what he had expressed two minutes before. Nothing was expected of him, in fact he was deliberately kept back, for it was feared that his quick wits might in the future engage in dangerous rivalry with his brother. So he ate sweets and discussed clothes with the chambermaids, who petted him like a lap-dog.

But Louis, with scarcely any more education than he, was expected to join in discussions on the troubled state of France. He was never left in peace, he was harried about by the Frondeurs from place to place. He was often without any proper tutor; this put him at a disadvantage even with boys younger than himself. Beside his brother he was apt to seem stolid as a block of wood.

'How amusingly different they are,' said Queen Henrietta, and bit her lip on her exclamation, for there might well be a reason for that. Louis was unmistakably a legitimate Bourbon, but scandal had suggested that Philippe, so dark, intelligent and Italian-looking, was possibly a son of the Cardinal Mazarin.

Philippe too had caught hints of the rumour. In all personal questions he was acute, restless and eager; with all except his brother, his mind was passionately interested, his heart unconcerned. He could not decide if it were more effective to be the genuine first prince of the blood royal or the secret bastard of an Italian adventurer. But Louis smacked his head if he described himself as the latter, even if they were talking unheard at night on those scrambling visits they were always paying to different places. They might stay in a palace, but the furniture was often so scarce that they had to share a bed. This equal companionship made Philippe very proud; but he had a nervous horror of being touched while he was asleep, and to avoid this would lie so near the edge of the bed that sometimes he would roll out and bump on the floor. Louis thought it fun to sleep together, as they had pillow fights in which naturally he came off victorious. What upset his pride more than the scarce furniture was that the sheets were sometimes torn. He put his toe in a hole in one and ripped it right up, and then thumped Philippe for laughing, for he himself was furious. 'What is the use of being a king in ragged sheets?' he demanded.

'Then it does not matter if I am a son of Mazarin,' retorted Philippe, forestalling his brother's reply with a bolster.

But Louis had his effect. From infancy Philippe's habit, both natural and instructed, was to look up to this superior being who had always been just two years older, taller, stronger than himself; and was in addition, as he was continually reminded, his King.

Now his little cousin Henriette had come to give him his first taste of superiority. He played with her on the great terrace which looked over the river and away in the distance to the roofs and towers of Paris. They would sit on the marble rim of the big fountain, and Minette longed to take off her hot black clothes and twiddle her toes in the water, and then with a delicious shock, slide right into it. But Philippe was horrified when she said so.

She had with her a quantity of the paper boats that Charles had made for her, and sailed them on that round sea where the water-lily leaves were desert islands. She pushed off her

24

frail fleet, blowing at them with her cheeks puffed out like an infant Boreas in the corner of an ocean map, and watched their precarious voyages towards the perpetual rain of the fountain. Once beneath it they staggered drunkenly, and if they could not escape to the shore of the basin's brim they became waterlogged and sank. This was an exquisite sorrow; yet the relentless admiral continued to urge fresh armadas to the discovery of new Americas, while Philippe's high voice pattered against her ears, incessant as the drops that pattered on the water-lily leaves and splashed within the fountain.

'Can you keep a secret? You must never tell it. To your mother? No, certainly not. Nor anyone. If you do, they may kill you.'

'I think I would rather not hear it then, cousin.'

'But you must hear it. I've promised you now, and princes have to keep promises. I'll whisper it.'

But suddenly he considered that she might remember it, and some time she or someone else might twit him with being a bastard. Secrets could only safely be told to those about to die. He had a fleeting vision of the joys of absolute power; then asked her, 'What do you do for your spots?'

'What spots?'

The dangerous secret soared out of her reach – or was it that spots were a kind of treason?

'Why – just spots. Our chambermaids sometimes tie raw beef on our faces at night to make our skins good, but that makes a horrid mess. When I am grown up I shall use face cream like old Skim-the-Milk – that is what they call the Cardinal, you know, but sometimes his pets have licked it all off by the morning. He is always having new pets, for they come from hot countries and die over here, however warm they are kept. The last was a sort of monkey with the longest tail you ever saw, and it wore a velvet coat and sat on his shoulder and smelt just like him.'

'Does Mazarin smell like a monkey, then?'

'No. The monkey smells like Mazarin, for it is bathed with the same perfume.'

She could never afterwards look at Mazarin's exotic pets, some quick furtive monkey in a gorgeous coat or brilliant plumaged bird that spoke in a human voice, without being reminded of the gaudy little creature now beside her, so alert, so alive, so full of intelligence and enjoyment of it. Yet at the time she hardly noticed him, she ceased to hear what he was

25

saying, for the sun's long rays had slanted down towards the fountain, behind it a cedar spread its darkness like a thunder-cloud, and against that cloud new colours suddenly gleamed out in the falling shower.

'Cousin, look, look! Is it a miracle? There is a rainbow in the fountain!'

Charles heard the happy cry as he looked out of his mother's window on to the gardens to where the two small figures, crouched on the fountain's edge, made the only move-ment in the rich light of that still evening.

Before him the terrace sloped down to the broad river, all round it were the woods. It would be pleasant to walk there now, walk on and on, thinking of no plan, thinking of nothing in particular, until at last he would find himself in some village where a sturdy sunburnt girl, with breasts big enough to fill both his hands, would bring him a long drink of cooled wine. But any village here after the recent fighting was likely to be a heap of ruined hovels, and the girls, if any, more starved than sturdy. There was no reality in daydreams even of the most physical nature, and what he really wanted was to go to Ireland.

Everything had been arranged; he had already sent on his baggage, and Ormonde the Lord-Lieutenant was raising the wild Irish on his behalf.

But his mother made difficulties, implored him to remain with her, to marry Mademoiselle and use her money to raise an army in France with which he could conquer England. It was useless to point out that England was too proud a nation ever to forgive him for invading her with a foreign army. Queen Henrietta had no more sense of nationality than most princesses of her time, and no more reason to have it, since her mother was a Florentine Medici, and her father a semi-Spanish Frenchman; her sisters-in-law were the English Eliza-beth of Bohemia and the Spanish Anne of Austria, Queen Regent of France; her elder daughter was princess of a Dutch state, and her husband, half Scot, half Dane, had been King of England. Europe in fact was represented in her mind as a large family party whose servants spoke different languages, rather than as a concourse of nations, each with a distinct sense of individuality.

Nor did she grasp that England as an island had advanced further than the rest in this sense. She had never begun to

26

understand the country where she had spent most of her life, though she still continued to declare that she would always look on it as her true home.

'Then let us hope I may find it so,' her son now replied; whereupon she wept stormily, declared that he used her words against her, that he did not trust dear Lord Jermyn, and she did not trust that odious Hyde who had led him to withhold his counsels from her so that he never spoke nor listened to her, and all she could do now to help him was to hide her head in a convent and pray for his soul, and doubtless in that too she would be accused of meddling.

His mother's voice was majestic and sorrowful, it wrapped her in a mourning robe of violet velvet, it trailed five yards upon the floor. It was the voice of La Reine Malheureuse, as she never ceased to sign her letters to the day of her death.

Charles, moodily staring out of the window, heard only her voice and not her words.

Women scolding him, weeping, demanding his affection – some prophetic instinct, born of a self-knowledge that he strove to restrain, told him that this was what he would most suffer from all through his life. And he did give his affection, that was what made it so damnable, and it was only Minette who did not repay it by plaguing him to do something 'for her sake'.

'Pity she must grow up,' he thought, and waved to the child, who was dancing up and down on the edge of the fountain and never saw him, so eagerly was she gazing into the prismatic shower.

He turned towards his mother.

'Better to lose my life in this enterprise,' he said, 'than waste it in shameful indolence.'

The Queen looked with love and despair at the tall black figure. He was a man now, she could not hold him to her. In one of those flashes of dispassionately clear sight that sometimes troubled her certainty in herself, she saw that if she could so hold him, idle, at a foreign Court, it might well ruin him. There had already been too many scandals concerning him for one of his age.

She made a great effort to yield gracefully.

'Dear son,' she said, 'I hope that you will always think as you have just spoken.'

And she let him go, with not more than two more painful scenes and a farewell banquet at the Palais Royal, where the

27

food was seriously delayed by the difficulties of etiquette, since the King and Queen-mother of France and the King and Queen-mother of England were all too polite to go in first to dinner. There they stuck for well over half an hour, bowing, curtseying, protesting, apologizing, and all but fainting from exhaustion and hunger, while delectable hot smells were wafted to them through that impassable doorway.

CHAPTER FIVE

They were all back in Paris; all except Charles who was with James in Jersey, where the islanders were loyal to a man, and the brothers were free to stroll about on shooting expeditions with their dogs and guns, and on Sunday to row over in wind and rain to church. Then, much later, Charles was in Holland; and the Queen hoped he would go to Scotland with the Covenanters, and Lady Morton said that if he did so he would be betraying his best friends, for both the Marquis of Montrose in Scotland and Ormonde in Ireland were enemies of the Covenant. Her husband, the Earl of Morton, was with Montrose.

James returned to them, and was very sullen and unhappy that he was not allowed to go to Scotland too. He said his brother was jealous of him because the islanders in Jersey had liked him better; and that it had been just the same in the old days when they were with the fleet, Charles had kept him in the background and not let him see any of the fighting.

'You talk nonsense, James,' said his mother, 'of course your brother could not risk both your lives.'

'He should not have risked his own then,' said James. 'They told him to keep down in the hold, and he would stay on deck all the time, just to see the battle.'

She complained that he put on airs because he wanted to be important, that his tone to her was deplorable. When she criticized his Aunt Elizabeth of Bohemia for being a neglectful mother, James said, 'Well, I had rather have a mother who was fonder of her dogs than her children, than one who is fonder of Lord Jermyn.'

He had many invitations from the French Court, but had to refuse because they involved too much expense. He wanted to joint the French army, but could not afford to buy the outfit. He lost his good looks when he was peevish and unhappy; two long lines pulled down his nose towards his mouth and gave him a narrow pinched look. He talked grandly of taking an army of French mercenaries to Ireland, but he had not enough money to go himself to Brussels when he quarrelled with his mother. However, he borrowed it, and off he went for a long time, and when he came back he never apologized properly.

Minette ran away and hid whenever she heard that a messenger had come for the Queen of England, for he was sure to bring a black-sealed letter and weeping and wailing, and perhaps another black dress. Her sister Elizabeth had died in prison in England, of grief, it was said, for she had pined away ever since her father's death, and had wept her heart out on hearing that her brother Charles had thrown in his lot with the Covenanters, and thus thrown over her father's friend, the noble Marquis of Montrose.

And within two months there was another death, of the Prince of Orange, husband to her elder sister, Mary, who had been devoted to his mother-in-law, Queen Henrietta. The Queen said to Lady Morton, 'It is of no use to think and plan, to love one's children. God does not mean me ever to know anything but sorrow any more.'

'I cannot think God would be that spiteful,' said Lady Morton in her blunt Scots accent, and the Queen remembered she was talking to an unbeliever.

Within a week, however, she was dancing round the room, catching up Minette to embrace her, having long mysterious talks with Morton, telling everyone mid laughter and tears that she was now a grandmother, since the Princess Mary had, a week after her husband's death, given birth to another William, Prince of Orange. Mary wrote to her mother that the baby was small and sickly, she began to doubt if she would ever rear him; and the Queen grew wild with impatience to go to her daughter and grandson who were lying ill among unsympathetic foreigners. Since the States-General rudely refused her hospitality, she would go disguised as a washerwoman. She would not be deprived of all her rights as mother as well as wife simply because the world had chosen to worship Cromwell.

But one anxiety drove out another. Montrose had landed in Scotland with only three men, to raise the country on the King's behalf. But Lady Morton said that the King had himself rendered that impossible. How could he have done so?

Minette could not understand, dared not ask. Her beloved Morton's face was like a statue.

And then there came the messenger with the letter bound with black ribbon and sealed with black wax, but it was not for the Queen, it was for Lady Morton whose husband had died, fighting for Montrose.

The letter demanded her instant return, to see to the affairs of her children and her estates. She took it to the Queen and laid it before her. 'Your Majesty sees that I have no choice,' she said, and her voice was so quiet that Minette held her breath. The Queen rose and kissed her. A strange hush lay on the scene.

As she left the room, Lady Morton woke from the spell that had been laid on her by royalty, by its misfortune, its charm, its complete, unquestioning acceptance of her service. For the first time she counted up the years since she had seen her husband. It caused her no surprise that her intense family loyalty had been swallowed up in her devotion to her royal mistress. She disagreed with her, frequently disapproved of her, she had on occasion been unjustly blamed by her; but it had no more occurred to her to leave her service for that of her family than it had done to the Queen herself. Other people's affairs, their troubles, their children had taken up all the foreground of her mind.

Now, like a nurse of the human race that has been carried off by the fairies, after seven years she found herself on earth again, and knew, not only that her children needed her, but, suddenly and desperately, how much she needed them.

But in saying goodbye to the Princess she broke down and wept; and Minette, seizing the advantage, begged her not to leave her for other children.

'But, Princess, you have your own mamma, and they have no one but me.'

'But my mamma is a Catholic, and you do not wish me to be brought up a Catholic.'

'And if I stay, would you be a Protestant?'

'I don't know,' said the child uneasily, 'but there would be more chance of it.'

Lady Morton regarded the infant Machiavelli with some severity.

'Whatever religion you may assume,' she said, 'never bargain with it.'

Suddenly she caught the child up on to her knee.

'Do not,' she said low and hurriedly as though she were ashamed of her words, 'do not let them put you into a convent. Remember your father died for the Church of England – when you were born, his first care was to have you baptized in it – it would, I think, have broken his heart to see you a nun.'

'Oh, but Morton, indeed I do not want to be a nun. When my brother is on his throne I am to go and live with him, and he will give balls for me at his Court, and you will come and live with us too.'

That last night Morton stayed longer than usual with her pupil after putting her to bed. It was her custom to sing her to sleep with the songs of her husband's country, long wild stories to a mournful tune, very different from the French songs her mother would sing when she was gay, of little girls who went to the woods to pick flowers and met the King's son there. But she liked Morton's best, for there were more adventures in them.

Tonight she sang of a bold robber chieftain called Kinmont Willie who had done a raid over the English border, and rode his horse back through the flooded river where not one of the English lords dared follow him. It was just after that, said Lady Morton, that her father's elder sister Elizabeth of Bohemia was born, and her grandfather, King James of Scotland, asked the old Queen Elizabeth of England to be her godmother and give the little Scots princess her name; but the old Queen, who by then was exactly like a witch with a great hooked nose and little eyes sunk on either side of it in a long face painted red and white like a dish from China, 'and indeed she was so terrible to look at that she had broken the last mirror she had looked into, and forbidden any other to be brought into the Palace for the rest of her life – well, the old Queen, the old Queen – now what was I telling you about the old Queen who cut off your great-grandmother's head?'

The governess's head had nodded sleepily over the child's bed, and now jerked itself back like a startled horse. It was the last thing she had intended, to remind her little charge of the much more recent tragedy in her family, and on the last night that she was with her. But Minette had no intention of being so reminded. She said firmly, 'You were telling me of the old Queen and the baby Princess who was called Elizabeth after her, and of Kinmont Willie. Tell me more of Kinmont Willie.'

'There's no more to tell but that the old Queen was so angry at his raid into England that at first she refused to stand gossip, as your grandfather King Jamie called it in the good old Scots way; but they patched it up, and that is why your father's sister, the Queen of Bohemia, is called Elizabeth.'

And why was she called the Winter Queen? Did she sit on a throne of snow with a crown of icicles on her snow-white hair? But the child knew it could be for no such excellent reason. She stared into the darkness behind the kindly and reassuring face of her governess, and repeated droningly:

> *'I wadna' ha' ridden that wan water*
> *For a' the gowd in Christendie.'*

She had had to ask what each word meant, but that did not destroy the magic. Now she lay with closed eyes, pretending to be asleep, for she was afraid that Morton would cry again if she kissed her goodnight. Under her eyelids she watched that tall upright form for the last time lean over the candles and put out the light. There was a click as the door closed, she sat up with a start, began to call to her to come back, and then did not. For a moment utter darkness surrounded her, then in the glimmer of red light from the fire, of grey light from the window, the room took on an unfamiliar aspect; the walls had disappeared, the corners of furniture were transformed into rocks and castle towers, that glimmer-ing patch of polished floor was a river that flowed on into darkness.

Some night she would get into a little boat made of paper and she would sail down that wan water, out through the walls of her room which had melted away into nothingness, out of the Palace, out of France, to England where Morton would be waiting for her, and Charles on his throne, or per-haps even further to some undiscovered country.

Morton had gone. That mattered most. Other people put her to bed, and nobody sang her to sleep. And Montrose was dead. He had been taken by his enemies the Covenanters, and barbarously executed before anyone had time to protest.

Minette was glad that Morton was no longer with them when this news came.

CHAPTER SIX

They heard that Charles was taking a Scottish army into England, then that he had been defeated at Dunbar, then that he had rallied, that he had marched victoriously right into the south-west and the country had risen for him to a man, that Cromwell was assassinated or had committed suicide, that Charles had been crowned at Westminster, then that all his forces had been utterly routed at Worcester, and that Charles was fleeing for his life with a price of a thousand pounds on his head and a death penalty on whomsoever helped his escape. Then they heard no more.

With every week that went by, it became the more improbable that he should still be alive; for how should a man so recognizable as Charles with his unusual height, strongly marked features and dark foreign colouring, find his way right across England to the coast and so escape, when the whole countryside was out looking for him, expecting the reward of a fortune for his capture? So the crowd of kind inquirers that thronged to the English Queen told each other in the corridors, and then, on entering her apartment, composed their features to as much hopeful cheerfulness as was consonant with sympathy.

Mademoiselle was often there, and spoke more warmly of him than she had ever done. How gallant he was, how courageous, and with a certain gaiety beneath his grave air! He was a true grandson of France's greatest king, Henry of Navarre, whose granddaughter she was so proud to be. 'I used to tease him,' she said, 'but he would have understood, would he not, that it was only play between cousins?'

There was an odd, almost wistful note in her usually confident voice. Years afterwards Minette could remember it, but at the time she was too young to recognize it. She knew only that Mademoiselle had taken pleasure in snubbing her brother, who might now be dead.

'Yes, you were unkind to him,' she cried, was aghast at her boldness and fled from the room to escape the scoldings and punishment that was sure to fall upon her. But with royal generosity Mademoiselle must have defended her, for she

33

never heard of it again; and when she next saw her the child embraced her fondly in penitence and gratitude.

Four weeks passed, five weeks, six weeks. To Minette, looking out at the autumn rain falling in the courtyard, it seemed that they had been waiting for years, all her life, for something dreadful to happen. A man rode into the courtyard, and she thought, 'Now they will say he is dead.'

But the messenger was from Charles, who had landed safely in France, and was on his way to them.

They drove out to meet him. Queen Henrietta's charming rascally brother, Gaston d'Orléans, the father of Mademoiselle, was in the coach with Minette and her mother and James; and he talked all the time, acting a comic scene of the Roundheads' amazement at hearing of Charles' safe arrival in France, for they had believed by now he must have lain among the unrecognized dead at Worcester. Minette never took her eyes off her uncle's flexible eyebrows and fluttering hands, she believed all that he acted, and thought that Cromwell had really choked on a sausage when he heard the news.

They stopped the coach, and saw three men riding towards them who looked like servants. One was very tall, with a dark yellow furrowed face like a gipsy, and no hair that could be seen. They did not know him at the first instant, then, as he got off his horse, even Minette could remember that no one else moved just like that, so lazy and yet so quick.

Her mother gave a little shriek.

'Charles! What have they done to you!'

'It's this walnut juice,' he said, 'it won't wash off,' and, as he took off his hat and knelt for her blessing, they saw his hair had been cut very short and badly, for it was different lengths, but none long enough to curl. His clothes were rough and ill-fitting, he was the oddest sight. Minette did not want him to come and kiss her; she pretended not to know him, and hid her face in her uncle's scented sleeve, and he twirled round on his high heels and called out, 'Hey, what is this! Your Majesty has grown so ugly that here's a finicky little sister who doesn't know you!' At that she was dreadfully ashamed, and all the more when she saw how James flung his arms round Charles, and how glad the brothers were to greet each other. She wished she had not missed her chance. Tears began to run down her face, but luckily everyone was too busy to notice; they were all getting into the coach, and still Gaston d'Orléans talked and laughed, and twirled his

34

cap in his hand, and then stuck it on again right over one ear, and made jokes about Cromwell, and when other people talked too much for even him to get a word in, he pulled out a little pocket-mirror and made grimaces at it, for he was as restless as running water – even in his sleep he walked and talked. And James asked a thousand questions, and Charles answered 'Yes' and 'No', and asked about James' chances for the French army.

Minette at last grew weary of staring at the rough grey cloth on his knees; she looked up at his face and found his heavy eyes regarding her with a certain amusement. She was sure he had known that she had only pretended not to recognize him; he would despise her always.

The first thing he did when they got to the Louvre, was to ask Lord Jermyn for the loan of one of his shirts, and he seemed quite pleased when Lord Jermyn said he would make it a gift. Now that he stood bare-headed, his mother called out that he was a Roundhead and crop-ear, and then her laughter choked on a sob as she told him that she could not ask him to stay to dinner, and that as soon as they did have a meal together she would have to charge his share to his account. But they soon managed to be merry over that too.

He looked much older and he was very tired; he fell asleep in his chair as he was telling them his adventures, which had been fantastic. Men had looked him in the face and remarked that he was very like the description of the King; he had hidden in a tree while the enemy searched below; he had been disguised as an old woman, as a gipsy, as a gentleman's servant who did not know how to turn a spit when told to do so, and as a Roundhead with better results, for he had gravely rebuked his company for swearing. He did so now, in a twanging nasal whine which curled up his long nose so that he looked uglier than ever.

Yet even Mademoiselle showed admiration of him this time. She would walk for hours with him in the long gallery between the Louvre and her own palace of the Tuileries, for she could not go out in the air that winter as she was suffering from a swollen face. From the way her aunt of England talked about it one would have thought it had swelled on purpose to spite her. But Mademoiselle's own vanity was no whit disturbed by it; unconcerned, even when she had to wear a bandage over her cheek, she would stride beside her cousin, trying to match her step with his. She had as long legs for a woman as he for a man, but though he seemed merely to stroll along, it was difficult for anyone to keep up with him.

The Queen had prepared her elaborately for the ridiculous sight of Charles with his hair cut short, but on the contrary she found that the last two years had greatly improved him. He was no longer the gawky youth who could neither dance well nor talk French properly. He had grown stately, even majestic, his dancing was extremely graceful; he was older too in worldly wisdom and knew now that his cousin's nose was not as big as her fortune. Perhaps she knew that he knew it, for she was still apt to parry his compliments with sarcasms. She was always wanting to convince him that women were as good as men, but had an uneasy suspicion that the conviction would only bore him. She herself had attended councils of war, and if only the nobles would again drive out that insolent upstart Mazarin she would then take her share in the actual fighting. And in imitation of her flighty father, she stuck a hand into the pocket of her mannishly cut riding-coat, twirled on her heel, and whistled a song that half the street boys in Paris were singing:

> 'A wind from the Fronde
> Is blowing, blowing, blowing,
> And Monsieur Mazarin
> Will be going, going, going.'

Then she would get her chance to show that glory and great deeds were not yet dead, whether for man or woman.

'That is why, my cousin,' she said with her air of frank condescension, 'I like you better than I did. It is not merely that you have acquired an air, that you can hand one to one's coach without tripping over one's gown, and no longer refuse ortolans and fall on mutton like a wolf—'

'I still prefer mutton, though,' he interspersed, 'even when I had to cook it myself. Did you know I could cook? You should engage me as one of your scullions, cousin.'

But she ignored the unworthy interruption – 'it is because you have faced hardships and dangers equal to those of a hero of old.'

'How do you know they were not greater?' said Charles. 'No hero of old ever had to wear boots too tight for him. Try it, my cousin, on rough woodland ground on a wet night; try slashing them with a blunt knife and stuffing them with sodden

36

paper, and all the time knowing that to escape death or capture you should be walking all night at the rate of five miles an hour. They took all nobility out of me, I can tell you. I lay on the ground and begged to be left till the Roundheads found me.'

But Mademoiselle would not admit that courage could depend on well-fitting boots. She began to suspect that the King of England was not after all a true hero.

The sufferings he had to endure from the Covenanters in Scotland moved her most. In that uncivilized desert he never saw a woman nor a pack of cards nor a violin, and the ministers had had the insolence to rebuke him for smiling on a Sunday.

He would not have run much danger of that rebuke now. After the first excitement of his arrival he had grown very glum and silent. James rushed in to tell him that Jersey, their own particular island as he called it, had surrendered to the Parliament. Charles looked at the ground, and said not one word. James was so excited you would have almost thought he was pleased at the event, but then he was proud of their beloved islanders, and the magnificent resistance they had made. One could see why he was the more popular of the two brothers; he was so much more youthful in nature as well as years, his fair handsome face flushed as he chattered to that grim figure that sat so still.

But Charles scarcely answered those who spoke to him, and, though he would tell amusing little anecdotes of his escape, he would mention no names nor actual details to anyone, not even his mother. When she reproached him for his lack of confidence in her, he did not answer. She said, in the girl's hearing, that he was thinking of Mademoiselle; James said to Minette that he was thinking of Scotland.

Once the child plucked up courage to ask which it was. She had climbed on his knee, but he had not noticed her; at her question however he looked full at her, and gave a short unsmiling laugh.

'Which am I thinking of? Of Mademoiselle, of course. I don't wish ever to think of Scotland again. I was preached to death there by wild Covenanters.'

He had been a mere prisoner in their hands, and without the privacy of a dungeon; they had preached as many as six sermons in a day at him, and sometimes forced him to do the preaching and confess publicly his repentance for his sins, his father's and his grandfather's, so that at the last he had added truthfully he was very sorry also for ever having been born.

Their passion for rebuke had even led them to scold God; his one happy memory was of the prayers after the defeat of Dunbar when his allies told the Almighty how mistaken He had been not to support His own side, and how much He would suffer for it.

In order to gain these hateful allies, he had had to forsake his true friends both in Scotland and Ireland. And what had it all come to? He had been crowned King of Scotland certainly, but now that his army had been destroyed, Scotland no longer existed politically. His chance of England seemed ruined for ever. Ireland, which might have been a complete country, compact by loyalty to his service, he had left to be ravaged by Cromwell's soldiers until she was a mere plague-stricken desert where the very name of England was a curse.

And Montrose, his father's friend, his staunchest ally, was dead, shamefully executed by the Covenanters; and men blamed him for it; sometimes even he blamed himself. But Montrose in his last letter to him, written under sentence of death, had not blamed him.

The magnanimity of those we injure is not however of much comfort. He recognized dully that that letter placed Montrose in one class of men and himself in another. He would never again utter high sentiments to his mother about it being better to lose his life than waste it in shameful indolence. They were not his style now. He would leave them to the 'heroes of old' of his cousin's schoolgirl imagination; and to those men who, like Montrose, though born into this cynical and venal age, yet somehow had managed to resemble them.

He pushed Minette off his knee, repeating, 'Of Mademoiselle, of course. She has the best violins in France. I am going to ask her if we can dance to them tonight.'

Mademoiselle encouraged her aunt's hopes, if not her cousin's. Queen Henrietta said she must dress her niece's hair for a ball at the Louvre, and Charles must be page, and hold the flambeau for them – 'And I will lend you my diamonds, now I have got them out of pawn,' she cried, clapping her hands like a young girl. So in her bedchamber at the Tuileries Mademoiselle's vanity was fed by a queen to dress her hair and a king to hold the light, while at her feet a little watchful princess sat on a stool, hugging her knees, and silently paid her the supreme compliment of envy.

Charles held the flambeau in its long silver case, the end balanced on his hip, the light a little behind him; it threw strong shadows on his face, exaggerating his dark and heavy features almost to caricature. In the centre of the mirror Mademoiselle's face shone in a high light, as clear of shadow as an enamelled miniature. She looked only at that, and thought, 'Tonight, when I sit on the dais, the young Kings of France and England will sit at my feet. Shall I marry the King of France, or shall I have the Emperor instead?'

The Queen went on busily patting and smoothing her niece's auburn ringlets, and twisting in them those royal jewels that she had not yet sold, and all the time she talked of England and how happy she had been there with her dear husband. As she spoke she looked as she had done in the early months of her bereavement when there had been a new calm about her, for then her passionate love for her husband, after long years of torture, had been at peace. She could bear no more for him, plan and question no more, nor strive with all her will and brain and charm to influence him for his good. There was nothing now that she could do but love, and the purity of her emotion, purged of all conflict, had given her face the repose and selfless abstraction of a saint. That expression now returned as she looked back upon her married life and canonized its every moment.

'In all our life together,' she said, 'I only had one quarrel with King Charles, and in that I was to blame. Shall I tell you how it happened? Well then, I was, you must remember, a quite young girl, only fifteen, and I fear very spoilt and wilful. England was a strange country to me, I could not speak a word of the language, and King Charles' French at that time was worse than this boy's here two years ago; also he was very shy, and there were misunderstandings. I feared he was not in love with me, and I was so homesick I would cry myself to sleep at nights, longing for my mother to come and say good night to me.'

'I cannot swallow all this new talk about love, especially in connexion with marriage. For my part, I think it ignoble.'

The slightly rasping voice seemed to issue from the mirror; Minette stared at it, aghast. But the Queen answered her niece with deceptive mildness, 'Yet even thirty years ago I

39

was ignoble enough to wish my husband to love me, to be glad that he had beautiful eyes.'

(But in memory those eyes had a reproachful look. A trick of expression, the droop of the sad, curved eyelids – that was all. He had never reproached her.) She flung back her head and laughed with such vivacity that the face of her niece below her in the mirror looked by contrast as if it were made of painted wood.

'Little wretch that I was,' she exclaimed. 'How all the solemn English councillors stared at me! I was determined to show them I was a daughter of the greatest king France has ever known. There is a silly story that he said Paris was worth a mass. Well, I was not going to consider England worth a single Protestant service. I refused to be crowned according to the rites of the Church of England, or even to walk in the Coronation procession. I had no one to advise me, I thought I was a heroine to deny myself the pleasure of walking beside the King, and seeing everyone think how pretty I looked and how young to be a queen. One can say these foolish things, my dears, now one is old and ugly.'

They laughed and protested, except Minette who sat gazing up into her mother's face in the mirror, praying her to go on.

'But this,' said the Queen, 'is not what I was meaning to tell you. It is only to show you that I thought myself very important, and that all my servants encouraged me to do so.

'Then I heard one day that the King had complained of them and was sending them all back to France. He came to tell me so himself; he sent away the women who were with me and locked the door. His face was pale and stern. I was terrified, yet I was more angry than afraid. I heard the clatter of their departure in the courtyard, I rushed to the window and beat on the glass, shrieking to them to remain with me. King Charles seized my wrists and dragged me away from the window – I screamed and stamped, but would not budge an inch. I remember thinking with that despair that only the very young can feel – for to them each moment lasts for ever – that I was being held prisoner in a hateful foreign land, alone against the whole world. And then, all in an instant, the King had flung his arms round me and was telling me he loved me, now in English, now in bad French. Yet we understood each other very well at that moment – indeed it was from that moment we knew that we loved each other, and in its good time that knowledge prevailed.'

40

She had reached her conclusion, lamely. She had meant to show her niece what a wonderful thing was the love of a husband such as hers had been, such as her son would be. But she could not now feel that it was of so much importance what Mademoiselle and her son should do. She had pressed her hand against her heart so that beneath her bodice she could feel the stiff folds of her husband's last letter to her. It had lain there for over two years, and would do so now till she died. 'Dear Hart,' it began; so all his letters began; and it was true, she had been the pulse of all his thoughts and actions, of all but one, the greatest of all, his thought of God. How jealous she had been of that omission!

Her mind darted here and there, seeking escape, for it had got caught in a tunnel where at the very end, as at the wrong end of a telescope, she saw a tiny picture of a black figure laying his head upon a block. Once her thoughts were entrapped in that tunnel, they huddled together, fighting each other in the dark. She had held fast to the right, to God, to the Church; had this indeed helped to destroy her husband? Sometimes when off her guard she would hear a voice say it inside her, and then she would make some sudden movement, smile, or sing a snatch of song, do anything that would wrest her thoughts away, even as just now she had flung back her head and laughed after she had said, 'I was glad that he had beautiful eyes.'

Beneath her, the mirrored eyes of Mademoiselle, bright and curious, watched her aunt's lips move silently, and thought that her troubles had certainly cracked her brain a little.

King Charles moved the flambeau on his hip so that the shadows leaped sideways across the glass, and Mademoiselle's nose sprang into prominence in silhouette against the darkness. Mademoiselle's feet shifted and tapped on the floor like those of a restless horse; all her attention was withdrawn from her aunt as she asked her tiresome cousin why he could not hold the light as before.

The Queen's voice came out of the shadow, strained and harsh, 'Never have to say to yourself, "It was my own doing," for they are the most terrible words in the world.'

All present, even the child on the stool, knew this to be an admission of some secret and perhaps sudden remorse. But Mademoiselle preferred to be offended rather than be made uncomfortable by a pity that she found difficult to express.

'Why should your Majesty give me this warning?' she asked.

41

'Do you fear I should refuse the obvious advantages of a match with your son? I have had no chance to do so – no one has ever made love to me in person, and as I am not bad-looking, I can only suppose it is because people are afraid of me.'

'The present occasion is hardly suitable to a proposal,' said the torch-bearer, 'you would surely, Mademoiselle, prefer a larger audience.'

At last he had spoken. Minette loosed her grip on her knees and breathed in relief. At last, too, the faces in the mirror had moved, passed each other, vanished beyond its dark and shining surface. Mademoiselle was laughing and rapping at Charles' knuckles with her ivory comb, and the Queen, leaning against her niece's shoulder, was saying, 'Isn't he an incorrigible rogue? What shall we do to punish him?'

'Make him dance in tight boots,' cried her niece, shaking out her skirts with a great swish and rustle. 'Cousin, where is my fan? And I have forgotten my handkerchief.'

'Let me bring you your memory,' he protested as he searched the room, 'there cannot be much of it to carry.'

He flung open the door into the corridor, where their servants were waiting with torches. Off they went down the passage; the sound of their scurrying footfalls, their laughing voices, the swish of Mademoiselle's satins, floated back to the doorway where the Queen and Minette stood and watched their moving circle of light, until it went round the bend in the corridor, leaving at that corner a glimmering point, an echo, then nothing.

CHAPTER SEVEN

The ball was not a success from Queen Henrietta's point of view. She had exasperated her niece by sending her off with Charles in that obvious fashion; and then Charles quite suddenly attempted to prove his ardour in a manner that startled and offended Mademoiselle, who could swear like a trooper, but was more inherently bashful than most nuns.

She considered him inferior to herself, coarse, lazy, indifferent to all good qualities, inadequate for all her ideals, and yet he made her feel awkward, inexperienced and at a loss. The result was that in the renewed wars of the Fronde

42

Mademoiselle joined with the Prince of Condé against Mazarin and the royal family; and she went into action wearing in her hat a battered old feather that had been worn by her grandfather, Henry of Navarre. Was there ever anything so hysterical? demanded her aunt of England of her aunt of France. That girl had lost her head completely; a pity it was not her hat.

And Charles now devoted all his attention to an unscrupulous Parisian adventuress who had infatuated even staid old Chancellor Hyde, and rooked Sir Kenelm Digby of an unconscionable amount of money.

Queen Henrietta decided to consider only the spiritual welfare of those she loved. If she could help her eldest son embrace the true faith, he would have France and Spain as certain allies, and the wealth of the Papacy to help him win his throne. (But at this thought her small hands clenched, her head pounced forward, for the worldly motive had obtruded itself like the bright head of a snake.) At least her youngest, her child of benediction, as she called Henriette, should be brought up in the full grace of God.

She longed to found a religious house of her own outside Paris and there start a convent school, which would educate her daughter. She had been house-hunting indefatigably for some time, when one day she came rushing into the friendly convent in the Rue St Antoine, exclaiming that she had found the very place. A pretty house had been built at Chaillot by the most Christian Queen, Catherine de Medici, who had done so much for religion. It was approached by the Cours la Reine, where the gilded and painted coaches promenaded at evenings, as thick as gaudy moths under the summer trees; it stood on a little hill close to the river, the gardens were full of huge chestnut trees, brought long ago from India.

'Oh, Mam, let us go there at once!' cried Minette, and quite forgot that this new and enchanted palace might turn into the convent of Morton's warnings which was to hide her for the rest of her life.

But there were legal difficulties; the nuns must pay a large sum for the property within twenty-four hours, and neither they nor the Queen had a tenth part of the money.

And the Archbishop of Paris, a spiteful old man who had never got over the slight at Queen Henrietta's wedding nearly thirty years ago, where he had not been chosen to officiate,

43

now avenged it by saying that exiled queens who meddled with politics were the wrong sort of lodgers for convents.

But the Queen, undeterred, bustled round her furniture in the Louvre, putting labels on whatever she could spare for the rooms at Chaillot. 'Mère Angélique shall have this comfortable chair – I know she suffers from sitting on hard seats. And this writing-table will just fit into the window in my private sitting-room. Now you, my child, what would you like to take with you to your own little room at Chaillot?'

Her faith was rewarded; their obstacles melted away. Just before the twenty-four hours were up, a very fat business man, a friend of Mère Angélique, called to say he would guarantee the money for the property. He stood there in the hall, talking to her in a bluff cynical voice, pulled at his nose, and said that business was bad and money was very scarce and he didn't really know where he would get it from but it might turn out quite a paying proposition, and he expected all masses for his soul to be said free. At which the nuns, cooing round him, laughed and clapped their hands and called him the finger of God.

Queen Anne, with genuine affection, was delighted to see her sister-in-law's pleasure, and snubbed the Archbishop. So on a midsummer day the English Queen stood in the gardens at Chaillot with her little daughter beside her, awaiting the arrival of her greatest friend, Mère Angélique, and a dozen or so of the nuns from the convent in the Rue St Antoine.

Here came the coaches and the familiar faces, lit out of their accustomed placidity by the excitement of their journey – 'Only think! the holy Vincent de Paul came himself to see us off!' They ran over the gardens like a flock of birds, and the Queen had to clap her hands in summons. 'Now you must follow me,' she said as though she were at a children's party, and she led them through all the rooms – 'Yours, you see, are on the quiet side, overlooking the gardens. You do not see the road at all from here.'

But, no, they had taken the vow of poverty; they could not sleep in such splendid rooms, only in the garrets, and so they did, to the Queen's intense disappointment, until she had removed nearly all the comforts she had so carefully placed in their apartments.

The school was started, the English princess, as its first pupil, was a good advertisement, and the Queen hunted up

44

all the richest well-born children she could find to help with the expenses.

In this feminine society, guarded by great trees, in the quiet content induced by her friend's companionship, she discovered happiness greater than any she had known since her husband's death. Here she had a home of her own apart from her sister-in-law's hospitality and the appalling politeness it involved; here she was ruler, benefactress, almost saint.

Her feelings were more acute than her understanding; she did not perceive that her delight in her placid surroundings was due to their contrast with all that she had known; she hoped with her wonted energy that her aspirations might be fulfilled in her favourite child.

So, to begin with, she insisted that her daughter should learn humility by waiting at table on the nuns. They found it embarrassing, so did Minette when she spilt the soup, and knew that the other little girls in the school were laughing at her. Then she was baptized again, this time into the Catholic Church; the name Anne was added to Henriette in compliment to the Queen of France, and Father Cyprian was ordered to prepare a manual of religious instruction for her, bound in red leather, with her new initials H.A. stamped in gold on the cover.

Father Cyprian taught her her catechism with the other children. She loved the gentle old man; she liked being led into the chapel by her mother's hand, which she sometimes lost among the mourning veils, and found again with a satisfactory sense of reassurance that anything so small and soft and yet solid and compact, so firm and decisive, so playfully caressing, in fact so essentially her mother's hand, should still be there among the mysterious mass of thick black folds. She felt herself of unique importance in being led into the chapel by a mother so much more royal and more tragic than anybody else's mother.

The Protestant side of her family and of the little court of exiles were terrified of the Queen's designs upon her daughter. Was it possible that she intended her for a nun? The Princess Mary wrote from the Hague to protest, so did Elizabeth of Bohemia. Everybody warned each other, told King Charles, and Charles told his Chancellor, that somebody should take steps about it.

Morton had spoken to Minette of a convent as of something forbidden, secret, naughty, yet unutterably dismal and rather frightening. But this prison of her governess' Protestant imagination receded further and further in her mind. There was nothing dark and secret about these sunny gardens, these little girls with whom she did lessons, played and quarrelled, nor was there about the laughter of the nuns, more carefree even than that of the children they taught.

But perhaps there was about Mère Angélique, not dark indeed, but secret, the sort of secret thing that you would keep in the hidden drawer of a cabinet. Her small pupils fought for the privilege of putting flowers on her table, and she would smile graciously down at them with a lovely remembering look. Minette never believed it was them she was thanking, it was somebody far away and long ago.

Somebody had long ago given flowers to Mère Angélique, given her jewels and horses, and balls and picnic parties for her pleasure; she had been (so her father confessor had told her) 'petted like a bird of the Indies.' That somebody had been the late King of France, Louis XIII, brother to Queen Henrietta. This silent and lonely man, who had cared for nothing but hunting and was as dry and yellow as a withered leaf, had flared up at the end of his life into an almost selfless devotion to this girl of seventeen. He called her his angel; she was virtuous and proud and did not want to be his mistress. The Cardinal Richelieu had feared her influence and worked against it; she took the veil, and her only regret in her retirement, as she confided to her friend, was that it had given pleasure to that terrible enemy. She still loved to talk of King Louis with Queen Henrietta, who had privately thought her brother a bore, and was rather apt to remind her religious friend of his gaucherie, his long dull stories of dogs and horses, his slightly ridiculous admiration of virtue in the women he loved. And Mère Angélique would laugh with her, but very gently, and pull the reminiscences back to their emotional aspect which had given her her strange moment of importance.

'I think that was the only time in his life the poor soul ever knew true feeling. Have you ever thought it odd that that was the time when our Queen Anne, after remaining barren for twenty-three years, at last became enceinte?'

Should she tell to the dead King's sister what the King had once said to her? 'When my child is born, it should resemble you, rather than the Queen.' But would it be such a triumph?

46

The Queen might think it indelicate, worse still, absurd, in a middle-aged nun.

And now she hastened to protect her precious secret by hurrying on unwisely.

'He used to write down everything I said to him and everything he wanted to say to me, in case he forgot.'

'That is a common symptom of calf love. I do not think my brother ever grew up properly. Do you remember that stupid dog of his, Pinchot, and Louis telling him, "Now, Pinchot, die for the King." And Pinchot paying no attention to him but just scratching for fleas!'

The slumbering trees, heavy with dark foliage, brooded over the sunlit grass. In and out of their shadows moved the two women as slowly as two black swans swimming on an emerald lake. Old stories, old jokes, old torments, agonies, and indecisions had melted long ago, and now only added their spiced flavour to the warm inertia of late summer, the pungent scent from the box hedges, the droning sound like a large bee from the arbour where a nun was reading to an old blind lady.

And because she was thinking of her differences with her sons, and because the lot of mothers was hard, the Queen sighed, and looked sadly about her at two white butterflies circling up into the shimmering sky, and remembered a fat elderly woman who liked to play the lute though very badly, because it had reminded her of the time when she had played the lute as a little girl; and said, 'My poor mother! She may have been unwise, but her sons were not good to her.'

No one had been good to Marie de Medici; not even herself. When she had heard that her mother was coming to pay her a long visit in England, she had walked round her rooms, saying, 'Farewell now to my liberty.' Had she, too, disappointed her mother, even as she herself had been disappointed?

She gave herself a little shake and said, speaking rather fast, 'Well, thank Heaven, my daughters at least have always been devoted to me. Do you not think that it is men who make all the trouble in the world?'

As if to furnish immediate proof of it, one of the nuns came rustling over the lawn to tell her that Chancellor Hyde had called to see her on urgent business. The Queen turned on Mère Angélique, who was shocked to see her gentle friend and confidante transformed to an angry, alert and frightened woman. Her voice was high-strung, taut with expectation of battle. 'What is it now? He always brings trouble. A pettifogging lawyer – all he ever did in the war was to write a book about it.'

But even as she spoke she saw her husband's opinion of Hyde as though written in the air against that rose bush, whose petals had fallen in a pattern like lacework on the ground. 'The truth is I can trust nobody else.'

This was the penalty of knowing all his letters by heart, that phrases in them were apt to rise up and strike against her. For an instant she stood quite still, looking at the ground, then in a gentler tone, 'You should pick up those petals,' she said, 'they will make excellent potpourri,' and went to her sitting-room to give audience to Chancellor Hyde.

Queen Henrietta sat at her writing-table in the window that looked over the gardens to the broad river, and in the distance the grey towers and roofs of Paris; she sat in one of the old green leather arm-chairs, stamped with the medici monogram, that Queen Catherine had left there. They would do till she could get better. The Catholic Queen had been her father's mother-in-law and his greatest enemy; but like herself, she had been truly devoted to religion; so much so that it was believed she had poisoned that fiercely Protestant Queen, Jeanne d'Albret, mother of Henry of Navarre. Queen Henrietta preferred to disbelieve that story, and to forget that her grandmother had been a Protestant. She thought rather that if only all rulers in Europe had been as firm as Queen Catherine in stamping out heresy and revolution (which always went together) she herself would now be sitting on her own throne in England, instead of on this comfortable but shabby chair, to give audience to Chancellor Hyde.

Chancellor Hyde was gouty and fat; his face was drawn in circles, two decisive round chins, pouting round lips, a magnificent bulge of round forehead, and bushy grey tufts of eyebrows over round bright eyes.

It was no pleasant errand to him to visit this clever stupid Frenchwoman who had always been jealous of his influence, first over her husband, then over her son. She had fought for a despotism that had become impossible in England since the days of the Tudors. Henry of Navarre had restored the French monarchy at the very moment when it was failing in England, and his daughter, a truer Bourbon than her father, could not believe that times had changed, or that countries differed. She never recognized that the English upper and middle classes

48

had begun to take the lead over king and nobles; she regarded the Puritans as a mere band of fanatics, alien to the true spirit of the country, who wrote rude things against actresses and so got their ugly ears cut off; she never saw, not even when she had been impeached of high treason as the 'greatest Papist in the land', that to the majority of English minds Popery meant Spanish armadas, Popish spies, a persistent terror of the rack and *auto-da-fé*.

Thinking of these things, and of the love that this woman had so truly borne towards the husband she had ruined, and of the difficulties of his task, which caused him to fidget and mutter a curse against his young master who had devolved it, as he did most unpleasant tasks, upon his shoulders; thinking also (though he had no wish to do so, and was irritated at such illogical irrelevances in his orderly mind) that his royal mistress had been the prettiest little French kitten when first she had come to England, but that she had gone off very early (certainly the Dutch painter Van Dyke had always flattered her on his canvases) and that, at any rate as far as he himself was concerned, the Dowager Queen in her mourning robes and with her protruding teeth was no more than a dumpy plain little old woman, and when she directed that vicious glance at him she was indeed no more than an ugly old cat; so thinking, fidgeting, wondering whether this moment were really as important as he had feared (for what could any one man do to alter the course of history?) he burst out on an impulse of despair rather than of hope, 'Ah, Madam, what can I say to you? For we desire the same things, yet cannot see how we may go the same way to get them. And those most dear to you are those I would give my life to serve; yet at no time, I think, has my service been pleasing to you, and now I know that it will give offence.'

But his eloquence failed. She bade him be seated, a concession she thought politic to accord to his gout, but then told him to bare his point without any further courtesy of salute before the duel.

He sat heavily, blinking at the floor, wondering why it was that with such quick wits as his mistress possessed she invariably chose the wrong kind of men for her intimate friends; fops turned religious like that sentimental fool, Walter Montagu (the late King could never abide him); lap-dogs, lady-killers who curled their moustaches like that barber's block, Jermyn, doubtless her lover, who had actually wanted

49

to sell Jersey to the French, and had made bad jokes on the good old name of Hyde when he protested he would not part with one foot of English earth. Such was her choice of men. She had never got on with himself. His voice when he spoke again was cold and formal.

'Madam, I am a lawyer. Let me state the case as in a court of law. England is by now an obstinately Protestant country. If she could ever be induced to take a king again, it will have to be a Protestant king, and with the security of Protestant heirs. Madam, it was his Majesty's last wish that his children should be brought up in his religion, it was his first care that the Princess Henriette should be baptized into it, and it was your promise to him, Madam, that his wishes should be regarded. Is his martyrdom and death a reason they should now fall into neglect?'

Now he had said it. She sprang to her feet, and he actually thought for an instant that she would strike him. Twice she began to speak, then, choking on her words, she turned about and deliberately looked from him to the window where she could see nothing through her maze of tears until a small slouching form came dawdling down one of the paths, kicking at a pebble, her skirts held up almost to her knees; whereupon the Queen's efforts to repress her rage were transmuted by the minor effort to refrain from shrieking to her daughter to hold her head up and remember her backbone.

'I tell you, sir,' she burst out on a high note of passion, 'all my life I have been torn here, torn there. I know well you think my religion helped in England to destroy my lord the King. Yet abroad I am suspected as the wife and mother of heretics; I have been told again and again that had my faith been strong enough to convert them, I should have been given all the money and armies necessary to win the throne again. My sister-in-law of Bohemia wishes my daughter to be a Protestant – very good, but my sister-in-law of France is continually demanding proof that she is being properly instructed in the Catholic religion. Even you, sir, must consider the Queen of France is in a better position to help her than the other. Sir, my husband trusted you. Let me do so too. I will tell you – so great is the love she bears to me and my little daughter that her dearest wish is to marry her to her son King Louis, and see her Queen of France. Will you tell me then that it is a wise and politic thing to bring her up as a Protestant?'

She leaned forward, scarcely breathing her words. Her eyes

50

shone. 'The prettiest French kitten' was once again recognizable, a kitten that sees a ball dangled before its nose and only waits to draw itself together before it pounces on it. Hyde shot a glance at her in amazement. Here was the secret of eternal youth, that Queen Henrietta should put more faith in the romantic friendship of a somewhat foolish elderly woman who had always let her emotions run away with her, than in the iron policy of her minister Mazarin. Would *he* think a penniless little exile, however pathetic, a suitable match for the King of France?

But he was quick to seize the handle she had given him and secure a secondary point. If these were her hopes for the Princess, then she could not object to giving her royal word that at least she would not place her in a convent.

The Queen was caught. She went scarlet. This came of trusting anyone, of speaking her mind. Forgetting all that she was wont to say in praise of the English, she hit her hands together and cried, 'Has there ever been one spark of chivalry in your nation?' They had hated her from the beginning; all they cared about was this new dead negation of all faith, love and beauty that they had made into a religion and called Protestantism – good God, what a word! She was a criminal because she had gone to church, because she had sung and danced and loved to act in masques. She wondered the flowers themselves were not forbidden. 'The very weather protested when I entered your capital, the rain ruined the procession. And that first terrible night in England when I was put into an old bed, a bed that your Queen Elizabeth had slept in! None of my attendants, however old, had ever seen such a bed, yet it had been assigned to me in compliment as a relic of glorious antiquity. Oh, you English, so barbarous and so sentimental!'

And now she was laughing, but crying as she laughed, as indeed she had been doing through most of this outpouring. The embarrassed Chancellor, breathless, battered, as if trying to hold up his head against a tornado, and, what was more, hold the thread of the matter at issue and discern how he could find a path back to it through all these circumlocutions, did by a stroke of genius, that was largely the result of exhaustion, perceive that his best hope was to meet her on her own ground; though that was to him no ground at all but mere winds and gusts of passion, obscuring mists of memory and fantasy, showers of tears extinguishing all hope of sense.

51

He knelt, and sinking his head upon her hand he said, 'Madam, the cards are all mixed up. At present they are against us. But we are gamesters who were first engaged by conscience against all motives and temptations of interest. We must play out the game, and help each other in it as best we may.'

Her orgy of emotion had left her feeble, almost indifferent. A little weary smile crept round the corners of her mouth. Englishmen liked to talk in phrases borrowed from the card-tables or tennis-courts; they were so simple and serious in their use of them that even grave lawyers like Chancellor Hyde were apt suddenly to seem like children. That after all was what she had liked best in them, and best of all in her husband, who had depended upon her with a child's utter trustfulness.

But that way madness lay. She must not think of that helpless, undeveloped strain in Charles that had persisted in him ever since he had been a backward, sickly baby, unable to speak or toddle until he was past three years old. She alone knew, as though she had been his mother, what courage had been needed to make himself a man. When she thought of the sad, bewildered child in him, always too gravely conscientious, too slow-thinking to understand the minds of others, it was unbearable; she did not know which way to turn, for a horrible picture danced before her eyes of his state in prison, ill-treated, neglected, dirty, so that at forty-eight he had looked an old man past seventy. And a part of her had found relief in that she had not after all, in spite of her frantic efforts, seen him then.

The sharp division in her mind threatened to cleave her brain. In dull attempt to bridge it, she stared stupidly at the stout man before her, and tried to give her consent an appearance of graciousness.

'You have my promise, sir. I will not give my daughter to God.'

She sank back in the green chair that still bore the Medici monogram, she pressed her hand to her head and hardly heard him go. Nowhere in this world was there any peace.

In the garden below, Mère Angélique walked with one of the nuns. Looking down on her with affection, tinged with exasperation that she should waste her time with that shallow de Vaudois, the Queen longed for the selfless calm of the conventual life. She noticed the two shadows below were longer

52

than when she had walked there with her friend; the sun was sinking, time was passing, soon she and Mère Angélique and even her little daughter Henriette would all be dead, even as poor weak Charles and his beautiful eyes were dead. Why then did one struggle, since only God endured?

CHAPTER EIGHT

One night in the Palace of the Louvre King Louis' faithful servant, La Porte, came to him, and told him he must get up and dress, and fly with his mother and brother yet again. He was hurried into his clothes, and his teeth began to chatter, for it was a cold night. He kept repeating to himself it was a cold night, for he would not admit another reason for his shivering, and that was a low murmur that swelled and then subsided and then grew again and came nearer and nearer, from every side that he could hear, all round the Palace, hemming him in so that he could not believe he would ever find his way through it and escape. This was the second time he had had to get up and fly in the middle of the night; it was an odious habit, unbecoming to a king; he found he hated to go to bed, to have the lights put out round him, lest, in looking into the darkness, he should see La Porte coming towards him with a candle in one hand and the other held round it to protect the flame which tossed and flickered up into his face, struck against the open black cavern of his mouth and the whites of his round frightened eyeballs.

That was how he had seen him on a frozen night in January, when he and Philippe had been hurried into cloaks, shawls, feminine things, with no time to dress properly. They had been taken down a stairway that nobody used, and out through a little private door into a side street where their horses had stood, slipping and sliding on the icy ground; they had ridden all through the night as hard as they could to Saint Germain, and, when they reached it, there had been no food, no furniture, worst of all, no fires. And the next thing he had heard was that another King, his uncle, the King of England, had been executed by his own subjects.

These dismal memories of his first flight beset his mind as he sat on the bed, and La Porte thrust his legs into boots which seemed as though they would never get on. The murmur suddenly became a roar, so close to his ears that it must surely be within the Palace. He started up, kicking over the second boot, calling out 'What's that?' in a cry that was all but a shriek, for someone was at the door, scrabbling to get in. La Porte clapped his hand over his mouth, the doors were flung open, and there stood his mother, Anne of Austria, Queen Regent of France, her face white, her hair dishevelled, her mouth open, her speech stuttering, unable to come clearly. She stumbled across the room to him – 'Get back into bed,' she said, mumbling her words so that they were hardly audible, 'the people are in the Palace.' She pushed him back on the bed, she pulled off his other boot and thrust them into a cupboard, and she and La Porte tore off his clothes between them, pulled on his nightgown, and hurried him under the bedclothes.

'Understand,' she whispered fiercely to him, 'you are in bed, asleep; you have done nothing else this night. If they thought you were escaping, they might tear you in pieces. Lie still, breathe deep and quiet, keep your eyes closed.'

She spoke close to his ear, standing between him and noises that were coming nearer, up to the room itself.

Hardly had she done so when she was back at the door again, and he heard her open it, go outside, and speak in quiet though urgent tones.

'The King is in bed, asleep. You can see for yourselves that there has been no thought of his leaving the Palace this night. Enter then and look on him; but quietly I beg of you. Do not wake the child.'

And then came incredible sounds of shuffling, snuffling, whispering, of people scraping into the room and pausing, then approaching him with shapeless, furtive tread, passing close to his bed, leaning over him, breathing over him, stinking breaths of garlic and age-old clothes and unwashed bodies. As if his eyes had been wide open, he could see their starved faces, ferociously inquisitive, their filthy rags, their procession of gaunt diseases. And he, their slave, had to lie still and pretend sleep, for fear of this pack of dirty wolves that pattered past him.

'Breathe quietly, keep your eyes closed' – no easy thing when his heart was leaping like a trapped rabbit in his fear and anger. They had caught him in his own palace, hemmed him in, prevented him from leaving it. Louis the Gift of God they had called him, and this was how they treated him!

54

What sort of King was he whom the rabble could command like this?

'Think of the King of England,' said a small voice inside him, and he did, of the uncle he had never seen, who had let himself be beheaded. He should never have done it. Anything but that. The shock had echoed through the world. Far away in India a king had decreed that anyone who ever mentioned the crime should be executed with torture. That was the way to rule, as kings still could in India. If King Charles had killed himself in prison it would have been better, for then people could still have thought – 'At the last moment they would not have dared – no people would dare kill a king in cold blood, after trial, like any of his subjects.'

But now royalty would never be safe again. Louis could have sworn at his uncle for failing to keep his throne or his head. He had made things more difficult for kings ever after. He had let down his class. Whenever he thought of it, he became rigidly royal and would cuff Philippe for some disrespect to the throne; he could not do that now, and wondered anxiously what was happening to Philippe. He was a plucky little devil when put to it, and might easily show fight unnecessarily.

He must have lain here for hours, and still the people were going past him, their prisoner. If only he could escape from them once again, he would never come back to Paris; he would leave the mob here to howl as they would, they should not get at him again. But here they were now, close over his bed, closer; he thought he would choke, scream out with rage and disgust as though rats were crawling over him.

'Do not press so near,' said his mother's voice quite near him, 'you will wake the King.'

When she was even a little excited or angry she became shrill; but now when Louis knew her to be trembling with nervous rage, her voice was low and calm, reassuring him as well as those half-savage intruders.

The light was stronger. She must be standing by him with a candle. A wave of her perfume flowed over him. He had always hated perfumes, and she used the same as Mazarin's but stronger; now, when it was combined with the stench of the crowd and the growing airlessness of the room, he thought he would be actually sick. And why should he not be? Why should he not wake up and say he felt ill and needed air? Hundreds and hundreds had now seen him lying asleep. But

55

he knew he must not dare, that the report that would run back along the crowd that was waiting to see him, might confuse and irritate their suspicions, and in an instant rouse them to a dangerous fighting mob.

The slum people of Paris had rushed out of their holes in the early battles of the Fronde to fight with sticks and knives and stones; and now here they were in the Palace, in his bedroom. He must keep still and not mind that his foot had gone to sleep, for it was safer not to risk even a movement, he must keep his eyes closed against that light which suffused his eyelids with a red angry glow, so that they burned and itched to open. They fluttered on his cheek – then for an instant when he felt no one very near him, he let them lift the least little bit and saw the broad dark back of his mother with the candle in one hand and the other on the bed curtains which she had half drawn, and beyond her a face that gaped in a toothless grin, and then others, like faces seen in a nightmare – but they were coming up to his bed, he did not dare look; his eyelids closed fast again. He had to lie cowering, afraid to look on his people – 'By God,' he swore to himself through clenched teeth while his lips seemed merely to close in the peaceful smile of a boy's deep sleep, 'I will never look on them again if I can help it.'

When he was small he used to like to play at being a valet, and pretend that La Porte, his valet, was the King. La Porte had not approved of that, he thought it disgracefully lacking in royal dignity. But what was he doing all the time but playing at being a king? – pretending it, that was all it was. The whole of one winter he had had to wear his last year's coat, too short in the sleeves, because his mother could not afford to buy a new one. But Mazarin, for whom all these wars were fought, never had to go ill-dressed. Mazarin might be banished, but he would never be uncomfortable. And his mother loved him best, better than her son Louis, King of France. (Tears of indignant self-pity began to tingle in his eyes, until checked back by terror lest they should show through his lashes and betray his shamming.) Nobody loved him really, except La Porte, and Philippe, silly little fool, who was no better than a girl. He would not care if people loved him or not, but anyway, nobody should bully him and order him about; they would find that out later, let them just wait, that was all, Mazarin and his mother, Mademoiselle, who used to infuriate him by taking him on her knee and calling him

56

her little husband, she and her silly father, who had both of them dared combine with his cousin the fierce Prince of Condé, and taken up arms against the royal troops. They were as much responsible for his lying here, cramped and cold, not daring to stir or sneeze, as were these ugly gutter rats that scuffled past his bed. They too would see, they would all see – what would they see?

He had shut his eyelids tight now so that rings revolved in the red darkness, great suns, one after the other, each larger than the last. For a moment the Queen, bending over him in an attitude of maternal solicitude for his slumbers, very impressive to the passing crowd, wondered if her son had really fallen asleep. For a moment he had fallen, not into sleep, but into a deep and dreamlike peace; he had ceased to hear and smell what was round him, he heard nothing but the rustling, whispering silence of the woods and smelt nothing but the sharp fragrance of wet bracken; a yellow leaf drifted idly through the still air and brushed against his cheek. A few weeks ago when it was still early autumn, he had been taken hunting in the woods in the Val de Galie, and was told that they would stop for a slight collation at Versailles, a hunting-box built by his father, which had lain empty ever since he used to hunt here.

Towards sunset they had come to a clearing in the woods and clattered through an archway in a high red wall into a weed-grown courtyard. There before them in the midst of a prim garden that had been left to grow wild, stood a pleasant red-brick house with slender pinnacles whose faded gilding had caught the last rays of the sun. Swifts flew in and out under the pointed roofs of blue slate; they were the only people who had lived here for years. The box hedges were ragged and unclipped, the stagnant moat was thick with green scum, tall evening primroses straggled across the paths and even in the cracks of the garden wall. There never was so quiet a place. The delicately built modern house was like a card castle; a toy that had been carelessly dropped in the forest, neglected and forgotten.

Louis' father had grown so fond of it that his first instinct, in pleasure or in sorrow, was always to go to Versailles. He had given his gayest hunting-party here for the angel he loved; when she left him to become a nun he had retired here to nurse his grief; in his last illness he vowed that if he recovered

57

he would abdicate and spend the rest of his life here in contemplation, and the company of four Jesuit fathers.

His younger son Louis did not know all this; nor did he think of his father, whose sad, sickly face he could barely remember. He had looked up at the deserted house and the forest trees behind it in the pale September sunset, and heard the horses trampling in this courtyard which had lain quiet for eight years. Far away, a horn echoed in the forest. He had thought how he would like to live here, removed from his palace of the Louvre and the evil-smelling streets of Paris and their treacherous populace.

And now once again the memory of that little house in the woods where his father used to escape swept over him, calming him at first; then suddenly it rubbed against his other fancies, causing a spark that flared up and set his brain on fire. Certainly he too would escape to Versailles, but to no little hidden house; he would build a palace there so superb that people would come across the world to see it; he would surround it with gardens as far as the eye could see; he would desert this fickle, filthy city, move his whole Court there and live in his own world, remote from any other. A king would be absolute monarch at Versailles, no one could question his will; the mob would never reach him there.

It was all he could do to prevent himself from rolling over and biting the bedclothes in his ecstasy at this sudden and superb discovery of his determination to be king indeed one day and do exactly as he liked. He would have wars, in which he would conquer all his enemies; ballets, in which he would take all the chief parts; fireworks; feasts in the gardens, with whole mountains of caramel and marzipan and all the trees hung with crystallized fruits (he had always wished they grew in orchards). People might call him greedy, but it would have to be behind his back – what was the use of being a king if you could not be greedy? He would hunt every day, he would ride in the forest at night, all night if he chose. No one would dare to scold him or tell him he must not do this or that; Mazarin would not be there; his mother would be in the background, adoring him; Philippe would be there to exclaim and admire, afraid even to pat the fiery horses he rode, amusing him with his mimicries, especially of old Skim-the-Milk, and his funny stories, and his tricks on other people – but he would never dare then to play them on himself.

In this construction of his kingdom he had almost ceased to

notice the steps that went past him, until it struck him that for some time they had sounded more straggling and separate; then came one with a limp, a horrible hop-jiggety-hop, and at last, very slowly, that too died away. The doors closed softly, mockingly softly, still pretending not to wake him; someone gave a great sigh that turned into a sob; his mother's arms were round him, her large soft bosom was all over him, her breath came in the quick pants and little shrieks which, as Louis knew from experience, heralded an attack of hysterics. He jerked himself away from under her weight, scrambled to his feet, and standing on the bed in his nightgown, he raised his clenched fists above his head and shook them at the doors through which his people had passed.

CHAPTER NINE

The Prince of Condé, cousin to the French king, had been acclaimed throughout Europe as the greatest captain of his age. The generals Turenne in France and Cromwell in England later disputed this claim with him; but neither did anything as spectacular as Condé, who at the age of twenty-three had inflicted a crushing defeat with his infantry on the Spanish armies at Rocroi. Till then they had been thought as invincible as the Spanish armada had been a century earlier. The prestige of the French prince was therefore enormous. In ordinary life he was nobody – uncouth, and even unpleasant in appearance, for he took no care of it; his nails were dirty, his hair was ragged and untidy, and with his great nose and restless, discontented eyes he was apt to look rather like a brooding vulture. But in battle this changed completely. A fiery light shone in his eyes, his voice was cheerful and caressing, he acquired a charm that seemed indeed magic, for he could then do what he liked with men, and send them to certain death as gay as he was himself. The greater the carnage, the happier and more confident he seemed.

His cousin La Grande Mademoiselle had a passion for Corneille's plays, where the heroes were superhuman, of iron will, driven by desire of glory, vengeance or power, but never by the softer passions. They were above love, as they were above pity or remorse for the suffering they inflicted. She wished to resemble them, as Condé undoubtedly did, and dismissed a maid from her service because she married for love.

In the wars of the Fronde, Condé was against Mazarin, and therefore the Court. Turenne had on one occasion to rescue the person of the King from Condé's armies; it was even thought that his sombre and fiery ambition aimed at seizing the throne for himself. In the meantime Mademoiselle realized that, largely owing to Mazarin, she had come no nearer to being Empress nor yet Queen of France. She had passed her twenty-fifth birthday, and that was an advanced age for so great a princess to be unmarried. Her complexion was beginning to coarsen; she spent more time at her mirror and with less satisfaction.

King Charles had returned distinctly improved from his unfortunate campaign in England, but was still incapable of a true appreciation of her. She hoped for examples of forlorn and desperate courage, and he talked about wet boots. She compared him unfavourably with Condé and exclaimed 'Thank Heaven!' when the civil wars broke out again.

Her father was of no use in them. Mademoiselle took charge, she rode at the head of the troops; she took Orleans practically single-handed by the sheer force of her personality, and returned to Paris to be hailed with shouts of joy as the Modern Maid of Orleans. Nicknames went to her head, she saw herself as Queen of France, the new Joan of Arc, and all the superhuman heroes and heroines of Corneille in one.

When Condé tried to enter Paris his army was cut off at the gates of Saint Antoine by the King's. The carnage was terrible, the streets were full of wounded and dying; Mademoiselle ran to her father and cried, 'Condé will be killed. What can we do?'

'I have got a terrible headache,' said Gaston, 'I really ought to be in bed.'

Nothing she could say could induce him to take any other action. He felt quite sick, he said. He should not wonder if he had been poisoned; perhaps it was those mushrooms last night; but no, he did not think it necessary to take any medicine – medicines were so upsetting – as long as he could sit over the fire, and not be troubled—

'For God's sake, then, go to bed,' she screamed at him, 'and pretend to be really ill. Do not disgrace us more than is necessary. I will save Condé myself, single-handed, as I took Orléans.'

60

'There you go again! Always play-acting. Always being the heroine. All the fault of these pompous plays. I detest tragedies. I'd rather any day look at little dancing boys dressed as monkeys.'

'I do not act the heroine, I am of birth so high that it is only natural to me to do what is great and noble.'

But the originator of this birth made a grimace at her, and she burst into tears. He had often betrayed his friends, sometimes herself. She knew that part of her difficulties in marrying were caused by his unwillingness to let her vast fortune go out of the family. And yet he stood there with his eyebrows raised quizzically at her, looking like a handsome, mocking, petulant boy – just as when he had played long matches at battledore and shuttlecock with her when she was a child, and paid her his 'debts of honour' (for he had always let her win) in little jewelled and enamelled watches. In those days he had treated her as a boon companion and an equal, he had laughed delightedly when she gave herself airs, he had introduced his younger mistresses to her and she had been convinced that they were as good as they were pretty.

She did not want to remember those days, she did not want to cry as she always did in this humiliating womanish fashion in their quarrels; she wanted to tell him how she scorned and hated him. But as always there was that imperturable barrier of his indifference. There he was now putting out his tongue in the mirror and rubbing it with his laced handkerchief to see if it were furred; he was actually getting amusement out of his rôle as an invalid; he really did not care what anyone thought of him. She turned and rushed out of the room, down the stairs, out into the street.

Alone, unattended, jostling past wounded or dying men, men that sometimes she knew, she ran to the Bastille. She saw the Duc de la Rochefoucauld being led along by his young son and some other men, then she saw that he had been terribly wounded in the face, which was streaming with blood. 'His eyes,' sobbed the poor boy in answer to her question, 'a musket ball has gone through the corners of both his eyes.'

She could not wait. Hers was no woman's part. She must pursue her mission.

The air in her nostrils was like wine; the streets through which she ran were no longer just the streets of Paris that she had known since childhood, they were the field of glory that

61

she had been born to tread. Phrases came in and out of her mind – 'I am of birth so high – so high—'

She had reached the Bastille. Once again she would show what a great princess could do single-handed. She stormed and browbeat those in charge until she induced them to turn the heavy guns on the royal troops.

Thus she enabled Condé and his army to enter the city in safety; and thus, as Mazarin exclaimed when he heard of it, she herself killed her husband. There was no hope that Louis would marry her after that. Condé was now the man she ought to marry, so her friends all told her; and she pretended to laugh at the notion, to protest that it was altogether too romantic, that she was not a schoolgirl to imagine that he would come for her like Amadis for his Oriana on a palfrey, and run over everybody he met on the road to win her. There was also another objection; for Condé was already married.

There had been nothing self-interested in Mademoiselle's action. Like most of hers it was one of unpremeditated impulse. In moments of crisis, she said, the soul shows its nobility by hastening to the aid of what is noblest. Condé was fighting against the King's army, but Condé was the greatest captain of his age, he had covered France with glory, and it behoved France in the person of Mademoiselle to testify her gratitude in that sudden and inconvenient hour.

'I am at my best when things go badly,' she said, but she spoke too soon. It became the turn of the royal troops to enter Paris, the turn of the boy King to be hailed as the saviour of his country. Mademoiselle lost her nerve, she fled in undignified and unnecessary panic, in disguise, in continual tears; her father would not shelter her lest he be associated in her disgrace, no one would welcome so dangerous a guest.

She reached an old broken-down mansion where the grass stood knee-deep in the courtyard, the windows were boarded up, and spiders swung from the ceiling. It was two o'clock in the morning; she was cold, worn out with fatigue, she had ceased to feel fear or even hunger; only a negation of all hope or interest, a supreme desolation. She had taken her own road, and this was where it had let her. The end of her flight was, she realized, the end of her reign of glory.

Soon she would begin to plan again, to improve the place until she could hold some sort of Court there; to build a theatre even before the workmen had finished with her bedroom; to read, to keep a diary, and to declare with her ac-

62

customed naïve courage how her many resources helped her in her retirement, so that she never missed the Court ceremonies in which she had been wont to take such keen and controversial pleasure.

But in that pale and ghastly hour she could foresee nothing of the compensations she would perforce make for herself. Six years of exile were before her, of perpetual quarrels about money with her father and stepmother, of matrimonial projects which would come to nothing. Condé would express his gratitude, he would even wash his hands when he came to see her, a remarkable tribute; but Condé's wife, despite her continual ill-health, would persist in living on.

It seemed to her afterwards that she had known all this at the moment when she had stood in her new home and smelled the dust thick all round her, and a great spider ran down to the end of his web to stare at her. 'I knew it all then,' she said to herself; and another memory hit on his mind like a blow, the memory of her own face staring at her from a mirror, bright and unaware, and behind her the voice of her aunt of England croaking her ill-omened warning:

'Never have to say to yourself, "it was my own doing," for they are the most terrible words in the world.'

CHAPTER TEN

The wars of the Fronde were now over, and Cardinal Mazarin was reinstalled in absolute power in the capital whence he had been driven three times. With her astonishing resilience Paris recovered with a bound into gaiety. Street songs against Mazarin and the Queen were increasingly good-humoured, if as disrespectful as ever. After all, why shouldn't the poor widow have her lover, and the populace welcomed him in that capacity with a frankness that shocked the decorous Queen.

Louis had grown into a handsome boy; Mademoiselle into an old maid. No one saw or remembered her, but here was a new young King who sat his horse well; people threw down their work and ran through the streets at sound of the horn to see him riding with his nobles and Court ladies in their feathered hats and velvet dresses to the hunt; they stood a whole day in a sweating crowd and fought at the end of it to get even standing room at the back of the theatre when he put on one of his stupendous ballets. The price of the tickets was enormous, and one might swoon and be trampled in the press at the entrance, but at least it was all equal; even the reporters had to pay and wait for hours for their seats. And then the ballets themselves were marvels of costly splendour and modern machinery, and the most splendid sight in the whole show was the young King himself. Monarchy justified itself, there was no revolution; and the Cardinal Mazarin gave a ball in honour of his nieces at his palace, the most magnificent in the world.

At the ball, the youngest princess of the royal house of England made her first appearance in public at the age of nine. It was a critical moment for Minette, preceded by many anxious months. Queen Anne, on her visits to her sister-in-law Queen Henrietta at Chaillot, always sent for her niece, gave her a picture, or better still a little wax figure of one of the saints, patted her hair, and asked her questions out of the Catechism. Then, sailing with majestic ease from one world to the other, she would try to persuade the Queen of England to bring her little daughter to Court. In her girlish friendship with Henrietta, the younger, smaller, quicker-witted woman had plagued and teased her but never ignored her as her dreary young husband, Louis XIII, had done. She liked to think how charming it would be if her son were to marry her friend's daughter and thus unite France to England and reinstall the Catholic faith in that lost island.

But Queen Henrietta, who was clear-sighted enough into the error of others, expostulated that Henriette was still so delicate, had suffered so from convulsions as an infant, and excitement was so bad for the sensitive little creature, above all, the child had no clothes fit to wear.

And Minette, trying to look strong and insensitive, would stand clenching her hands to prevent their trembling while her fate rolled backwards and forwards over her head. Cousinly criticisms (Mademoiselle had said she was not pretty), infant convulsions, no dowry, no dresses, all pointed to a convent as a more likely career for her than a Court.

But at last Queen Henrietta had been induced to make an exception for this very special occasion, since her youngest son, Henry, Duke of Gloucester, was also to make his first public appearance at the Court of France. He had lately been released by the Commonwealth from Carisbrooke Castle in the Isle of Wight, where he had lived a private rather than a prison life with his tutor and had been known as Master Harry Stuart. The arrival in France of this fair shy boy of thirteen was the event that Minette had longed for all her childhood, but now that it had come it was overshadowed by the terror and delight of her entry into the world.

And he, after his long seclusion, was more bewildered than she.

'Take your sister's hand,' said the little bustling Frenchwoman who was his mother, 'and lead her into the ballroom. She has to appear in the ballet this evening, and you must reassure her.'

His sister Elizabeth had for long been his only companion, and had died. It was strange to find this also was his sister, the little foreign girl in a glittering Court dress, with whom he could only talk in formal, halting French, and she in uncertain English. He took her hand, which was as cold as ice.

'Have you never danced before, my sister?'

'Not in public, my brother,' she replied in her soft tinkling French voice, 'and I have to speak a piece of poetry. If I forget it I will disgrace the ballet.'

Her smooth fair hair was combed straight back from her high forehead and fastened at the back of the head with a circlet of pearls, but fell in loose ringlets at the sides of her serious, oval face. The two children, strangers till that moment, kept close together for protection. Around them burned thousands of candles; their heart-shaped points of flame rose all over the vast room, wavering a little here and there, sinking ever a little lower as the perfumed wax spent itself.

'When they are all burnt out it will be dark,' said Harry, not knowing, like so many solitaires, when he spoke aloud. This effulgence of soft light that left no shadows anywhere was the most marvellous sight since his release from captivity. It fell on the gold plate, making it look black and dull in places, but it transformed the chandeliers and goblets of Venetian glass into irridescent bubbles that at any moment might float through the air and dissolve. The room was alive with faces that looked kindly upon them, their smiles shone, their hair glittered with jewels, their clothes were sparks and rivers of light.

James too was to dance in the ballet. He looked after his young brother and sister, took them to the banquet table and sat beside them. He was a man now, strong and confident; he was the only relative in this new world that Harry could at all remember. The last time he had seen him they had been play-

ing hide-and-seek with their sister Elizabeth one spring evening years ago in the garden at St James' Palace, where they
had all been imprisoned; and James had hidden for so long
that he was never found, for he had escaped, and left England
disguised as a girl. He showed Harry how he had nearly given
himself away by his immodest manner of sticking up his leg
on a table and pulling up his stocking.

'I was dressed up as a boy when I ran away from England,'
said Minette, 'and I slept under a hedge.'

'Can you remember it then?' asked Harry.

That was not a fair question. Why should she not remember
it when everyone else remembered and told their adventures?
She changed the subject with a certain dignity of manner. 'Do
you like these scarlet sugared apples? They are better if one
licks them all over, but one can't do that here.'

They admired the castles and ships and systems of the
planets, all made out of sweetmeats which would later be cut
up for them to eat. But they grew very tired waiting for this to
happen.

People noticed them with pleasure; they were alike in their
transparent colouring and look of brittle delicacy, alike also
in an unconsciously wistful smile, which made ladies declare
they were a pair of infant cherubs, not long for this world.
They swept off Harry after the banquet in a swirl of satins and
cooing questions and little pleased laughs. Minette had a
glimpse of him later in the evening; he looked bewildered, a
trifle foolish, and in his hand was an exquisite little mermaid
of marzipan and sugar which he held so tight that her breasts
had begun to melt.

James was now an officer in the French army. He had seen
action under Turenne and acquired so good a reputation for
leadership and personal courage that the Irish soldiers, who
had been banished from their own country and taken service
in Spain, had begun to desert to the French army in order to
be under him. He had four mules now to carry his baggage,
and as many horses as he wanted. He had always been more
popular in France than his brother Charles, and was now of so
much more consequence that Charles was only treated with
tolerable consideration when James was present.

Tonight even that vicarious courtesy was denied Charles, for
people seemed to avoid him. He stood a little apart from his
surroundings, looking on at them with occasional amusement

but no personal interest. It would have been easy in that company to single him out as the exiled King.

James joined him, full of gossip of the three young nieces of the Cardinal, who were also making their début this evening. Two of the Mancini girls had enough good looks and high spirits for three; James had heard that Olympe was King Louis' favourite, but he himself wanted to know what Charles thought of Marie.

'I don't,' said Charles, and his eyes rested heavily on the full bosom and flashing eyes of her sister, Olympe. There was a girl indeed.

> *'Pan's Syrinx was a girl indeed*
> *Whom Jove transforméd to a reed.'*

But no reed would suffice Olympe. A plum now, or a pineapple, its barbaric head tufted with plumes.

'They say,' said James, 'that they and their brother—'

'They always say that,' said Charles impatiently, 'it is time someone thought of a new vice,' and he turned to speak to the Cardinal himself, who was passing them with a sleek bow. But Mazarin contrived to ignore him altogether while he addressed a few affable words to James. Then, apologizing for leaving them, explaining, indicating his master's wishes, he hastened on to the side of King Louis, his voluminous robes flowing in measure to his suave movements.

'I am useful to him as a mercenary,' said James uncomfortably; 'as I have to earn my living that way,' he added, 'it is a pity I can't do so fighting for our own countries.'

This remark seemed to throw Charles into a profound depression, and James accused him of unreasonable gloom. Charles gave a slight shake to his shoulders, which made him look like a great dog come out of the water. 'I have some sort of reason for it,' he said, and lowering his voice, he told James briefly that Mazarin had that day concluded a treaty of peace with Cromwell, recognizing him as Lord Protector of England. He could therefore no longer afford shelter to the Protector's enemy in France.

'So I must pack and go,' he concluded, 'though where I don't know. The number of countries where I am not an undesirable alien are growing few. Well, I've not yet tried Ethiopia.'

James was flushed and excited. He wanted to resign his commission, to tell that smooth red fox exactly what he thought of him.

Queen Anne was feeling very sorry for her nephew, King Charles, and anxious to be nice to him. James had more charm, while Charles was still apt to be odd, uncouth and abrupt as when he had been a lanky boy, and lazy and stupid too to a point of almost unnatural indifference – but even he would recognize his misfortune in being turned out of France. Did he yet know of it? She fancied there was an unpleasant awareness in her nephew's dark face this evening, though that might easily be because he needed a new suit of clothes. It was indeed all very tragic, but Jules, who knew everything, had said this peace with the arch-traitor was a stern necessity.

A stout shabby man with a red face was looking hard at Charles. Did he know that Charles must go? It would be terrible if Queen Henrietta should hear of it tonight. She moved her fan backwards and forwards in restless agitation.

'You find the night very hot, my aunt?' asked Charles. 'Will you let me fan you?'

'Who is that fat man next to the Marquis of Ormonde?' she asked.

So that was the trouble. Charles looked at Hyde, leaped to conclusions, and supposed that his mother had again been complaining of the Chancellor to his aunt. How these women cackled!

'Oh, that is the naughty man who does all the mischief and sets me against my mother,' he said, intentionally loud enough for both his mother and Hyde to hear. It would have been hard to say which blushed the deepest, but the Chancellor had the advantage in his naturally ruddy complexion.

'The young fool!' he growled inwardly as he moved away; but reflected that Charles' position at the moment was one to render desperate an older and wiser head than his. This touch of paternal tenderness was complicated by a painful sexual jealousy, for he, the only completely sane and honest adviser as he believed that King Charles had about him, and moreover, middle-aged, much too fat, and a martyr to poor man's gout, was yet acutely, degradingly in love with a woman whom he could not but beseech the King for his own sake to abandon. His heart told him that his persuasions in this matter were disinterested; his flesh told him that they were not. And the grave saturnine scrutiny of his young master held, he knew, the same opinion as his flesh.

68

'Ah God,' he thought as the fiddles teased and tingled through the brilliant, murmurous air, 'to be twenty-three again, and slender and six feet two, to be a King, with no crown indeed, but with the hope of one, and the certainty of new adventure and the power to please women—' – his prayer died on the last retarded note of an old Court dance that Rameau had composed to please King Louis XIII and the nymph he had sighed for and never won, she who was now abbess in the Convent of Chaillot – 'and what,' Hyde asked himself, 'have you, old fool, been dreaming of?'

Minette had been standing beside her mother and aunt, watching her brothers. She saw Charles smile at James' indignant affection after Mazarin had passed them, and longed to do anything that would bring that smile on herself.

At the flight of the three people he had offended, Charles found his small sister looking up at him.

'Mam says, Sire,' she volunteered, 'that Chancellor Hyde is puffed up with pride. And that is why he is so fat,' she added.

Charles nodded down at her and continued in a sing-song:

> 'Chancellor Hyde
> Wears his breeches so wide—'

'Oh yes. Go on.'

> 'So wide, so wide,
> He can't find anything inside,
> Although – but James, let me take you aside.'

And taking James by the arm, he swung him round and whispered what was evidently another couplet, at which the brothers laughed long and loud and swaggered a little, slapping each other on the back. Their satin cloaks were swung across their shoulders, they were taller than most people round them, to Minette they looked very splendid.

'Why must you go away?' she said to Charles.

'Who told you I was going?'

'Philippe. He said it was a great secret.'

'The insect! He must live inside the keyhole. In that case it is all over the Court.'

'He forgot about it very soon, he had so many other secrets.'

They had all seen Philippe for an instant before he had been

69

snatched up by a repressive tutor, twirling, hopping, shrilling a high wordless chant in the middle of the bare dancing floor, an imp of darkness blown in the wind of his own delirious excitement. Lights, music, people looking, and he in his best clothes, these were God to Philippe of France.

'The filthy little ape has been ogling me the whole evening,' said James.

'Don't flatter yourself. I saw him give some attention to his own countrymen, young de Guiche for one.'

Minette stared through the open door into another room where bright figures were moving in a formal rhythm that answered to the tripping, swaying sounds in the air. She could just see the heads of the musicians bobbing and swaying too in the little gallery. The whole world was dancing. But soon all these people would be still, silent, looking at her. She began to pray that a thunderbolt might strike the palace, and the ground swallow them up, or that the common people would rise suddenly in another revolution and drive them all out.

'Is it nearly time for the ballet?' she asked, and then, 'If your Majesty will excuse me, I feel sick.'

'We will go into the gardens,' said Charles, 'and you can say your part to me out there.'

He led her out of the glare, the buzz and clatter, the press of people, almost stifling to one so much below their height. The scent of tuberoses and jasmine lay heavy on the darkness, the numerous lights could only make wreaths and patterns against it, the music stretched outwards into it until its last fine-drawn thread fainted and failed. But now they heard the fountains, a rush of silver sound without the colour of melody, rising and falling like the song of nightingales hidden in the darkness. And now they saw the full moon as it rolled slowly out from behind a tall black tree.

'There are the Children in the Moon,' said Minette.

'Some people say it is a man with a bundle of sticks and a dog,' he replied, 'but I only see a face, rather on one side and lackadaisical, with the mouth a little open.'

'Oh yes, and then it is like our Aunt Queen Anne.'

'You are a pert baggage. Now say your piece.'

She said it falteringly, and he could not correct her as he did not know the lines. He felt her tremble, and put his hand over both of hers to still them. 'Wait,' he said, and after a moment, 'Now say it.' this time she arrived safely at the end of her lines.

70

'That is perfect,' he said, 'and that is how you will say it. Now do not think of it again. I want you to think of me. I am going away, and I wish I could take you with me.'

'Take *me*, brother!'

'Yes, you and Harry, both; but I have no place for you, nor for myself neither for that matter. But I am the head of our family and your King, and I want you to remember it. I leave Harry in your charge. Help him to obey my wishes, for others will not help him, least of all our mother. She will want him to enter her Church, and that I cannot have, so he will have to defy her.'

'Am *I* to defy her then too?'

He could not demand of a child of nine that she should repudiate her mother's religion. He and Hyde had agreed that in the face of the Queen's passion and resolution this was impossible. He had no home as yet to offer her – they would have to leave things as they were. It was intolerable that his chief worry at this moment was not as to where he should go and how get his bread, but the fact that he was leaving his young sister and brother in the power of these women, his mother and aunt. And Harry of Gloucester, after James, was his heir. The boy was tenderhearted, easy to be wrought upon by feminine affection. His little sister might help to counteract the influence of his mother.

'No,' he said, 'there are enough family quarrels as it is. But you can make Harry feel what a fine fellow he is when he upholds my will. Remember this – if he becomes a Papist it will set up a counter-action to the Crown which would draw all my Catholic subjects and sympathizers to his side against me.'

'Oh, sir, Harry would never do that.'

'No, but others would do it for him. The Church of England is for the King of England. Keep him loyal to both.'

'And I too. I will be loyal too.'

He laid his other hand over hers so that they lay between both his. 'That is the old way they took the oath of fealty,' he said, and his smile made but little change to his heavy, melancholy face. She stood there looking up at it in the moonlight, knowing that she would not see him again after tonight.

The night was full of scurrying, faint-coloured shadows, of murmured voices and high shrill whispered laughter like the squeaks of bats. These things disturbed his blood. On such a night it was hard to fix his mind and will on the religious upbringing of two children. Somewhere in this quivering, scented darkness was La Châtillon, languishing in someone's arms, breathing her teasing whispers into someone's ear. Whoever was with her, that fat madman, Sir Kenelm Digby, or possibly even old Hyde, he must ferret her out tonight.

'You must go in now and be dressed for the ballet,' he told Minette.

Once indoors again, free of Charles' presence, in the loud solitude of lights and bustle and people talking, not to her, the effect of his strong personality was to confuse and distress her. Unwillingly, inexplicably, she remembered Morton crying because Charles had deserted Montrose. She gazed at the bright candle flames that Harry had so admired; it seemed to her that they were the thoughts of all the people round her; and she prayed that her own, which were of love and a desire to protect her brother from death, despair and dishonour, might burn steadily until her candle were out.

Her mother thought it was fear of the approaching ballet that made her look so grave.

She dressed her herself for it, while odd, half-clad figures rushed about, shrieking and tittering. They turned out to be chiefly the Mancini girls, of whom Olympe was making the most noise. Philippe too was chattering like a parrot to his greatest friend, the young Comte de Guiche, but his elder brother, who had more to do in the ballet than anyone, was quiet and serious. Not all King Louis' future cares of state-craft and warfare would ever produce a moment of more urgent importance to him than this.

Opera-singers had been brought from Mantua to join in the performance; an experiment of the Italian Cardinal's. Queen Henrietta did not approve of this admixture of professionals, but they stood about together in little quiet groups, and behaved much better than the royal and courtly amateurs.

They heard the violins tuning up, and while the Queen put rouge on Minette's white cheeks, she chattered to her about the masques she had acted in in England; how she had worn an antique sword in the rôle of an Amazon, and how awkward it had been to manage, but nobody noticed when she tripped over it. Then she took Minette's face in her hands and said, 'Hold your head up. Do not look at the faces in front but at the very back and speak to them only, so that they may hear every word. King Louis will not listen to you. He has far too many pieces of poetry to say on his own account.

There is nothing to be afraid of, and I do not expect my daughter to be afraid.'

The music had begun, the chief actors had disappeared, the Queen had to go to her place in the audience. She was more frightened than Minette, for she knew how high were the stakes on her behaviour. King Louis was just at the most solemn and self-conscious age of boyhood, when it mattered desperately that one should do the right thing. He would never forgive his little cousin if she did anything to weaken or spoil or, terrible thought! bring ridicule on the ballet to-night. And always at the back of the Queen's mind was the hope that he as well as his mother would wish one day to make Minette the Queen of France. The close-packed faces of the audience made her shiver; she could not believe that she had confronted them with equanimity when she herself had acted so often in England. The buzz was deafening, an alarming rumour went round that the reporter for the *Gazette* had not been able to edge his way in.

Charles, returning from the gardens rather late, had to stand at the very back of the hall, but, on account of his height, was able to see over the heads of the others. Gorgeous spectacles on the stage were apt to bore him. He found himself computing the probable cost of all this magnificence of costume and stage setting and wondering how far it would go to fit out an army. 'That is the attitude of a poor relation,' he told himself.

His young cousin of France had just appeared in his fifth part and an entire suit of gold. He was really impressive; he had the true sense of the theatre, for he gained something on the stage, a majesty and power that attained an almost superhuman quality in the final tableau where he appeared as Apollo, surrounded by the nine Muses. The beauty of this group caused an involuntary exclamation to rise from the audience; on its breath Apollo soared into verse of considerable length, announcing that he was the conqueror of the world.

Louis believed the words he spoke. The sea of admiring faces before him, the rapturous applause that followed his every entrance or exit, his every speech, aroused in him an almost bewildering self-confidence. This then was his true self, a king, a god among men – not a boy who was told to do this and that, and shivered frightened in bed between torn

73

sheets. His nobles thought themselves above their King. He would show them how far he was above them.

No less than his little brother he was dependent on an audience. His exaltation was inspired by the crowd and in its turn swept back and inflamed the crowd. There appeared something prophetic in this tall young golden god who proclaimed his victory over his enemies and the dawn of a golden age for his country. Patriotic fervour joined with personal; an emotion of hope, pride and triumphant joy caught the close-packed audience, they clapped and shouted in thunderous applause, and those that were seated rose to their feet.

It was at this moment that Minette had to detach herself from the group and come forward to say her piece. She stood there in the front of the stage, looking absurdly small and childish, holding a lyre in her arms. The people paid no attention to her, they were still applauding the Sun god, now once again enthroned in the centre of the group, and only a very few realized who was this infantile figure.

A hot rush of anger mounted to Charles' head as he perceived what an agonizing moment this would be for any actor. The applause at last died down; there was silence which, to Charles, who was staring helplessly at the stage, seemed to last about ten minutes, so certain was he that the child, confronted with this vast audience, would find herself unable to say a single word. He saw Olympe Mancini, who represented Music, smile at the King with one black eyebrow raised; and cursed for a bitch the beauty he had admired.

Just then an odd thing happened; a thin strain of music from one of the violins went tripping up into the air all by itself. As it ceased the figure on the stage, so small and still it looked almost like a doll, began to speak. With a little stiff gesture she pointed to the crown of roses and myrtle on her head and explained that she was Erato, the Muse of love and poetry, that her race was royal and divine. Her voice was small, but each word fell clear and rounded as a drop of water, and Charles noticed them now for the first time.

> 'C'est à moi qu'on s'addresse,
> Quand on veut plaindre tout haut
> Le sort des grandes personnes
> Et dire tout ce qu'il faut
> Sur la chute des couronnes.'

She was looking to the back of the hall which had remained lighted; he felt certain that she had seen him and was speaking to him. She would not think of the sense of what she was saying, the fate of great personages, the fall of crowns; it was not of these things that she spoke, but of her affection and her trust in him. And a sharp ache reminded him that he was going away and would not see her again perhaps for years, that by then she would love others more than himself, and would be unable to love anybody with the same unquestioning simplicity that she could now give.

At this instant it was nothing to him that he was also leaving La Châtillon.

CHAPTER ELEVEN

Queen Henrietta regarded Mazarin's treaty with the regicide as a direct insult to herself. It was not pleasant to be dependent for her bread on a power in league with her enemy. She wrote to England to demand her pension as widowed consort. Once again, as when she had begged for a last interview with her husband, Cromwell reminded her of her refusal to be crowned. She who would not be the wife, should not be the widow.

Mazarin conveyed this message when she visited him in his palace in a small green room, the colour most fashionable in modern house decoration, surrounded by curious carvings in jade and ivory, by courteous coloured figures a few inches high, smiling the placid, eternal smile of China. In this marvellous shell he had created for his smooth person, the Cardinal told her the rude words of the brewer's son who sat on the English throne. She saw in them the most dangerous blow that had yet been dealt to her, a threatened charge of illegitimacy against her children. She went very white; she began with dignity, 'This outrage does not reflect on me, but on the King, my nephew,' and looking hard on the ruler of her nephew's kingdom, she continued, 'who ought not to permit a daughter of France to be treated as a concubine.'

His eyes, she noticed, were brown like velvet, and like velvet quite opaque; there was no feeling nor intelligence behind them, as though when he looked at her he did not see her; did not see, certainly, the woman who was the rightful Queen of England but only an elderly, shrill, complaining woman in widow's weeds, protesting that she really was a widow. She tried to control herself, to lower her voice: it seemed to be cracking. Her thoughts had all scattered, they went whirling round her, telling her preposterous, unimportant things that yet filled her mind to the exclusion of all else – that this oily Italian thought she had not made a good wife, had done nothing but quarrel with her husband and his country. She heard a strained falsetto say, 'I was abundantly satisfied with the late King, my lord, and with all England.'

She returned raging to the Palais Royal where she found her youngest son and daughter bending over a copy of the *Gazette*, reading the full enumeration of the charms of the débutante Princess Henriette, who had proved the fairest budding flower of royalty, an infant angel whose beauties and divine grace added lustre even to the inimitable splendours of the young King's court.

'Is it really true?' cried Minette; and Harry laughed at her, telling her that newspapers always wrote like that.

'But, Mam, I am to do a new dance all by myself in the ballet because I dance so well, and, Mam – ah dear little Mam, do listen – the ballet is to be given in the public theatre to all the people of Paris, whoever can get seats.'

The joy of the rising stage star shone in her eyes. It afforded no pleasure to her mother. Not all her angry arguments with Hyde had robbed her of her self-respect as had those few moments with a man who must indeed be a devil since he had made her feel so like one. A desire to act, to strike, to destroy, tore at her breast.

The two children stared at each other, hushed and frightened, suddenly aware of her mood. 'Oh, what can I *do*?' she murmured, hitting her hands together, and her eyes rested on her youngest son with a sombre, almost malevolent expression. He had already begun to supply the answer to her question, so fatal to her temperament.

As Charles had foreseen, she had at once considered how well suited Harry would be to a brilliant career in her Church. But Harry, with one of those disconcerting changes common in early boyhood, showed no intention of remaining sweet and studious or even delicate. The French Court, having spoiled him, now complained of his rudeness and high-handed ways. Harry did not care; he revelled in his lessons in fencing, riding and dancing, and in his popularity with other boys at

76

the Academy, who taught him how to use their wicked catapults, and fought with him and laughed at him and nicknamed him the Shoemaker, thus dispelling in chaff the depressing effect of Cromwell's threats to apprentice him to
'some honest trade'. His tutor said that he had got into a bad
set, and not touched his books for three months; the Queen
said that he needed the discipline of a strict boarding-school.
She tried to force him to enter a Jesuits' college.

She was not, it seems, quite sane at this time. Her grief had
left her whole, more of her whole self perhaps than she had
ever possessed before or since; for one great sorrow can fill
the heart with an absorption that itself gives peace. But the
bitterness of this new stroke from her enemies was corroding
her heart, fretting it away in little pieces. So many small things
troubled her now, she seemed always tired but could not bear
to rest. She wondered if Lord Jermyn noticed how unbecoming her heavy black was to her now that her eyes had got
so sunken, and yet she would not abate it by so much as a
softening piece of lace. It was an unfair advantage in men
that he should still be floridly handsome in his full-blown
middle age, though he drank far too much. She had found
herself maliciously pleased to observe a pimple on that classic
nose, until Harry remarked on it, when she boxed his ears.

Anglican services were now given in the private house of
Sir Richard Browne, who was still nominally ambassador
from the Court of England. Harry would look in on his way
to or from games, glowing from exercise and the new pride
of strength and mastery over his limbs, the new pleasure of
companionship. In the shabby little group of exiles gathered
together in Sir Richard's house, he met the men who had
known and fought and suffered for his father; he was bound
to these new, yet life-long friends by their devotion to a common cause, of which this form of worship was the symbol.
He could not take the Sacrament without remembering that
promise he had made before he was yet nine years old, to
his father, who was going out to die. He had promised that
he would be torn in pieces before he would give up the English Church, or let himself be made king while either of his
elder brothers were alive.

The Queen came to hear of Harry's attendance at these
services, and set the converted abbé, Wat Montagu, on to him.
Even young Philippe was allowed to put his finger in the

pie; he came with his tutor to argue with Harry, and told him confidentially that all good Catholics were saying, 'What Henry VIII destroyed, Henry IX will restore.'

'What do you think of that now? Isn't a crown a better bait than a Cardinal's hat?' And he went on to whisper obscene inquiries as to Harry's relations with the bad boys at the Academy – at which Harry showed that he had at least learned their language, for he called him a grinning bastard and hit him in the face, and Philippe howled, not from the pain but anxiety; for 'Christ in heaven!' he moaned, squinting sideways at his nose in a horrible fashion, 'will it, oh will it swell?' There was a scene with Philippe's mother, with Harry's mother, with both their tutors, there were scoldings and punishments and letters.

One day everybody wrote to King Charles at Cologne; some descriptively, Lord Jermyn guardedly, the Queen discursively, telling her son not to lose his head and get excited, but think the matter over quietly; Harry loyally, signing himself 'Your Majesty's most affectionate, most obedient and most humble brother, subject and servant.' And in answer came five letters from King Charles, also all written on the same day in a sudden fury of energy. He told Jermyn he disbelieved his neutrality and was so full of passion that he could not express himself; he told his mother that she evidently did not wish him ever to return to England; he told Harry that if he did not continue to obey him, 'this shall be the last time you will ever hear from, deare brother, your most affectionate brother, Charles R.'

And on top of this undeserved threat, 'Wot Mot', as Harry irreverently called the English abbé, scolded him in front of the Marquis of Ormonde for his untidy hair, and drove him off to have it brushed as though he were a child. But it was his last exercise of power.

The Marquis of Ormonde had been sent by Charles with orders to take Harry away to join his brother. Even Queen Henrietta saw that she would have once again to admit defeat.

Through all this Minette trod delicately like an unhappy kitten, and so treading, on tiptoe, with head over shoulder and wide watchful eyes, she came one day down a corridor in the Palais Royal, and looked out of a window on to the courtyard and saw Harry, who was going away, run out to say goodbye to their mother and beg her blessing before he left Paris. The Queen was then just stepping into her coach

78

to go to Chaillot; she stopped as the boy knelt before her, and said something to him that made him spring up and stand rigid for a moment, then turn and rush into the hall, just below the gallery where Minette was standing. She heard Wot Mot come fussing up to him, asking what the Queen had said to him, and then Harry's voice, loud and strange, replied, 'She said what I now say to you, get out of my sight, and never let me see your face again.'

And down the road to Chaillot, making a cloud of dust between the two tall rows of trees in the Cours la Reine, went the Queen's coach, bearing her to vespers, to the sweet singing and the peaceful faces of the nuns who adored her as a saint.

Ormonde had come into the hall; she heard his pleasant Irish voice asking Harry if he were ready; and he answered, 'Yes, but I have not yet found my sister.'

Then at last she turned and called down to him, 'I am here, Harry.'

He ran up the stairs to her and flung his arms round her; she pulled him down on to the window-seat beside her and cried, 'Oh Harry, don't go, don't go away.'

He told her he must go – 'You are only a girl,' he said, 'so it does not matter so much if you are a Papist. You are for our mother and France, but I am for Charles and England. Look, you can see for yourself what he says.'

He thrust a letter under her nose, and read in a strained, harsh voice, oddly like Charles' own when he was deep in earnest, ' "Doe not let them persuade you either by force or fine promises. For the first they will neither dare, nor will use, and for the seconde, as soon as they have gott you they will have their end and will care noe more for you." '

'You hear *that*?' he said in his own voice, looking up at her.

In the window-seat where they sat the light came sideways on to his face; it looked sharp and flat as though cut out of paper, dark on the one side, on the other a burning white.

She cried, 'Oh no, but indeed they care for you. My mother says one must not listen to Charles when he says things like that, that his troubles have made him harsh and bitter, and one must pray for him.'

'Well, you can stay here and do it. I am going to him. He is a man, and he treats one like a man. He doesn't scold and tell one to brush one's hair. They say my aunt is coming to speak to me tomorrow. I can't stand any more of it.'

79

He stood up before her, poised for flight; he was free; he was going to Charles, he was going to their lively laughing loving elder sister Mary whom she had never seen, he was going to their Aunt Elizabeth, the Winter Queen, the Queen of Hearts, who romped and rode and hunted with them, he was going to all that family of jolly cousins who teased each other and did not mind being poor and did not have to be separated from each other even though they too were exiles from their kingdom.

'Oh take me too,' she begged. 'Charles wants me to be of the Church of England too. Indeed I am as English as you are.' She was trying to speak in English, but in her haste her tongue stumbled and tripped over the hard words, she burst into tears and flung heself down by the window-seat where she buried her head in her arms in a paroxysm of sobbing. She knew Harry could not take her, that it had been difficult enough for him to get away himself, but that her mother would never let her go, for her mother loved her as she did not love Harry. The pitiful tangle of human relations had early twisted and hurt her heart.

Harry knelt by her and tried to comfort her, he hugged her and rubbed his head against hers and told her they would all be together when Charles went back to be King of England. Then he went, and Minette looked out of the window and saw that all this time the cloud of dust that was their mother's coach had got smaller and smaller in the distance down the long road to Chaillot, until it was now no bigger than the white puff-ball of a dandelion clock and just as she had seen this, it disappeared.

CHAPTER TWELVE

Minette was nearly ten when that happened; at eleven she renounced the world because King Louis snubbed her at a dance. His mother had told him to open the ball with the princess of England, when he wanted to dance with Olympe, the Mancini girl, who had lately married the Comte de Soissons. At sixteen, Louis preferred a woman of the world, older than himself, whose marriage had made her forbidden fruit, to a dish that his mother put regularly in his way like something wholesome to eat at breakfast. The boy stuck out his under-lip and said out loud in front of everyone, 'Madam, I do not like little girls.' The Queen of England tried to cover it by saying that Henriette had hurt her foot and would not in any case dance that evening, but the Queen of France furiously insisted that Louis should dance with his cousin. So dance they did, hating it and each other, and in her ears the King's words fitted themselves maddeningly to the tinkling music: 'I do not like little girls, little girls.'

It was of no use to please her kind aunt Queen Anne if she could not please the King. She must please everyone, she must dance and dress so well that no one could possibly notice she had a crooked shoulder, or remember that she had no dowry; thus only could she keep her place in the world – if she could not, she must take the veil and live all her life at Chaillot, whose trees and lawns threatened to enclose her, as in a green prison, in the midst of that glittering ballroom. But before the end of the evening the prison had become a sanctuary, even a playground, where she would be with her friends, safe from the scornful glances of Olympe Mancini, now Comtesse de Soissons, and her tittering whispers to Louis, just loud enough for her to hear – 'Well, was she as dull as ever? And have you won her heart all the same? That is what these dances are for, you know.'

All the applause and praise that had been lavished on Minette after her performances in the Court ballets only made her now the more dashed by her humiliation. Queen Henrietta decided that not only was this Court life far too exciting for the impressionable child, but that Queen Anne's stupidity in forcing her on her son was ruining the brilliant hopes induced by her good will.

So Minette stayed continuously at Chaillot and became, like many girls after a precociously worldly childhood, deeply engrossed in a rather serious, sentimentally religious convent-school girlhood. She walked with the other girls up and down the grass paths by the rivers; they showed each other their embroidery stitches, listened to the nuns' stories of the saints, vowed never to marry but to take the veil at the same time as the particular friend of the moment, walk up the aisle together as brides of Christ and remain inseparable for ever. Worldly ambition had lost all its charms for her, she assured Mère Angélique. She looked back on her brilliant début at the French Court as at a far-removed and frivolous past. There were relaxations. She learned to swim and enjoyed

81

splashing and shouting with the others in a backwater of the river better than any ballet. She made her first great friend.

Some ironic law of compensation must have decreed that about four years after Harry had run away from his mother, Louise, the brilliant and artistic daughter of Elizabeth of Bohemia, should run away from hers; should come to her aunt of England in order to embrace the Catholic faith and be entered as a novice in the convent of Chaillot.

She had left the Hague on foot, quite alone, before seven o'clock in the morning, causing twenty-four hours of frantic anxiety and scandal before a note was discovered, pinned to her dressing-table, in which she gave the reason and destination of her flight and directions for her luggage.

'What else was there for me to do?' she asked in her cynical fashion. 'Who wants to marry a princess without a *dot*, with scores of poor relations, all of royal blood, all borrowing money, all saying they must go in first to dinner?' Elizabeth, her eldest sister, a beauty as well as a philosopher, was going into a convent too, a sham one, said Louise a Lutheran imitation. 'If one must take the veil, one may as well do it artistically; and, by the way, that is a very pretty summer-house in the garden, do you think they would let me have it for a studio?'

She was dressing herself in dilatory, absent-minded fashion, looking out of the window more often than in the glass. Minette was showing her cousin her room at Chaillot; she sat on the bed in the midst of a delightful confusion of half-unpacked clothes and haphazard talk; she marvelled that Louise's mother had let her grow up so untidy, and that Louise could ever have left that gay scrambling life at the Hague.

Something of its unquenchable vitality blew into the still, sweet, slightly stuffy air of Chaillot, whose exclusively feminine emotions had so contented her. Now once again and more vividly than in her childhood, she was thrilled by the practical jokes and impromptu theatricals that had shocked the English Puritans at the Hague, 'the songs, dances, hallooing, and other jovialities' of the enormous family of Palatines too large to be distinguished from each other without the help of nicknames. Rupert le Diable (because of his hot temper) so closely resembled Louise that she was mistaken for him when she acted a man's part in a play in his clothes. They mixed up half a dozen languages in their talk and letters and spelled in a manner all their own.

And how the three clever sisters teased each other! They had told Louise she did her hair with her paint brushes, and she had plagued Elizabeth for her unphilosophic annoyance when her nose got red by suggesting that moment for a visit.

'Do you expect me to go with this nose?' Elizabeth had cried, and Louise had retorted, 'Do you expect me to wait till you have got another?'

Then there was the Sophia Charles and James had talked of, who made such merciless fun of her governesses.

'Charles wanted to marry Sophia,' Minette said, 'he thought she had more wit and common sense in her little finger than Mademoiselle in the whole of her long body. Please, cousin, do not tell anyone that, especially my mother.'

And for the first time Minette experienced the delicious thrill of sharing dangerous confidences with a grown-up girl. It was short-lived. Louise turned frowning from the window, fingered something at her neck, said with a queer husky angry laugh, 'Oh – Charles! Sophie pretended to have a corn on her toe rather than go on walking in the woods with him – we laughed at her for making up such a vulgar excuse, and she said, "Well, it isn't so vulgar as his telling me I am handsomer than his mistress, Lucy Walters." *That's* not the way for a prince to propose.'

Louise sat there, swinging the slipper on her foot while the sunlight slanted across her changing face. Her untidy hair, her inquisitive nose that quivered at scent of a new idea, had assumed a dangerous importance. Why had her voice gone hard at mention of Charles? Alarm and antagonism mingled with Minette's first attraction to her cousin, but there was no time to question or quarrel, for Louise was rattling on about Sophie and the Elector of Hanover, whom she would marry if she got the chance, and would not try to make into a king as their mother had done – 'and all because *her* mother teased her by calling her "goodwife Palsgrave". These mothers! But you know that the first instinct of maternity is to eat its young.'

Minette had not known. She felt that a bucket of cold water had been emptied on her head.

These fortunate daughters of Elizabeth of Bohemia evidently thought their fascinating mother very silly. They were irritated at her sitting up at a ball till five in the morning with the utmost zest merely to watch the dancing, when at her age she should have been in bed or at least bored; they wished she

83

would snub her young adorers, and not address her old ones with endearments such as 'ugly filthy camel's face!'

The Winter Queen of Minette's childish imagination was rudely shaken on her throne of icicles and hearts. Was this the woman to whom all her brothers and her sister were so devoted? But 'Oh yes,' said Louise, who at last divined something of her bewilderment, 'other people's children do adore her. And so does my brother Rupert adore your mother; he says those years of his boyhood at her Court in England were the happiest he ever spent. Yet your brothers have all quarrelled with her. One must remember,' finished Louise, 'that one man's aunt is another man's mother.'

And she promptly adored her darling Aunt Henrietta, who stood up to all the storm of protests from the Hague, where Queen Elizabeth as the outraged mother declared she would rather her daughter were dead than a Papist, and demanded that she should be returned to her forthwith. To which Queen Henrietta replied that she saw no more reason for returning her niece Louise to her mother than Elizabeth had seen for returning her nephew Harry to his.

Louise was passionately Protestant in her Papistry. She and her sisters had pulled everything to pieces between them and with the help of wits better than their own, for the philosopher Descartes kept up a continual correspondence with the intellectual Elizabeth; and Gerald Honthorst the artist had found Louise his most remarkable pupil. He had often sold her pictures for her, sometimes as his own, for they then fetched higher prices, and helped with the family expenses in the pleasant modern red-brick house at the Hague.

Louise's turbulent spirit, laughing and sad, unthinkingly cruel, unconsciously binding the child's ready devotion to herself by a process of destruction, swept Minette's along with her, taught her to probe and question, doubt and dissect. Seen through her eyes Louis did not count; he had no genius; Mazarin was the only real man of the French royal family, 'he *is* one of the family, isn't he?' and Harry, instead of a hero, was a young jackanapes who gave himself such airs that the States-General had demanded his withdrawal from the Hague, 'and why? well, I believe as much as anything, excepting always the fear of Cromwell (for one says now the fear of Cromwell as one would the fear of God), it was because Harry would mount his horse at the foot of the staircase instead of in the courtyard. There is a sort of private

84

royalty about him as though he believed himself to be King more than his brother.'

Even the martyred King Charles came in for a dry reflection from Descartes that his death would no doubt enhance his reputation, 'and I dare say,' she added, 'if his son the second Charles had had the luck to be killed at Worcester, one might even be able to think of him too as a martyred hero.'

There it was again, that sneer, that wry hatred, where before there had been only good-humoured execution. The two girls had avoided the subject of Charles since their first meeting; now suddenly it could not be avoided. It was not true – but what was it that was not true?

'What has Charles to do with you?' cried Minette. 'You've never loved him, so you don't know him.'

Even in the onslaught of a quarrel, Louise would always pursue any side-track that might lead to speculation. 'Is love then necessary to knowledge? I should have put it the other way round.'

'I don't know. I don't care. I know that love is more necessary than knowledge.'

'Now, there,' said Louise, 'you have I believe said something really new.'

At fourteen Minette could and did attack, but was defenceless. Five years ago she had stood in a garden at night with Charles, and he had put both her hands between his and had told her that that was the old way for a king to take the oath of loyalty. She had not seen him since, but it was still true; she would give her life to guard him from death, despair or dishonour.

But, 'You beast,' was all she could say.

'What in the world is the matter with you, you silly child?'

'You poison everything. You are like a snake.'

'The serpent in Eden, I suppose. Well, even you will have to know the difference between good and evil some day.'

'Charles is not evil.'

'I dare say not.' But her sneering tone snapped as if it were a piece of ice. She began to shake and cry, 'Don't hate me so, Henriette. I cannot help hating Charles. I don't want to, I've tried not to. I want to love God, it's all I can do now, isn't it?' Her laugh was more dreadful than her tears.

Had Charles not been kind to her? Had he made her love him and then left her quite negligently? Minette had heard of his doing that – a sort of carelessness, she thought. He would go on being just as kind if he stayed.

Her thought came clear through her troubled, questioning eyes. 'Heaven!' cried Louise, 'do you think I was in love with *him*!' and in a storm of protest and self-justification there tumbled out the secret of her bitterness against Charles and against the world, the reason why it was not worth taking seriously and the best thing to do was to retire from it with as good a grace as one may.

The Scots Marquis of Montrose had been a friend of Louise's brother, Prince Rupert of the Rhine; there had been something akin in the temper of the two men, though Rupert never had that unearthly calm that marked Montrose. He had paid a visit to the Hague and at once of course was friends with Louise's mother; she persuaded him to stay on with them far longer than he had intended; she called him Jamie Graham, and sometimes (oh, horror!) in her irrepressible passion for nicknames, Gentle Jamie. It was a little painful to Louise that his grave courtesy, which inspired so many with awe, even fear, should be in no way perturbed by her mother's affectionate familiarity. Queen Elizabeth commissioned Gerald Honthorst to paint his picture that she might hang it in her chamber, and Louise in secret commissioned him to paint a miniature of it that she might hang it round her neck.

Her love for Montrose was a religious fervour. That side of his life had ended, he thought, not so much with the death of his wife as with the death of his king. He was dedicated; he told Louise he could not love her; and he did. She could not believe her bliss, even the parting could not destroy it, nor yet the news of his death. For peace and happiness had shone in his face on the way to execution so that his enemies were cowed at the sight of it as at something holy; and the men and women assembled to throw stones and abuse at him fell sobbing on their knees. A far ray of this strange light seemed to have touched her also; it shone in her eyes and she walked on air, knowing that death itself was not greater than the love of such a man.

Then bitterness crept in to corrupt it, and she could not bear the desecration. Young Charles had failed to support him; he had allied himself with the Covenanters who were his enemies, and thereby betrayed him. Yet she knew her hatred to be a betrayal of Montrose's love. He had blamed no

86

one. In her efforts to achieve a like immunity she turned frantically to God.

So here she was at Chaillot, pulling Minette's world to pieces. The child was so quick, so appreciative, it was delightful to see her flush with that little intake of the breath, her eyes opening round and blue on all that she told her. She had vowed to herself not to tell her of Charles – and yet was it not better to open her eyes? It was so easy for Charles to be loved by scores of silly sensual women. Of what use could the love of his little sister be to a man like him? 'Love him if you will,' she cried, 'but know the truth – that he is utterly selfish – that he may be brave in battle but he will always surrender to the easiest way.'

'That is a lie. You don't know what he did when they had begun to threaten my father's death. Against his orders Charles wrote to Cromwell, he sent him a blank sheet of paper signed with his name to be filled up with any terms Cromwell might chose to dictate to him – he offered to give himself up, to abdicate his rights as heir to the throne – so long as they would promise not to kill my father. He never speaks of it – I heard you using the phrase "carte blanche" the other day, and it is a new piece of slang to you, that is all. You don't know that it was started years ago when Charles gave himself into his enemy's hands for the sake of our father – you just sit there and call him selfish and think you can kick it all away – but they all advised him to join with the Convenanters and not Montrose – my mother did too, and you do not blame her.'

Louise had a maddening way of not answering directly. 'People noticed he was different after that. If he did a heroic thing in his youth, then he knows what he has done since. He can go back on other people but he can't go back on himself. Like Cæsar, he has crossed his Rubicon.'

The swinging slipper hung still. (Had it been balanced there in that position on the tip of her toe ever since her glancing, flickering talk had first set Minette's brain on fire in the midst of scattered heaps of clothes?) Even out in the garden Louise was so untidy that her clothes seemed to be just dropping off her. They were sitting on a carved stone seat, and behind them a big syringa bush sent waves of hot scent over them as the breeze played through the wax-white flowers. Minette sat with a spray of it in her hands, pulling at the petals. As each one came off between her fingers she saw it large as a sheet of paper, wax-white and blank, and scrawled across the bottom of it her brother's signature in bold black writing, in vain attempt to buy their father's life.

Girls in flowing full dresses walked up and down the grass paths between the flower-beds, in and out of the shadows of the great trees, their arms round each other's waists, their heads bent over the latest gossip. Véronique de Soulanges had cribbed answers in class; Mère Angélique had snubbed Amélie de Festubert; the little Foletier had brought her pet squirrel into school in her pocket; glancing at the two figures on the seat, they said how the princess Henriette's *flamme* for the princess Louise was nearly over, for there they were quarrelling again.

A pair of girls went softly past behind the stone seat and decided that the quarrel was all about nothing, nothing to do with life at Chaillot at all.

BOOK II

HIGH NOON

CHAPTER THIRTEEN

La Grande Mademoiselle returned to Court after an absence of six years. Though she was only just past thirty, her hair had begun to go grey. Yet she herself seemed not a day older; she jumped from her coach like a schoolgirl when she came to meet her aunt the Queen-Mother of France after her exile, asked if she still thought her a very naughty girl but promised to be good now, and laughed boisterously over the supreme joke of having opened fire on the King's troops at the battle by the gates of Saint Antoine.

She insisted on her aunt telling her that she had forgiven her; to which Queen Anne replied that if her niece's throat had been within reach of her hands at the time she would most certainly have strangled her; but all that was now over. Mademoiselle was entirely satisfied. She took the friendliness of the royal family and the Cardinal at its face value; Mazarin was charming to her; he went out of his way to hand her to her coach and joked over the old days of the Fronde.

'You do not find me such a dreadful enemy now, I hope?' he said, smiling. He promised that he would make her 'establishment' (i.e. her marriage) his own particular concern, and made some coyly insinuating remarks to Queen Anne on the similarity between Mademoiselle and Monsieur, as Louis' younger brother Philippe was always called.

Mademoiselle was consumed with curiosity to see the royal brothers. Queen Anne was on her way to a fashionable watering-place and expected her sons to join her at any moment. At last King Louis came in, flushed and merry, his boots muddied to the thigh. He greeted Mademoiselle cordially, apologized for the mud and said that Monsieur was coming in the coach. They had had an adventure. As they came through the forest, shots came out of the trees, and one hit the back of the coach.

Louis had stopped it, and ran into the woods with the others to see if they could catch the robbers, but never saw one.

'You ran after the robbers! And Philippe—'

'No. Philippe had shoes on, and did not want to get them muddy. He has made himself very elegant in your honour,' he said, turning to Mademoiselle and looking much amused. 'You would not believe how many bows and rosettes I counted ... him in the coach. I wish we had caught those fellows. They must have run away when they saw it was the royal coach.'

He had grown into a fine young man, tall and handsome, and what was more important he was now at his ease, no longer stiff and anxious, but full of pride and pleasure in himself. Mademoiselle had heard how he strode into the council chamber, hatted, booted and spurred, as he was starting for the hunt; forbade the grave old men to pass an economy measure that would interfere with his pleasures, and broke up their meeting. Such high-handed measures delighted her. She looked at the splendid youth and thought of 'her little husband'. Somehow she did not think she had better refer to this, although she had been pleasantly reassured by King Louis' humorous innuendo about his brother's wish to impress her.

She began to feel excited, as she always was by any new project. She had thrown away her chance of the throne, but she might still marry the heir to it. Then she who had always been Mademoiselle, the greatest spinster in France, would be known always as Madame, the wife of Monsieur, the greatest gentleman. What could be more fitting?

Monsieur entered. He was very small but did not at once appear so as he was perched on red heels four or five inches high (no wonder that for their sake – or hers – he could not face a swampy forest); he was a miracle of elegance in grey with a good deal of lace; his greetings, gestures and easy talk were charming and assured. As he bowed to her, Mademoiselle noticed what a fine head he had; it was his head that had been particularly compared to hers. His very smallness attracted her, and the dainty precision of his gestures; he was so neat, complete and gay; sentences flowed in pretty profusion from his lips, all nicely rounded, finished, hitting off his meaning with delicate yet audacious strokes. He reminded her of her father in that, and of her vow as an enthusiastic schoolgirl never to marry anyone who could not talk as well as her father. And, like her father, nothing could put him out of countenance; when Louis teased him about his shoes and the robbers, he re-

90

taliated by implying that Louis was a hearty he-boor who plunged into the deepest mud on purpose; told how Louis had been trying to make an acrostic on a certain fair lady's name and had not been able to manage it without his help, and mimicked the hearty simple type of fellow who contrives to drop artful hints as to his prowess at games or in the field by going into contortions of manly modesty on behalf of his wits. 'I'm afraid I'm not much good at these writing games. I'd rather – ha ha – stand up against old d'Artagnan with his foil unbuttoned any day.'

But Louis could not bear chaff, he gave Monsieur a violent kick from behind, so that some of that 'manly mud' was after all plastered on the fly-away skirts of Monsieur's pretty coat. Furious, he rushed at Louis and there was a sharp scuffle; the Queen shrieked lamentably; they stood sulkily with red faces, all their princely assurance shattered, revealed as two angry boys. Louis attempted a dignified apology, which unfortunately turned into the statement that if his mother had not been present he would certainly have thrown his brother out of the window.

The Queen stormed and complained to Heaven that there had been a quarrel like this only a week ago, and why? just because King Louis had discovered his brother eating meat on a fast day – and was it because of his piety? No, but his greed, because he had not had meat himself. This pointed to Louis as the chief culprit, but it was Philippe who was most scolded, told that he would be beaten as he was when a child if he could not show more respect to the King his brother. At this Philippe gave an involuntary glance at Louis as if in appeal, and Louis seemed very uncomfortable, shuffled the controversial boots and muttered to his brother what seemed like a suggestion that they should both get out of this for God's sake. And out of it they got, leaving Mademoiselle convinced that all standards of behaviour, manners and etiquette had utterly deteriorated since she had left the Court.

Though Monsieur was thirteen years younger than herself, a head shorter, and as effeminate as she was masculine, she saw nothing incongruous in the idea of their marriage; and he on his part was quite glad to coquet with it, as with any project that could enhance his importance. So he frisked round his ungainly cousin like a little dog, a poodle to be exact, that has been clipped and curled and belled and beribboned until it bears as slight a resemblance to a dog as he did to a man; his hair was a frizzed foam of ringlets, his mouth a scarlet bow and his eyebrows a pair of lacquered brooches; even his eyes, full, black and lustrous, had the appearance of ornaments stuck in the middle of his face. Yet perhaps the Queen and Cardinal were more accurate than they had intended to be, for there was a sort of similarity between the unlikely pair and one that enabled them to get on much better together than with their more normal partners of the other sex. Both loved to dress up and went together to masked balls and fairs; Mademoiselle as a warrior in silver armour, and Monsieur as a girl with long fair hair. On one occasion they arranged a masquerade in which everybody went as monks and nuns, and ran through the streets in their costume. Monsieur told Mademoiselle delightedly how a monk had tried to make love to him as a nun, and how the monk had turned out to have a lovely white hand and most feminine arm. The masquerade caused a good deal of scandal; Queen Anne was horrified at the insult to the Church, and conveyed acidly to Mademoiselle that she should have kept her young cousin out of mischief.

'She treats us all like children,' Monsieur agreed, and was very sympathetic; in fact he kept silence for nearly five minutes while Mademoiselle poured out her latest grievance against his mother. The Prince of Condé, now also reconciled to the Court, had come to call on the Queen, and her aunt had sent her out of the way in the crudest manner, telling her to go out and take a walk as though she were a little girl, she who had been Condé's saviour. Tears of disappointment and injury stood in her eyes.

'Is it possible?' said Monsieur in a neat little voice of surprise. 'My mother, you know, has no tact, and I find it difficult to believe she was ever a great beauty.'

That was another point of resemblance, that they both loved gossip. Both also had a swollen, at times even an apoplectic, sense of rank, and could spend hours happily discussing the insolence of Madame This in taking precedence of Madame That, the craven baseness of Madame That in yielding precedence to Madame This. There was a scandalous report that James, the young Duke of York, had allowed one of the lesser French princes to go in to dinner before him, and Monsieur and Mademoiselle clattered about it as though he had deserted his troops in battle. After that, Mademoiselle would never so desert her rank as to allow precedence to any of her English cousins; if people showed themselves so unworthy of their privileges they would have to forfeit them.

And urged by a tiresome, half-fearful prick of curiosity, she added, 'And my little cousin, the baby Henriette, what is she like now? As meek and good as ever, I suppose. I hear they thought of putting her in a convent – it is much the most sensible thing to do with her, for she can have no hope of an establishment for herself.'

Monsieur was, for him, oddly non-committal on this subject. Mademoiselle stood strained and ill at ease, wishing she had never introduced it, or else that she could hear a great deal more about it; hear that the Princess Henriette had taken vows of eternal chastity, or had run away with a groom, or had been disfigured by the smallpox. The moment passed and the silence of Monsieur, and with it that chill shudder of foreboding within her as though someone, possibly the Princess Henriette, had danced on her grave. There could be no need to worry about that dull little girl, who of all these new up-starting youngsters about the Court, was the least likely to prove a dangerous rival.

The most prominent of these, and in her opinion the great cause of the deterioration of manners, were the Cardinal's nieces, the Mazarinettes. These bold and beautiful Italian girls led the fashion in wild extravagance, love of showy display, contempt of etiquette or anything that might cramp their free-dom of speech and behaviour. 'Vicious' – 'rude' – 'bad be-haviour' was the Queen-Mother's verdict on them; she dis-approved of this perverse modern insistence that girls will be boys. But she could not discountenance them.

King Louis had tired of Olympe, but now entertained a more genuine and romantic passion for her sister Marie, who was not voluptuously beautiful, but had been broken-hearted when he was ill with enteric, together with thousands of his soldiers, in Turenne's victorious campaign against the Spanish army. Marie did not care to dress as a man nor to caress blackamoors, and in comparison with her sisters seemed to Louis an angel of purity. He actually told his mother and Marie's uncle, the Cardinal, that he wished to marry her. Queen Anne regarded a legitimate connexion with her lover's family as a shocking dishonour, and said so to Mazarin with-out at all perceiving how she offended him.

Mazarin was indeed in a difficult position – that a niece of his should sit on the throne of France was a dream beyond even his ambition; but Marie would owe him no gratitude for

93

her exalted position, for he had always snubbed her and kept her in the background as the least likely bargain among his nieces, while she in return hated and flouted her worldly uncle. Olympe had openly been Louis' mistress; if he should then proceed to marry her sister, Mazarin would be as unpopular with the country as in the worst days of the Fronde. He had no mind to be driven out of Paris yet again.

Queen Henrietta of England, through all her long retirements from Court, never took her eye off the course of events there. She considered them so far encouraging that she permitted her daughter, now aged fifteen, to appear there again and much more frequently. It was not at all likely that a marriage between Louis and Marie de Mancini would actually take place, but its project had frightened Queen Anne and might well make her hasten to marry her son to someone more suitable. Moreover, the affair itself showed Louis to be possessed of a heart as well as sense; neither he nor Marie wished for a liaison, their love was tender, curiously youthful, they talked for hours together but in front of other people and mostly about books. Louis had discovered that his education had been neglected in his boyhood during the troubles of the Fronde and was anxious to correct it, especially when he had the studious Marie to help him. These new and gentler tastes made it seem more probable that he would come to appreciate his young cousin of England than when he was in the first crude flush of adolescence. Marie would be merely the stepping-stone, decided Queen Henrietta, indefatigably optimistic.

Marie was, but not to Queen Henrietta's daughter. It was Mazarin's dearest wish that Louis should eventually be lord of Spain as well as France. There was now hope at last of peace with Spain and an alliance between the young King of France and the Spanish Infanta; and this gradually became a certainty even to Queen Henrietta. She began to make overtures to the Duke of Savoy, to the Grand Duke of Tuscany for the hand of the Princess Henriette, but both failed to respond.

'The Queen of England is wild to marry her daughter to someone or anyone,' wrote La Grande Mademoiselle in her diary, digging her pen into the paper so that the fierce strokes looked like upturned swords, 'and King Louis said to his brother, "as you are so fond of her you had better take her, for no one else will have her." '

She looked at the words with satisfaction, they appeased a dull cloying anxiety that seemed always to cling about a corner of her heart. She had written again and again in her diary that she had no particular wish to marry, but she had two very pretty stepsisters just growing up, and there had actually been talk of marrying one of them to King Louis. That would have been intolerable; she was quite relieved, where once she would have been bitterly disappointed, to see that the wind had now set towards Spain.

'You, I suppose, are very sad about it,' she said to her little cousin of England, looking her up and down.

'It would be scarcely loyal not to be in love with King Louis,' replied Minette.

Mademoiselle stared at her, astonished that she was not the same little girl as she had left. She had expected everything and everyone, including herself, to be the same as six years ago, for like a true Bourbon she had learnt nothing and forgotten nothing.

'You have changed more than I,' she said, 'indeed everyone tells me I am exactly the same, except that my complexion and figure are better.' (The Princess Henriette on the other hand was still much too thin.) 'King Louis too is greatly improved, he is so much taller and bolder. I always said he would make a fine king when other people thought him backward and too timid.'

She had already said this in front of the King and thought he could not have understood her as he had given no sign of pleasure. So she repeated it now in a clear voice as the King and his mother went past them to dinner, followed by Monsieur, who winked, frowned, nodded, and crooked a heavy ringed little finger at them in a mysterious manner.

'What is the matter with Monsieur?' asked Minette. 'Has he some practical joke on hand?'

'Oh, I don't know. He has always something in his head. He has heard that Miss Gordon and I are dressing as Breton peasants in silver tissue and pink ribbons in the masque tomorrow night and insists on copying it in every detail. I have no doubt he will make a much better girl than I.'

And taking Minette's hand she led her up to the doorway, where she dropped it and passed through first into the dining hall.

This caused a sad commotion; she had taken precedence of the Princess Henriette who, besides being equally with herself a granddaughter of France, was daughter and sister to the Kings of England. Mademoiselle excused herself by saying that she had not seen the Princess Henriette for so long that she had still thought of her as a child and had merely taken her hand to encourage her as she would have done in the old days, and the princess herself had shown a simple pleasure in her action.

But 'it is said that you passed before her,' the Cardinal told her drily.

Only Monsieur, with whom she had planned the proceeding beforehand, took her side and exclaimed that things had come to a pretty pass when foreigners who were dependent on them for the very bread they ate expected to go in to dinner before them. Queen Anne flew into a passion and shrilly rebuked her son and Queen Henrietta, who of course came to hear of it, wept bitterly. Mademoiselle felt uncomfortable about that, but in any case it had not been her fault but Monsieur's, who must have spoke out of no real partisanship to her but a mere love of mischief-making, for he had ever since been ingratiating himself with the Princess Henriette.

'And much joy may she have of him,' she breathed as she wrote in her diary how childish, flighty and unworthy she had found her cousin, so that she no longer entertained any thought of marrying him.

Minette was grateful for Monsieur's attentions. Her re-entry into Court life was like a progress on egg-shells. Queen Anne continued to pet her, but she was made to feel that pretty behaviour was a necessary condition of her very existence. She wished often that she could have taken the veil with Louise at the convent at Mauberge. Louise had not stayed at Chaillot; Mère Angélique had refused to accept her noviciate because, if she did not prove to have a vocation, it would be difficult to say so to one who was a princess and the niece of their foundress. Her own opinion was that Louise needed more qualifications for the veil than her discontent with the world. 'When you pray as fervently as you paint,' she told Louise, 'I will believe in your vocation.'

So Louise went to Mauberge, where the Abbess had not the same scruples as Mère Angélique, and Minette begged to be allowed to go too, and at last Queen Henrietta achieved her desire. But it did not after all afford her much satisfaction, for her daughter's pious wish had been inspired by her niece rather than herself. In any case it would be foolish to encourage it just yet.

King Louis had fallen through, the Duke of Savoy had

fallen through, the Grand Duke of Tuscany had fallen through. But there was the first Mademoiselle in France playing her cards as badly as ever, offending the King and the Queen-Mother every time she opened her mouth, and who knew what prize might fall to Henriette as a result of her elder cousin's bungling.

Said Monsieur, progressively, to the Princess Henriette:

'She snaps my head off.

'She thinks I belong to her.

'She is tall as a grenadier.

'I always liked you best, ever since I first saw you and thought you as small and dainty as a doll. We make a very pretty pair, don't you think?'

CHAPTER FOURTEEN

One Saturday in Lent the Cardinal gave a banquet. There was of course no meat, but the variety of the fish and ingenuity of the innumerable ways of cooking it made the feast richly indigestible. After dinner they danced, and after that he led his guests into a gallery where, arranged on long tables, was a priceless collection of jewels, carvings in jade and coral, curiosities from China and the antique age. He announced that these were the prizes in a lottery in which everyone present would receive a prize and no one would pay for his ticket. Mazarin in fact was giving away the main part of his famous collection.

This from a man who would not give the smallest preferment in the Church without a heavy bribe, who had spent so much time and industry as well as wealth in the patient and judicious amassing of these bibelots that he was now casting from him, caused speculation that was not wholly flattering. Some whispered that these extravagant displays of wealth were very vulgar, that if they were to increase at this pace the old nobility would soon be completely ousted by the new rich; it was not observed, however, that any of these critics refused their lottery tickets. Others considered it an act of propitiation rather than display; Mazarin's power was weakening, he had lost ground with the King ever since he had refused to allow his marriage with his niece, and with the Queen ever since the gout had begun to cripple him; the efforts he had made to pre-

serve his erect carriage and youthful complexion were ludi-
crous, but now at last he had to realize that an old man is
only charming when he gives presents.

Mademoiselle was not one of these detractors. She had
fought to drive the Cardinal from France, she had had her
matrimonial chances wrecked by him again and again, and had
lately been offered as consolation prize the hand of a deformed
idiot boy and incurable drunkard who happened to be prince
of Portugal. Nevertheless, she believed Mazarin to be her
friend; she had been flattered by him, she was now enchanted,
she walked about, her eyes round with surprise and pleasure,
exclaiming at his generosity and his magnificence. He took
herself and the Princess Henriette by each hand to lead them
round the gallery. Then he said to the princess, 'Look well at
each present and see what you would choose – it may be the
lottery ticket will know your thought.'

The Princess Henriette stopped in front of a little Greek
lady in terra-cotta who sat upright upon a couch in an attitude
of eternal delicate repose. 'How pretty she is,' she cried, 'she
has been waiting all these centuries to receive her guests, perhaps for Monsieur Aesop to come and charm her with his
fables. Ah, why have we no poets like that now?'

'You had best ask Monsieur La Fontaine,' said the Cardinal;
'in the meantime let her wait, for here is one whose gay hour
has arrived,' and he showed her a statuette of a dancing faun.

Minette's desire to pay the right compliment to her dis-
criminating host faded in an astonished delight. She had never
seen the figure before, yet as with all things that make an
integral part of our lives she seemed to recognize it, to know
even the melody to which the creature danced for ever in a
land where the sun shone through clusters of golden grapes,
and nobody was ever sad or poor or angry or ever went away.
Somewhere or other she had once seen little boys with goats'
horns like this dancing round the rim of a golden cup. 'Oh!'
she gasped in a pleasure that had suddenly been stabbed with
a memory she could not catch; for one instant she had seen
her mother's head, grey, old, untidy, utterly abased; the next
it had slid into the recesses of her mind while before her eyes
the faun danced on.

It was the Cardinal who paid compliments now, telling the
Princess Henriette that her classic grace in dancing had made
the Court believe in the existence of a golden age when all the
world was young. He then devoted his attention to Made-

moiselle, but it was too late, he should have done it first. Her cousin's schoolgirl pedantry had already irritated her; the English princess was always seeking to please, a sycophant, a poor relation. She could see through her host's childish ruse of making her choose what had already been decided on as her prize, and was not going to comply with it. She was annoyed moreover that the dancing faun had not been allotted to herself, for she had always been devoted to dancing; as a child if she were not able to dance she would hop and leap about by the hour together, and once she had danced all night until her shoes were quite worn through, and only at a gardener's wedding. Wherever she looked she could see nothing quite so distinctive and unusual, so perfectly appropriate to herself as the dancing faun.

She became aware also that wherever she looked she saw strange faces, some that did not even know who she was, and many that were too young to have any adult memory of the war in which she had played her glorious part. It seemed such a short time ago.

'The tall Mademoiselle', that nickname had always pleased her, but another had fallen on her sharp ears that evening and made an echo in her heart like the toll of a bell. 'Who is that?' someone actually asked; and the whispered reply crept after her, 'That is the King's cousin, the old Mademoiselle.'

The presents were given; the excitement, the exclamation, the rush to gloat over the prizes and compare them with those of others made the gallery seem like a long cage filled with gaudy parrots all fluttering and squawking. Monsieur could not contain his envy when he saw Mademoiselle presented with an enormous diamond which someone had told him was worth £4000; but she herself did not seem pleased, she tossed her head and said, 'Then it is a pity the Princess Henriette did not win it, for she has told me she prefers money to anything else, and would doubtless sell it immediately.'

Monsieur leaped upon her motive with his uncanny quickness. 'You would like then to exchange with her? I can arrange it.'

He was clutching a Persian jar of attar of roses, he was flushed and happy, eager for more fun, he danced up to Henriette and said, 'My cousin, Mademoiselle wishes to exchange her present with yours. She had a diamond worth £4000 and knows you would prefer something you could sell for a good sum.'

Minette was looking at the dancing faun; its secret glancing smile had seemed to repeat the Cardinal's words, 'Here is one whose gay hour has arrived.' She had taken it as an omen that the troubles of her family would soon be over and they would all be dancing together in peace and prosperity. She looked up to see Monsieur hopping in front of her, his glance full of mischief, his smooth sallow hands fluttering over his precious jar as if longing to escape from their load in a flight of airy gestures.

With his words she was reminded that Charles had been turned out of Holland as well as France, and was now serving in the Spanish army as a means of earning his bread, though often he did not have enough to buy his next meal. Ignoring Monsieur, she walked across the gallery to the tall woman dressed in red and black and white.

'I hear, Mademoiselle, that you wish to speak to me. Will you tell me what it is you have to say?'

It was the second time Mademoiselle had been surprised by her little cousin. She said in a conciliatory tone, 'Only to ask if you wished to exchange presents.'

'That was not the message as I had it. Did you tell Monsieur I would prefer something I could sell?'

Mademoiselle regretted her attempt at conciliation. 'I am a bad enemy,' she had written of herself with some complacency; when there were attacks she was accustomed to make them herself. She felt a rush of fiery pleasure as she saw that this thin pert scrap was actually demanding battle; this pauper, whose brother had only wanted to marry herself for her money; who stood for all that she hated and despised and vaguely feared in the new bright Court of upstarts and toadies that had so strangely altered from the one she had left only five or six, though it might have been fifty or sixty years ago.

'If you care most for money,' she said, 'you are merely in the fashion I suppose, and I have been away too long to have learnt the fashion. But even as a child you thriftily asked me for money instead of a doll. Your royal name approves you. It is amusing to see how generations of Kingship cannot eliminate the Steward.' She laughed loudly and added, 'You know my way. I cannot resist a joke.'

But nobody knew her way. She was not, as she had been for six years, the head and centre of her own admiring Court, still less the warrior princess of earlier days, whom great captains had been proud to hail as an ally, and the populace as

100

the true Queen of France. She was merely an astonishingly rude stranger, a too tall, elderly girl rather than a woman, whose clothes and air and speech were all subtly out of date, a trifle ridiculous. Those near to her joined nervously in her laugh, those further off expressed in delighted whispers their horror at her behaviour.

Minette's hands clutched the dancing faun, forgetting what they held, itching only to lift and throw it with all their force in Mademoiselle's face. What would happen if they did? Morton had once said to her, 'If a thing is true, say so. It is not only right, it is the best way to save your face.'

'It is true,' began Minette, hardly knowing what she was about to say, 'it is true I wish I had more money – and you, more charity.'

She turned away, still holding her head very high, yet walking with an unconscious flowing grace that made all her movements seem liquid and inevitable like those of water. A murmur of approval followed her. She was slight and pale as a snowdrop, but she could show fight, she could provide amusement, and this rendered all the more piquant the delicious spectacle of the elder woman's jealousy.

She found that the Cardinal's eyes were resting on her, and wondered if he were angry. She was responsible for this disturbance at his banquet, she had deliberately sought out her cousin, she wished she had not. 'It is always better to leave things alone,' her mother always said so, and never did. And the Cardinal had been no good friend to her family. Still, he had thought of the dancing faun for her. On an impulse she went up to him and thanked him. 'Now that I have seen it, it is as though I had always wished for it. I do not know how you could have known that, but you have, and I am grateful.'

Her voice was low and tender, it created an intimacy between them, it was as though a child had said, 'I will tell you a secret.'

'If she keeps that quality,' he thought, 'it will be a charm more potent than all the fat on Olympe's shoulders.'

'You answered your cousin well,' he told her, 'but do not make an enemy of her.'

'It seems I have no need to, sir.'

'You are wrong. She has a good heart and I believe some affection for you. It is not she whom you have to fear in this Court.'

'Who, then?'

He did not answer for a moment, and when he did it was not an answer. He said, 'You do well to wish for money. Without it you will have neither pleasure nor power nor yet peace. It is like salt, you can taste no meat without it. It has taken me a lifetime of industry to amass my fortune, of which this collection here has been its most treasured part. I had intended to leave it to my nephew, Alphonse, the most promising of my family – I had felt confident of him as my successor. But the other day as you know he was killed by accident in a schoolboy romp at the Jesuits' College, when he took his turn to be tossed in a blanket. So you see, Princess, it is a poor discovery to make late in life that salt, by itself, is useless.'

His smile twisted his rouged cheek; he bowed with less than usual of his insinuating grace, and as he left her she could perceive by his walk how his limbs were aching.

'Undoubtedly I am ageing fast,' he told himself, 'I chatter to a little girl with thin arms whose family is a nuisance.'

The sympathy of women was notorious (the fussy devotion of Queen Anne was becoming a great trial), but this quality that was now budding unconsciously in the English princess of fifteen promised something deeper, more magical, possibly dangerous. He found himself still speculating on it and its future effects as he prepared his praises for the new ballet the King had composed on Cupid and Psyche.

But Louis received them ungraciously. He was telling Marie de Mancini how she had inspired the theme, and was in no mood to be interrupted by her uncle. Her great eyes glared up at him like a hungry fledgling whose choice morsels are being snatched by an intruder.

He passed quickly, finding the predominance of callow youth this evening very trying.

'How dare a disgusting old man like that speak of your Cupid and Psyche!' exclaimed Marie.

Louis was rather embarrassed. He had always been accustomed to Mazarin, he did not know what he would do without him; nor did he quite know what he would do with him if he persisted in living very much longer. It was not enough to compose and dance in ballets, to arrange hunting parties and lead the Court. He had told Marie that before he had met her he had only cared about being good at games and sports; but that now she had made him want to be a great king. But her fierce sympathy with him would allow of no half measures –

102

why should he not turn out his servant, Mazarin, as though he were a footman?

She was dark and thin and dry; her eyes seemed to burn up her face and her passionate sincerity to make a void round them. She and Louis could sit in their window-seat as in an enchanted circle, unobservant of all around, speaking only of themselves or the Cupid and Psyche they had chosen to represent themselves. It was not possible this moment should ever end, that they should ever part and Louis marry anyone else.

But as they thought this and spoke it in every line of their unconscious bodies – Louis flushed and boyish, leaning forward to look into her face; and she, pale and stiffly upright, rigid with emotion – they saw a servant speak to the Cardinal, who scarcely waited to apologize to those with whom he talked before he left the gallery.

'That will be the messenger from Spain,' said Marie, and they both fell silent.

For some weeks now the Court had been making preparations, buying new clothes and horses, talking of the journey Louis would make through his kingdom, to end at the most southern point close to the Spanish frontier in his meeting and marriage with the Infanta. Even that had not at first dashed Marie. She had thought she was going too. She had pictured herself wandering through strange towns and forests and waste places with Louis where anything might happen to prevent that dreadful ending to the journey. There would be a breakdown of the commissariat, they would be separated from their chaperons, from her particular old dragon, Madame de Venel, whom Louis had teased almost out of her life (he had given her a box of sweets which he had filled with live mice).

They would lie under the forest trees and the stars, and Louis would say, 'I care nothing for my throne – let us ride away together and never come back.' Or – for somehow that was a little difficult to imagine – they would be carried off by robbers and she would save his life; and all France as well as his nobler instincts would demand that he should marry her in gratitude, whatever his mother and Mazarin might say.

But today all these miraculous possibilities had vanished, for she had been told that the Cardinal intended to send his nieces safely out of the way when the Court moved. She had not yet told this to Louis, their moment of happiness had been too precious to spoil with bad news – twice he had asked her, 'What is it? You are thinking of something – tell me,' and she had said, 'Not yet – there is something else I want to talk about first,' for always they had so much to talk about there was never time to tell it all.

But now another messenger had come from Spain, and the Cardinal had left the room. Word by word, letter by letter, his business marched inevitably forward to the Spanish marriage-treaty with its terrible heritage of the Spanish succession, preparing the path to those long wars 'that would first exalt and then exhaust France and leave in her the seeds of revolution. But Marie could see only a very little way down that path, the first few steps in fact, that would lead Louis on a triumphal progress through his kingdom, fêted everywhere, visiting strange places like the seaport of Marseilles and the savage mountains of the Pyrénées, until he reached Saint Jean de Luz and his bride; where at so vast a distance of time and space he might even have forgotten about herself.

She told him then that she was to be left behind.

He said sadly, 'My mother told me last night. I did all that I could, but it is hopeless.'

' "That you *could*" – *you?* – You are the King!'

'So I said. I said I would marry you. She wept and stormed, you don't know her when she is like that, it is terrible, she screams at the top of her voice. I was firm, and then I told Mazarin. But Marie, it is of no use. The people would drive him out again, and you. It would means the wars of the Fronde over again, and that I will not have, even for you.'

'But I *hate* my uncle. Why should I be linked with him? Did I ask to belong to this family of toads and vipers, heartless schemers, minds like muck-heaps?' – and she flashed out one or two disclosures of her sisters' vices, shocking Louis by her outspokenness. She was really too violent, they would have so few times left in which to be together, and here she was spoiling them by arguing that he could very well marry her if only he would be brave like herself and defy everybody. He *was* brave, he *had* defied, but it was she who did not care whether France had another civil war or not.

'You are more of a foreigner than your uncle,' he said sullenly, and at that the hot tears began to smart and ache in her eyes, but she would not cry, she stared in front of her, blinking to keep them back. She saw nothing that she stared at, only the massive walls of Bruages where she would be sent with her sisters, a desolate sea fortress in dry land, left stranded like a derelict ship, for the sea had receded for miles round it and it stood solitary and meaningless in the middle of salt marshes. So would the tide of life recede from her, rush joyously in the wake of the King's bridal progress and leave her stranded, derelict. Like those who in fatal moments see their wraiths, she had a sudden vision of her own form, young, angular and sudden in its movements, walking alone upon the walls of Bruages, looking out across the grey marsh where the seagulls swirled and cried. She believed that through all the years to come, nothing would quench the fire in her veins; she would find her only relief in violent quarrels with her sisters.

Louis was speaking to her, but she had not noticed what he said; he was pushing something cold and hard into her hand.

'Take them up quickly,' he was saying. 'People will think you won them in the lottery. Dear Marie, do not cry. I cannot bear it if you cry.'

It was a string of large pearls in her hand.

'They are beautiful,' she said in a choked voice, not looking at them but at him, whose eyes were full of tears.

'I shall never love anyone as I love you,' he said, 'I would die for you, and I cannot live with you. Life is cruel, I wish I were dead.'

He was young and strong and handsome; death was nothing but another journey, a little more exciting than even the one he had so shortly to go. He did not see Marie on the walls of Bruages; he saw himself going gaily through his kingdom while his heart was breaking, and he longed to put his head down in her lap and cry.

She said, 'Sir, you love me – you weep – and you will leave me.'

She spoke clearly, quite unaware of those present. A young man with a dark grave face, carved like a cameo, who had been looking at her and the King, heard her and turned away.

'You have dropped your pearls,' said Louis, who had flushed to his forehead, suddenly aware how conspicuous she had made him. It was time to go. He must speak to others. Marie should have noticed these things. It was for women to have tact and understanding, to make things easier, not more difficult.

'I have ignored everyone else the whole evening,' he said,

105

'I am the King, I must not behave like a love-sick stable-boy.' But he should not have had to explain that.

He left her. He spoke to the Prince of Condé, to the Venetian ambassador, to the Princess of England. She was talking to the grave young man who had observed them when Marie had so unfortunately forgotten to lower her voice. His face, Louis noticed with some annoyance, was remarkably beautiful. The Princess Henriette introduced the obscure stranger to his notice, saying that Monsieur Racine was a poet who wished to write for the theatre, speaking of such trivial matters so as to make things easy for him, to cover his confusion and distress as he tried to struggle back into the daily current of his life.

Her eyes avoided his, and yet he felt that she had seen all that he felt and was sorry for him; her voice was murmurous and caressing, like water, he thought. His heart had been scorched by Marie's fire and now she bathed it. He looked at her suddenly and anew. She made no demands of him; he had been expected to marry her, he had once refused to dance with her, and she had never reminded him of either. Why had he always been so sure he would not marry her? But of course – his wits were wandering – she was a pauper and an exile.

CHAPTER FIFTEEN

As Marie de Mancini left the gallery, Mademoiselle recognized the pearls she now wore as those belonging to the crown of England. The Queen had lent them to her many years ago when she had decked her out for a ball. She remembered her aunt's sycophantic chatter as she twisted the jewels in her bright hair (it was still just as bright where it had not turned grey), flattery to which she had scarcely troubled to listen, because she was thinking how she would sit that evening on a dais with the kings of France and England at her feet, and neither of them quite good enough for her. And now those pearls, that the dead King Charles had given long ago to his queen in the happy days of their marriage, had been sold for King Louis to give to this cuckoo's brood that were trying to oust the best families in France.

The restlessness and self-satisfaction that had beset Mademoiselle all that evening was at once appeased. It was true then, and she had not been unjust, that family would do anything for money. In triumph and reproach she stared at her aunt, who did not notice her, she too was looking at Marie's brown neck, encircled by her pearls. She had kept them till now through all her privations and demands for money, that she might still have a present worthy to give to her daughter Henriette on her wedding to King Louis. She could not give that as a reason for refusal when King Louis, himself asked leave to buy the pearls of her.

The death of Oliver Cromwell some months previously had made no difference to Charles' fortune. It had come too late, she said, like all good things that happened to them, and so, though there were precipitate Royalist plots that met a premature death, and many upheavals and disturbances in England, yet none promised any real hope of a return of the King. Chancellor Hyde had said all along that there was nothing to be done but wait until the natural course of events in England would swing the pendulum of public opinion towards his restoration. But now the natural course of events had removed his chief obstacle, and still the pendulum, though wobbling frantically under Cromwell's son, refused to swing. Monarchy itself had probably ended in England – and now she had seen King Charles' pearls on the neck of Louis' little upstart.

She could plan and struggle no longer. Submission to God's will was the only guide for the conduct of life, and she drove post-haste to Chaillot to acquire it. All the talk and bustle about the journey south, all the preparations for the Spanish marriage were an unbearable humiliation; she could not endure to go too and see her daughter suffer, so she told Mère Angélique.

'She does not seem in great danger of suffering,' said the Abbess drily as Minette's voice came shrilling through the trees, now in snatches of song, now in squeals of ecstasy as she sported herself in that newly fashionable plaything, a swing. Glimpses of her blue silk skirts flashed in and out of the sunlight like the darting flights of a kingfisher.

Above her head the chestnut branches towered to the windy sky, they had spread their green fans and lighted a thousand candles to the glory of God; the air was full of blown blossom, of the shrill calls of birds, of the hopes of a princess of fifteen

107

who had no dowry, but at whom the King of France had looked as though he saw her for the first time.

She did not notice the two black figures walking on the lawn, she did not hear her mother answer the Abbess, 'That is because she is still a child without any thought of such things as her marriage. She has never looked on the King as anything but a playmate.'

'Then where would be her humiliation if you take her south with the Court?'

'They would not leave her in ignorance, everyone would be laughing at her disappointment – and at mine.'

So the Queen's health was very bad that summer, and as for some reason the air of Chaillot did not just then agree with her, or perhaps it was Mère Angélique who did not, she retired in exceedingly low spirits to her new country house at Colombes. It was a pretty place, the air was soft and sleepy with the cooing of the doves that had given it its name. But this summer Minette hated it. She had thought that everything would be different this year, and everything was exactly the same, only much, much more so, she complained in a long letter to Louise at Mauberge, who answered her with a few philosophic remarks that read like rather stale texts. Friendship then was one of the things that did not stay the same, at any rate not in absence, and disillusionment was added to Minette's bitter disappointment at not going south with the King. For the first time she knew she would not be shy of him and he would not be bored with her. If she had gone with him on this long pleasure journey through France while the voracious brood of the Cardinal's nieces were left behind at Bruages, who knew what might have happened? But she had not gone. She was here at Colombes with her mother, as poor Marie was at Bruages.

They heard disputes as to the order of precedence to be observed at King Louis' wedding; there was no one of equal rank with Mademoiselle to bear the train with her; and Minette's hopes ran high again. A long friendly letter came for the Queen from Mademoiselle – the famous shops on the pier at Marseilles had proved disappointing, and she had got nothing there that she could not have bought just as well in Paris; also she found it very annoying the way the galley slaves were allowed to walk about the streets, clanking their chains.

'Does she say nothing about me, Mamma?'

'She hopes you are well, my dear. What else should she have to say?'

'I only thought – then does she say who will bear the train with her?'

'Oh, that. Yes, here is a postscript all scrawled across. What a coarse heavy writing it is. She has sent for her two stepsisters at her own expense. And she was always so terrified of their getting more notice than herself! I always said that girl was the sort of fool who would cut off her enormous nose to spite her own face.'

'But why shouldn't she have sent for me? I am a granddaughter of France. Even her stepsisters are to go to the wedding, and I am not to go!'

She hit her knuckles against the furniture and wished it were her cousin. Her mother at once became more calm, controlled and competent than she had been for many months; she told Minette firmly that she would have been miserable on this journey, with less money than a chambermaid to make an equal show with all the magnificence around her, that Mademoiselle was so jealous of her that all the Court had remarked it and looked on it as a joke, and that she ought to regard it as a compliment that she should already be considered a dangerous rival.

Exhausted by her outburst, Minette lay curled up in her mother's strong arms, her cheek against the broad white collar of stiff muslin which was the Queen's only relief to her widow's weeds; she reflected that after all she was far happier here with her, and 'Coo, coo' chanted the doves outside the window, nodding their heads in agreement, curtseying through the glass with respectful sympathy to la Reine Malheureuse, curtseying to herself in acknowledgement of her loving and dutiful resignation.

It was disconcerting, unnatural, an undoubted visitation of the devil, that she dreamed that night of her mother's face distorted with weeping in that shocking moment when as a very young child she had first seen her cry; that in her dream she leaned over that sobbing countenance and said to it, 'I hate you, I hate you.'

The leaves fell in the river and drifted downstream, the rain made miniature fountains in the water, which grew too cold for bathing, the Queen made her put a shawl round her shoulders when she went into the garden, the summer died a natural death in floods of gentle rain, there was no hunting

109

nor dancing, they heard that the King's wedding and return with his bride would not take place until next summer, the world seemed to stand still with nothing more to look forward to than the medicines she had to take for her cold.

Then in midwinter, after nearly seven years, Charles paid them a visit.

Mazarin was completing the Treaty of the Pyrénées at Saint Jean de Luz; and Charles had gone all the way there to see him, and crossed the border into Fuenterrabia to see the King of Spain, for now that the wars between France and Spain were over he hoped to enlist either or both of these countries in his service.

The cold hall at Colombes was full of bustle and exclamation when a tall man walked into it and kneeled before the Queen to ask her blessing. Minette was behind her and drew back still further to observe this stranger who was her brother. She was surprised to see him so old and worn, battered was the word that came to her mind, and she did not think that he had brought good news.

He rose, looked round him, and his eyes rested on the Gordon girl who was standing close by the Queen. She was just seventeen, and fair, a pretty creature, but Minette fancied that a shade of disappointment flickered across that quick, weary, disillusioned glance as he said, 'And is this my little sister?'

The Queen rushed on the chance of a joke, 'Yes, take her and kiss her – has she not grown into a fine girl?'

The Gordon girl blushed and giggled, and straightway Charles, in the middle of embracing her, looked up and said, 'You are making fun of me. This is not Minette.'

Minette by now was laughing so much she could scarcely come forward and curtsey. 'I failed to recognize you last time, sir,' she said. 'Now it is your turn.'

'No, for I saw through your plot, but you denied me even when you knew me, you feminine Saint Peter, you should blush to hear the cock crow.'

'You did not look so clean then,' she admitted as she kissed him.

That guilty secret of her childhood had slid into a joke, making for greater ease and companionship; she had a notion that many other things would do the same when she had talked them over with this man, so much older than herself and so different. Now that he had embraced her he held her

110

away from him, looking her up and down with shrewd eyes under their heavy lids; and she felt there was nothing that she could not share with him.

'I thought you would be a grown-up young lady,' he said, 'and here you are still a baby. You must give her something, Mam, to make her fatter or they will say we are so poor we have to starve her.'

Minette's impression had been right; he had no good news; neither Mazarin nor the King of Spain would do anything for him. Mazarin with polite irony had even refused Charles' proposal of marriage with his niece Hortense, on the score that as long as the first spinster in France remained unmarried a modest Cardinal must not look as high as a crown for a girl of his own family.

'There is no doubt I am the most ineligible bachelor in Europe; no one will marry me, not even Bablon, though I intend to ask her every day.'

'Bablon' was their nickname for La Châtillon, who was then a visitor at Colombes and a very pleasant one. She joked and flirted with Charles; she was painted too harsh a red and white which emphasized the lines like faint scars between her nose and chin, but she still looked beautiful, especially by candlelight when she wore a yellow dress. She would then sit at the harpsichord and sing duets with Charles, which Minette accompanied on her lute, watching them both in childish admiration. Mademoiselle had not liked Châtillon, she had said she was overdressed and that her adventures would make a stranger chronicle than the wars of the Fronde – this added to her fascination for the girl.

The visit could not last. Mazarin came to hear of it, and Charles was warned that he must not stay in France, even in the privacy of his mother's country house. Cromwell was dead, but Cromwell had left England a powerful country, and France must not offend her. Charles must be off on his travels again and see what he could do to get food for himself and his followers. He could no longer serve in the Spanish army now it was at peace. He was out of a job again. Young Harry talked of becoming a tennis instructor, and James of marrying an heiress; unfortunately he had fallen in love with old Hyde's ugly daughter who was one of the Princess Mary's maids of honour.

Charles had quarrelled with Mary, he did not know how it was. Perhaps they were all embittered for lack of anything

111

pleasant to tell each other; or perhaps he had taken too much from Mary and taken it for granted. She complained that he was as arbitrary as if he were indeed a reigning monarch; and he that she was being damnably inconsiderate and tiresome over her love-affair with Lord Jermyn's nephew which was causing jealousy and scandal.

'But perhaps poor Mary really loves Harry Jermyn,' said Minette as they walked in the frost-bound garden for the last time before he went away.

'That is your criterion, is it not? And when will you yourself fall in love, or have you been so all this time with someone?'

'I used to think I was with King Louis, but it is so long since I have seen him.'

'Be faithful a little longer. You could not choose anyone more useful to me.'

'And that is *your* criterion. Shall I always submit my passions to it? How furiously cold it is!' She began to dance up and down in front of him on the crisp white grass, singing a song she made up that moment. 'Who will you choose for me, my pretty pander?'

Her brown and white spaniels, Lulu and Poilu, pronounced Pulu to rhyme, danced too, jumping against her and barking; they thought this a game entirely for their benefit. Lulu was very feminine, with a tail like an ostrich feather and melting eyes. She pranced round Pulu, who was larger and more stately, but now condescended from his manly dignity so far as to make little rushes at her, rolling her over, once even making her bounce into the air and turn a complete somersault. They scampered across the lawn and Minette after them, for she had suddenly remembered that she must show Charles her swing, though the air was too icy now to rush through it. She sat in the swing however, scraping up the frost on the grass with her pointed clog, while Pulu ran about, rubbing his nose in it and yapping at the sting it gave him; then he jumped into her lap, and burrowed into the little muff she had made for herself of green quilted silk. She wore a mantle of pale green velvet and white fur that had belonged to her aunt, and was out of fashion. Lulu had already taken shelter with Charles, and had her nose well in the shelter of his elbow; he rubbed her silky coat the wrong way and pulled her ears, teasing her, calling her 'little absurdity', 'nice little beast', 'Madam Oddity'.

Madam Oddity crept further down his arm; she had her head well into his cuff now; it was wide enough to hold her bodily.

'When she has puppies,' he said, 'send me all you can spare. The more I see of men, the better I like dogs.'

He stopped playing with her, and rested his hand on the rope of the swing, where it showed a dark and mottled purple from the cold.

The wrought-iron gates on to the road were drawn in black strokes against the steel-white background. The freezing air was silent now that the doves no longer cooed in the garden but huddled in their dovecote, and the autumn gales no longer rushed through the trees. Their branches stretched like skeletons against the iron sky. Everywhere was a frozen suspension of life; nothing moved, no bird called, it was impossible to believe this cold scene would ever burst into leaf and flower, or that anything would ever happen again. Minette rubbed the blue tip of her nose, Charles moved his hand from the rope and put it in his pocket.

'Let us go in,' they said, and yet they lingered. Once they were indoors other people would cluster round them and they would have to talk about plans, and then Charles would ride out through these gates and it might be seven years again before they next saw each other. But out here the world stood still for a little time. She remembered the gay hopes she had entertained in that swing as she had flown through the warm air and the falling chestnut blossom, and she no longer regretted their disappointment, for if she had gone south with the Court she would not now have been sitting here with Charles.

'Write to me,' he said, 'I shall like to get your letters.'

'I shall have so little to tell. I will give you messages from La Châtillon and any new songs that I can find.'

'When I next get any money I will send you a present. What shall it be?'

'A new saddle. Oh, but you will not have enough for that – no, do not think of it. I wish we could have ridden together here. The frost has been as cruel as the Cardinal. And once I thought I liked him.'

'You will think that of everyone some time or other.'

At sixteen it is fascinating to find that one is anybody. 'Am I so foolish?' asked Minette, not caring what she was as long as Charles had noticed it. He laughed and shook the rope,

113

wriggling the swing till she jumped out of it. He said, 'Louise is right about you,' and Minette was wild to know what Louise had said, but he would not bother to remember it properly – 'only that you are a soap bubble.'

He had paid a visit to Louise in her convent at Mauberge, and she had welcomed him very kindly. Minette wondered if she had forgiven Charles or forgotten Montrose; she had grown very jovial and had entertained her cousin royally with amusing talk as well as good food and wine. 'What was it she said, I could have wished I'd thought of it myself, something about one man's aunt being another man's mother.'

'Oh!' whispered Minette in a little gasp, it was so strange to find that all that had happened between her and Louise two years ago had all died away, leaving nothing but the echo of a joke. Should she tell Charles of Louise's passionate outcry against him? It would most probably only amuse him. She had begun to learn from him that the only thing to do with life was to 'be merry and then they will forgive you everything, even poverty, perhaps even so far as to feed you, which is all that forgiveness is worth.'

'Is poverty a crime?' she asked, and burst out with her story of the dancing faun and Mademoiselle's atrocious behaviour. But she was quite right he said. Life was too short to be measured by anything but success. 'I am a king and must cadge my meals where I can. It is no help to be royal. Neither does it help to have an anxious eye, a cautious tongue, a too eager embrace, a too quick agreement in opinion. These do not make for good company, and to be good company is one's only excuse for living at all in such circumstances, or indeed perhaps in any.'

'And so, if they say, "I suppose you have come here for your dinner," you reply, "What else should I come for in this company?"'

'Yes, my apt pupil. What's the use of an old hat if you can't cock it?'

She thought that now at last she would have no more fear of the terrible tall Mademoiselle's scorn or the wicked little Monsieur's mischief-making, or even of Louis' contemptuous indifference, for she was now secure with Charles; they at least would appreciate each other and be amused at their efforts to cock their hats against the world.

She learned this lesson only a few weeks before it was no longer necessary.

114

CHAPTER SIXTEEN

The ice had melted in a thaw colder than any frost; Charles rode out from Colombes on a raw winter's morning. There before him lay the road to Brussels, and at the end of it a worse prospect of discomfort than any he had known. He suddenly decided to turn his horse's head in the opposite direction, and pay a brief visit to his uncle Gaston d'Orléans at Blois. It would be amusing to see the old scoundrel again and prolong his visit to France by a few days; he did not suppose he would ever come to this country again.

It was twilight when he reached the Loire, a wide, soft-flowing expanse of water with brown woods rising like mist from its shores. He first saw the towers of the château as a reflection that glimmered in the water. At some distance a man stood upright in a boat; he pushed it along slowly with a single oar, leaving a long dark ripple of reflection that nearly touched the white-mirrored towers. He was the only living thing to be seen in that grey and silver solitude. The scene was as quiet as though the château had been deserted for many years, and the river would never again be a bustle of summer traffic, of merchants' boats and floating pavilions, hung with gold and crimson, where musicians played and the princes of that land took their pleasure; as though all the brisk life that had once boated and hunted and reigned and loved along that river had now departed, leaving only an empty château and its image in the water.

But the château was far from empty; the cold dusk was soon shut outside, and Charles stood in the hall at Blois in a warm brilliance of candle and firelight and Gaston's welcoming exclamations. Gaston's second wife sighed over him and blinked her fat white eyelids in expression of sympathy as she informed him that he too had his troubles; for herself she was a martyr to the vapours and would not have the strength to dine with him that evening. Two or three shy, pretty girls in their middle teens were pushed forward to him, made to curtsey and speak nicely to their cousin. A bustle of orders and preparations was in progress at the further end of the hall, and Charles, sniffing the divine perfume of roast partridge,

115

knew that whatever else happened in this odd world, he was at least certain of his next meal.

They sat at dinner in a room where the walls had been decorated under Queen Catherine de Medici in a scroll-work of dull, chalk-like pinks and blues; the colours looked thick and unwholesome like those of toadstools – perhaps partly from damp. The painted panels of cupboards were a maze of devices in which little faces suddenly peered out at one as though they had that moment chosen to become visible.

Gaston told Charles that a whole roomful of secret cupboards was concealed behind such panels in the chamber adjoining the Italian queen's private chapel; and that there she had kept her marvellous collection of perfumes and cosmetics, and poisons too – so they said in the next reign.

'I dare say it's true. She was an extraordinary woman. The old duke of Bellegarde remembered her very well – ah well, it's an effort now to remember him. One grows – one goes. People will be forgetting you and me next, just as they have forgotten the Court of the Valois, the Vicious Valois – it is the fashion now to call them that. But people still had manners then, and wits were valued. No doubt they overdid it. I found some hair restorer in a Venetian glass bottle the other day in that secret cupboard and might have tried it – but who can tell it isn't poison? A pity they were so versatile. Have you heard of anything good for the hair in the course of your travels?'

He talked in a desultory, jerky way, suddenly remembering half-way through dinner to ask after his sister, Queen Henrietta, and whom was she converting now? Odd, how fanatical she was; so different from their father, King Henry – 'Paris is worth a mass,' that was a good story, it showed you what he was like. But women always made trouble. Their grandmother Jeanne d'Albret had been a fierce Protestant and, though doubtless she would refuse to acknowledge it, that was where his sister's intolerance came from. For his part, like all modern and enlightened minds, he was mercifully free from it.

The wine was excellent. Tray after tray of food was collected from the table and carried up to Madame's room. 'Eating and praying are her only consolations for having married me,' said Gaston.

He talked of his pheasants, of which he was very proud, and complained of his young nephew King Louis' inconsiderate behaviour in shooting as many as fourteen of them when he

116

stayed for the night on his way down south this autumn. And then he would walk in the gardens without a hat, and so Gaston too had to go uncovered, until he had to put his gloves on his head for protection against the damp. It had been an unlucky visit. His chef had been so flustered that he disgraced himself – 'tepid leather for every course. And Mop here' (he pointed at the prettiest of his two daughters; the third had turned out to be a friend who was staying with them) 'had her face stung all over by gnats. We used to call her the little queen – no hope of that now, hey Mop? Those gnats should teach you not to leave your window open when a king comes to stay.'

'Leave your door open instead this time,' suggested Charles; and found rather to his surprise that Gaston encouraged him to flirt with her. It gave him the first hope in his prospects for many months; for Gaston had sometimes shown gleams of almost uncanny cleverness, and it might be that some prescient sense told him even now, when Charles' future looked blacker than it had ever done, that there was a chance it might prove worth while to secure him as a son-in-law.

The young lady's own attention was far more occupied with the Prince Charles of Savoy, a pleasant quiet boy, only a little older than the girls, who had been staying in the house for some time and was treated as one of the family. They tittered and talked in undertones with him, trying to make him behave badly too, while he smiled in embarrassment, and stared with a boy's envious curiosity at the adventurer king. When an opportunity came he plied King Charles with shy questions, not knowing what to ask, but hoping to make him tell how he had fought in Spain, fought on sea, fought and lost all in his remote island kingdom of England. Most of all, he wanted to hear how he had wandered for six weeks in his own country with a price on his head; 'but you will never get him to tell the truth about that,' whispered 'Mop'. 'My sister, Mademoiselle, says he tells different stories about it every time, and someone said that it is for fear of betraying those who helped him, and my father said, "How odd." ' She giggled wildly as she shook her frizzed bush of hair, for she thought whatever her father said must be humorous; and also she was trying to distract the boy's attention from their long lean gaunt visitor, who was far too old to be interesting.

Gaston apologized for his daughters' manners; their mother, he said, only saw them for ten minutes every morning, when she told them to hold up their heads, 'which, as you observe, they never do.' They and their little friend, Mademoiselle de la Vallière (she was the fair one between the two dark, and as quiet as the sisters were lively), were incurably childish, would play all day in the woods together, and never wanted to go to Court with Mademoiselle, his eldest daughter. But now they were to join her at Saint Jean de Luz and act as train-bearers with her to the new Queen from Spain. 'But my daughter is determined they shall not lodge with the Queen-mother and so put her in the background. She writes her orders about it every week or so.'

His laugh made him look much older than when Charles had last seen him, and yet there was still that suggestion of the handsome careless boy about him. He swaggered, he flourished, but he was fatigued. He spoke of the last time he had been in Paris, the first time after years of exile. It had tired him to death, he said; everybody had been so wearisome that he had been glad to get back to his country estates. Here he had held his own Court, encouraged the latest artists and writers. 'That Italian boy Lulli who is now writing operas in Paris was a fiddler in my daughter's service long before the King took him up.'

When the whim took him, Gaston had drifted down his beautiful river for days on end, stopping at some charming island or wooded bank, perfumed with thyme and honey-suckle, to make his camp for supper and the night.

'Where could you find a better life, more free, more go-as-you-please? And yet, too amiable, One requires a something by way of contrast, the salt of danger, agitation—'

'A spice of treachery,' suggested Charles.

'True, very true,' sighed Gaston, too happily unconscious of sin to take the remark to himself.

Not all his pleasures as absolute prince at Blois had made up to him for the lack of his greatest amusement, that of be-traying his friends. He could do so with such lightness of heart that it amounted to supreme innocence. When he broke his written oath he excused himself because he had not given a verbal promise; when he broke his spoken word it was be-cause he had given it with a mental reservation; when he had to make a decision he at once fell ill; when he had to fight a battle he went to bed and left his daughter to do it; when he left his friends in the lurch he asked them afterwards how

118

they had fared as unconcernedly as if he had done his utmost to help them.

Though he had hated Paris in that last belated visit, he could talk of nothing else; of the plots and the barricades and the street fighting in the old days of the Fronde, of the minor excitements of parading the streets in disguise – 'No one knew me, I did not know myself, and that is the charm of masquerade – you are Paladin, Charlemagne, Amadis of Gaul, you are a low lousy beggar slinking through the filthy slum, you are life itself before it has yet decided what person it will be in you—'

His voice broke off, his eyes became vague and dreaming, he was seeing himself as a great prince, a hero; that was why they looked slightly glazed. To the essentially practical mind of his guest it seemed an odd form of absolution to bring comfort to anybody. But such moments could buoy up Gaston's spirit when he heard himself described as a monster of perfidy and even cowardice. No one, he told himself, who had such aspirations could possibly be base of soul; it must be that others were too gross of spirit to understand his; besides he never had an unkind impulse, even his wit had never been known to hurt others. His heart was as naturally good as his intellect – only the times were so confusing, one's relations with other people so involved; he was always ready to start an enterprise, and then saw its difficulties, and had to change his mind, draw back and extricate himself as best he could. Whereupon there would follow all that tiresome chat of your 'word' here and your 'word' there. As though your word were an unyielding block of stone, for ever fixed at the base of a rock of unchanging circumstance – whereas all it was in reality was the reflection of a mood of a passing impulse, of a conglomeration of the needs and events and demands of a crowd of characters that fluctuated with each shifting moment.

So he said to Charles as they sat by the fire after dinner, appealing to his nephew in a nervous half-fearful way that Charles might have found uncomfortable, but that the warmth of the fire on his legs and the admirable working of his digestion permitted no exterior emotion. A needy wanderer of nearly thirty, he had been kept from despair at his persistent failures only by his immense physical vitality, and his sense that even a beggar, if wise, need not be deprived of physical pleasures.

The elderly child before him reminded him of that other son

119

of France, Louis' young brother Philippe, now growing up, but still a child, and apparently always to remain one.

If he were ever to establish any relations with France it could only be now by marrying Minette to him. The thought almost disturbed his comfort for a moment, but common sense quickly dispelled it. There was no need to consider what was impossible in the present state of his fortunes; even though Philippe, it was said, showed a greater liking for his English cousin than he had yet done for any woman.

The light of the leaping flames licked upwards at the fantastically carved chimney-piece. The first of the Valois kings, Francis I, had had it made for that room. And the last of the Valois, the curled and scented son of Catherine de Medici, Henry III, had stood in the little side-room off the passage, which Charles could just see from where he sat, and watched his guest Duc de Guise, who had stood warming himself at that fireplace, when men rushed in and stabbed him to death. Then when his rival was dead, King Henry had come and put his foot on the body that had been the most splendid man in France, and said, 'He does not look so tall now he is dead.' This was the more dreadful because King Henry had admired manly beauty so greatly that he could never love a woman.

Charles, remembering that murder of a century ago, and finding his attempts to borrow even as much as five pounds from his uncle fall lamentably flat, was content to sit back in somnolent amusement at Gaston's reflections and reminiscences, and through them all that thin strain of question: as though, in looking back over his life as a whole, Gaston still hoped to discover something in it that might correspond with his early dreams of what it would be. The blurred colours and tortuous tangle of his mind had found a fitting home in this painted palace, where the memory of old treacheries hung about the air like a stale perfume used by the Italian queen and her strange son.

As if conscious of it he came back and back to the subject of treachery, 'and yet,' he said, 'it is life who plays the traitor to us all, takes our best hopes and fairest promises and turns them against you. You try to make it a romance, a high adventure, and it falls down into farce. The only thing is to laugh at it, to make a grimace before anyone should have a chance of grimacing at you.

'Look at my daughter – not those two gigglers at dinner – but my elder, Anne Marie Louise, our young lady of France,

120

our Mademoiselle. She was the prettiest child, her nose was not too big then, and her liveliness was enchanting. Even the King, my poor sour-faced old brother, would cheer up a little when she rushed at him and hugged him and demanded that he should give her one of his hound puppies. She had taste too; she always chose your best English hounds, and she was the only female I ever saw, child, girl, or woman, who could keep up with them in this country.

'But she became overgrown, and remained it. Everything in her has been exaggerated, and fixed. She makes trouble wherever she goes, and I am certain she will commit some incredible folly before she grows quite old. And yet, so short a time ago—' for a minute he was actually silent. His mind was whirling round his daughter's childhood 'so short a time ago'; then suddenly his lips twisted in a sarcastic smile, it had reached still further back, to his first wedding, to the blonde sheep who had so surprisingly produced that eldest daughter.

Such a fantastic muddle as it had been, that wedding, all mixed up with his friends' crazy conspiracies on his behalf, which were bound to end in their death. It was not his fault that the only way to get out of it was to give their names to Cardinal Richelieu; and after all he had exhausted himself pleading in vain for mercy for poor Chalais. Poor young Chalais, so gay, so good-looking, how he had adored that boy! They gave him a second-rate executioner, and it took twenty blows to kill him; and then they accused himself, Gaston, of heartlessness because he danced and smiled just afterwards at his own wedding. Was there any use in going to it as though it had been Chalais' funeral? He had not wanted the wedding ('though indeed,' he said aloud, as if pursuing some argument, 'my first wife had three virtues: she was silent, she was an heiress, and she died on giving birth to her child'), but one had to go through with a thing properly, damn it, when one came to it – dance – laugh – and who wouldn't have laughed at those two women in the wedding procession who actually came to blows and then scratches on a question of precedence – 'Remember how we took cockfighting bets on the warlike hens?'

Charles, who had not then been born, nodded as if in rememberance of the scandalous incident, while Gaston jumped out of his chair in ecstasy at it, kissed his finger-tips to the ceiling, thrust them again into his pocket, flapping it against his side, and spun on his thin legs before the fire, sending two goblin shadows across the patch of floor where the Duc de Guise had died.

In such extravagant gestures he could dispel the memory of that strong boyish neck, mangled by the executioner. Poor young Chalais – 'beautiful, beloved, betrayed,' he murmured, so that Charles meditated whether his uncle, whom he had always thought on the verge of going off his head, had now really done so. Certainly he was very ill; at the end of that pirouette he had collapsed in his chair, his face twisted with pain, and stared at his guest with the helpless eyes of an old man.

When Charles left him next day, in a cold drizzling rain, both knew that they would not meet again. Death lay only a few weeks ahead for Gaston; a more unexpected fate awaited Charles.

CHAPTER SEVENTEEN

While Cromwell had lived there had been something to hope for; now it seemed that nothing had the power to change Charles' fortunes. His credit was at the lowest ebb it had yet touched; he dismissed his servants, he pawned what plate he had left, he could not buy a warm coat.

He did not mention any of this in his letters to Minette. Hers were at first childishly formal and full of majesties and protestations of loyal obedience, which made him chuckle as he sat reading them in his threadbare coat and chilly lodging. But they soon thawed under his easy example and his petitions that there should be less loyalty and more news of what she was doing. She must be furiously bored if this wet weather went on much longer; for his part he was so idle he could find nothing better to do than write to her, while Harry, industrious lad, played tennis. He sent her songs which she must learn to sing before he saw her again.

'God knows when that will be,' sighed the Queen, for none of them had any idea, and Charles himself gave no hint of it, that all through this 'idle' time when he was writing nearly every day to his little sister of songs and romances and pet dogs, he was in close communication with the most powerful party in England, and as the spring advanced it became certain that General Monk, with the army that had once been Cromwell's, intended to bring him as king to England.

The news of this came so suddenly that it astounded everybody, but even Queen Henrietta, once so credulous, now so suspicious of good fortune, had to believe in the marvellous change in her son's fortunes when she heard that that careful nation, the Dutch, who had been so inhospitable to Charles, were hurrying to get in their presents to him before anybody else, showering money and pictures on him, a royal yacht and a state bed.

Now at last he and his sister Mary had something pleasant to tell each other; he led her by the hand into the room where lay a great portmanteau, bursting open with £30,000 in gold, which had been sent by the English Parliament to buy clothes for himself and his suite. At that miraculous sight their hearts melted, their quarrels were forgotten, Mary burst out crying with happiness and flung her arms round his neck, begging him not to leave her behind, but to take her back home too to England.

La Châtillon looked a trifle disconsolate these days, particularly when they heard that the bold, beautiful Mrs Barbara Palmer was with him at Brussels and that he would take her with him to London. Minette wondered sometimes if he loved Barbara more than herself; her anxiety must have shown in her letter, for he wrote to her, 'I love you as much as possible. Never fear that others who are present shall get an advantage over you, for, believe me, the love that I have for you cannot be shared.' And he told her to choose the ribbons and trimmings and feathers for his new summer clothes in Paris, so that she was almost consoled for not being with him and the rest of the family at Brussels. 'If you only knew how often we talk of you and wish you were here,' he wrote.

She went with her mother to hear the Te Deums sung at Chaillot, and then to Paris to receive their friends' rapturous congratulations. The Queen was too much excited to sleep; she rose at dawn to write letters to her son, begging him to remember in his good fortune those who had suffered for him and his father. 'All this is from God, it is written by His hand, one can see it plainly,' she wrote, and Charles forbore to answer how much His style must have improved.

He entered England with his brothers on the last day of May and his thirtieth birthday; there was never a happier omen. He took four days to reach his capital through the crowds that cheered and danced and sang and lit bonfires, and sent out representatives of every trade and profession to express the joy of the whole nation in his return. Through it all he found time to scribble notes to Minette; how stunned and deafened he was at the clamour and business so that he hardly knew what he was writing, but had managed to get her present before he left Brussels and commissioned his sister Mary to forward to her by one Mr Progers. It was a green velvet saddle, embroidered and laced with gold, far finer than any she had ever had.

This bewildering change in Charles' fortunes had come while the French Court were far away down south near the Spanish border. There was little chance to show a change of front to him after the years in which he had been refused even the right to stay with his mother on French soil, culminating in the combined rebuffs of both France and Spain this winter. Mazarin hastily wrote to offer him a choice of his two remaining nieces, but with no success; and Hortense reproached him bitterly for having prevented her from the crown of England.

As for Mademoiselle, when she heard of Charles' triumphal entry into his kingdom from which he had been exiled for thirteen years, of the universal joy that acclaimed him King more surely than all Monk's soldiers, she flung herself on her bed and sobbed, 'I have been a fool.'

Mazarin, in a last attempt to repair his own mistake, suggested that it was not too late to repair hers. She replied with dignity that it would ill become her to marry a man in his good fortune whom she had refused in his bad; the Cardinal, however, understood her sentiments and took care that Charles should know the change they had undergone. Charles laughed, and let it be understood, in an equally roundabout fashion, that he had no wish to marry a woman who had snubbed him so often.

On an evening in early June, just before King Louis' wedding, Mademoiselle took a walk along the riverside at Saint Jean de Luz, away from the little seaside town and towards the Pyrénées. The highest mountain there, which is called the Three Crowns, was blotted out by clouds, and this she took for an omen. She had failed to marry the Emperor, the King of France and the King of England. She had begun to think

124

that personal relations were very difficult, and surely marriage the most difficult of all.

She was not, however, thinking of the Emperor Leopold, far away in Germany; nor of King Louis, who in three days' time would enter the dark church at Fuenterrabia, glittering in robes of cloth of gold, encrusted with jewels, to be united to the heiress of Spain; nor yet of King Charles, disporting himself in London with Mrs Barbara Palmer; but of her father, Gaston d'Orléans, who had died last winter, neglected almost alone. His wife had rushed away from Blois as soon as he was dead, and there had been no proper ceremony at his funeral. King Louis had said to Mademoiselle, smiling, as soon as he had got through the proper expressions of condolence: 'At last my brother is satisfied. You will see him tomorrow in a mourning mantle five yards long in honour of your father.'

Even in death Gaston had been only a joke. He had never counted as much, whether for good or ill, as he had hoped. Now his chief importance was that his titles and estates would pass to Philippe, who would henceforth be Duc d'Orléans.

But to Mademoiselle, Gaston had always counted; and most when she had been a child. He had once arranged a children's ballet especially for her – a Dance of Dwarfs, in which they trotted about to the music very happily though in no particular pattern, and played with parakeets which were loosed from their cages for the purpose. Even now Mademoiselle could feel annoyance with one of the very little girls who had cried and screamed with fright when a bird had got entangled in her ruff, perhaps because the little girl had later married the Prince of Condé, and though so often ill had never died.

'Yes, I shall never marry,' she decided, but still she was not thinking of the Prince of Condé, savage, strange and shaggy, whose life she had saved in battle; but of those nights in her childhood when she had wakened suddenly to see her father standing by her bedside, the light behind him glinting on the jewelled cap that he wore cocked right over one ear, throwing long shadows down the dark disapproving face of her governess. He would show her the box of curiously shaped comfits that he was turning over and over in his pocket; tell her of the banquet he had escaped from, where the King his brother had looked so white that they had nearly carved him up in mistake for a cold boiled fowl – for he had been bled four times last week and that was enough to make anyone look chicken-livered; crow at his own witticisms, spin on his heels, toss his cap in the air and collapse in helpless laughter on the side of the great bed. To the child, sitting up in it before him, it was as though a gigantic painted top were humming in the dark room; she would clap her hands and gaze on him enraptured.

On her way down south with the King and the Court last autumn they had stopped for a night at Blois, and she had last seen her father. He had been odd and ill-humoured, had given them a bad dinner and grumbled because King Louis shot so many of his pheasants. Then at four in the morning he had waked her by coming and sitting on her bed and talking about himself. He was old, he said, though he was only a little over fifty; one never knew what might happen; if he died, who was to look after the two girls? 'Their mother is no use at all,' he said, and he had looked appealingly at his eldest daughter. But there was no more of a mother's qualities in the woman now past thirty than there had been in the little girl he had used to wake up in that very bed in order to provide himself with his most admiring audience.

She had so often cried with helpless vexation before him; now his appeal had placed her in the position of power, but she did not like it. In one moment her anger, her hatred even, and with it the fascination he had always had for her, all crumbled away and left her cheated, disappointed in some way. It did not occur to her that he wanted her to take his head in her arms and try to comfort him. A brilliant and angry light had gone out of her life; she thought that everybody really was stupid, commonplace and pitiful, that there was nobody in the world capable of acting consistently on the grand scale.

But she had promised him she would do what she could, and would now insist on her stepsister carrying out her very suitable engagement to the Grand Duke of Tuscany instead of philandering any longer with her hopes of the young Prince Charles of Savoy who had been so imprudently encouraged to stay at Blois this winter.

And her mourning for her father had been magnificent. All her vast retinue had been put into black, and later she had had her apartments hung with grey, as was usually only done by widows. She had said she would never marry until she could find someone who talked as well as her father. Now she thought her widow's grey had mourned both her father and the husband she would never have.

126

Above the distant mountains the sky was clear, and a single star had just begun to show in it. 'I follow my star,' she said to herself; it was a tired old formula; she had been glad to forget it, but now it stuck in her head again, and all at once she knew why.

The more ordinary and commonplace relations of humanity were not for her; but there were others, and she was born to discover them. She would found a community of friends who would live in the country, keep sheep, write poetry, visit each other every day for conversation and plays, sit under trees, and lead a life immune from care and anxiety, concerned only with the best things in life. There would be but one condition: none of them were to marry nor have lovers; the community would be entirely celibate. She could not imagine why no one had had so excellent an idea before. It must be that she was in advance of her age; and in symbol of it she stalked on with a swinging stride in front of her women, who found the rough road very hard going in their thin shoes.

A Basque peasant passed them, driving his ox-cart. The two great milk-white heads of his oxen were yoked together; their four eyes looked out sleepily from beneath their shaggy sheep-skin covering and red fringe. On their backs were strong linen cloths of red and blue stripes. The driver stared in surprise at the tall lady with the bright resolute face, who marched towards him like a soldier, in a white and crimson dress that was getting muddy round the skirts.

When she returned, she wrote a letter full of her project to her former governess, Madame de Motteville, who was one of the greatest friends of the Queen of England.

The letter was passed round and caused much general amusement.

CHAPTER EIGHTEEN

On a blazing hot day at the end of August when the city lay scorched and sweating and smelling in the sun, and the Seine was too bright to look at, King Louis rode in state into his capital after more than a year's absence. The whole population of Paris turned out to see him. Queen Henrietta and her daughter had been given a balcony at the Hôtel de Beauvais, close by the gates of Saint Antoine. The blare of trumpets, the

127

rattle of drums, the thud of horses' hoofs, the march of men, approached them like the throb of a million pulses made audible in the hot air. 'They are coming! They are coming!' the mutter swelled into a savagely exultant roar, there was the flash of scarlet and steel in the sunlight, the lines of pike-heads glittered as far as one could see, then came a white bride in a golden chariot, and on either side of her King Louis and his brother in golden armour on white horses whose harness glittered with jewels.

'Look, my child, look!' sobbed the Queen, who had become hysterical at the thought that this was how her son Charles had ridden back this summer into his capital. 'It is the return of the Golden Age.'

So they all thought – that hoarse, half-starved, wolfish crowd below who seemed to have gone mad with joy at sight of the god-like figures.

Thrones had been erected under a great arch in the middle of the street by the gates of Saint Antoine, on the very spot where, eight years ago, a battle had been fought to keep King Louis out of his capital. He had time to remember this during the hours that he sat with the rest of the royal family and received presents and addresses of welcome in the full glare of the August sun. No doubt Mademoiselle also remembered. She had got a shocking headache from standing so long under the appalling weight of her Court train. Bands played, speeches were made, people fainted, but only those of the plebeian sort among the crowd, and none of the show figures disgraced themselves.

The glare dazzled Minette. She became hardly conscious of the scene before her; she shut her eyes and saw gold rings revolving against the red darkness; they came spinning upwards, larger and larger; then came a gold cup, whirling round and round, and on its rim were two little golden boys with goats' horns and hoofs, who danced and beckoned to her.

'Are you feeling faint, my love?' whispered her mother, but did not wait for an answer, for life was too exciting for there to be time for anyone to feel faint.

'Philippe is certainly handsomer than Louis,' she continued, 'would you not be proud of him as a bridegroom? He never takes his eyes off this balcony, he is looking at you all the time.'

Her daughter opened her eyes; she saw, in a dazzle of gold and dust and shimmering heat, a figure seated triumphant upon a throne, a figure bright and still as an image in a church,

128

whose one sign of humanity was that his eyes were turned towards her.

It was at this moment that Minette grew up; for it was at this moment that she was recognized to be grown up and of importance. It is the unimportant who are kept back longest as children, discouraged from taking their place in the world, since there is no place for them to take. She had been one of these, but now that was changed.

Mazarin had advised King Louis to do all that he could in the future to cultivate the friendship of King Charles. In this, he admitted that he had bungled matters himself in not backing that dark horse. It was too late now to do anything with Charles direct. Refusing all belated offers of marriage, the happy bachelor had set sail for England, and now reigned with every appearance of security in the kingdom that Cromwell had made twice as powerful as it had been in the days of Charles' father.

But his youngest and best loved sister was still in France, and in her now lay the only hope of attaching his personal interests to that country. Moreover, she had just reached the interesting age of sixteen, had grown much taller and more elegant than when the Court had last seen her a year ago; and the Cardinal remembered to have observed in her a promise of singular charm. Before King Louis' brother, Philippe, had left Paris with the Court last year, he had told his mother that his cousin of England was the only woman he could ever think of marrying; and he had been fobbed off 'as usual' as he indignantly told himself. All the show and pomp of Louis' wedding made him long to be a bridegroom too. And now this dramatic change in his English cousin's circumstances had abundantly justified his choice.

Everyone felt that here was the opportunity to encourage a normal taste in him, and create a personal link with England. The Dowager Queen of France wrote the most flattering proposals of marriage on behalf of her son to the Dowager Queen of England; and the first thing she did on her return was to drive over herself to Colombes and conduct the English Queen and princess in person to Fontainebleau, to be introduced to the new young Queen of France.

Now it was that Minette had to step forward and take her place in the world, which had suddenly become more important than anyone's in France. The King's wedding at Saint Jean de Luz had taken place in June. For a year it had occupied the foreground of men's minds, but now it was in the past, a settled fact; there was little more to say about it except for those who had seen it to tell their friends at home how they had missed the most marvellous spectacle of the age.

Yet somehow it had fallen a little flat. It had all been most carefully prepared; the Spanish Court settled on one side of the river, the French Court on the other, and an island in the middle was entirely built over with a pavilion, designed by the artist Velasquez, where France and Spain could meet in perfect neutrality. Covered galleries were raised above the streets of Saint Jean de Luz between the church and King Louis' house and that of the Infanta, so that France might visit Spain, and God, without descending to the earth among the common people.

There was all this, and a handsome young king who was the fresh hope of a tired nation, and a young princess who at once adored him. And yet it was somehow disappointing; it all went so exactly according to plan, there was never a touch of that surprise which makes for drama. The new young Queen was adequate; she was not pretty, but she was not ugly; she did what was expected of her, behaved admirably, though rather stolidly. She was as hide-bound by Spanish etiquette as if she had been kept in swaddling bands all her life; she never said anything that came fresh and at first-hand from herself; when Mademoiselle in her brusque fashion asked her suddenly if she had ever been in love before, while at her father's Court, she replied after a moment's stare (the result merely of bovine surprise, for she was not offended), 'No, for there were no kings there.'

Over only one thing did she show spontaneity, and that was food. Her eyes would light up at the sight of her favourite dishes; she could not speak as she watched their course round the table, and they would fill with tears if the tit-bit she had hoped for herself were taken by anybody else. This simplicity however belonged to a sweet nature. Louis was pleased with her dog-like admiration of himself, and still more with the fact that she represented Spain. Her mother-in-law was very fond of her; not only was she docile and obviously virtuous, but she was Spanish like herself, daughter of her brother, King of Spain, brought up in the land and the ways for which she herself had always been homesick through all her life in France. There were now two queens of Spanish birth and up-bringing in France. Enclosed in the traditions of their etiquette, the Dowager Queen, Anne of Austria, and the new Queen, Marie Thérèse, seemed stiff, old-fashioned and dull.

The little Court of the Dowager Queen of England was far more popular. She was so merry and good-humoured, her daughter so pretty and gay, their manners were so charming and informal that visitors crowded there from morning to night; and Minette got a sore throat from talking so much. Never had she known her mother so companionable. She laughed over the new royal bride, declared how fortunate it was that Louis' boyish appetite seemed to be increasing rather than diminishing with the years, 'for they can always find something in common by counting up how many dozen oysters they can contrive to swallow between them.'

This gossipy confidential chat made Minette realize she was of full and marriageable age more than anything that had yet happened.

Her mother's tart observation was sharpened by the fact that if Charles' fortunes had changed a year earlier, as many people had expected they would after the death of Cromwell, Minette might well have married Louis himself. The changing values of the marriage market thus permitted a spice of disappointment even in the midst of her triumph that here at last was a proposal for her daughter, and from the brother and heir of France; one, moreover, that would allow her to keep her child at home with her, safely wedded to a Catholic prince.

'You have always been fond of your cousin, my child?' she said a trifle anxiously. 'I remember your playing together so happily with Philippe in the gardens at Saint Germain when you were almost a baby. He always took far more notice of you than Louis ever did.' And she assured her daughter that Monsieur's now ardent love for her was proof that he had outgrown his boyish vices. Minette was supposed to know what she was talking of, but her mother's words did not convey a great deal; if it were a question of whether she would have to be jealous of men or of women, she did not see that it would make much difference.

She had however very little time to consider or compare; she was rushed from one thing to another, amused, flattered, bothered as usual by Mademoiselle who was as restless these days as a jack-in-the-box. She was furious when the Princess Henriette was taken for a ceremonial drive through the city in the same coach as the King and his brother and wife and mother, in order to show that she was now to be considered

131

one of the family. And the old question of precedence caused trouble again at the banquet that Mazarin gave in honour of the English princess, when her attempts to waive her rights caused almost as much disapproval as did Mademoiselle's refusal to budge from the doorway. The Princess Henriette was showing herself the daughter of a new age in this modern carelessness over etiquette. Three diehard dukes however still cared enough about it to prefer banishment from Court rather than go in to dinner after some foreign princes.

Mademoiselle, in defence of the old standards, quarrelled with her cousin and both her aunts and Monsieur.

'Poor girl,' said Queen Henrietta complacently, 'she is losing her looks very fast now. It was a good thing Charles never married her. Louis' patience with her is extraordinary.'

Louis was patient, rather dangerously so to anyone who knew him; but no one did as yet, nor did he himself.

And Minette was now secure against Mademoiselle's tantrums; her only emotions were those of excitement and anticipation.

What did she anticipate? Well, first and foremost, there was the ball that Monsieur would give in her honour at the splendid country house the King had just given him at Saint Cloud. A new white dress was being made for her to wear at it, sewn all over with pearls and diamonds. She would peep in at the two tailors who were at work on it in a long, low room, their heads and shoulders hunched over the shimmering waves of silk. Monsieur came with her to see it, and said that his aunt's taste amounted to genius. When she told him she had designed it herself the admiration in his eyes deepened to an awed respect.

'But my mother has been trying my hair in the new way, frizzed out on either side of my face, and I am to wear it like that at the ball.'

'She is always so right. That will give it a becoming width. Your face is the prettiest in the world, but there is not enough of it.'

Gone was the thoughtful schoolgirl, the smooth hair combed back from the high forehead. Here was a young lady in the height of the new fashion, her face no longer a grave oval framed in long ringlets, but a laughing triangle between two frivolous clusters of little curls. For the first time in perfect confidence, in a bliss of gratitude so great that she longed to hug the good God for it, Minette stood before the mirror,

132

ready dressed for the ball, and realized that nobody could possibly guess she had a crooked shoulder; that, at any rate in this dress, she might indeed be called beautiful.

The Court had been gorged with shows and spectacles that summer, but not till now did it enjoy its keenest sensation, when their king's brother led the English princess by the hand down the long gallery at Saint Cloud. Here were all the elements of surprise and drama that had been lacking in the entry of King Louis' bride into their world; here was this 'poor child' who had been living on charity, whom even minor princelings had refused to marry, suddenly translated to the centre of diplomatic attention and courted ardently by the highest bachelor in the land.

This prince of nineteen, who had not long since been called 'the prettiest thing in France', appeared exquisite in dove colour, which he had chosen 'that a cloud might accompany the moon'. The wide skirts of his coat fluted out from him like wings; the jewelled bows on his shoes appeared to have just alighted there, a pair of fireflies in their flight; love-knots, ribbons, laces fluttered round him like an attendant cloud of minute Cupids. Indeed it appeared a condescension in him that he himself put his foot to the common ground, so lightly and joyously he trod, he might as easily have walked on air.

His eyes sparkled as he looked at his princess, who was also not made for earth. Her shining dress floated round her and seemed to bear her along, her face was radiant with pleasure at the change in her fortunes, expectant of an answering pleasure in all those who looked on her; and therefore they gave it, touched by such simplicity.

The pair passed on, hand in hand; murmurs of soft applause followed them; they compared her to his guardian angel leading him to virtue and happiness; they quoted with tender raillery a rough joke of the young King who, in the flush of his marriage with his substantial bride, had remarked that his brother was in the devil of a hurry to marry the little bones of the Holy Innocents.

His description struck people as appropriate to more than her thinness. There was an unearthly childishness in her fragility, in her fair skin that flushed so easily, in the clear gaze of her innocent and confiding eyes. There was in her the attraction of the immature and the impermanent; nobody expected her to last long.

Monsieur, whose nose was as keen as a setter's in such matters, could perceive that his brother's wedding had been quite put in the shade by the expectation of his own. Louis had had all the fun and dressing-up, now it would be his turn.

'Look at de Guiche goggling at you,' he whispered. 'He is furiously jealous of you for he adores me.'

'I had hoped he adored me and was jealous of you.'

'Oh well, it is odd how these things get mixed up. Not as odd though as my wanting to marry you. I have never felt like this about anyone before.'

Indeed he was trembling with excitement. He felt he was trying something new and daring; something so strange as to be quite immoral. The incredible had happened. Monsieur had fallen in love with a woman. 'But it is because you are not a woman,' he told her, 'because you are a sprite, as cool as a flower, and you never plague a fellow, you let one alone.'

He was in the wildest spirits. He longed to show off to her, to make her see how he, butterfly as he was, could outshine all the people present, could make them fear him worse than Louis their king, and only by the power of his wits, his satire, his deadly observation. He had taken the prevailing fashion of writing characters, but acted them impromptu instead, and with uncanny cleverness, enhanced tonight by the excitement of performing before the Princess Henriette. The subjects of his parody stood about the room in helpless fury, each convinced that he or she alone was causing the mocking peals and titters of the audience.

Surrounding him, a small crowd of pretty young men pranced and gushed and gesticulated, demanding their favourite portraits.

'Give us the nice young girl in the confessional.'

'No, give us the old lady flirting with her footman.'

'Give us the Rape of Lucrece. Enough of this cruelty to contemporaries – give us a classic study.'

He improvised a bed out of three chairs and a cushion, removed in pantomime every garment that it was possible for a modern young lady to wear, and even produced one of the new little brushes for cleaning the teeth, brandishing its ebony and silver handle like a conductor's baton in time to his grimaces and spittings and splutterings.

Minette was reminded of Charles showing her how their lively cousin Sophie had acted her gaunt governess, half-dressed, cleaning her teeth with a piece of rag on a raw cold

134

early morning, while she corrected the shivering Sophie's recitation of Pebrac's *Precepts*. That had happened before Minette was born; and now Sophie was married, and they had only just heard from the Court of Hanover that she had given birth to a little boy whom she had christened George. That was an odd uncouth name to choose, there had never been a George in the family, nor in any English royal family.

But Sophie had married right away from the family; she had not wanted to marry Charles, she had pretended to have a corn on her toe rather than walk with Charles, and now she and her Hanoverian little George would never have anything to do with England. An uneasy regret stirred at the back of her mind; she wished Sophie had married Charles; it would have been so pleasant to have a sister-in-law who could make them laugh as Monsieur was now making them – no, not quite as he did, for there was an apprehensive quality in this laughter.

Monsieur's Lucrece was a cruelly comic study of a simpering prude; Tarquin's entry, invisible, inaudible, was inferred only by her scandalized exclamations. Roars of applause greeted her coy remonstrances and rose to a thunderclap at her final faint utterance when, lying back upon the three chairs, she breathed, 'you have done a shameful thing' – pause, then in a whisper, half-asleep – 'Do it again.'

Minette, horribly embarrassed, suddenly discovered she was near to an open door-window; now, at the end of the 'portrait' when everyone bustled round Monsieur in laughter and praise and scolding which was really praise, she could slip out unobserved.

The garden stretched away in the moonlight as far as she could see. She went up a grass path between cypresses that rose like black fountains on either side of her. Their shadows lay across her path. She stepped in and out of them, and wished she could see her own governess again. But that she would never do now, for years ago her mother had come into the room and said, 'Henriette, my love, you have lost a very good friend,' and told her that Morton had died far away in England. And now Minette was at last to go to England, quite soon, this very autumn; and she would see Charles there as King in all his glory, and James, and Mary, and Harry, to whom she had cried, 'Don't go – oh, Harry, don't go away!' But she would not see Morton.

And this, known so long as a sad but gentle ending to something precious, which had after all ended for her a long time ago, swelled suddenly in her heart until it filled the whole of the present. The white stillness of the night, the black cypresses on either side of her, and now, as she walked on, the whisper of the fountain she was approaching, all said the same thing, 'Morton is dead. I shall never see her again.'

CHAPTER NINETEEN

It was horrible, unpardonable, not to be endured, of all her sons he had always given her the most trouble, she had never trusted that girl, never, and now she knew what to think of her meddlesome mischief-making old father, for she had never trusted Chancellor Hyde either, and James was a fool, he ought never to have been allowed to be alone for one moment, he would ruin them all over again just as they had begun to know a little happiness; whatever happened, whatever they might pretend had happened, she for one would never acknowledge that creature as her son's wife, she would go instantly to England and leave no stone unturned to prevent it if it hadn't yet happened and annul it if it had, and in either case if the woman entered Whitehall by one door she would leave it by another.

In some such way did Minette learn from her mother of James' problematical marriage to Anne Hyde, daughter of Chancellor Hyde the Earl of Clarendon, maid-in-waiting to Princess Mary of Orange, and the ugliest girl Charles said he had ever met. Whatever had possessed James? The rumour was that he had married her before his brother's restoration, about a year ago. Queen Henrietta's view was that no pre-restoration marriage could possibly count; nevertheless she wept and stormed and despaired. She would delay their visit to England no longer.

But several things happened to delay it, and there was nearly another family quarrel over her demands that the Princess Mary should come and stay with them in Paris and all travel over to England together; while Charles, who was in a hurry to see his sister, insisted that Mary should waste no more time but go to England direct from the Hague. 'For God's sake settle it between you then,' implored Mary, who had already suffered as a peacemaker between her brother and mother. Charles won, and Mary crossed without waiting to go round by Paris. The Queen was bitterly disappointed; and then suddenly real sorrow fell on them like a thunderclap, dispersing these peevish squalls and showers. Once again a messenger in black came to the Queen of England, carrying a letter with a black seal. The Queen's face was livid; Minette knew in that instant that she too had the same thought, that they would not after all be going to England, for she dreaded to put it more directly than that, even to herself, even with the letter being opened before her eyes, so soon to answer her. Nor could the Queen wait for that answer.

'My son is dead,' she whispered, not daring to ask it, but striving to propitiate fate by stating the final calamity as though it were inevitable.

Her son was dead, but not Charles; it was her youngest son, Harry Duke of Gloucester, who (it had been thought at first) had caught a chill while playing tennis at Hampton Court, had then been discovered to have the smallpox, and in two or three days had died.

'Let me never look upon your face again.' Minette could not forget the torn, angry voice of the boy, repeating their mother's last words to him; could not forget the cloud of dust that was their mother's coach growing smaller and smaller down the long road to Chaillot, while she clung to Harry in the window-seat of the Palais Royal and begged him not to go away. But he had gone, he had ridden out of the courtyard with the Marquis of Ormonde, and now they would never look upon his face again. She did not know if her mother remembered what she had last said to him – perhaps she could not, and keep sane.

The Queen exhausted herself in storms of weeping, in rage with the English doctors who had not bled Harry sufficiently to take down the fever in time, in repeating the paeans of praise that all England seemed to be exclaiming over the dead prince. He had become extraordinarily popular in the short time since he had been there, and since the news of James' unfortunate marriage had leaked out there had been many hopes that he might come to be Charles' successor.

But Harry was dead, James was married, his wife was about to give birth to an heir; and now, though even James was showing a wish to try and back out of it, and even his father-in-law, old Hyde, now Earl of Clarendon, demanded to have the marriage annulled and his daughter shut up in the Tower

137

for her treason in marrying his master's heir ('He has gone clean mad,' his friends declared, and it was Charles who had to console the old man), yet Charles had decided that it was too late to do anything about it, and that James would have to lie as best he could on the bed that he had made and with the woman he had put in it.

James was on board at Calais with several ships to escort them across the Channel; he had been put in charge of the Navy and was very proud of it, for the English Navy was the best in the world, he said. He seemed to regard it as a personal slight to his seamanship that the crossing, in a dead calm, took two days.

There was no state entry into London, the Queen could not bear that; so they crossed the river from Lambeth almost privately in the evening, and Minette saw grey shapes rising from the mist across the water, and lights like sparks, making no distance, and was told that she had come in for the first of the November fogs.

The visit to England had really begun, it danced by her, the most brilliant patch of happiness she had known, and it ended as it had begun in a thunderclap of sorrow.

She often tried afterwards to tell what had made England so like fairyland even in the months of November and December. It was true the climate was abominable; her mother was always complaining of the damp which penetrated to her bones – heavens, how they had shivered in the dark-panelled rooms at Hampton Court where, in spite of the great fires, the wooden boards seemed to have been laid straight on top of the wet lawns outside. The Queen, who was very rheumatic, had then found some consolation in her long exile to her own country.

It was the people who made England so pleasant; their gaiety, simplicity and informality. Charles was made to be their king as none other could be, Minette declared; he was so easy and natural with all those round him, there was no ceremony, and she had never been with people who laughed so much. From the very first morning it had been like that. She had been too tired to dress properly and attend her mother's reception, so she had just put on a coloured print wrapper and a mob-cap and run along to her sister Mary's apartments, where she had sat playing card games with her and James and all three talking all the time, when in came Charles with the French ambassador's secretary, taking his arm in the most friendly manner, to pay her a surprise visit, and there they had all sat as though the secretary were one of the family, making the silliest jokes in the world.

And the secretary, also delighted with this informality, wrote home that Monsieur had never seen his hoped-for bride so lovely, not in her most gorgeous robes, not even in that white dress that had surprised the Court into an almost awe-struck admiration, as when he had seen her in her cotton wrapper of a thousand colours.

The French ambassador was the Comte de Soissons, hus-band to Olympe Mancini, who had come over to arrange the terms of the marriage treaty with the English King. Monsieur urged him again and again to conclude it; he was thrown into a fever of agitation by the reports of Minette's instant popularity. The crowd was enchanted with her simplicity and eagerness, her childish pleasure in all she saw, her adoration of the King her brother; they called her 'our own princess', remembered with indignation how as a baby she had had to fly from their land, and vowed never to let her go again. People wrote poems to her, and not merely the Court poets; a gentleman at Court, Mr John Evelyn, presented his wife who had written a delicious character-study in her praise; and many men fell seriously in love with her. They heard in France how the Duke of Buckingham had completely lost his head over her; to add to all these immediate rivals, several foreign princes, attracted by what they now heard of the English princess's charms, began hastily to make proposals for her hand. The French Court chuckled and whispered that these very suitors had been considered by Mademoiselle as possible 'establishments' for herself; the height of their pleasure was reached when they heard that the Emperor Leopold, who had been the pinnacle of her ambition, had sent two separate envoys urging King Charles to break off his negotiations with the French prince and give him his sister in marriage.

Monsieur grew pale and thin with anxiety; he could not eat nor sleep. It was strange to see the toy prince racked with so genuine an emotion. Jealousy was a potent factor in his composition. He thought of the English princess as the most beautiful and desirable thing in the world, destined for him from childhood by his own choice when others had ignored her, and now, just as she was coming into his possession, she was in danger of being snatched from him by the greedy hands of late-comers. When talking of other matters, his eyes would suddenly fill with tears of self-pity and longing. Even Louis, who generally treated him with an elderly brother's hearty brutality, was concerned for him; so was Mazarin for France. They began to press the suit on England and heard to their consternation that it was being strongly opposed by King Charles' cousin Prince Rupert.

Rupert of the Rhine, as he was always called in England, had, as the result of a quarrel with his eldest brother, sworn never again to set foot in his home at the Palatinate. He followed Charles to England at the Restoration, as was only natural, for he had come as a boy to the Court of his uncle, Charles I, and remained with his brother Maurice to fight for him all through the Civil Wars. Though only eight years older than Charles, he seemed of the former generation, indeed of an age yet more remote. He was of gigantic stature, with a face of sensitive (in his youth almost feminine) beauty; his manners were of an arrogant simplicity; and his career was the despair of his mother, Elizabeth of Bohemia, who had declared no child of hers should roam the world as a knight-errant, and saw them all do it, but none so much as Rupert.

All this belonged to an heroic past, but the restless experimental curiosity of his mind to a scientific future – of which the world was only just beginning to feel the promise. Loyal, fierce, abrupt, melancholy – an artist, a scientist, an engineer, a buccaneer who conned his ships better that his mates, a dashing cavalry leader, a crack tennis player (one of the four champions of England), he was too full of contradictions to be understood.

'The man is a strange creature,' said old Hyde, who had again and again been baffled and offended by the Prince, but summed his final judgement in no harsher phrase. And 'Rupert the Devil' he had been nicknamed by his family; 'that diabolical Cavalier', the 'Wizard Prince', 'that ravenous vulture' by the Puritans, who had had a superstitious terror of this their most dangerous enemy; 'the Prince of another world', he had been contemptuously dismissed in Paris. So he seemed, here in London, where he lived his life rather apart from the Court, occupied chiefly with experiments in his laboratory.

There was something odd in all that family, perhaps it was merely that, in a life unsuited to it, they were artists. He told

Minette that Louise was very happy at Mauberge and had kept up her painting; she had done many pictures for her convent church and for others. She always attended midnight mass for the pleasure, she flippantly said, that was afforded her by the heavy black of the shadows on the stonework, the tapering candle flames, the black and white forms of the nuns – such a scene as never failed to give her fresh taste for painting.

Minette, like all the English Court and royal family, stood in considerable awe of 'Mon cousin'; she longed to ask a thousand questions of Louise, but could venture no further than – 'You knew Montrose?'

Characteristically, Rupert would only tell her how he had met Montrose in a Yorkshire inn after the battle of Marston Moor, and that he had been very nice about Rupert's white dog, Boy, who had just been killed in action.

'I left him tied up with the baggage,' he said, 'but he must have got loose, for he followed me into battle, and was found dead on the field.'

Neither Rupert's spirits nor his reputation had ever quite recovered from that first smashing defeat at Marston Moor; till then he had been thought invincible, so much so that the white dog was held to be his familiar spirit, fed on human flesh, who whispered instructions from the devil; the Roundheads rejoiced as much at the death of 'that accursed cur' as at the defeat of his master. Since then Rupert's talisman had been no lively, barking, tail-wagging familiar, but the letter Charles I had written, charging him to fight that battle, whatever the conditions and the chances, even certainties of failure. To the end of his life he carried the letter on his person, a secret vindication of his character, which he could never bring himself to use.

As disinterestedly as he had fought for his uncle, he now took up the cause of his little cousin, urged that the character of the French prince was no fit one for her husband, and advised instead the alliance with the Emperor Leopold. But his opinion was held to be unpractical, that of a dreamer, a disappointed man. Charles as well as Louis felt that the alliance between France and England was too advantageous to be lost, and the other suitors were rejected.

Charles talked with Minette in the rain-sodden groves of the Home Park at Hampton Court; they strolled back through the warm red brick courtyards of the Palace in the winter's twilight, seeing the little windows dotted irregularly above them, bright with candlelight – a delightful homely farmhouse of a palace, where their father had collected so many beautiful pictures.

He remarked that certainly of all unhappy marriages those that were made for love were the worst, since that was too rarefied and indeed too rare a foundation for such a superstructure. And he took trouble to explain the superior purpose of her marriage. She was to unite France and England and make her brother strong against the world. She was proud of it, and would not have given it up to be any Queen or Empress living.

But Charles would not comply with Monsieur's clamour to have his future bride returned to him as soon as possible. The family must all be together for Christmas – who knew when they would be all together again? Great preparations were made for mummers and carol singers and all the joys of an old-fashioned Christmas such as had been forgotten in England through the grey years of the Protectorate. In that cruel winter long ago, the shivering child that Minette could just remember had lain in bed under a single blanket on the very day that her father King Charles had been beheaded in London; and on that day a soldier of the Parliament had been sent down to Glastonbury to cut down the sacred thorn tree that had blossomed there every year on Christmas Eve ever since, it was said, Saint Joseph of Arimathea had planted it there from a piece of the true cross. Now, miraculously, the sacred tree had begun to shoot up again and gave every sign of being ready to flower by Christmas.

Queen Henrietta sent for a branch to be brought to them at Whitehall in time for Christmas Eve. She was in a wild flutter of excitement, sometimes weeping and calling herself 'la reine malheureuse' as she looked on the scenes of old and happy days; sometimes in joyful inspiration prophesying England's return to the glad days of the old faith when it had never been thought a sin for people to be gay or for miracles to happen. She would have agreed with Selden, if she had read him, that it never was a merry world since the fairies left dancing and the parson left conjuring; as it was, in a burst of indignation over the fallen maypoles, she recalled those exquisite spring mornings, sharp with dew, when she had risen before the sun was up and gone a-maying with her husband in the woods round Westminster.

'And I too!' cried Mary, 'I can remember going too that last year before I left, and how you jumped off your horse to pick a branch of may and stick it in your hat.'

'I never liked that hat,' said the Queen, appeased and reflective.

Mary had kept them up talking till it was nearly morning – 'it is too late to go to bed,' she said in imitation of her Aunt Elizabeth of Bohemia who was always quoting Shakespeare, 'to show how English she has remained, I suppose,' said Queen Henrietta with a pounce at her embroidery, for her hands were never idle. But Mary steered them safely past her Aunt Elizabeth, on to a holiday voyage she and Charles had taken long ago down the Rhine in a barge, incognito, and their secret so well kept 'that not above half the country knew of it.' Her long ear-rings tinkled as she tossed and turned her head, for she was very vivacious although she looked so languid; her lazy eyes would scarcely open and then you saw they were laughing at you. She had lately had her portrait painted in Turkish dress which suited her very well.

She had once paid a visit to her mother in Paris when Minette was still a child and most of the time at Chaillot; 'do you still carry about your letters unfinished in your pocket for days until they get all crumpled and dirty before you send them off?' Minette asked, for that was what had most struck her in her elder sister. Mary scolded her for her impudence, chased her round the room and tickled her, but it was still true; Minette searched her pocket and found a letter to her little son William who was now ten years old and already took his responsibilities as Prince of Orange very seriously.

'How shocked he will be at this rag!' cried his mother, holding up the tattered paper. She was worried about him, he was so cold and formal, so unlike all of them; but then he had had so much ill-health, no doubt he would grow out of all these drawbacks together. James showed a particular interest in his nephew, for he had acted as godfather at his christening, in spite of Mary's protests that the clumsy boy would certainly drop her baby. He had been christened William instead of Charles as Mary had wished, because her mother-in-law, odious woman, had considered the name unlucky.

'She could not say that now,' said Mary, looking with

affection at her eldest brother. She went to bed too happy to sleep, she said; when she woke in the morning she felt heavy and dull; by evening they knew she had the smallpox.

Minette was sent to Saint James' Palace to be out of the infection. James, who had not seen Mary that day and was therefore comparatively safe, came and sat with her, looking out of the window on to the garden where long ago he had played at hide-and-seek with his brother and sister.

'That was where I hid the evening I escaped,' he said, 'there under that thorn bush. It was all in blossom then. I shall never smell that thick scent of blackthorn without feeling those shivers down my spine as I crouched there, turning the key of the garden gate in my pocket to make sure I had it, and hearing Elizabeth and Harry go calling through the garden and then away into the house, saying they had given me up – and then, so close to my bush I could have touched him, one of the guards, his legs black against the dusk, laughing at them for not being able to find me again.'

She noticed the melancholy lines in his long face. Here he was safely back in the same place again, at home now, and not in prison. Surely that mattered most.

But his marriage had continued to give trouble; his mother still refused to acknowledge his wife and persistently tried to lead Charles aside in order to discuss 'this unfortunate situation'.

'There is no situation,' he had answered, and it became a family saying.

Only this sudden danger to Mary had reconciled the Queen to her son's wife. People only stopped worrying about something when there was something still worse to worry about. Did they *want* then to be unhappy?

Minette stared into the darkening garden, her eyes smarting with tears. There, by the bare thorn bush that spread its black twigs against the wintry sky, she almost fancied she could discern the forms of the two children who long ago on that spring evening had looked for their lost brother. Both now were dead; and at this very moment Mary might be dying. 'Oh why must things change?' she cried, 'now that we are all here and happy, why can we not all stay here for ever?'

Charles wrote scraps of notes to Minette from Mary's bedside; doctors and counsellors implored him to consider his safety and his kingdom, but nothing would induce him to leave her; Mary had stood by him when he was in need, and now he would stand by her. The doctors were determined not to repeat their mistake with the Duke of Gloucester, so they bled her repeatedly, and she died, not of fever but of exhaustion, on the Christmas Eve when they were to have held such high festival.

She was twenty-nine; she had been left a widow at nineteen, she had been passionately in love with her husband, and devoted to her brothers. At thirteen she had left England to be a bride in a foreign country, and her sad father had ridden his horse along the shore for several miles to take his last sight of her. Now at last she had had her chief wish and come back to her home and family; nor did she live to see her son destroy her brother.

CHAPTER TWENTY

If Monsieur had shown anxiety before, he was now in agony lest death should prove a more formidable rival than even the Emperor Leopold. The formalities of the marriage treaty had been concluded; there was nothing to keep the princess in England, where the smallpox was rife; and in shrill terror for her safety he wrote beseeching, commanding, entreating her immediate return.

Now that the time had come for her to go, she clung to Charles and begged him to put off the marriage, to keep her with him. Mary's death so soon after Harry's, and in the height of their happiness, had given her a shock. She was frightened of leaving those she loved, of living with anyone so fantastic as Philippe. She had thought she knew him so well and could get on with him so easily, and now, quite suddenly, she did not feel she knew him at all. It was useless for her mother to tell her how her influence would make a man of him – 'I would rather have one ready made,' she told Charles, who laughed too heartily to give much comfort. Nor did it reassure her to hear how desperately Monsieur was in love with her. It was just this that made her nervous. How should she treat a love that was looked on as amazing, unaccountable, almost unnatural?

She asked Charles, who shrugged his shoulders and said he did not know much about being in love. She knew him well enough by now to be neither shocked nor surprised by his answer. She was no longer jealous of his mistresses, there were too many of them. She had begun to understand as well as to believe that his affection for her was not a thing that could be shared with them. But not all the growing wisdom and knowledge of the world of sixteen and a half years could keep her from clambering on to his knee, together with a couple of spaniels already in possession there, from burying her face in his coat to hide her tears, for he was so bored with women crying on him (they always did it he said until he had to give a new title or pension to stop it) and saying, 'But what am I to do?'

'Keep friends with Louis,' was the extent of Charles' matrimonial advice.

But he was charming to her; he gave her presents, he promised to write often, he hated to let her go, and he let her see it.

The Duke of Buckingham headed her escort to the ship; at the last moment he discovered some pretext for coming on board. He behaved preposterously, and the princess could only regard his antics with the chilled eyes of sea-sickness; she had never felt so unromantic in her life as when her adorer described his emotions towards her, and then picked a jealous quarrel with the captain whom he thought too attentive to her. They had a wretched crossing, as always when Queen Henrietta was on the sea ('it is tempting Providence and defying Jonah to send you with Mam,' Charles had said, and was well justified). The ship was driven back on the rocks and the royal passengers had to be taken off in a small boat at Portsmouth.

The princess was so ill she had to be carried on shore. She was almost relieved to discover spots on her chest. If she too died of the smallpox it would settle everything, and at least she would not have to cross the Channel again. In blissful indifference she heard faintly of the storm of anxiety and protest Monsieur had raised on the news of her illness; of the duel that the Duke of Buckingham had fought with the captain as soon as they got on shore; she was not even much disturbed when the Duke burst into her room in order to prove his devotion to her even in infection, and swore that he would follow her to France even as his father had followed Queen Anne of Austria. This reference to her aunt struck Minette as utterly absurd, she laughed feebly and feverishly, the Duke seemed to her as unreal as a gigantic dragon-fly whirring

146

round her; the doctor came to drive him out, 'but he must have a net to catch him,' she said, 'he must be sure to get a net,' and then she suddenly became quite clear-headed and determined through her fever, and told the doctor – Charles' own doctor whom he had sent all the way from London to attend her – that she would not be bled, for if she were she would die as her sister Mary had died, 'and it is not yet time,' she said. Her mother came and wept tears of relief, for she had not got the smallpox after all, it was only a bad attack of measles, and now she would be sure to recover.

She did recover; the voyage began again, with no worse trial this time than Buckingham's tempestuous attentions. Minette was just beginning to feel strong enough to appreciate them by the time they reached Havre, but by that time the Queen was afraid of the scandal they might cause and hurried to send him on in front with messages to the French Court of their arrival. The royal family came to meet them, attended by a body of guards, and escorted them in pomp to the Palais Royal.

It was true, Monsieur had grown quite pale, or perhaps it was that he rouged less, and so much thinner that he seemed considerably taller. What was still more surprising, he had grown almost silent, listened to every word of the Princess Henriette's whether to himself or others, and never took his eyes off her face. For a few minutes they were alone, and then, still in silence, he flung his arms round her and kissed her almost clumsily. There was in him at this moment a help-less, blundering quality, that of a boy in love for the first time, so unexpected that it touched her oddly.

'I thought you would never come back,' he said, and she put her hands on his shoulders and kissed him, vowing to herself that she would never let him know she had not wanted to come back.

'You did not like my Lucrece,' he said, and she could not think at first what he was talking of. 'Oh yes,' he told her, 'I saw you go out into the garden to avoid speaking to me. I see everything, everything that is to do with you. Will you not see a little too? See how women have sickened me, always teasing one to pay attention to their charms or their virtues? If I could tell you how women have pestered me! And to one who absolutely demanded that I should make love to her, I replied languidly – "If you will first permit me to put on my gloves." Yet they go on. Only you are different. I feel I can

147

say anything to you. Beside you, all other women seem like false fat slugs.'

Minette, moved by his evident sincerity, saw all that he asked and rather more, saw how clever and witty he was (and who would have suspected such depths of satire beneath that lightly mocking exterior?), saw something bitter and pathetic in his experience as the pampered plaything of a Court that had been encouraged to spoil him in every way; saw that all her fears now seemed very foolish. With Monsieur so fond of her, it would surely only be her own fault if their marriage were not happy. 'Her own fault' seemed to her, as to most of us, the least of all possible dangers.

Nor could she perceive in Philippe's strange new timidity a fear of her and his relations with her, that made the previous months of suspense and longing seem like an exciting dream whose awakening he could sometimes even regret. His emotions then had nothing to feed on but imagination; now, he was faced with reality, and for the first time in his life he was real enough to be terrified of it.

Events seemed to have conspired together to prolong his agony – Lent, the mourning of the English royal family, the long illness of the Cardinal Mazarin, who was surely dying but, good God, how slowly! He did it in the grand manner as authentically as if he had been born a great prince. All the right gestures were made. He quoted Horace; he left his vast fortune to King Louis who left it back to Mazarin's family; a comet appeared in the sky, 'It does me too much honour,' said the great man, ironically smiling on his death-bed.

Only Queen Anne disturbed these amenities by fussing over him with uncontrollable demonstrations of grief and affection. Her English niece could not understand how the great Buckingham, father to her susceptible Duke, could ever have fallen passionately in love with her; and yet it was true, for her mother had told her so too, had seen it happen at her own wedding with her own bright observant eyes when she had been a precocious minx of fifteen. The present Duke had become so troublesome that Queen Henrietta had asked Charles to recall him. Monsieur could not bear him for his height, his handsome looks, his arrogant way of looking at him and his adoring way of looking at the Princess Henriette.

Yet Monsieur had never felt dissatisfied with his own appearance before; he knew it to be of perfect beauty on a small scale and had always delighted in its porcelain finish.

Now he was uneasy and lacked confidence; but his friends did not lack it. Marriage would soon cure him, they told each other, and awaited his return to them with complacence.

Monsieur's state of nerves could stand no further delay and he was married to the English princess very quietly, on account of her mourning, on the last day of March. That night he sat on the side of the great bed in their room at the Palais Royal and talked as though his comparative silence of the last weeks were a dam that had suddenly burst and loosed a torrent. What was it all about? She lay stunned by it at first, for she had been strung up to anticipation and had to adjust her mind to this unexpected mental onslaught.

Mazarin had died at the beginning of the month; it was he that Philippe talked of as though he had been thinking all this time of him alone. 'He may have been my father,' he said, 'who knows?' If so, he had shown small affection for his son; he had been careful only to keep him in the background, to have him brought up by women and encouraged to behave like a little girl.

'They laughed at Louis when he was afraid of horses – nobody laughed at me. I loathe hunting, he loves it, but he did not at first. He loathed it too when his horse ran away with him. But a King of France must be brave, and his brother must not get in his way. When we quarrelled as boys it was always I who got beaten, and when we do it now I get mocked. I could be as good a soldier as Louis any day and better – he does not always show sense – but when I showed it at Dunkirk they were very careful to take away any chance of power from me, they told me to go and walk on the sands with the ladies and eat sweets, and so I did, and splashed them with sea-water too, that was fun, ha, ha, the silly hens, squawking and spluttering.'

In the midst of his laughter he flung up his hands in a sudden wild gesture. 'Is it my fault' he cried, 'that I am like this, what they have made me, all of them, all, but especially my fool mother and that old man who lay dying, dying, dying, always very politely, and Louis very polite too, but thinking "Will he never die?" until at last he is dead, and next day they come to Louis and ask who now is the chief minister, to whom are they to refer in future, and he says, "To me." Just that. Two little brief words but they will sum up his whole reign for you will see, he means to be king in every particular, the greatest king France has ever known, and he

149

will be it, I know him. He is determined, he is relentless, he is superb. He see one thing only and marches straight to it. I am much cleverer than he, but I will never do anything. We used to be friends, we were always quarrelling but that was nothing, he always stood by me against anyone else. But now he thinks me childish, effeminate, all the things they have been careful to make me, so that he may march on and leave me behind. He is to be Louis the Great King, and I am to be his lapdog that he may have something to kick out of his way.'

It was as though a doll had cried out in torment. And through all his wounded vanity and self-love and the penetration that had suddenly stabbed through his own disguises, making him burn to disclose and enlarge himself, one thing showed clear to Minette, and that was that he might not after all be very much in love with her, but that he certainly loved one person in his life, and that was his brother.

She had sat up in the bed, hugging her knees, watching him in perplexed dismay. She did not know what to say to comfort him, she did not feel she was there, nor that he would hear her if she spoke.

'They should not have married me to you,' said Monsieur, 'they should not have married me at all.'

CHAPTER TWENTY-ONE

Some people considered that Monsieur's love for his wife lasted a fortnight; others held this to be an extravagant estimate. She had aroused a boy's love in him which attained its height when she was out of his reach; it could not grow to man's estate. For a time he alternated between envious admiration of her and self-contempt or at least self-pity, self-adulation, and at all times self-intoxication, so that he would stand in front of the mirror for hours, asking for sympathy that he was not taller, or for appreciation of his eyes, his nose, so much better than Louis' long Bourbon nose, or his teeth, so much better than Louis' teeth, 'which, do you notice, are already turning black?'

Had Minette married straight from the convent and her mother's country house, she might well have been broken on the revolving wheel of his vagaries. But her visit to Charles now stood her in good stead. He had counselled nothing, he had treated the subject of her husband as negligible, but the result of her companionship with his robust cynicism was now to make her feel that she would not be dashed because her husband had talked about himself all through their wedding-night, nor even because he was occasionally irritable and spiteful.

She observed sagely that whereas Charles' affection for women was apt to wane in their absence, Philippe's had thrived on it. It was a relief to her when he began once again to turn to his former companions, the pretty young men who knew so well how to respond to his moods with just the right amount of teasing to make their sympathy amusing, and the right sort of slang phrases to express their pleasure as they fluttered with affected cries round his collection of old paintings and beautiful or odd antiques. He already showed a curious and discerning taste. To his friends he bragged of his princess's perfections, and was anxious to show them too, as though she were a discovery suitable to find a place in his new cabinet of buhl and gilt.

Minette thought it unconventional, but no doubt symptomatic of the strange new freedom of married life, when he brought the Comte de Guiche into her room as she was being dressed, at the moment when one of her maids was putting on her stockings.

'Did you ever see such small feet?' Monsieur cried to him, 'and look at her toes, as straight and white as though she had never worn shoes. You know what the toes of most women are like, cramped, deformed, a bunch of radishes, ugh!' He was so eager that he did not notice Minette's laughter as he held her foot, turning it this way and that to display it until she was nearly upset off her chair.

Over his frizzed and beribboned head she met the eyes of de Guiche, and saw in them a new and burning gravity.

But the handsome de Guiche and even Monsieur her husband were only part of the surrounding crowd. With that acceptance of her luck that comes to adventurers whose lives go up and down, she flung herself with whole-hearted gaiety into her new and surprising position as virtual queen of the French Court.

The real new Queen, Marie Thérèse, ate too much and moved too little to be healthy; lethargic and inclined to melancholy, hopelessly bewildered by the quick play of wits around

151

her, she was always pleading indisposition to avoid fulfilling her queenly functions. These in consequence devolved upon 'Madame' as she was now known, the first great lady in the land, the wife of the King's brother. She had often to represent the Queen of France at State banquets, at the reception of foreign ambassadors or even princes.

In a few weeks, in a few days even, she became the fashion, as not even the showy Mazarinette girls had ever been. Her popularity represented a change of taste. People were getting tired of parvenus; in any royal assembly at least half the ladies present were the daughters of bankers or shopkeepers, and the young King did not object to dining with a wealthy man who had been a valet. All this had been amusingly modern long enough to begin to be stale. And then the King had tired of Olympe, and Marie had failed to marry him; almost they had begun to be looked on as back numbers of the Court *Gazette*.

But here was a new Queen of the Court who was a princess by birth as well as marriage, as informal and careless of etiquette as ever her rivals had been, but polite in a strange new fashion, for she could not bear to hurt the feelings of others. This she had learnt through her early training in adversity, that snubs and slights give a bitterness from which great misfortune is free. The change of front that all men and nations now showed towards her and her family did not make her despise them. Charles had shown her in what it was a reasonable attitude. She learned her lesson earlier than he and therefore more unconsciously and less cynically. 'What's the use of a new hat if you can't cock it?' she adapted his phrase as she tried on one of her many new hats at the mirror, big shady hats to give protection from the sun while riding, with coloured plumes that swept over the edge in a becoming curve. The small face beneath it looked like that of an elf peeking up from under a wide branch.

It was this childish quality in her that delighted the Court and astonished strangers; it also tore at her mother's heart and made her protest, sobbing, when a few days after the wedding Monsieur carried off his bride from her to his palace of Saint Cloud. Queen Henrietta was not at all well satisfied with whatever information on her son-in-law she could extract from her daughter; her grave face made Minette more uneasy than she would otherwise have troubled to be; she felt herself threatened by unknown responsibilities, perhaps even dangers,

152

and she too cried on leaving her mother and begged that she might stay.

But the gardens and river at Saint Cloud were enchanting; a new cascade, a rippling stairway of water, had been added, all for her, and indeed 'these gardens were all made for you from the beginning,' Monsieur told her, 'before you were born.'

The fortnight was not yet over.

By the time it was, Louis was telling her the same thing of Fontainebleau. He wrote to her in a pretty, complimentary style, begging her to persuade his brother to join the Court there immediately; he rode over to add his personal persuasion; he too walked with her beside the cascade, and told her his plans of one just like it at Versailles (but there was no hill there to cut the steps from) and of great lakes that he would have surrounding the palace (but there was no river there to supply the water). It did not matter; difficulties only made it the more amusing; he would have the most magnificent palace and grounds in the world there before he had done.

He had taken his new Queen and the Court to see the place last autumn just before Minette had left for England, and she had been delighted with the poor dead King's 'card castle' as Louis had called his father's shooting-box, that delicate rose-red house that they had come on so unexpectedly in the heart of the woods. She thought it a pity to send whole armies of workmen to build a vast palace and gardens and waterworks all round it; she had a notion that she would never see Versailles quite as charming again. And indeed she never did.

But Louis was full of new energy. He must build, he must alter, he must reconstruct everything, and show how great a king he could be. He did not mind how hard he worked now that he was his own chief minister, and his own secretary too, for he insisted on going into every detail himself. He did not mind if Fouquet, his Minister of Finance, prophesied to others that such energy would not last six months. He had his own suspicions of Fouquet's financial honesty and was biding his time with him. He did not mind if the nobles laughed among themselves at his slaving like the meanest clerk. He had his own plans for dealing with the nobles. He would pay them back in time for harrying him about in his childhood, preventing him from any of the proper education of a king, while they used him as a mere pretext to exploit their own

153

power. It was as absolute on their estates as the power of any Eastern despot. Very well then; he would see to it that they did not stay on their estates. He would wield a force stronger than arms, the force of fashion, to make them struggle for the privilege of remaining harmlessly near him at Court. To do that he must make his Court the most brilliant and magnificent in Europe.

'I am very stupid,' he confided with genial modesty to his sister-in-law; he knew that his best chance in carrying out this stupendous task he had set himself was to be very thorough. So he must get up early and work all the morning; and then he could have the rest of the day free for hunting and water-parties and balls and ballets. He made notes of everything. He questioned Minette closely as to the literary leaders of the day in England, for it was important that he should know all about art and letters as well as everything else. He had been told that there was someone called Miltonius who, for all that he had been on the wrong side in the late wars, was likely to be thought a great poet. But Minette, even when she had extracted the Latin ending, led him right off the scent, for she had never heard of Mr Secretary Milton's verses, and declared he was only a prose writer of poisonous political tracts, which would certainly not outlast their day.

She was eager to give him all the information she could; she wished Charles were there to help them, and Louis wished it too, to please her. But he did not approve of Charles' methods, or apparent lack of method, in kingship. It was all very well for him perhaps to be so easy-going and natural with his people. They knew how lately he had been a beggar. They had put a brewer on the throne. 'But if my people ever did that, they would not put a king on it again.'

He, too, had suffered from his people – his brief contact with the very scum of them had been sharp and close. He told Minette how he had had to lie and pretend to be asleep while the mob shuffled through his bedroom. He knew now what the rabble were good for. They should work in their thousands and tens of thousands, as hard as the slaves of the Pharaohs, to build him huge palaces far removed from them.

He also knew of what the rabble were capable. That was what they themselves must never know. They must be kept disciplined, put to work in gangs, under soldiers, under an iron regime in all matters, even those of the least apparent importance, an order, a habit of obedience in thought as well as deed, so as to leave no room for doubt or hesitation.

And suddenly he broke out, 'Your father committed one shocking error. He should never have let himself be beheaded. He should have killed himself first. Now your family will never be secure again. The golden rule has been broken that decrees a king should stay on his throne and his head on his shoulders.'

No one had ever mentioned Minette's father to her except in a sighing voice as the Blessed Martyr. But Louis, walking up and down on the lawn at Fontainebleau with his eyes fixed on the grass and his under-lip thrust out, was talking to her so earnestly that he had forgotten her.

'Charles says,' she answered, 'that his travels and troubles have taught him how to stay on his throne.'

'Yes, because he has learnt to stay as much like a subject as possible. He lets ease and familiarity be the rule – the liberties you tell me people take with him are astounding – but it may be that in England, now, it is the only way. The English are good at compromise. They will put up with a king as long as he is not too much like a king. But if he has no heir and James comes to the throne, it will not be so easy.'

'Why, what is the matter with James?' she asked with some indignation.

'I don't quite know,' said Louis, intent on his own problem. 'Here at any rate it is another matter. Once let the King lose his hold over the imaginations of his people, once let them see him as a mere good-natured foolish kindly gentleman, and they will turn and tear him to pieces. I know. Your mob is one of hucksters but mine is of starving wolves.' And he added, lifting his head at last and staring at the new fountain that sent a jet of water nearly ninety feet into the sky, 'Here they may spit and squall, they may even murder – but they would never try a king and condemn him to a death on the scaffold.'

Louis' conversations with his new sister-in-law were not often so serious.

He scribbled notes to her in verse, and she tossed back answers to them, they were read aloud amid the laughing applause of the crowd; this game formed the nucleus of a play and they began to write it together. 'But aren't we rather stupid to be so clever?' asked Minette. 'Our new man Molière can write it so much better.'

'*My* new man, you mean,' cried Philippe, for Molière had taken service under his name and protection and had won an instant success at Court with his daringly witty comedies. Nothing quite so 'modern' had ever been seen before; they made Louis feel that he had indeed introduced the dawn of a new age. In imitation of Louise's quaint caricatures, Minette drew a very bad imaginary portrait of Louis as Apollo, driving his chariot up the clouds of sunrise, with Molière, Lulli and La Fontaine harnessed as his steeds.

'There is not much chance for my glory,' he said, 'if you are to be my artist!'

He was very gay, he was charming at first, not only to this merry new sister, but to his brother, whom he chaffed and thumped in a more friendly fashion than he had ever shown towards him. Philippe was in high feather; he strutted and preened himself, he felt he was nearly equal to Louis, indeed in some ways superior, since he had married a woman that Louis obviously admired so much more than he could his own wife. But this pride was rudely dashed when Louis began to discuss the symptoms of the young queen's latest indisposition and to speculate whether they were the result of too much fruit or of the coming advent of a dauphin. Philippe became moody and consulted a sorceress in great demand at Court, who had already sold him some cosmetics and told his fortune. These efforts to emulate his brother's vigour did not have much immediate result. He still had a partly nervous dislike of sharing a bed, and it was fortunate for Minette who was a light sleeper.

The nights in the convent when she had read long romances of Launcelot and Amadis of Gaul, with a stolen candle clutched in her hand, had had a bad effect in accustoming her to do without sleep. It became more and more difficult to lose herself in unconsciousness now that her life grew more and more exciting, with King Louis her constant and easy companion, King Louis whom she had thought of till now as a contemptuous boy, a polite host, a terribly superior young man.

And a crowd of new people danced across her closed eyelids in a many-coloured frieze; surprising, amusing, all different, alike only in one thing, that they all liked her. She was grateful to everybody; wherever she went she seemed to be holding out her hands, receiving presents and thereby encouraging more. 'Whatever she talks about with you,' said one, 'on how-

156

ever slight a matter, she seems to be asking you for your heart – and what is more, you have to give it.'

King Louis teasingly repeated this, to her indignation. 'But it is true,' he said, 'even Mazarin felt it, for he told me that he once talked to you just as any foolish old gentleman might do with a sympathetic young girl. Poor old Mazarin,' he added, with the beginning of a chuckle which grew grave on him as he said thoughtfully, 'I do not know what I should have done if he had not died then.'

'Oh, you would have escaped from your Mazarinage, never fear,' she answered, with that wicked little laugh that was so new in her. It made him regard her a trifle anxiously, aware that he too had fallen victim to her dangerous gift of intimacy. He said things to her which he would afterwards have regretted had he said them to anyone else. But she did not remind him of his confidences in the exasperating way of many women. He felt that what he said to her dropped deep into her heart as into a pool of clear water, and would lie there undisturbed until he had need of it. The fancy surprised him, as did all his present thoughts about his sister-in-law. He had thought he knew her so well, too well for interest, and suddenly she was quite new to him. He spent hours in her company discovering this. 'You are so different from other women,' he told her, 'I can say anything to you.'

There are apt to be formulas in love-making; the masculine Louis had fallen on the same one as his effeminate brother, for in both cases it was the sense of ease and companionship that attracted them. But Louis did not yet know that he was love-making, nor did Minette.

Others knew, de Guiche for one, so that he avoided her company, fearing his own emotions. Even the young Queen noticed them, told Louis plaintively that she was afraid she was not as clever as his brother's wife, and wept when he did not deny it.

The spring opened early into high summer; by the beginning of May, Minette was bathing in the river with those ladies who were adventurous enough to join her. With laughter at their difficulties they helped to dress each other on the grassy bank and rode back through the trees, where they would be met by King Louis and his brother and other gentlemen, who would escort them back to supper or else bring supper with them, for the young King delighted in picnics and the freedom they gave from etiquette. They would ride home under the

157

stars, later and later as the weather grew warmer and Louis the more aware that he was indeed an absolute monarch, with no one who could gainsay his will – certainly not a whining wife or a disapproving mother. He was in the flush of his new and self-assumed power, his escape from his 'Mazarinage', and his determination to accept no other tutelage. Certainly he would not submit to being told at what hour he – or his brother's wife – must come home to bed.

For one glorious summer before his life settled down, hardened, became in time unalterably fixed in the mould that he himself prepared for it, for this one brief summer he was king indeed, as only the very young can imagine royalty. He had the power to create enchanted groves of trees hung with sweetmeats, rocks of caramel and marzipan, rivulets of champagne and brandy; to command fireworks and gigantic figures of flame to march across the night sky; to dress up as all the greatest gods and heroes in turn, and dance and act to the deafening applause of multitudes; to picnic on the river or in the forests and stay out in them as late as he liked, till the dawn if he chose.

And this summer was Minette's reign. When they hunted, it was naturally the King and Madame who led the chase; when they danced, it was the King and Madame who opened the ball; when they acted, the King and Madame divided the leading parts. On her seventeenth birthday in the middle of June, an open-air ball was given in her honour under the illuminated trees; a whole anthology of Court poems sang the praise of this midsummer princess; and the King gave her first one present and then another and then another, for each time he thought of something still more appropriate to her; a pair of embroidered riding gloves of Spanish leather, a necklace of bright stones, a volume of La Fontaine's new fables bound in white velvet with the royal fleur-de-lis of France stamped in gold on the cover and surmounted by the wild rose of England, conqueror of all hearts in France. For if Louis were the sun, the English princess was his sister the moon, reflecting his glory.

On a lawn at the edge of the lake at Fontainebleau, preceded by nymphs in classic draperies who strewed flowers and sang praises before her, she appeared as the goddess Diana. The Seasons offered her homage in fantastic dance and procession; from her eminence she could see their forms reflected in the torch-lit water; among their upturned faces in that wild

158

flare she distinguished those of Monsieur, of the Comte de Guiche, of her pretty English friend, Miss Stuart, of a new black-eyed beauty among the young Queen's ladies, and a new blue-eyed one among her own, of Marie de Mancini who was soon to marry the High Constable whom she detested, and to leave the Court.

Now came Louis as the bright Spring, leading a train of Lovers; Joy and Abundance attended him, and before his face the weird forms of Winter, War and Discontent fled away. He knelt at her feet, he crowned her Queen of Beauty, and placed the round orb of the world between her hands.

It really could not have looked more marked, thought their respective mothers and mothers-in-law and his wife and her sister-in-law among the audience. The three legal queens put their heads together in conclave against the reign of this usurper, though her own mother did not protest too much. Queen Henrietta's delight and pride in her daughter's success made her live her own happy and popular youth over again; she declared that Henriette's behaviour was nothing but the natural result of thoughtless high spirits – she had said all along what a mistake it was to remove her so young from her mother's care. Queen Anne protested to her that Henriette was taking Louis away not only from his wife, but his mother.

'That is inevitable,' answered the Frenchwoman drily, 'we cannot keep our sons in leading-strings all their lives; that we cannot is perhaps our tragedy rather than theirs.'

Her reason was always sound when she did not apply it to herself. She could listen dispassionately to Queen Anne's shrill maternal jealousy, to her complaint that Louis had walked alone in the gardens all last evening with Henriette; she tried delicately to recall how her sister-in-law had once walked in a certain garden at Amiens alone with the late Duke of Buckingham. A cry had been heard, and the people who came on them had discovered the fair young queen from Spain in great confusion, the English duke enraged. There had been a scandal; there was some story of diamond studs that she had given him; Buckingham had had to go back to England, but it was said that he had sworn to return to France and spend the rest of his life in her service. Death prevented that; he was assassinated by a madman, and Queen Anne was left lonely in France until Richelieu recommended to her notice his young Italian secretary, Mazarin, by pointing out that there was a look in him of the late Duke of Buckingham.

But there was no chance now of shaking the virtuous indignation of this stout widow by any reminder of the past. She had quite simply forgotten it, and would have stared aghast had she been reminded how she had clung to her husband's little sister that last night before Henrietta left her to be made Queen of England; how she had begged in shy whispers 'for news of you in England – and – and of all whom you may see in England.'

That tender fluttering hypocrite had been a soft and easy prey to her emotions, very different from her high-spirited Henriette, decided the fond mother. Nevertheless, she wrote a word of warning from Colombes to her old friend Madame de Motteville, begging her to keep an eye on her daughter, 'my other little self,' and to stand her friend – 'I am sure you will know what I mean.'

So Madame de Motteville gave Minette good advice, while Queen Anne scolded her and Queen Marie Thérèse sulked; and to all Minette was perfectly polite, affectionate and gay, with the happy ease of manner that went with her sense of freedom from them all; and continued to do exactly as she liked. Queen Anne was bitterly disappointed in the docile little niece she had so carefully trained to be her daughter-in-law; she had thought her other niece Mademoiselle had proved impossible for such a position, but Mademoiselle would not have had one-tenth of the power that this child was taking to herself.

'If you had been my daughter-in-law you would have behaved much better towards me, and my son would have had a sensible wife.' So she unburdened herself to Mademoiselle for over two hours, sitting by her niece's bedside when she had a fever, which rapidly increased under this bitter and belated triumph.

'Madame is everything now and I am nowhere,' said Monsieur to his mother, for he too had begun to complain; he had even sought out his mother to do so, a rare act in him, as he had always resented her preference of Louis. His attitude as a jealous husband was unusual; his complaint was not that his brother had taken away his wife, but that his wife had taken away his brother; that Louis paid no attention to him now at all, 'and after all he never saw Henriette was pretty and clever until I had chosen her; he says openly to all the courtiers what a fool he was, blind and deaf, but he never thinks of saying that *I* wasn't. He forgets me altogether, he treats me just as coolly as though I were not her husband, as though I were not there at all.'

And he turned from her to stare defiantly at himself in the mirror; pulled out his ruffles, adjusted a love-knot, tweaked his cravat, did all he could to assure himself of his personality. His mother's placid face crumpled up like an angry handkerchief.

'Is that true?' she asked. 'Does he tell the Court he was a fool not to have appreciated her earlier?'

'Yes indeed, Mamma, and then they all say she is the true Queen – well, she cannot be the Queen without my being the King. But for me she would have married the Emperor Leopold and gone right away, and I only wish she had, for people are talking to her or about her all the time, and de Guiche follows her about like a dog.'

Suddenly he swung round on his high red heel, so sharply that it looked as though that slender pedestal must surely snap beneath him. 'And you know, Mamma,' he said on a lower and more unhappy note that his aggrieved whine had yet sounded, 'Louis was nice to me at first, grateful to me for discovering her when he had not the wit to do it – but now he is rude, offensive to me. I think he hates me, I catch him looking at me as though he wished me out of the way. What have I ever done to him that he should wish that?'

He sounded on the verge of tears; at any hint of sympathy he would have wept outright. But Queen Anne had none of her rather flabby softness of heart to spare for her younger son.

'At least, thank God,' she breathed piously, 'the Queen is almost certainly with child. There can be no question of repudiating her now, even if Louis can be so wicked as to wish it.'

'And what about *me*?' shrieked Philippe, 'is it not even a question as to whether it is possible to repudiate me?'

He flung away, feeling that his manhood had been outraged.

CHAPTER TWENTY-TWO

Louis and Henriette were at last made aware of their feelings by first seeing them in the distorted mirror of others' jealousies and suspicions. They agreed that these were absurd, unnecessary, and above all old-fashioned, that people had not yet grown accustomed to this new reign of fearless youth. But they also agreed that perhaps as people were still so stupid they had better be more cautious, and they rode in the forest of Fontainebleau till three in the morning to discuss how cautious they must be. At least, that was how it began.

'I must speak to you,' said Louis, low and imperiously, as they glided down the river on a painted barge under an awning of green silk worked in silver. The music of a new gavotte played on the violins trembled over the water; the sunlit ripples thrust outwards on either side by the barge seemed to dance to its rhythm, and their reflections on the awning cast upwards from the light on the water danced in partnership with them – 'ta, ta ta *tum*, ta ta *tum* te *tum*,' hummed Minette, beating time with her fingers, 'do you see, sir, there is a river of music above us and beneath?'

'I can never get your attention. Let us ride ahead of the others when we go home through the forest.'

'Why, we are always doing that. Mademoiselle de Mortemart said that all the Court must have developed a new arm muscle by now from holding in their horses so as not to catch us up. And I said—'

'What insolence!'

'No, I said "What discretion!' And there should be a new book of Loyal Anatomy showing the Maid of Honour's Knee from curtseying to us, and the Courtier's Neck from staring at us, and the Knife-Grinder's Tongue from talking about us.'

'It is not always wise to be witty. Who is she?'

'You should know, for she is one of your Queen's ladies, and very handsome – black eyes and always laughing.'

'I remember now. I dislike the type.'

'Then I need not do so.'

'Be serious. I am out of humour. They have been plaguing me again.'

She had no need to ask who 'they' were, nor why. 'You must not talk to me so much, sir,' she said, happily certain that she would not be obeyed, and then, seeing he was to be teased no longer, 'But why should we trouble? It is only old people who do not understand how fast the world is changing. Even my mother who is an angel, generally, says that young people in her day did not have a tithe of the freedom that we have now, and that we should have scandalized everybody if we had lived then.'

162

'We seem to have scandalized them now,' said Louis, 'and there is no sense in doing that when there is no reason for it.'

'Then how would it do if you were to pretend to be violently in love with someone so that no one could suspect you of being too much interested in me? The Mortemart now – she is just the person.'

'That is an amusing idea, more like the stage than real life.'

'And so is our life,' she answered on a sigh of pleasure, and indeed (as she remembered long afterwards) the whole of that scene upon the river – the dance music, the shining forms of the courtiers, the banks of dark forest, the foxgloves in its depths that caught the setting rays of the sun and gleamed out like upright spears of purple flame, all struck her as strange as well as beautiful, like a scene in a play.

'The Mortemart is no use,' said Louis' voice, 'since she is one of the Queen's ladies. If I am to have an excuse for coming to see you so often, it must be one of yours.'

'Miss Stuart is the prettiest.'

'She is a minx, she might make mischief.'

'Oh, if you want a nonentity you cannot do better than Mademoiselle de la Vallière. She is pretty enough to be plausible – she looked quite well as one of the nymphs in Diana's train.'

'Did she? I could see no one then but Diana,' replied Louis courteously, and added in his more thoughtful and intimate voice, 'yes, she would do.'

Minette at once thought that she would not, but could not at once think why. Louise de la Vallière sat at some little distance from them, gazing at the water. Her colouring was very fair though she was not otherwise very pretty; her expression was sweet and pensive.

'Her father is not noble,' said Louis, 'it must be owing to her mother's family that she is at Court. But that need not prevent my choice. Even the best earth requires a little manure occasionally.'

'She is very simple,' said Minette, 'it would be cruel to hurt her.'

'I am not going to hurt her. I will only pretend that I am in love with her.'

'Then she will fall in love with you and find out it is pretence and be broken-hearted and die, cursing us both.'

'Dear sister, what a drama! It is only a game, and one that we may never even have to play.'

163

They could talk no more then. The barge drew into the shore where footmen awaited them with the supper-baskets and their horses. The servants kept themselves in the background that the picnic might be the more pastoral; even the musicians were concealed among the bushes. Princes of the blood handed the refreshments and burned incense to keep off the midges. There was a great deal of joking over this casual service, there was even a little mild horseplay.

In the centre of a ring of ladies, seated on the grass, their skirts spread round them like vast flower petals, King Louis stood and dangled a sugar-plum in his hand, demanding who would catch it. They called out for it, laughing, protesting they were starving, holding up their hands with a flutter of white fingers and flash of rings. Suddenly he tossed it to Mademoiselle de la Vallière, who had not joined in the playful contest. She looked up, startled; her eyes were like a wild doe's, thought Minette, and again she wished she had not mentioned her to Louis, but then she thought what difference could it make? None, between herself and Louis, for there was nothing between them, they were only friends, great friends.

She threw a stone into the river, and it made a circle, ever larger and larger; the rim of it gleamed like a curved thread of fire in the sunset; it would never stop growing, it would go on widening outwards until it reached the opposite shore. Engrossed in this, she forgot Mademoiselle de la Vallière, and only ceased to watch it when she felt that someone was watching her. She raised her eyes to meet Louis', and was surprised, disconcerted even, as though it were someone different that looked at her out of his eyes, someone new, and yet never had she felt so intimate with him. There with that crowd of chattering courtiers between them, he was by her side in a solitude as deep as that of the forest where they were so soon to ride.

'So soon,' 'so soon,' she thought, while the horses were led forward and she drew on her gloves of green leather with the silver-fringed gauntlets, his birthday gift to her. A groom held her white horse, the King hastened forward to help her to the saddle. For one instant the whole scene before her, the green glade among the trees, the gay figures of men and women and horses, dark against the rich light of the sunset, all seemed charged with a breathless importance, so that she longed that it might last for ever; that for ever she should stand here and

164

King Louis hurry to her side while she thought, 'So soon am I to ride with him alone in the forest.'

The instant passed; she was in the saddle, they were together under the great trees, they were riding home in the cool of the evening. A last ray of sunlight slanted through the leaves on to the jewel in her hat; elsewhere it lingered only as a green reflected light; the paths through this branched cloister glowed dull red from dead beech leaves, a reminder of earth, as was the sharp fresh smell of it turned up under their horses' hoofs. Otherwise they seemed to be riding under the sea, so cool and dim and green it was in the sudden hush after all the talk and laughter at supper. Louis had pulled in his horse to look at that transitory gleam that had slipped sideways from her hat on to her face.

'I never knew before,' he said, 'that there were red lights in your hair,' and then in sudden impatience, 'How many other things have you concealed from me? Is it to tantalize, to reproach, that every day you show me more what I have missed?'

The gleam faded, the strange familiar face was now in shadow. He jerked his reins, whipped up his horse, and both rode on in silence. But his voice that had sounded so oddly, a voice troubled, perplexed, even angry, still rang in the ears of both, so that neither dared speak again. Yesterday he could have said cheerfully in public what a fool he was not to have seen earlier that the Princess Henriette was the most charming of women; now, suddenly, this had come true, not only to his mind, but to his heart. The silence of the forest seemed to throb and echo with his regret. 'I have been a fool, a *fool*,' said the thud of his horse's hoofs in his ears. And he jammed his hat more firmly on his head, and set his horse at the gallop, calling to his cousin to keep up with him in the curt, gruff tones that he had used in speaking to her when he was an ungracious boy.

'He is angry because his mother has scolded him – his wife has wept – his brother has whined,' so Minette said to herself and tried to take it seriously, to remember there must be no scandal between the King and the wife of the King's brother. But above all this her heart was singing high and shrill, 'He is angry because he loves me, and it is too late.'

Even 'too late' was only a word among other words invented by the mind. Louis loved her above all other women, that was all that mattered, and as they raced together through

165

the darkening forest, 'can this indeed be happening to me?' asked a shy child who still lived deep inside her, a child that had had to pretend she had hurt her foot because King Louis would not dance with her, because King Louis did not like little girls.

The night was magical. There was no real darkness. The light turned from green to silver, the leaves turned black, their small shapes still clear-cut above them against the luminous air. The hot dark red of the paths had turned black too; the earth had burnt itself out, there was no glow left in its cinders; 'dust and ashes, dust and ashes,' said the thud of his horse's hoofs in King Louis' heart. A moonbeam slid through the branches, it struck white fire from the silver embroidery on the saddle that King Charles had given 'his dearest Minette'.

In a clearing of the forest where two riders met, a pool of light encircled that strange pair for one instant as they rode through it from darkness into darkness, flying as if to escape, but from whom if not themselves?

For Louis' thoughts were pursuing furies, hitting him here and there, so that he turned his head this way and that as he rode, reminding him that he could have married his cousin a hundred times over; that his mother, who was now using all her power to separate them, had thrust her again and again on his unwilling notice; and that it was himself who had thrown away what he now valued more than all his kingdom. He had won through to that kingdom through all the wars and rebellions; he had mastered his nobles; he had wedded with Spain; death had rid him of Mazarin, and he owned no other check on his power; he had even defied his mother. Yet all this had turned to dust and ashes in his mouth, since he had learnt too late to love his cousin.

His horse shied violently, and he had some difficulty in quieting him. They had come suddenly on a wide open space where giant rocks stood as if waiting for them, their black distorted shadows thrown across the moonlight, their stillness unnatural at the first sight so that the riders as well as the horses were startled into a fearful apprehension. They had seen the rocks once before by daylight, but now in this pale glare they were like primaeval beasts turned to stone; some of the largest had indeed the appearance of huge idols.

Louis persuaded Minette to dismount with him and examine the monsters. They hung the reins on the spike of a withered tree, and then walked among the rocks; but Minette did not

166

like to do so, she felt they were being watched by things unnatural and unfriendly; 'they are too still,' she said, and knew
that it sounded ridiculous, but Louis was too full of his
thoughts of her to notice what she said.

'I am the King,' he said, 'I can do what I like. Who is there
to tell me that what I like is wrong? I have already shown the
Pope I can put him in his place.'

'There is God,' said Minette perfunctorily, stepping hastily
out of a wet patch of bog.

But Louis had not yet begun to think much of God.

'The Queen is unhealthy,' he said, 'if she should miscarry –
she might easily die in childbirth – well then, if so, what
should prevent my marrying you? Nothing, except my brother,
and he is nothing. Your marriage could be annulled. If it has
not been consummated then there is no law whatsoever against
it, and I do not believe it has been consummated, I *will* not
believe it—' He stopped suddenly and took both her hands,
looking with a hard defiant expression into her face. It seemed
to float before him, grey-white in the shadow of her hat, a
moth's wing of a face, and now, as it upturned towards him,
the moonlight touched it and hollowed out her eyes so that
they looked dark and mournful.

'Minette,' he said softly, as if trying the sound of it, and
indeed it was the first time he had ever spoken or even noticed
the pet name that once all her family had called her, and that
now only Charles still used, who had first invented it. It was
a moth's wing of a name; it fluttered on his lips and left them
gently, very different from large full-blown names like Olympe
or Marie Thérèse. He had never thought of names before, of
thin moonlit fancies such as now beset him, reminding him
of what had once been said (and he had hardly listened at the
time), that Minette had been born of a sigh and a tear, of a
single night together torn from the strife and separation of
the civil wars, of the adieu that King Charles had then bade
his beloved wife. A sudden fear rushed on him; he flung his
arms round her thin shoulders, pressed his mouth down on to
hers, and mumbled through his kisses, 'You shall not leave
me. It shall never be adieu between you and me.'

He felt her arms round him; her hands touched his neck.
'You love me?' he demanded.

'I have always loved you.' It was so gently said, it was no
more than if a moth's wing had brushed his cheek – and
then she laughed. The unexpected sound gave him a little

167

shock, cooling his spirits. He had felt so much a man, afraid only for her fragility, for that tender appealing loveliness that made everyone who was charmed by her feel afraid for her.

But her laughter made him at once fear for himself; it transformed her from a wraith to a mocking sprite, and him to the self-conscious boy that he had once been. What could she be laughing at in such a moment? Was it possible she could be laughing at him?

She was almost as quick to perceive his angry suspicion as he to feel it, yet did not stop her laughter lest he should know she perceived it. 'Always,' she repeated. 'Ever since you would not dance with me.'

And across the anxious frown that had carved a black upright furrow between his brows in the moonlight, there danced two fingers, light as elves. He caught at them and put them in his mouth, bit them a little to punish her for startling him; then the sense of what she had said dawned on him, and he wrenched her hands so sharply that she cried out – for he had forgotten that he had refused to dance with her. The recollection, which evidently delighted her, brought him back with a curse to all his angry determinations, made him shout them among those listening shadows. Other people might have to abide by their mistakes, but not he. What should one brief year count in a reign as long and glorious as he intended his to be? A year ago he was free and could have wed his cousin. Then he would free himself again, and her too. He would contrive it somehow. Had he not shown this summer that he was absolute monarch?

And the Sun god too, thought Minette, the Lord of Time. Yet could even Louis roll back the seasons to a year ago and make it as if that year had never been? 'There is God,' she had said, and her foot had squelched irreverently in the mud, she had thought more of it than of her words; and yet it was true, there was God, there was time, one thing following after another, unseen until it came, but then inevitable. Even Louis could not alter what had been.

She wished he would stop talking. She did not want to look back and regret, to look forward and plan; it made all their happiness unhappy, and just when they had discovered it.

'When did you know you loved me?' she asked. It was of far more importance than annulments, divorces, dispensations. And then suddenly her attention swung to what he was saying, and she saw Philippe sitting on the side of their bed on their

168

marriage night, talking, talking, talking, a doll that had come alive and discovered in itself a soul in agony, a soul that could feel love – not for her but for an all-powerful elder brother whom he resented and worshipped, feared and adored, to whom he looked always and confidently for support and protection. The only true emotion in that little wizened heart of Philippe's was for his brother; was she to poison and make evil his one pure possession?

'You cannot,' she said suddenly. 'You cannot make Philippe annul the marriage and then take me yourself as your wife. The humiliation would torture him – and it would come from you. I think that would kill him.'

'Does that matter?' asked Louis between his teeth.

'You know that it does.'

At that moment Phillippe was nothing to him but the weak obstruction to his wishes; the ties of affection and pity were unbearable restraints, unworthy of a great mind. But reason as well as instinct told him it was impracticable, that the odium he would incur would weigh down his whole reign – 'and you would hate me,' she said, 'for making people hate you.'

How well she told his thoughts. 'You are a witch,' he said, and took her in his arms again, caught fire again as he kissed her, sat down upon a ledge of rock and pulled her on to his knees. At least, he urged, their secret love need hurt no one. 'Secret' struck as a mockery to both; they thought of the hundreds of watching eyes that had seen them ride off into the forest, that had seen them so ride off a score of times before – but there had not then been the secret. Now, when they returned, riding into that glare of torchlight, all who looked on them would know all that had happened. And what happened would not be merely a love affair between the King and a great lady, it would be incest, for the ties of marriage were thought to make relationship as near as the ties of blood.

It was this that made Louis hesitate, even while he demanded and implored that Minette should give herself to him, now, in this moon-enchanted forest. Their love, he said, was above all laws; but Minette was not thinking of laws; she was thinking in exultation, 'this is I, the Princess Henriette, and no other, chosen out of all the girls that ever were or ever will be, to be living now at this moment, to be in King Louis' arms and to hear him say he loves me.'

She turned her face so that she might look up into his, and said, 'It has all come true. Long ago I used to pretend that you and Philippe were two little golden boys, dancing fauns, who beckoned me to come and play with you in a golden land where grapes dropped into our mouths, and now it has come true.' She could have bitten her tongue on 'you and Philippe,' she hurried on, hoping that he would not notice. But 'you and Philippe' remained buzzing in her head and, she knew, in his. 'It is you who love him, not I,' she cried. 'If you must betray him, it is for you to say.' And sinking her head upon his breast she began to weep passionately, for she knew that she had said the very thing to make him renounce her. She would refuse him nothing, she had told him so, she had kissed his hands as in fealty and said that she would rather die than disobey him. Now she knew that despair had urged her to this abandon, for that it would not be required of her, and if it were, Louis would hate her always.

Long after the Court of France knew her no more, a very able man observed that above all the people of her time the Princess Henriette knew how to distinguish between people. It was this knowledge born of sympathy that now made her distinguish Louis' permanent desires from his ephemeral, even while she sobbed like a child with her head inside his coat. Her hat had fallen on the ground beside them, its jewelled clasp winking upwards. Louis clutched her to him, he felt the tears smarting in his own eyes, he felt that fate had been against him from the beginning, that he was of all men the most miserable.

For it was true, he could not after all take his brother's wife, either in defiance or deceit.

CHAPTER TWENTY-THREE

It is unfair to put Armand, Comte de Guiche, in the category of Monsieur's friends; he was very different from those shrill, witty, perpetually young men. Rather, he represented the schoolgirl's ideal of the romantic hero; 'supernatural' was Madame de Sévigné's word for his lofty abstracted air, his long silences, his quite preposterous good looks. From the first everything about him had been a little too good to be true. He was of one of the best and most interesting families in France. Everyone loved his father, the splendid old Maréchal de Gramont; everyone adored his uncle, the Cheva-

170

lier de Gramont, the most daringly fascinating of rakes; everyone respected his aunt, Madame de Saint Chaumont, the most reliable and sensible of women; everyone admired his sister, the Princess of Monaco, who had soon left her husband's lonely rock in the Mediterranean and was of the gayest and most popular at the French Court.

It was all too easy for young Armand. He was the same age as the King, and far more strikingly handsome; he was a bit of a poet, a bit of a musician, and he had shown a quixotic courage in the Spanish wars; by the time he was twenty-two it was difficult for him to know what he wanted to do next. He was spoilt, but gentle; women fell hopelessly in love with him, but he remained aloof. Marriage had disillusioned him, but in a way to make him mildly misogynist rather than a rake. The enormous prestige of his uncle in that career was no doubt discouraging.

While still a boy, shrinking with a boy's fastidious nervousness from his too early marriage, he had been flattered by Monsieur's adoration and became in his turn attracted by the mixture of the butterfly and the wasp in this extraordinarily pretty little prince. It was impossible to de Guiche to enjoy any relationship without idealizing it; he spun daydreams of a kingdom in Languedoc where Philippe would be prince and he chief adviser; their Court would revive the poetry of the old troubadours in a land where their speech was not yet forgotten. Philippe was enchanted. De Guiche was Louis, grown doubly beautiful, unfailingly kind and charmingly fanciful. Whomsoever he married he had sworn he would always love Armand best.

But he married his cousin Henriette, and it was Armand who was unfaithful, for he turned in sudden revulsion from Monsieur to Madame. Everyone knew it would happen. In the English princess there was just that touch of the unusual, of unlikeness to other women, that was certain to appeal to him. The Duke of Buckingham had offered to bet a pair of gloves with Minette that the first person who fell in love with her after her marriage would be the Comte de Guiche. The circumstances of this wager, on a heaving sea under an iron-grey ice-cold sky, had not encouraged her interest in it; and the immediate violence of the events that followed, sickness, storm, shipwreck, and then a fortnight's fever, had obliterated any memory of it.

It had only entered her head again when in one of their

rehearsals for a scene together, in the Ballet of the Seasons, de Guiche asked her suddenly if nothing had ever touched her heart. She had said something or nothing in answer – she was laughing and in a hurry for them to go on with their parts. But he was staring at her, his dark eyes looked wild, and she noticed how strangely the pupils were dilated.

'I feel myself in great danger,' he had said in a low tone, and left the room.

Even then she did not believe in his passion for her. She did not want to believe it, for one thing; her life was crowded enough. In the strong light of Louis' attention she saw herself as never before; every gesture and glance of hers had a new significance since Louis was watching it. There was no need for de Guiche to hold a candle to her mirror. She wished he would not show his admiration in these abrupt and inconvenient ways. King Louis had come into the room and asked what she had done to de Guiche that he should come rushing down the passage and scarcely stay to salute him as he passed. He had been exceedingly ill-humoured all that evening.

Louis' renunciation of her had at first given her an added glamour. She was now indeed his sister the moon, Diana ever chaste and ever fair, with whom he could be on terms of tender and sparkling intimacy as long as he did not allow himself to cry for the moon. Louis prided himself on his control; besides, there were plenty of other people with whom he need not be controlled. Here Olympe de Soissons once again proved useful; all the more in his perverse, half-angry mood, because she had lost her charm for him. She proved that Minette was the only woman in the world for him, and he could wring exquisite sorrow from them both by telling her so.

He felt himself so much the more in love with her since that night in the forest that he began at once to show caution; and in a boyishly exaggerated, foolish way that made her nervous, for it surely could not deceive a soul when he swung round suddenly from talking to her to stare at Mademoiselle de la Vallière and address some forced, perfunctory remark to her. He admitted that he found it exceedingly difficult to think of anything to say to her, she was so stupid; and Minette's fears for her began to be realized, for here at least was one soul simple enough to take his stares at their face value. The girl blushed and fluttered, she could not take her eyes off him except when he looked at her, when they were at once fastened on the ground. Minette warned him, 'It is not fair, the poor

172

child thinks you are in love with her, and everyone else is laughing at her.'

There was a strong vein of hardness in him, he could not consider the feelings of the 'poor child'. He only said, 'But I hope they are thinking it too. They ought to. I bored myself admiring her little dog for ten whole minutes last night.'

'Yes, and they saw the boredom as clearly as they heard the talk – "What long ears he has!" – "What a silky coat!" – "What is his name?" – "What a pretty name!" '

'You don't think I act well enough?' inquired Louis politely.

It was as though a cold finger had just touched her heart. Like a general at the first sight of the enemy, she at once summoned her forces; she smiled at him and said in a low tone, 'Dear Louis, I could not wish you to act any better.'

A hot look flamed up in his eyes; he put his hand on her shoulder heavily, weighing her down. She had the power to awaken his passion for her again as strongly as ever, and rejoiced at it. But of what use to encourage what must be frustrated? This was the way to lose what at all costs she must keep, his essential trust and friendship – the whole purpose of her marriage. So she tried desperately to steer a middle course, to entertain him, assure him of her deep and constant affection, but not to tease his passions.

It was all the more difficult because, as she now discovered with pleasure and amusement, she was instinctively a flirt. The desire to please was so strong in her that she would exercise it on people for whom she did not care a straw – and yet for the moment that she talked to them she really did care; she imagined what they felt, and held herself responsible that the feelings should be pleasant; she could not bear to hurt, snub or ignore; her natural instinct was to like people and wish them to like her. Everyone who spoke with her felt that he or she had some special reason, unshared by the multitude, to like the princess.

And de Guiche felt it most of all. Other people told her that he had lost his heart and was losing his head, but she replied flippantly that he was too supernatural to be really in love – he would insist on going off for forty years or so, like Guy Earl of Warwick, to fight dragons and Saracens for his lady rather than settle down comfortably with her. She said it too to Louis to allay his jealousy, but it did not come out so naturally the second time, and she felt resentment with de Guiche for causing these unnecessary difficulties.

He himself knew the danger of running counter to the King. He kept out of Madame's way as much as possible – and then, just as she had been saying to Madame de la Fayette, 'What did I tell you? De Guiche was never really attracted by me; he was only working up a little scene of his own to see if he could act as well in tragedy as in pastoral comedy!' – just as she had said this, and the game of Court life had settled down into a regular procession of the King and herself across the board, followed in due course by all the other pieces – then de Guiche began making his odd irregular knights' moves across to her again; surprising her with unnecessary little notes, charmingly worded, but all about nothing. His conceit annoyed her – how could he expect so much interest from her when he must know all her attention was centred on King Louis? (An admission that did not even strike her ingenuous thoughts.) He must after all have been deceived by the blind of the King's pretended interest in Mademoiselle de la Vallière and so thought it safe to pay attentions to herself. But as she thought this, standing in her room at the Tuileries, where she was trying on a new dress of primrose-coloured silk, her head jerked back and she drew in her breath so deeply that the fitter measured her waist an inch narrower than it really was, thereby entailing endless later alterations. For this was what had come into her head so suddenly and clearly that it was as though she had seen it written on the wall above the mirror. 'Is it I who am deceived?'

At once she reminded herself of Louis' evident boredom with Mademoiselle de la Vallière, of the annoyance that he had expressed with her clumsiness whenever he paid her attention. Yet now that she came to think of it he had been very patient in overcoming that annoyance, for certainly the girl had not overcome her bashfulness. Minette had indeed wondered if there were not an element of cruelty, as in a boy who tortures a bird, in the interest with which he had observed the helpless flutterings of this white dove. But perhaps it was not cruelty that inspired the interest, or not more cruelty than, as she had already learnt, might well exist in love.

From then on she could not help watching, wondering, whenever Louis even looked at la Vallière; and yet she knew that it was the last thing that she must do, since the courtiers would all be watching herself. For the first time the new fierce publicity of her life began to grate on her. Always she had to be on guard, gay and good-humoured. And in discovering

174

this side she also found that she was very tired. The continual round of festivities grew more and more exhausting.

It had been a remarkably fine summer, but by early August the heat of the day had a dusty and weary quality, and the nights were often stifling, grey and overcast with cloud. She could not sleep. She would lie rehearsing long scenes with Louis in which she taxed him with deceit and double dealings; begged him to be straightforward with her; or even arrogantly assured him that he need not be so afraid of her. By the morning she would know how she had wasted her time. She would never say such things to Louis. She had not the right to say anything at all. They had agreed that they could not be lovers, and therefore what business had she with any other love that he might take to himself?

'Yes, but if only he would be frank with me—' 'After all, I am responsible for the poor girl—'

She knew that such sentiments were cheats; that her hot indignation of the night was her true feeling, when she had longed to slap Louis' face for his humbug and la Vallière's for her ill-breeding. For to Minette it seemed the height of ill-breeding that anyone should so expose herself as did this girl. Whatever Louis' feeling might be, a cold amusement in his artifice, a passing mild interest in the flirtation, or the beginning of a genuine love-affair (Minette would count up all the different possibilities on her fingers each night), there could be no doubt now as to those of Mademoiselle de la Vallière. It was true that everybody was laughing at her; there were bets as to whether she would cry or swoon next time the King spoke to her. One evening the Court Fool, who had been performing acrobatic feats in the middle of an applauding circle, leaped up from a double somersault, pointed at her, and said in a comically dolorous whine, 'She's not clapping. She's in love, and not with me. There's bad taste for you. She prefers the King.'

There was suppressed laughter, the Fool was told to go on with his tricks; he pretended to be abashed, and stood on his head to save his face. King Louis looked at la Vallière with interest, 'to see if it is true,' thought Minette. Every drop of blood had ebbed from the girl's face, she trembled violently, and at last her eyelids, which had seemed almost closed, opened on the King, and she gave him the look of a wild animal at bay and stricken to death.

'Well, he knows now,' Minette said to herself, trying to find

175

satisfaction that that at any rate was settled. Louis, who so hated awkwardness, 'exhibitions', any loss of control or dignity in anyone, how could he ever tolerate a girl whose love was certain to make him ridiculous? The question was consoling; the answers, occurring suddenly in the middle of the night, were not. Just as she was beginning to doze, she would wake herself up to consider – 'Might there not be a charm in such complete surrender? She sees one thing only, and that is Louis. He must like that.'

And with an angry twist and a thump on the pillow that she had already turned three times (her head must be made of hot lead), she would tell it how unfair it all was – for she too could have seen only Louis if he had not been the adored brother of her horrid little husband; and she too had often wished to behave with the uncourtly abandon of a milkmaid, but had controlled herself for the sake of Louis, who now – good God, how ironical! – thought it so pretty to make a fool of oneself!

'Dear Madame, you look shockingly ill,' said La Grande Mademoiselle on her return to Paris after the successful achievement of her young stepsister's wedding to the Grand Duke of Tuscany. She had had a terrible time of it with Mademoiselle d'Orléans (she never called her by her father's nickname 'Mop'); the girl really seemed to have gone off her head. She had rushed at Prince Charles of Savoy, and told that bewildered youth that he had given her up for nothing but a little dirty money. When she was trying on her wedding-dress, she had torn it off and thrown herself on the ground and screamed. Mademoiselle had behaved with persistent kindness and firmness. She had offered to break off the match for her sister; but no, the girl would not have that either. The young Prince of Savoy had made no offer of marriage to her, so that Mademoiselle could not imagine how her sister permitted herself to think of him. At the last moment however d'Orléans had thrown herself with ardour into the preparation of her clothes, and gone off defiantly to her wedding.

'Poor Mop,' said Minette, remembering Charles' description of a lively curly-headed little wretch at Blois, who had romped and giggled with a shy courteous charming boy.

'Why "poor"?' asked Mademoiselle. 'It is not many girls whose stepsisters would take the trouble to secure them a splendid establishment, a trouble that no one has ever exerted on my behalf.'

176

She had once considered the Grand Duke of Tuscany an eligible *parti* for herself; and he had refused her cousin Henriette in her poverty, and been refused by her in her prosperity. Now this bone of contention between the cousins had been carried off by her young bitch of a sister, who had snapped at it without desiring it, for fear she might not get another. No wonder Mademoiselle thought marriage a disgusting affair; but she was no nearer to founding the imaginary kingdom that would get rid of all that. The chief difficulty was that she would have to leave the Court, its masques, its plays, above all, the amusing fairs in Paris.

She jerked herself from her chair as she said, 'My father always spoiled her disgracefully. On our last visit to him at Blois (you know, on our way south for the King's wedding – ah, but I forgot, you were not with the Court then, those were other days), he boasted to the King how well she talked and danced and sang, but she did not speak, not one word; and she danced very badly; and she refused to sing. And her face was all stung with gnats, so that she did not look at all pretty,' added Mademoiselle with a fine sweep of her arm, rounding off all the deficiencies of 'Mop' and thrusting her down beneath their feet, so that she was at last free to revert to her opening subject. 'But indeed I have never seen you look so ill. What is it? Are you with child? I must congratulate Monsieur—'

'No,' cried Minette, 'at least I do not think so. Perhaps. But it is too early yet to say.'

'I will ask you again in a month's time,' said Mademoiselle archly. 'But it does not do to get so thin. And your eyes look as though you had not slept for weeks.'

'These sultry nights – I detest the month of August, do you not too? And the Court has been so very gay—'

'I know, I know' – Mademoiselle had no wish to hear of any festivities in which she had not taken part. And she glanced critically about her to discover any new piece of furniture that she would not have chosen, or fresh paintings and decorations that were not to her taste. For the Palace of the Tuileries had been her home when she had reigned as Queen of Paris. On her father's death, his estates and titles had passed to Monsieur; and Mademoiselle's irritation at this found vent in descrying how her home had been spoilt. But today her concern for her cousin did not allow her to do more than point out that the blue walls had been more restful than this new pale green colour, and that Madame de Rambouillet

177

had always said that the sun should never be permitted to enter a salon.

In spite of Madame's protest she spoke to Monsieur, telling him he must have a better care of his wife. He was flattered by her assumption of the cause of Madame's indisposition; he almost thought it might be true. That sorceress La Voisin was an extraordinary woman, she knew a great deal more than palmistry. He was encouraged to visit her again. The young Queen would certainly have a child this autumn; she had been married to Louis for a year and two months now; it would be excellent if he could produce an heir in quicker time than his brother.

The doctor gave Madame opium to make her sleep and ordered her to stop riding and swimming and dancing and stay in bed all she could. It would be better to retire from the Court for some time.

Quite impossible; Monsieur could not be spared from the Court.

Then could not Madame go and stay with her mother at Colombes or even in the convent at Chaillot? A complete rest was essential.

The words sounded delicious. Her eyes wandered over the painted ceiling, where the reflected sunlight from the windows had sketched an odd little pattern. In her vast blue bed she seemed to be sinking into the sky. 'A complete rest', a sinking into oblivion, no need to think or plan or struggle, how perfect that would be! But would she have it at Colombes, with her mother asking her a thousand eager questions? Would she have it even at Chaillot, or anywhere, even at the ends of the earth, until she knew—

'I must know first,' she said to herself, and aloud, 'I must be here for the seventeenth. I cannot possibly get away till after then.'

'Why, Madame, what happens on the seventeenth?'

'Have you forgotten, doctor? Why, the seventeenth of August is the great fête that the Minister of Finance is giving at Vaux. There will be nothing like it in all the history of France.'

The doctor's large, soft face was that of a benevolent elephant, but now it bunched itself up in annoyance at this fine lady's prevarication, this tiresome clinging to yet another pleasure after so many hundreds.

'I dare say Fouquet will squander more money than anyone

178

else,' he said. 'As guardian of the nation's wealth he can afford to, ha, ha! But, Madame—'

'No, dear Doctor Yvelin, please no "buts". I cannot go till after then. Remember it would give offence, for the fête is to be in my honour. After that I promise you I will go.'

Immediately after the 17th Louis was to start on a tour of inspection into Brittany in company with his Minister of Finance. He would be away from the Court for some time, and so she too could bear to be away. And to herself she said, 'I shall know by then, surely I shall know by then.'

He grumbled at her that she would coax a reprieve from an executioner. He would have to yield, but on two conditions.

'Any conditions,' she crowed happily.

'You are not to dance, Madame.'

'Oh, Doctor!'

It was a wail from the heart. How was she to charm back Louis if she could not dance? La Vallière could not dance one quarter as well; she even walked with a slight limp. But her own dancing, and she knew it, was delicious. A bishop had said of it that she was nothing but wit, even to her feet. Could she melt the doctor's heart by repeating this, or was it too conceited? But before she could collect her plea, he had spoken again.

'And you are not to walk, Madame.'

'But Doctor, this is absurd. You mean me not to go at all. How am I to move about the grounds—?'

'If you do not walk a dozen miles or so in all and stand about for several hours in your thin slippers on the damp grass—'

'It has not rained for a month.'

'You can be carried in a litter, Madame; otherwise I wash my hands of you and send in my resignation.'

'In a litter! *I* in a litter! You mistake me for someone else. I was seventeen two months ago, not seventy!'

But he held to his point.

CHAPTER TWENTY-FOUR

To the Fête of Vaux then that La Fontaine made famous in his songs, the most gorgeous fête the Court had ever seen, and the last to be given by the ill-fated Minister of Finance, Madame, its protagonist, was carried in a litter.

179

Dr Yvelin's order had not been excessive; there were many who before the night was over wished they too could have obeyed it. A thousand acres of park and pleasure-ground had been given over to the fête, whole hamlets had been levelled to the ground, trees had been torn up, and streams turned from their course. Groves of great orange trees in square painted tubs had been moved out by engines. The cost of the supper alone, to feed six thousand people, was 120,000 livres. The steward, Vatel, controlled its vast organization; Minette had a glimpse of his pale, inspired face, as devout in his enormous task as that of any poet in the act of creation.

Her litter had been tastefully planned with cushions to carry on the design of her dress, and she made fun of it, comparing herself to a Chinese lady in her palanquin, or a gouty old English lord, or the Fat Woman at a fair who has to be moved about from one place to another. Perched between the two running footmen who bore the pole in their hands, she had the air of some lovely exotic bird, carried about in its cage; and few people had time to notice how ill she looked, so quick and gay were her smiles, her gestures, her snatches of talk.

The King hurried to her side with greetings and inquiries for her health. The latter were perfunctory, for he hated anything to do with illness, but his eyes opened on her equipage in a genuine impulse of admiration. But trouble was brewing in him, she could feel it at once; Louis was dangerous tonight.

'I must speak to you,' he said in a low tone. It was weeks since he had said that. She could have cried with joy. Even if he ceased to desire her with passion, he would still consult with her and they could always be friends. But it was not possible to speak then; they had to go into the house. Le Nôtre, who had designed the gardens, was introduced to the King; Louis praised his classic precision of taste, his contrast of green lawns with snowy marble, of dark cypresses with silver fountains. And then he complimented his host again and again on his magnificence.

Minette knew that he distrusted Fouquet. She thought the great minister had a nervously watchful eye this evening; all the time that he was showing the King fresh evidences of his wealth and taste he must be asking himself if he were making the right impression. She could have told him that he was not (clever men were so stupid), that Louis loved show, but that it must be his own show.

The royal compliments had a sinister sound in her ears. 'I shall not dare invite you to my house. I could never give such hospitality as yours.'

As he spoke Louis looked at the mantelpiece, a miracle of carving. His host then pointed out the ceiling, a miracle of painting. In the centre of both was Fouquet's emblem, a squirrel, punning on his name.

'What is the motto round it?' asked Louis in that exquisite silky voice that still made her afraid. 'Ah, I see, "Quo non ascendam? Where shall I not ascend?" Very apt.'

He turned to Le Nôtre, a huge burly man, whose kindly face was too full of power for anyone to notice its plebeian features. 'And what device, sir, can we find to do justice to your genius when we ennoble your house?'

'Three snails rampant on a field of cabbage, I should think, Sire,' said the designer. 'No, your Majesty, I am a gardener, and the son of a gardener. It would be ridiculous to ennoble me.'

His bluff voice was reassuring. It dispelled for a moment that breath of menace that seemed to hang on the hot air of the August night. Louis obviously liked him, made him continue talking, which Le Nôtre was delighted to do, telling his reasons for doing this and that at Vaux, his ingenious devices for surmounting certain difficulties, which gave him more pleasure than any easy perfection.

'When the very obstruction you have to surmount becomes the motive and centre of your plan, then, Sire, you can feel satisfied with the job.'

'I should like you to see my little hunting-box at Versailles,' said Louis. 'I have a notion something could be done with it, but they all tell me it is too difficult. There is no water near for one thing. Water is the soul of a garden, and your divinity has created it here.'

'It might be brought in pipes from Marley,' said Le Nôtre, who did not know what to do with a compliment. So he mentioned instead his allies in this his first great garden, Le Vau the architect and Le Brun the painter. The King made a note of the names.

While he was doing so his first gentleman of the bedchamber, the Comte de Vardes, came up and whispered to him. He was very tall, his head was magnificent, leonine in its great wig; he would have been extremely handsome had it not been for his too massive jaw, but even so his appearance was more superb than that of anyone round him.

'He makes them all look as though they should be walking on their heads instead of on those little pedestals,' thought Minette, suddenly seeing how absurd was the contrast of the huge wigs with most of the courtiers' thin legs on high heels.

Outside, the night had been turned into a fairyland of lights and falling waters; fountains, more elaborate than had ever yet been seen, produced a constant 'O – oh!' of delight from the spectators; they were twisted into patterns as intricate as lace; in one place they formed an iridescent archway round a grotto, where a huge shell of silver and mother-of-pearl opened to disclose a nymph, who recited to music a verse in praise of the greatest king in the world. She wore a scarf of green gauze; she could not be more than sixteen; everyone was asking who was this delicious child, and it was said that she was the daughter of Béjart, the leading actress in Molière's troupe.

A new comedy of Molière's, called *Les Fâcheux*, was acted on a stage erected out in the park. The actor-dramatist-producer was giving directions up to the last moment, when he had to go and change for his part. Minette's litter had been put down on its four short upstanding poles, and the footmen stood a little apart from it. The royal family and the princes and princesses of the blood had chairs placed in the front of the audience. The King watched the play with a more good-humoured expression than he had yet worn this evening. He had suggested a hunting scene in it to Molière, and talked about it as though he had collaborated with him through the whole play.

During the musical interludes of song and dance between the acts, Minette was conscious of uneasy currents in the crowd behind her, a continual shifting of people. All through the fête there had been a stream of people who came up to Fouquet with one thing after another, keeping him away from his royal guests; while on the other hand Louis was continually being engaged in little private conferences by men who spoke with that sad reluctant air which is generally the most effective in the betrayal of a friend. And he had had a brief conclave with the Queen-mother whose gestures had been emphatic and expostulatory.

Minette's position as an invalid, stationary except when carried by her footmen, in the midst of this whirling, pursuing

182

medley of people, made her oddly remote and yet clear-sighted; it was the position of the onlooker who sees most of the game.

And then suddenly she herself was in the thick of it. Her talk with the King came on her like a thunderclap out of the brilliantly illuminated night. The play was over, the audience dispersing to see fresh wonder. Minette had not yet ordered her footmen to remove her litter and, when ·the King approached her, those who were speaking to her drew back. She saw his face, set and quiet, like a cameo carved out against the background of torch-lit trees. He leaned over her litter, and suddenly she saw that his eyes were blazing. He said, 'I have decided to arrest Fouquet.'

'For God's sake!' she cried, then hastily controlled herself and spoke as low as he. 'Your host! In his own house? What in Heaven's name has he done now?'

'Now? It is not merely now. For years he has been cheating the exchequer, amassing vast sums for his own private use. Mazarin warned me. And now look at the proofs of his warning all round you, the insolent display of his thefts, the millions he has squandered on this single night.'

'For your pleasure,' she breathed, though she had little hope of that.

'For this triumph you mean. "Where may I not ascend?" Where not indeed? The crown is scarcely worth his plucking. I could never entertain him as he has me this night.'

'So you said to him, and people heard you. Is that going to be your accusation to him, that you are jealous of his wealth?'

'Madame!'

'Sire, I beg your pardon. But I do not understand. You have heard complaints of Fouquet's business methods before now. Why then is it tonight that you are so angry?'

He made an impatient exclamation. He seemed for a moment about to fling away, but he turned back to her. Through the turmoil of hot conflicting furies and desires tonight there was still this cool silver thread that drew him back to her side, made him want to know that she was with him, wishing him well in whatever he undertook.

'You do not know what I have heard tonight,' he said. 'Fouquet's corruption has been enormous – it cannot be dismissed as mere commercial morality. Things have come to my ears,' he stopped, he seemed confused, but she had never seen him so angry, nor so determined to try his power to the uttermost. And it was not yet six months since Mazarin had died.

The growth of the absolute monarch had been amazingly rapid, and might well develop into the tyrannical despot. In this personal fury with a rival who had dared offend him by a display greater than his own, there was something of the passion and caprice of a young Roman Emperor who tastes blood for the first time. But Louis' next words shocked her still more.

'It would be more convenient later,' he said, 'on that tour of inspection into Brittany; I could easily have him arrested then.'

Louis was proposing to lead his minister into a trap. Her pent-up irritation of the last few weeks was suddenly justified; Louis was a monster of perfidy, cruelty and moral cowardice; and it was not just because she was an 'injured woman' – odious phrase – that she had realized it, for this now had nothing to do with her, nothing at all, it was a purely disinterested, impersonal indignation that shook her with a fierce pleasure that here at last was a really good reason to quarrel with him. So busy was she proving to herself that her anger had nothing to do with her jealousy, that she missed her chance to speak, and he mistook her silence for the assent that he had been hoping for. 'We should get to Nantes in about two or three weeks,' he said, 'and my musketeers can do it there.'

'But you *cannot*,' she cried. 'Decoy him away on a friendly tour with you and then arrest him!' – to her intense annoyance she found his stare quelling her; she could not get out the half of what she had been preparing to say, and finished lamely – 'that would not be very glorious.'

'I have promised the Queen,' he said coldly (he always called his mother the Queen – his wife required more specification), 'not to arrest him here and now. She too takes his part, as she would that of any man who flatters her. Now you do too. He seems to have been universally successful with women.'

'I do not know him. Arrest him if you will, but is it necessary to take him off a couple of hundred miles or so first, and on a feint of friendship? Indeed, Sire, it is not to your honour.' (*Now* she could plant one of her weapons in a neat small phrase.) 'It reflects, Sire, on your courage.'

He did not speak. Her heart went cold. At last he said as if from very far away, 'At all events, Madame, there is no need to reflect upon yours.'

'I have been a fool, a fool,' cried her rebellious heart. Of what use was it to quarrel with him and turn him against her? There was her trust to Charles, her family, her country.

'Keep friends with Louis,' Charles had said, and this was how she did it!

It was too late to stop him; he had bowed, he had walked away. She could not jump off her litter and run after him, it would be too absurdly conspicuous. If she were that absurd La Vallière she could do it, and Louis no doubt would think it sweetly girlish and impulsive – but not in herself.

Till now she had not once thought of la Vallière all through her talk with him, and this was so unusual that a great hope leaped up in her aching and angry heart. Could this mean that her inner self, her womanly intuition, had divined that there was now no further need to fear La Vallière?

She at once felt strangely lenient to Louis. His anger with his minister was no more than natural, his plots against him, even his feline compliments to him, were the predatory gambollings of a young tiger, uncertain as yet of the extent of his claws. It was better to think of him as a young tiger than as a sneak. He would not really arrest Fouquet at Nantes; he would think better of it by the time he got there.

She was so exhausted by the time when even Monsieur would consent to go home, that it required a real effort to step from her litter into her coach; she sank back on the cushions, and put her feet up on the opposite seat with a sigh of thankfulness that at last the fête was over. Monsieur settled himself beside her in a twitter of appreciation.

'Now that,' he said, 'is my idea of a really good evening. I said so to Louis. I said that if only he could contrive to do things on that scale it would be worth while to attend his parties. He swore outright, and in front of our mother. He has no control. Listen, I have a delicious morsel of gossip for you – my dear, it is a pearl! Béjart's daughter – you know, the girl in the shell – they say that our Molière was enchanted by her this evening and declares he will marry her. But wait! that is not all. There is quite a good chance that she is his daughter – certainly Béjart was his mistress, so you see – and I have asked everyone about the other report. It is certain his enemies will do what they can to spread it, but what I say is, Art before morals, and God knows sex is dull enough without some variation of the theme, and in any case he is our man whom I discovered before my brother took him up, and we must stand by him.'

'I should wish to,' she answered, thinking of Molière's rugged yet sensitive face. He had looked at her in a very kindly way this evening; her humility was deep enough to be grateful for an expression of sympathy, even in the eyes of a low-born actor-playwright.

Still Monsieur babbled happily.

'There was an extraordinary amount going on tonight, I don't know if you grasped it. Fouquet has cooked his own goose, that's certain. Louis will never forgive him for this evening. But of course you know the true reason of his fury with him?'

'He is trying to make me say Louis is jealous of his wealth,' she thought, and was determined not to be caught out in anything that could be used against her in Louis' ears. So she murmured something about accounts and the exchequer.

'My angel, how dull! People do not trouble about accounts when they are in love.'

'In love?' she repeated.

'In love, cherub, in love. Have you indeed never noticed that your little nose has been out of joint these three weeks at least?'

'But what has that to do with Fouquet?' she asked slowly.

'Fouquet knew the pretty Louise, your Mademoiselle de la Vallière.'

'Only slightly.'

'So it was said. But others, tonight, said differently.'

'What do they say?'

'You heard nothing? This comes of your invalid habits. You cannot get any gossip if you sit still all the time on a litter.'

She was silent. Since it would give her pain, there was no doubt that he would soon tell her his news.

Sure enough, he fidgeted, waiting for a sharp response, then could contain himself no longer.

'Well then,' he said, 'there was a picture in one of the rooms at Vaux by Mignard, a pretty picture of a nymph, clad, you may understand, as a nymph should be, that is to say much as Mademoiselle Béjart was dressed in her shell. The nymph had large eyes, fair hair, an insipid expression, the features that any self-respecting artist would feel obliged to give any nymph. We come up to it with the King. "Behold!" says one of our party, "a portrait of Mademoiselle de la Vallière." '

'But was it?'

'I have told you it was not. Was all my innuendo too subtle for you? But it was like enough to any fairly pleasing, simpering young prude to insist that it was a portrait. Her figure was

186

flattered of course, one could not tell by it that she limps, but neither can one in real life until she walks – no more than I ever knew you had one shoulder higher than the other until I married you. But as to the portrait, when doubt was thrown on the matter, I said in an airy, confident way, "the opinion of the man who painted it should settle the question. Mignard told me himself that he was painting the portrait of Mademoiselle de la Vallière for a private commission." '

'In Heaven's name why did you?'

'I do not like profiteers. Besides, as a good husband, I am glad to further any love-affair of Louis' that is not with my wife. This little spur of jealousy has hastened it up considerably. Fouquet is doomed, but you need not fear for your gentle white dove, she will only profit by it. I fancy she is profiting at this very moment. De Vardes was to arrange it and he is a punctual pander. So he should be, as first gentleman of the bedchamber.'

He leaned forward to see how she took it. She sat silent. The coach jogged on. Behind the fussy outline of Monsieur's head, the square of grey dawn in the window grew pale in sunrise and the larks began to sing.

BOOK III

AFTERNOON

CHAPTER TWENTY-FIVE

The blue bed, the ceiling painted with rosy clouds and cupids, the square of wild autumnal sky in the window, had become Minette's world. She watched her mother move about the room quietly yet with that rather bustling, practical tread, or sit at her embroidery on the dais beside her bed, passing the needle and thread through the stuff in a soothing rhythm. The guardian presence made her a child again, whose only responsibility was to be good and take her next bowl of broth.

Her mother stayed in Paris for some weeks to nurse her daughter, for she was with child and, in these early months, seriously ill. Minette cared little for that; she was safe here in the great bed where she could act no more against herself as in that unlucky night at Vaux; and her mother did not ask questions. Visitors came from morning till night, until stopped altogether for a time by Doctor Yvelin. Then there were only letters to look forward to, especially those that came by the post once a week from England.

Charles wrote often to his dearest Minette, full of concern at her illness and begging her for God's sake to take some care of herself at last. He was 'very glad to hear that your indisposition is turned into a greate belly. I hope you will have better lucke than the Duchess heare had, who was brought to bed, Monday last, of a girle. I am afraid your shape is not so advantageously made for the convenience as hers is, however a boy will recompense two grunts more, and so good night, for fear I fall into naturale philosophy, before I thinke of it.

I am, Yours,
C. R.[1]

This daughter, christened Anne, was the second born to the

Duchess of York, and still no male heirs. But there was plenty of time, for Charles was not yet married.

One day the Queen began to read a letter from Charles, stopped in the middle of a sentence to compose her features to a decent distress, exclaimed, 'Only think!' – 'Well, well, I am truly grieved,' and at last told her who was dead.

Elizabeth of Bohemia, who had returned to her native country last summer, had caught a cold moving into her new London house ('How often have I said one should never move house in winter!' exclaimed the Queen, unable even then to resist a score.) Within a few days she had died 'on such a night of storm, wind and hail as has never been seen before.'

Elizabeth had left England as a lovely laughing bride of fifteen, with her long plaits threaded with pearls. Then the whole of London had crowded on to the shores of the Thames to see the daughter of the Scots King James pass from their land in a gallant company of ships, commanded by the Earl of Nottingham, who had been Sir Thomas Howard when he fought against the Armada. Two river banks alive with faces, from either side a continuous terrific huzza, this was the last she saw and heard of the city which had idolized her, until she came back as an old woman, privately with a few servants, creeping up the Thames in a single boat at night, that her lack of welcome might not be too conspicuous. She had outlived three generations of popularity, and had the sense to know it; lived retired; and died the following winter, after only a few months in the home to which she had longed all her life to return.

'And now I shall never see her,' said Minette. All her brothers and sisters had known and adored their bold and fascinating aunt; and she had always looked forward to doing so, lately with more certain hope, since she would meet her on her next visit to Charles in London. But now on a night of storm and hail the Winter Queen had left London once more and for ever.

Her mother sat reading the letter through again to herself, as if unable to believe that the lifelong rivalry, veiled as family feeling, was now over. The English Parliament had decided that Queen Henrietta's pension as dowager consort could not be paid unless she made her home in the country, and she had been looking forward with dread to living in the same city as her English sister-in-law. Now she realized that the dread had been a more than half-joyful anticipation,

190

She looked up from the letter at her daughter's voice.

'Do you remember, Mam, how I annoyed you by asking for a "fairy farm", as my Aunt Elizabeth had as a child?' A farm with all the smallest animals that could be found, Shetland ponies, bantam chickens, cows from Morocco no bigger than calves; so Morton had told her. And Elizabeth's godmother – the wicked old Queen with the nose like a witch, who had cut off her great-grandmother's head – had died because she sat on the floor and refused to go to bed. For that had been the bedtime moral of the story, and Morton had told it on the last time she had put Minette to bed, the night before she went back to England.

'They all go back to England and then die,' thought Minette, and wished that she had done so too, as Harry and Mary had done in the height of their happiness and home-coming. Elizabeth the Winter Queen had reigned in Bohemia for one brief season only; and now she wondered that her own title of the Midsummer Princess had not struck her as ominous last June.

May, June and July she had reigned, a royalty of long-drawn-out sunsets, brief nights, and early dawns, fresh with dew and exquisite with the song of birds. Then came the harsher pomp of August, poppies instead of the wild rose; the singing birds were silent, and silently the yellow leaves spun down through the still air. There had been a thundery night towards the end of August, the night of the fête at Vaux. The weather had broken for good after that, and as she watched the steady downpour of rain she told herself it did not matter, for the summer was over; there was nothing more to look forward to.

The great gardens of her palace at the Tuileries became a sponge of sodden lawns and wet leaves. She had heard there of the King's tour of inspection with Fouquet, of Fouquet's arrest at Nantes by d'Artagnan, lieutenant in the musketeers, and of the King's intended reform of the whole financial system. There were startling disclosures at Fouquet's trial, enough to hang him twice over, Monsieur declared gleefully.

Mazarin had left his public fortune to the King, and the King had left it back to Mazarin's family; and everybody had behaved beautifully. But Mazarin had had a far larger private fortune hidden away in various places, and Fouquet had kept it hidden. It was Colbert, a singularly honest intendant of Mazarin's, who informed the King.

Le Nôtre, Le Brun and Le Vau were already at work on

191

plans for the King's new buildings and gardens at Versailles. The Prince of Condé had taken Vatel into his service; 'No one could serve you more religiously,' said Madame, who had felt oddly more concerned for the steward even than for his master. Colbert was made Minister of Finance in Fouquet's stead. Louis secured the whole of the fortune that Fouquet had concealed, and was now the richest monarch in Europe, 'so that you would think he could afford to forgive,' said the witty young Madame at the Tuileries over her morning chocolate and copy of the *Gazette*.

Louis had learnt during his poverty-stricken boyhood that a king's first duty to himself was to keep a tight hold on the public moneys. Money was the great present difficulty of monarchs. The influx of wealth from America through Spain in the previous century had depreciated the standard of gold.

King Charles I of England had always been at his wits' end for money; and his son was now finding the same difficulty; as he complained to James, his whores cost more than his father's wars. He did what he could to pay for them with a wife; he entered into negotiations for the Portuguese Infanta and a dowry of £500,000, the cities of Tangier in Africa and of Bombay in the East Indies. So that no doubt she would be worth it, he observed. His sister had hoped he would make a romantic marriage, and was disappointed by the little she could hear of Catherine of Braganza. She was convent bred, not a real beauty, unlikely to hold Charles.

But Minette had lost hope of happiness for anyone. It was not the way of the world; and for herself she was lucky to have known three months of it. Monsieur, in wishing himself in love with her, had grasped beyond his reach and fallen flat in the mud; she now felt that she had done the same when she and Louis had sacrificed their happiness for the sake of Monsieur. She regretted also her concern for the King's honour in the affair of Fouquet. She would never again trouble about other people's business – Charles had said it was a great mistake – 'If you succeed in altering people, it is only for a time, and then they dislike you for their inconsistency.'

Louis visited her punctiliously; there was a special state call when he came to ask her congratulations on the birth of a Dauphin. Queen Henrietta was asked to be his godmother. Here was another Louis, the Gift of God, but she would have to choose something original for his second name. He had been born on All Saints' Day, so she suggested Toussaint, and

192

Olympe de Soissons whispered impiously that it sounded like a cough mixture. So short a time ago Minette would have thought nothing of repeating the silly joke to Louis; now she looked at his still face beside her bed and wondered if they would ever laugh together again.

His mother had taught him to be afraid of her laughter; told him that his brother's wife was as clever as he, and would be certain to lead him if he allowed her too much influence; even if she did not, people would think she did. This disturbed him more than the fear of incest.

La Vallière was still one of Madame's maids of honour, and Louis therefore came every day to the Tuileries to see her; but his wife and mother thought it was to see Madame. Their jealousy of her had increased in proportion as the reason for it had waned. It was Minette who was now the blind to La Vallière, the King's real love. She had been hoist with her own petard, as she had seen quoted in those long, rambling, generally indignant letters that Elizabeth used to write to her daughter Louise at the convent of Chaillot.

Fatigued and exasperated with the hypocrisy of Louis and, as she took it, of La Vallière ('why can that idiot girl never look at me without turning up the whites of her eyes?'), she had become very friendly with her former rival, Olympe Mancini, now Comtesse de Soissons, who like herself had been deserted and disillusioned. Olympe amused her, so did the Princess of Monaco, sister of de Guiche, and both smuggled into the sickroom innumerable letters from the lovesick Count. Letters were his favourite medium for love-making, and Madame's long illness gave him the best opportunity he had had yet. Their style was flowery; their subjects, the lady's charms and his emotions; he was apt to be more discursive on the latter.

'He has learnt in some romance,' said Montalais, the maid-in-waiting, 'that any lover worth his salt writes at least four letters a day.'

But Olympe more sympathetically read them aloud to Madame, who was very apt to leave them unfinished. The women buzzed about her bed; Montalais brisk, efficient, quick to disparage any sign of sentiment; the Princess of Monaco looking in for a moment like some brilliant mocking-bird, derisive at the sight of more letters from her poor young brother; Olympe de Soissons, superbly dressed, almost hysterically gay, and then with sudden abandonment telling them how she and her sisters were doomed to disappointment from

193

birth. Look at Hortense, who should have been Queen of England, married to a man so virtuous that she was obliged to run away from him, disguised as a man, after first taking the precaution to rob him. 'Such a sad life, I think. Do you not think it is a sad life when women cannot love their husbands?'

Sunk in rich Italian melancholy, her beauty was transformed from a Pagan goddess to a Guido Reni sorrowing Madonna. There was a tap at the door. A page had brought another letter. Once more she was eager, excited, a harbinger of joy.

The winter sun hung low like a copper ball above the mists of the river as the Comtesse de Soissons stood by the window to catch the last of the light, that she might read of de Guiche's tortured but eternally faithful soul. Behind her in the great blue and rose room where the colours were fading in the dusk, Montalais moved softly up to the dais, leaned over the bed, and peered into the dimness under the canopy. The small face there lay like a pointed shadow on the pillow, the eyelashes made a dark curve on the cheek, the lips were parted. Under Montalais' scrutiny Madame stirred, and murmured something incomprehensible about Shetland ponies and calves, then was still again.

The love-letter had done more than the doctor's pills and sent Madame fast asleep.

Piqued at the result of his letters ('My friend, you are a bore,' was Olympe's terse account of it), de Guiche freed himself from the clammy weight of his emotions, and recounted Monsieur's jealous reproaches to him, giving them an air so fantastic that they read like a tragi-comedy written for marionettes six inches high. Minette laughed aloud; thus encouraged, de Guiche aimed higher, at the King himself. Madame, he heard, giggled happily into her pillow when she learned that the King had written love-verses to La Vallière which he had tried on de Guiche's downright old father, the Maréchal de Gramont, without letting him know their authorship.

'Abominable, Sire, abominable,' had been the verdict.

Four letters a day did not exhaust de Guiche's energies. He had a notion, borrowed from one of his sister's admirers, a fiery Gascon, an extraordinary little man, the Comte de Lauzun, who out of sheer bravado and the fun of it had disguised himself as a servant and got into her household. De Guiche therefore disguised himself as an old gipsy woman, and with

Montalais' connivance came and told Madame's fortune in her apartments, where she now sat up in an arm-chair every day. Nobody recognized him but herself, and she nipped his hand severely when she crossed his palm with silver.

After this he frequently visited her without any disguise or other pretext, when he knew no one to be with her but de Soissons and Montalais; both of whom had a way of disappearing discreetly into the ante-chamber. He too was discreet, and could have small wish to be anything else when Madame had recently been so ill and so soon would be ill again and in worse danger for her life. It suited his temperament to etherealize what was already too delicate a creature for a more robust love.

The year had turned; there was hope of spring in the lighter days, in the bare twigs that shone purple with leaf-buds when the sunlight caught them. Madame was better and was now allowed to walk a little in the garden. She was grateful for this new interest coming when she had thought her life was over, since at her age she thought of life and love as the same, and of her first disappointment as her last.

But now she began to look forward to her life after the child's birth, to practise her lute and learn new songs for it; to wonder what she would wear when next she attended Court functions, and if de Guiche would still love her then; to think how sweet is light love and how sad, for when it passes it leaves nothing. Is it then love indeed, or is it oneself only that one sees mirrored in the eyes of the new love?

'Madame, your eyes grow round, and your lips are parted as though a cherry were dangling just before them. Will you not let me taste?'

'It is Monsieur de la Rochefoucauld's cherry. He told Madame de la Fayette the other day that lovers never grow tired of their conversation, since they speak only of themselves.'

De Guiche laughed, but a little uneasily. It was some time before she could succeed in coaxing him to tell again his sad story of his wife, which led, as always, to his boyish friendship with Monsieur and his new awakening through her.

'But you must not be too unkind to him,' she said, 'he loves you very much, and naturally he finds it hard and unreasonable in you to turn against him.'

He looked at her helplessly and muttered that it would be a

195

good thing if Monsieur could die before she really learned to know him.

A few days after that, Montalais came running to her mistress with a piece of news that she tossed delightedly before her.

'La Vallière is not to be found, Madame! The King came for her and she has disappeared. Now it is a wild-goose chase everywhere, and for what a goose! Who would think her light enough for flight, and with whom can it be?' She had always had her own ideas about that shy, soft type of girl – had there not been some former admirer of La Vallière's, about whom the King was perseveringly jealous? 'She told me all about it one evening when she was brushing her hair – you know the fatal effect that has on women.'

Madame did; she wondered how imprudent she herself had been when Montalais did her hair. It gave her an unpleasant shock to find how friendly Montalais must be with La Vallière, at whom she was always mocking.

It was early in Lent, and a new preacher, the Abbé Bossuet, was appointed to give a sermon before the royal family at the Louvre. The King did not appear in chapel; he was looked for; then it was discovered that he too had disappeared.

Late that evening Minette saw from her window a rider galloping up the avenue to the palace, his hat pulled down, his grey cloak drawn across the lower part of his face. He turned his horse to a side entrance and disappeared. She thought from the way he rode that it was the King. Then she heard his footsteps in the passage – a hurried almost blundering tread, closer and closer to her door, and 'Oh!' cried her heart, hammering against her side, 'what can it be now, and why should he be angry?'

Montalais ran at his knock and let him in. He took the door handle from her and pointed to the passage, then shut the door and advanced on Minette. She had been right, he was angry; there was a swollen blue vein that stood out on his forehead, she had never seen it before. He could not speak at once, he was recovering his breath, and then his torrent of words broke on her. What was it all about? Not La Vallière then – only de Guiche, and surely that could not matter. She ought to be relieved; but she was not, to hear Louis calling her faithless, wanton, a traitress and only because of de Guiche.

'But have you found La Vallière?' she asked, and then as he stared at her boldness she said, 'Yes, it is true I have seen de

196

Guiche sometimes and privately, but that is not important, I want to know about her.'

'It was your treachery that sent her flying from the Court.'

Her head had begun to throb painfully. 'I have never betrayed La Vallière. I have kept her secret even when both the Queens bullied me for receiving your visits.'

'Are you so lost to decency that you cannot understand? She knew your shameful secret, she tried to keep it, but she had sworn to have no secrets from me. I saw that she was concealing something and commanded her to tell me. She fled rather than do so, and I found her at Chaillot – the nuns had feared my anger and would not admit her – she was in a little waiting-room, lying on the floor, half dead with fright and misery – because of you.'

She was as angry now as he. 'What have my secrets to do with her? Why should you try to get them out of her? It is the most sentimental schoolgirl rubbish that ever I heard.'

Her heart was thumping wilder than ever, she felt rather sick; suddenly she realized that she had a better weapon than she had yet thought of using. She turned from him and leaned her head against the window-pane, saying, 'And if I miscarry it will be your fault, and I shall call the abortion "God, the gift of Louis." '

'You have no heart at all,' he said, but she had gained her effect; he had looked startled, and now a little shamefaced. She pursued her advantage.

'I will not have her here any longer to act as your spy on me. She has given me endless trouble. I am blamed for her sake, and now she carries tales to you. I will not take her back.'

He flared up again at that.

'You shall take her back – or I will publish your intrigue with de Guiche to the world, I will get you divorced.'

'That is not the way to move me,' she said coldly.

But he was not chiefly set on moving her. He seemed to forget all about La Vallière while he demanded answers to his questions – was it true that de Guiche had been visiting her, sometimes in disguise – had he been making love to her all this time, had she admitted love for him, was she his mistress, good God, was it possible? was the child within her a bastard?

Minette sank down on the window-seat; the cold spring twilight glimmered behind the trees; she could hear a thrush singing somewhere in the garden. She made a great effort to keep her head, to see what was the important thing to tell Louis in this rage of his that was so irrational.

'The disguise,' she said slowly, 'was a joke; there were nearly a dozen people in the room at the time. And since then it is true I have sometimes talked with him alone, but never really of love. You can see I would not be in the mood for it. And I am sure he has no serious feeling for me.'

Her tired voice expressed an obvious sincerity. He sat down beside her to look into her eyes, and could not doubt her.

'You do not know that he loves you?' he said, 'then it would surprise you to learn that today he quarrelled violently with my brother, admitted his love for you, and said that it was intolerable to him to stay and see you as his wife? He has left the Court.'

'Oh,' she cried, 'and now Monsieur will be so cross!'

He smiled slowly. 'I see,' he said.

'What do you see?'

'That you do not love de Guiche so very much.'

'Oh, but I do! At least I enjoyed his visits, and I do not want him to harm himself – he is so headstrong. But I suppose I love myself better, and I know that Monsieur will blame me for this quarrel.'

He put his arm round her. 'I will take care of you,' he said, and she marvelled at the inconsistency of lovers.

CHAPTER TWENTY-SIX

Minette's scene with Louis was the prelude to half a dozen with others.

La Vallière returned, threw herself at Madame's feet and implored her forgiveness. 'Montalais told you about de Guiche, I suppose,' said Madame.

'But, Madame, it was my fault that I could not keep it from the King. Montalais has been so good a friend to me, so kind and understanding—'

'I know,' said Minette dryly. 'She has been understanding with me too.' Always she had this wish to be very worldly-wise and ironical with La Vallière, and yet she liked her; she could understand Louis loving her, and his bullying her too, for La Vallière looked lovely in distress; the too meek face was

198

lit by a wild flame that flushed her fair cheeks and shone in her beseeching eyes.

'You are much more good than I,' said Minette, and meant to stop there but heard her own voice hurrying on – 'but it is easier for you, for you are more stupid, and besides the King is not your brother-in-law. It has all been too difficult for me,' she added with a sigh, and suddenly she wondered what she had been saying.

La Vallière caught at her hand, covered it with kisses and tears. 'Madame, I beg of you, let me go away. I cannot bear the King to come for me here in your own house, it is horrible, Madame, but he will have it so, lest the Queens should suspect.' She stammered, too shamefaced to look at her mistress, 'Ah, Madame, I cannot bear to abuse your kindness, and now I have betrayed you to the King—'

'Oh, as to that—' began Madame, but this time bit off her words before she assured her rival that the result of that had been to make Louis kinder to her than at any time since his love for La Vallière. She said instead, 'I am afraid you are not at all happy, Louise.'

It was odd to use that name again to someone so different.

A flood of grief answered her sympathy. Louise had never been happy since the King showed his love for her. She adored him, but oh, how much happier to adore in secret with no hope of return! Her conscience had been at rest then. Now it was a tortured thing; she could not confess, and what would happen to her if she were to die? If only she could expiate her guilt in a convent – but Louis laughed at that. Did Madame think he would ever let her go?

Madame did think so, but did not say it, when Louis had tired of La Vallière. She did not know him even yet or she would not have been so confident.

After Louis and La Vallière came de Guiche, stealing back to the palace secretly and dramatically to tell her that for her sake he had broken with Monsieur, who would probably ruin him, but that he asked nothing better than to lose all for her sake. Were any lovers as unreasonable as hers, to force their way into her room when she was prostrate with sea-sickness and measles, as the Duke of Buckingham had done, or now when she might at any moment give birth to her child? They must have a singular regard for her virtue.

She got rid of him, summoned Montalais, and the full vials

of the wrath that had been dammed in three previous interviews now burst forth on her maid of honour. Montalais was astonished, explanatory, apologetic, offended, outraged. She left the palace and obtained an interview with the Queen-mother of France, in which she told her that Madame had been keeping stolen interviews with de Guiche.

A slow and righteous fury exalted Queen Anne. All the kindness she had done to that little viper of England, whom she had nourished in her bosom, rose before her like a long procession of martyred saints. She had given the girl one of her sons, and the greedy upstart had promptly grabbed both. Now even the King could not suffice her; she must needs drag their royal name in the mud with any gentleman who came to hand.

She longed for her scene with Madame, but the danger of harming her son's heir forced her to transfer it to Monsieur. She scolded him almost as much as if he had been his wife, and wept over her ungrateful niece and incompetent son. He wept too, frightened by her, hurt by de Guiche, bewildered as to what he should do next. He had had a most painful scene with de Guiche. He felt it indeed hard on him that everyone who loved his wife should hate him for having done so first. His greatest friend now regarded him as a monster, and all because for once in his life he had been natural. He began to despise himself for the single lapse into the normal emotions, to wish that he had been consistent. (Louis was always consistent.) He wished that he too could have a baby, then people might sometimes consider his feelings a little.

In his perplexity he went to his mother-in-law at the Palais Royal. He was at his best with elderly women, when they were not his mother. Queen Henrietta was reassuring, admitted that her daughter had been very foolish – 'but have you not been a little foolish too? That de Guiche of yours must be a most disturbing person.'

And she smiled so kindly that Monsieur could tell her quite naturally how he would miss de Guiche and how unhappy their quarrel had made him. 'The things he said to me! And he loved me once. You are the only true mother I have ever had,' he added tearfully.

'I *am* your mother now,' she firmly told him, ordered Montalais' dismissal, led him back to the Tuileries and into his wife's room. Minette held out her hands and said, 'My dear, I am sorry you have lost your friend.'

He took them and said, 'We have both lost him. We must console each other.'

After this it was not surprising that Madame's first child was born prematurely at the end of March. But the event passed off very well, except in one particular.

'Is it a boy?' came a faint whisper from the bed.

'Madame, it is a beautiful little princess,' said a voice of elephantine softness.

'But are you *sure*?'

'The signs are usually unmistakable, Madame.' Dr Yvelin now sounded rather offended.

'Then throw her into the river!' exclaimed the invalid, and not nearly so faintly. All that trouble for nothing; and she would have to do it all over again – and over and over again, said her friends and physicians, who were never tired of assuring her how young she was and how she would live to have several sons as well as extra daughters thrown in.

Queen Anne was scandalized at the heartless flippancy of her daughter-in-law. They were all gravely disappointed that it was not a son; one could not have too many heirs, as child life was so uncertain that a proportion of seven dying out of ten was not an excessive estimate. But once the baby was born it was ingratitude to God not to praise Him for it, whatever the sex. The excitement of the childbirth had however softened her very much towards Madame. There was no chance of her stealing interviews or hearts while she was brought to bed, and she had shown great courage and endurance. So Queen Anne sought to console her by saying that, though she had not given birth to a prince, her baby might yet one day be queen, since her cousin the Dauphin, now five months old, would be a suitable age for her later.

On her first appearance in public Minette heard that the Maréchal de Gramont had obtained the command of the troops before Nancy for his son, the Comte de Guiche. Several people spoke to her of this honour with a sly commiseration; she was surprised and hurt that they should know so much about her affairs and assume still more. Her mother had given her many lectures on her imprudent folly, but that she had thought was the way of mothers. Now there was genuine warmth in her promises to behave with great discretion; all the more genuine because de Guiche was certain to be absent for a very long time.

Nevertheless it was with considerable misgivings that Queen Henrietta left later on in the year for England, in time to see Charles married to his Portuguese bride. He wrote a charming description of her sweetness and simplicity. Madame's English maid of honour, the pretty, silly Miss Frances Stuart, whom Louis had thought a minx, was sent over to be maid of honour to King Charles' wife. Her romping freedom of manners was an extraordinary contrast to the Portuguese guarda infantas, who sounded like half-Eastern barbarians; for they were afraid to go out of doors lest they should be seen by men, and refused to sleep in any lodgings that had been occupied by these monsters. Yet their appearance in their preposterously old-fashioned farthingales and foretops was sufficient protection for their chaste alarms. It was difficult to procure enough carts to contain them all – for there were nearly a hundred of them – and they and their priests buzzed round the Queen like a nest of hornets.

Catherine's 'fantastick Portugeese', as Charles spelt them, Henrietta Maria's bigoted French priests, Elizabeth of Bohemia's rude English ladies – there was always this same difficulty in different forms with royal foreign brides. Minette could count herself lucky in that respect at least, since her country was not her home.

CHAPTER TWENTY-SEVEN

The two leading salons of the day, remarkably different in character, were those of Madeleine de la Fayette and Olympe de Soissons.

Madame de la Fayette was a young widow, delicate, literary, refined, a relation of Mère Angélique, whom she had often come to visit in the convent of Chaillot while the Princess Henriette of England was still at school there. The girl had had a shy adoration for this older woman, married and out in the world, who yet talked to her about her favourite romances, and admitted her own passion for them. And La Fayette wrote romances too, which became famous. She had been brought up in the salons of the two great precieuses, Madame de Rambouillet and Mademoiselle de Scudéry, and now her own salon was frequented by the more exclusive brains of the day. Her chief friend from childhood, for they were at school together, was Madame de Sévigné, whom La Fayette blamed for wast-

202

ing her time and talents in writing so many letters – she herself could never be troubled to answer them.

But her particular genius in friendship was shown with elderly, remarkable, misogynist men. The talk was impersonal and often abstruse; there were difficult games such as acrostics and capping verses; sometimes the Duc de la Rochefoucauld, who hated other society, was persuaded to read aloud a few of those maxims that he had been working at for many years, forming and reforming the brief words until they attained a crystal perfection. He intended never to submit them to the vulgarity of publication, but his aristocratic prejudice was weakening under Madeleine's gentle persistence.

The atmosphere was not purely literary. The Prince of Condé, who seldom talked freely with women, was an intimate friend of his hostess; and the great general Turenne preferred to visit her rather than the Court, where he was deeply respected. The pleasant blue room, in the tradition of the earlier salons, was filled with flowers; the light was carefully shadowed and diffused, that of the sun by heavy curtains, and that of the candles behind cases of rounded glass. It was a dim, occasionally rather chill, intellectual refuge from the world of ambitious competition.

The salon of the Comtesse de Soissons was the hottest arena of that world. Here the interests were active and personal – high play and intrigue, whether in love or politics. Popularity was often the means to material advancement, and at all risks one must be interesting. The circle entertained a watchful regard for each other's misfortunes; their fearful pleasure in retailing confidences was that of the matador who enjoys exposing himself to the attack of the bull.

Minette observed this and trembled, for when she had been ill she had noticed that Olympe took it for granted that her relations with Louis had been the same as her own. The matter had only come up in joke – Olympe saying apropos of some fresh gaffe of La Vallière's – 'Thank heaven, we at least are out of it. Don't you agree that it is rather comfortable to be deserted?' It was impossible for Minette to answer such casual innuendoes with a protestation of her superior virtue; she had much rather let Olympe think what she chose than be priggishly assertive. It was only now, when no longer safely cloistered in her sick-room, that she realized she had given Olympe the power to tell others that the Princess had admitted a liaison with the King.

Olympe was still her friend, but the more she heard of Olympe's talk in her salon, the less security did that fact give her. These thoughts sometimes distracted her; though she tried to stiffen herself with the reflection that what did it matter? for these people who were so ready to believe the worst of their friends, did not think any the worse of them for it. They naturally preferred those who resembled themselves, and in Olympe's salon it was of more importance to be liked than respected. She forced herself by dint of her ready sympathies to take a lower standard than she really understood.

Under the constant stimulus of hope and fear the talk at Olympe's was often wittier than at La Fayette's, but of a wit so slangy, personal, and on the crest of the wave, that in a short time it would pass further out of date than any remote topic of academic discussion held in the rival salon. There, the danger was that the rare might become arid, and the impersonal wither into inhumanity; while in Olympe's, the heated surcharge of life was apt to over-ripen into rottenness. The former was most completely represented by the melancholy, baffled idealist, La Rochefoucauld; the latter by the Comte de Vardes.

This, the First Gentleman of the Bedchamber, was one of the most powerful and influential nobles about the King. He would lounge into Olympe's salon as though the place belonged to him, as its mistress undoubtedly did. As she sat at the gaming-tables, or talked to her other guests, moving about among them with a slow voluptuous sweep of her dress, he would stand against the chimney-piece, in his hand a glass of the strong canary sack from England which he preferred to the lighter French wines; his head back, his heavy jaw thrust forward, his blue eyes staring at her like those of a bull.

She never sought to impress him with what she said; admiring women who tried to air their wit before him seldom went on trying. His remarks were decisive, caustic, final; they went straight to the subject and blasted it. He was not young, but his great physique, the suggestion of brutality, of hard sense, uncompromisingly practical, proved compellingly attractive in this foppish world where many of the refinements introduced by the précieuses had begun to seem silly and affected. De Vardes' arrogance did not appear to be based on his personal success, but on an unconscious assumption of his superiority. He had the indefinable power to confer prestige; he seldom sought out people, and when he did it flattered them, even the highest in the land, even Madame, the wife of the King's brother.

Madame de Sévigné, as virtuous as she was charming, declared he was a rascal, but irresistible. Luckily for her, she never had to resist him. In love, as in talk, he attacked, conquered, and discarded. He would have had the utmost contempt for Madame's ladylike flirtation with de Guiche; she knew it; and was the more pleased that he could wish for friendship with her, who was, as he made her understand, too slight and fragile, too undeveloped even, in spite of her baby, for him to think of as a woman. A sylph of the Court was the popular description of her which he repeated with a wry twist of his full, hard lips, for he thought it a poor compliment. What he admired in her was her gaiety, her pluck, her funny, childish and yet clever remarks. She too began to despise de Guiche for his admiration of her as a sylph; it was much better to be seen as de Vardes had come to see her, the most shrewd and amusing woman he had ever known.

The quality of his mind struck her by its resemblance to Charles' (though perhaps tougher). That was a strong recommendation, so was his admiration of her brother. It was delightful to have someone to talk with about Charles, and that someone not a woman, whose first concern was always whether the English King were still in love with his wife or Lady Castlemaine, or whether Miss Stuart had already begun to put both their noses out of joint.

Charles had placed her in a very responsible position by suggesting that he and Louis should conduct their correspondence on State affairs through her. By this he hoped to keep her in Louis' confidence and of importance to him, independent of any sentimental attachment. Louis warmly agreed that the kingdoms would be drawn together in a far friendlier fashion through this gentler medium than through their respective ambassadors, who indeed seemed more concerned to keep them apart by their continual give and take of offence. 'These deliberate insults,' 'ces incivilités grosses et barbares,' were the more frequent subjects of their letters home. In reply Louis sent elaborate explanations, and Charles (through Minette) could say nothing for his servant who 'carried himselfe so like an Asse, but that it was a faute for want of good breeding, which is a disease very much spread over this country.'

But Charles was not always so conciliatory. Louis wished

to dispense with the naval salute that the ships of all nations were accustomed to yield to British men-of-war; it involved the right of search on neutral vessels in time of war, a dangerous condition, and he asked Minette to do what she could to remove it. But Charles answered violently that nothing would induce him to 'go lower than ever any of my predecessors did,' and – 'all I say is, my ships must do their dutyes, let what will come of it.' This required careful translation before it could be passed on to Louis.

But her difficulties carried a glowing compensation. Here was she, at eighteen, entrusted with the most delicate diplomatic questions between the two greatest nations of Europe. She listened to the politicians who discussed the foreign affairs in which she had been appointed so high a role, and included her only by courtesy; they did not know.

Young Ralph Montagu, the second son of Lord Boughton, came over on a flying diplomatic mission and brought her two letters from his master, one in French for her to show to Louis, the other in English, as always in Charles' private letters to her. De Guiche's fascinating scapegrace of an uncle, the Chevalier de Gramont, had also just arrived in Paris after a prolonged visit to the English Court, and had a store of scandal and jocular messages from Charles on his failure to find the Chevalier a rich wife as requested. In Olympe's salon the two men stood talking to her and the Comte de Vardes of the recent Anabaptist riots in London; the two French nobles were delighted with the rugged word, so characteristically English, hissing like water on hot iron; they were amazed to hear that this was but one among hundreds of Puritan sects, each convinced of its own solitary enlightenment by God. Only England could tolerate such a hurly-burly of half-maniacs, stubborn, independent, solemn, conceited.

'By God!' exclaimed de Vardes, 'what a proud race of crack-brained giants!'

At the other end of the salon a young man made a dramatic entrance by standing still in the doorway, flinging back his cloak and exclaiming, 'What do you all think of the latest news? The King of England has turned shopkeeper and is selling us Dunkirk. We'll buy London from him next.'

It was Bussy Rabotin, a clever, rather showy and disreputable cousin of Madame de Sévigné's. He would not be baulked of his effect, though Olympe had tried to hush him down, for he did not see Madame's slight figure in the midst of the group of men at the end of the room.

'You should stop that,' said a low voice by Madame's side, and she looked up to meet de Vardes' clear, hard gaze.

She had already tried. Louis had wanted to make Dunkirk part of the dowry that the English princess should bring his brother, but Charles had not then felt himself sufficiently secure with his people. But Dunkirk cost an appalling amount to keep up, and might easily prove an awkward foreign entanglement; he needed money badly; and old Hyde, the Earl of Clarendon, approved his idea of selling it.

Rather oddly, it was his little sister, bred as a Frenchwoman by her French mother, knowing England only as a visitor for three months and speaking English as a foreigner, who had urgently opposed this sale. It made no difference to her that Charles found Dunkirk a needless expense and possible nuisance. Those were men's arguments. What she saw was the ships full of French gold sailing up the Thames to deposit their load in the Tower as the price for an English seaport. What would all the Londoners, that proud race of crackbrained giants (her heart had warmed to de Vardes at that), say to it but that Charles was a pensioner of Louis, a spy in French pay?

She was eager to say all this to de Vardes, but felt it more politic to try and discover what he thought.

'Do you think the matter so serious?'

'Don't you?'

There was nothing to be got by this method. She shifted her ground a little. 'Is there still time?'

'The money is not yet sent.'

Ralph Montagu had left the salon, was leaving Paris early next morning. She must write at once. She asked leave of Olympe to go into her writing closet, and there wrote to Charles. She sealed it with her own private seal ring and sent it by one of Olympe's servants to Montagu's lodging. A note, sent back by him next day at starting, showed that he had received it safely, and she breathed in relief. At least she had done all she could, and she could not help it if it were not enough.

It was a good deal, but five million livres were more; the sale of Dunkirk was concluded, Louis set his engineer Vauban to fortify it, and people in England began again to say that you never knew where you were with the Stuarts, they were no better than bloody Frenchmen.

Minette found consolation in de Vardes' belief that King Charles' innately sound sense would make amends in time for any mistakes at the beginning. That revealing glimpse into his understanding both of her mind and of her brother's position brought them into much closer intimacy. Here was a man of the world who had shown her his advice was to be trusted; and it was what she often needed. She had never been able to meet Charles at Dunkirk after all this summer; she was seeing less and less of Louis; and to talk with de Vardes after Monsieur was like walking on a firm road after trying to dance over a quicksand.

He was astonishingly bold.

He told her that La Vallière's position in her household was a disgrace to the King, that he had remonstrated with him again and again, but that his royal master feared to risk the displeasure of his womenfolk. 'They daren't attack you,' he said, 'but they would tear that poor goose to pieces.'

It was the first touch of humanity from him on such a subject. 'I thought you despised women who yield to love.'

'That is a lie. (I beg your pardon, Madame.) But it is true I prefer an honest lust to a love that is promoted to its title merely as a reward for long service.'

He advised her to keep in as close touch with her brother as possible, 'for he is not only your natural protector but he is very fond of you – and he is not only that, but he is, in spite of his rather casual way of raising money, a man whom I for one would be proud to serve.'

At which she showed him some of Charles' letters to her, and he discovered a new cause of praise in them, his modesty; for she could not imagine, he declared in a burst of savage impatience, how boring it was to be first gentleman of the bedchamber to God. His restless vitality was like that of some great caged beast; he would prowl sullenly about Olympe's salon, yawn in open exasperation and break out in sudden rage to Minette on the contemptible tedium of life at Court.

If she incautiously chattered of these blasphemies she would ruin him, but he understood her too well even to ask her not to chatter. And he kept her informed of Louis' feelings for her, which were growing in coldness and distrust. This made her very unhappy, and if it had not been for de Vardes she would have thought herself quite friendless. Yet she was more admired than ever, and more for herself, now that the dazzle of her novelty had worn off. The young son of the Duc de la Rochefoucauld had long been desperately in love with her, but only now had her education advanced sufficiently for her to perceive it. They began a charming flirtation. She saw de Vardes' bold stare following her as she danced with the young man, and thought with a spice of pleasure that it was good for the great de Vardes to be a little jealous; he was so Olympian, so secure in his conquests and possessions; she heard that when he chose a woman it never dawned on him there should be any question as to her response.

And then, almost as soon as it had begun, the flirtation was interrupted, the Prince of Marsillac was removed from Court; she saw people whispering together when they looked at her. His father the Duc de la Rochefoucauld was very chilly. Madame's reputation, in fact, was beginning to be that of a delicately dangerous woman, sympathetic on the surface but essentially cold, a breaker of hearts, and, what was more alarming, of careers. Within the last year and that year occupied with the birth of her child, she had caused the withdrawal of at least two promising young men from the Court. Nor had she continued the improvement of Monsieur which had begun before his marriage; he too had been led by her lovely allure into disaster, for he had become more hopelessly perverse and vain than ever.

And now she was openly intimate with that notorious profligate, de Vardes. As for her affair with the King, it was clearly that which had hardened her; for she had made a fool of herself while she was still untried; she had lost him, and to an inferior rival with not a tenth part of her power to charm. This last she knew to be the most serious charge that Olympe and her set would make against her.

It was a relief that that terrible bright standard of personal success, which she had taken to be that of the world at large, was quietly ignored in the salon of Madame de la Fayette. Minette would have liked to see a great deal more of her than she did, but La Fayette did not care about Court life, thought Madame absorbed in it, and did not know that the shy schoolgirl who had been eager for her friendship lived on in the brilliant princess. In her salon Minette was grave and attentive, a little awed by the great minds to which she had the privilege to be listening. In this world de Vardes did not exist. It was

209

the more surprising when Turenne of all people reminded her of him.

They had been playing a game in which someone suggested a subject and each member of the company in turn said a sentence or two on it, as neatly and epigrammatically as could be done impromptu. This evening the subject was Friendship, an emotion that held a high position at the moment. The present speakers compared it with ivy, with rocks, and favourably with love.

'Friendship,' said one, 'is the only unselfish emotion.'

This spark blew Minette's smouldering feelings into a blaze. Was this true – in a world where Olympe and Montalais were friends? It was her turn next, and she had been nervously clasping and unclasping her fingers, choosing her words, when now she broke out in a rather breathless voice—

'The friendships of women are founded on distrust. They are to be commended in that they sharpen the wits more than the friendships of men, which are based on indifference.'

There was a rather shocked surprise in the laughter that applauded her. In what school could so young a princess have learnt such disillusionment? She perceived with horror that the Duc de la Rochefoucauld was to follow her; and he, though apt to be cynical in his epigrams, would not approve of it in her. He said, it seemed in answer, 'The consolation of friendship lies in this, that the opportunities it affords for backbiting are reciprocal.'

Certainly she had better have stuck to the rocks and ivy. She looked across the room at the strange, scarred face of her antagonist, but he would not meet her eyes. She tried to think she was a princess and had been insulted, but she was never very good at finding comfort in indignation.

Turenne had been sitting near La Rochefoucauld and, when the game was finished, walked over to her side. He asked if she had had any news lately of her brother James. She pulled her thoughts together and told him of James' intense interest in shipbuilding, and how hard he was working at the Navy Board.

'He had great industry always,' he replied, and spoke of him warmly as a courageous and intelligent lieutenant. 'He took an interest in everything and made a note of it; always had a notebook in his pocket. He took his work more seriously than many whose only chance of a career lay in the Army. If he carries on as he began he will do well. And yet,' he added, with that blunt simplicity that often made him pursue his thought in forgetfulness of the person to whom he was talking, 'I do not know how it is with the English soldiers, they are so often magnificent in their youth – they are brave, enterprising, enthusiastic, they make better young officers than those of any other nation, up to the rank of captain. But after that they are apt to become rigid, stupid – they are seldom good in higher command.'

Minette found herself rather oddly defending her father's nation with the example of Cromwell. Turenne freely granted the exception, 'but,' said he, 'you must remember that the late Protector was a most unusual man.'

'I hope so,' she answered.

But he did not notice the irony in her tone; he was going on to the next thing he had meant to say to her. It concerned herself, as she could see by the anxious and kindly way his eyes wrinkled up as he looked at her. 'I am a friend to your family,' he said, 'and your kindness as well as my goodwill has made me count myself a friend of yours—' He paused, and then with a smile: 'Friendship was the subject for this evening and I had nothing to say on it, and now again I find myself at sea.'

'You are displeased with me or you would not have begun so kindly,' she said in a light tone to cover his embarrassment; then added sadly, 'and so is the Duc de la Rochefoucauld, for he would not look at me.'

'La Rochefoucauld was not avoiding your eyes. He could not see them at that distance. His sight has given him constant pain and difficulty ever since his wound at the gates of Saint Antoine. He believes he is going blind.'

She had had no notion of that. Few people had, Turenne told her. His life had been singularly unlucky.

Minette was silent, thinking of this last stroke against it of her dealing. Who could have worked up the King's – or was it Monsieur's – jealousy against young Marsillac? It was as though she were attended by unseen dragons, who devoured those who approached her too nearly.

She heard Turenne say slowly, 'You do yourself a grave injustice, Madame, in your friendship with the Comte de Vardes.'

'But I *am* friends with him, sir, so what is the injustice? Unless, as I expect you wish to tell me, people think that we are lovers.'

'Yes,' he said.

'Please look at me. Indeed I do not wish to lie to you.'

'Madame, there is no need for me to do so. I discovered the truth in your face just now when you were looking at the Duc de la Rochefoucauld.'

She did not understand him. But he had known then, as he watched her face when off her guard, that she could not be the mistress of de Vardes, for de Vardes was a man who left his mark.

He said so now in his constrained and rugged fashion. She assured him for his comfort that she and de Vardes were not in the least in love, had even told each other they were not; men and women could be friends nowadays without that, for the world had grown far more free lately. ' "We have changed all that," ' she added, using a remark of Molière's that had at once become a catchword.

'And I have remained very old-fashioned,' he said, smiling. 'But, Madame, let me tell you, so has de Vardes. His ultimate concern with a woman can only be with her body. You will tell me that he is different with yourself, and I believe you, but nobody else does.'

This was a new blow to her, for she had thought herself secure, as de Vardes was a recognized lover of Olympe. She said so, and saw to her annoyance that her ignorance of the world astonished the old soldier she had thought so simple.

She said with a sigh, 'Well, I will be more careful.'

'Madame, if you concern yourself with only that you will know no peace. But think whether you can have no better idea of what a friend should be than what de Vardes can give you. You are unwise to trust him, that is certain. But I would say more than that – what I said just now, that you are unjust to yourself. You are of better worth than that, Madame, and you know it.

He got up and left her as abruptly as he had come. Since she was grown up, no one had spoken to her of her behaviour from any other point of view than that of her reputation. Her mother, it is true, had sometimes mentioned God, the Virgin and her patron saints, but rather as though Minette should be careful to make the best impression in that quarter also. But now, though Turenne had made no such reference, she felt that he had spoken to her of God.

212

CHAPTER TWENTY-EIGHT

Court life had become not so much a fashion for the French nobles as a necessity. It was an extraordinary tribute to Louis' growing personality, which steadily gained in intensity as it narrowed and stiffened, that he could already so impress it on these obstreperous lords. Most of them were older than himself; they had a short time since been ruling over their peasants as absolute monarchs, holding their own little courts in their own castles, hunting over their own countryside, and even making war when they chose as a change of occupation. But now these gentlemen knew that they were nowhere if they were not at Court. They had no occupation but that of waiting upon the King, and no chance of advancement unless they could attract his notice. Intrigue, which had begun to take the place of hunting and civil war, was fast becoming their only outlet for activity.

They did not give up their independence without a struggle, but that took on no such ferocious aspect as the wars of the Fronde or the rebellions of the last reign. It had become marvellously civilized, a genteel, underhand little war, whose battlefields were in the ladies' drawing-rooms and bedrooms, the corridors and ante-rooms of the palace, and one redoubtable attack against the royal power was even launched from the privy. This last was a skirmish of the wicked little Comte de Lauzun, who presumed to be the King's rival when Louis paid court to de Guiche's sister, the Princess of Monaco, in a temporary reversion from La Vallière's tenderness and tears.

Lauzun shut himself into the privy opposite the King's door at the time of Madame de Monaco's appointment; watched through the keyhole till he saw the king come out of his room and put the key on the outside lock, then re-enter, and shut the door behind him. Lauzun hopped out, turned the key in the lock, and took it back with him. Then through the keyhole he saw his faithless lady led to the door by Bontems, who tapped for admission; heard the King's voice telling them to enter; rattle, rattle, rattle went the handle, first on one side of the door, then the other; heard their angry whispers, saw their bent and bothered backs, heard suppressed exclamations from the lady and smothered bursts of royal fury from the other side of the door – for there was the King locked in and the lady locked out, and Lauzun sniggered in the privy as the baffled footsteps went slowly away.

He was gone long before the locksmiths arrived to release the King. But it was too good a story for the little man to keep to himself, and Louis sent him to the Bastille 'for having pleased the ladies.' But Lauzun was satisfied; he had certainly attracted the royal notice; people talked of him, if only of his extreme impudence, and from the moment of his release he began to be one of the coming men at Court.

A more usual method of currying favour was that of La Feuillade, who solemnly declared his wish to be buried at the feet of his royal master as though he were his dog. This did not prevent him from attacking one of Louis' favourite servants, the playwright Molière, by pretending to embrace him and thus contriving to rub the diamond buttons on his cuff across his face, scratching it badly.

The nobles hated this bourgeois writing fellow, whom Louis had appointed guardian of the tapestries in his bedchamber, and even permitted to snatch a hasty supper there when hard pressed for time during rehearsals. Molière helped to fight the King's battles, for he ridiculed the foppish courtiers in his plays until, as he himself coolly pointed out, a marquis was now as essential a butt in a modern comedy as a servant used to be in an old-fashioned one.

The 'Marquises' retaliated when the little Béjart gave birth to Molière's child, by hopefully pointing it out as the fruit of incest. Louis sought to silence them by standing as godfather to the infant, and asked Madame to be godmother. 'For,' said he to Molière, 'we have both already sponsored your plays, and have better reason for pride in that than in our own offspring as yet.' Molière had dedicated *L'Ecole des Femmes* to Madame; and read it to her in manuscript that she might suggest alterations, though he at once combated and refused to touch any particular she mentioned. He looked nervous and worn; he was never free of the Court for one moment, and admitted to his patroness that, sensible as he was of his great good fortune, there were moments when he could sometimes almost wish himself a strolling player again.

'It is terrible to be always on one's best behaviour,' he said.

His marriage had not made him happy. He was forty and worked to death, and she sixteen and a born flirt; so there

214

was not much need to seek any more recondite and hideous reason for calling it an ill-assorted union.

L'Ecole des Femmes had a furious success, but offended many by the passages which mocked at the idea of hell. The religious party at Court was gaining strength as Queen Anne grew older, more doubtful of her health, and more devout. It now gained support from an unexpected quarter; for King Louis got measles and was very ill. His mother frightened him into submission; he promised her to reform his way of living, to be an obedient son to her and the Church from henceforth, if only a forgiving God would see fit to restore him to health. The Church party also made good use of their opportunity.

A poor fanatic who thought himself the Messiah had been arrested with a few followers; and this moment was chosen by the judges to conclude their trial with sentences so horrible that, as Madame exclaimed when she heard them, one would have thought one was living a hundred years ago instead of in this most enlightened and sophisticated age. A woman was to be flogged naked on the scaffold, and Morin, the mad Messiah himself, was to be burnt alive.

She saw Turenne, but he was a heretic, a Protestant, and could have no influence. She saw La Vallière, who declared in a panic that she never, never meddled in politics or 'that sort of thing'. She appealed to de Vardes, and he said the King had a pious fit on, and 'would probably accuse me of being yet another Messiah myself, if I tried to save this one. These fellows like martyrdom; it's what they are out for – let 'em have it.'

She said angrily that it was a tragedy that everyone was not as enlightened as Molière. But de Vardes had set the example of damning Molière's popular successes as second-rate, catch-penny work. He thanked God he was not devout himself, but all the same Molière's play was a piece of bad taste, and his mind essentially commonplace and middle-class. So forcible was the effect of his brief contemptuous words that she nearly cried. For she could not bear to lose faith in Molière – that humorous mouth, those infinitely shrewd, sad, yet burning eyes, that broad comic nose – yes, it was true the nose was plebeian. But what did it matter since he did not care for the subtleties of the courtiers nor try to live up to them? And she realized, when left alone, that it was de Vardes who had disappointed her.

215

Her next move was to try to see Louis himself, but at that moment Louis' life was almost despaired of; and in the meantime the executions were carried out. So that when Minette had her interview with him, it was too late for her purpose. She sat by the great bed and saw his face, red, swollen, almost unrecognizable.

The doctors had warned her she might easily catch the measles a second time. Louis was touched by her visit, she could see, and tried not to feel glad that she need after all mention nothing controversial as its object.

'It was good of you to come,' he said, 'I did not think you would have cared.'

'Why did you think that, Sire?'

He said rather oddly, 'You have travelled a long way away from the little bones of the Holy Innocents.'

'But I thought they were just what you had no mind for.'

'I don't believe I knew my true mind.'

'It is a difficult thing to know,' she said seriously.

So simple and easy was it to talk together for these few minutes as though they had never ceased to be friends, that she began to wonder what had prevented this happening long ago. He told her that when he recovered he would visit his army in Lorraine.

'You will see de Guiche there,' she remarked imprudently.

'Shall I give him any messages from you?' he asked with dry irony, 'or is it unnecessary, since you correspond so frequently?'

A cold feeling crept up her spine, destroying all her newfound comfort. 'How do you know that?'

'A King is apt to hear things.'

A hundred eyes, a hundred tongues, all working against her. Was it worth it to undergo so much doubt and tremor, and all that she might receive letters full of passionate adoration that now embarrassed her to answer?

'What do you want?' she asked, 'I am quite willing to do it. Or why don't you do it? Tell him to stop writing – tell him that I will never write nor receive another letter, because I hate to displease you.'

'You mean that?'

'I do indeed.'

And she laughed in her relief, and exclaimed, 'So that is what it has been all this time! You have been so cold to me, and I could not think what was wrong.'

'Well, but you were so cold to me. I sometimes caught you looking at me as though you positively disliked me.'

And so she had, and why? for all the things she had felt against Louis were just as true now as they had been then, but now they had ceased to matter.

In a short time he was as well and handsome as ever, and, de Vardes told her. 'No sooner is he out of his bed than he is in La Vallière's.' The statement sounded a note of triumph, as if to inform her that hers had been short-lived.

Minette had an odd apprehension that the real battle was being fought behind all these open manoeuvres, and the real motives kept hidden. Who then were the true protagonists? She saw the first gentleman of the bedchamber standing beside his King, inclining his head graciously as he talked, so that he might not tower over him – and wondered if, behind de Vardes' courtly subservience and Louis' friendly confidence in him, there were not something watchful, perhaps suspicious, perhaps even hostile.

La Vallière suffered agonies of shame and remorse over the birth of her first baby. She nearly killed herself by keeping to her post as maid-in-waiting all through Mass and the early pangs of labour. When Minette noticed her state, she hurried her down into the house in the gardens of the Palais Royal which had been prepared for this occasion, and looked after her until the doctor arrived. The closest secrecy was observed. The house, hidden among the trees, could be reached by a private door through the gardens. Colbert, whose attention to his ministerial duties omitted no particular, himself carried the infant away under his cloak to have it baptized under a false name at the church of Saint Denis.

Louis was grateful to his sister-in-law. He had come back from Lorraine well pleased with de Guiche's frankness and simplicity. There had not been a trace of coxcombry in his manner, he had admitted to the King that his love for Madame had grown beyond what he had expected, that he himself would prefer to remain away from Court at present, and had asked leave to go on into Poland, and join in the war against the Russians. He had already covered himself with glory in Flanders, and the King gave him many honours. In a rather reproving tone he now told Minette that de Guiche was a fine fellow, upright and manly.

'And who but yourself has prevented me from showing

appreciation of it?' she retorted – 'and sent him off to fight hairy Muscovites in the snow at the end of nowhere? Did David tell Bathsheba she never really appreciated Uriah?'

This treatment delighted him; their companionship grew steadier and more natural day by day. It was a relationship well fitted to her; for neither her physique nor her temperament were suited to passion. Louise de la Vallière, religious, timid, virtuous in all her thoughts and beliefs, was yet far more 'made for love' than her mistress, whom all agreed and with some reason to call a coquette.

When she now talked with Louis, Minette was uncomfortably conscious of de Vardes' stare. He had told her that he had constituted himself as her watchdog, and she had been pleased at the time; for she was lonely and glad of the sense of guardianship, when there had been nothing particular to guard. But now that she was getting more friendly again with Louis, it was a nuisance. For a man so full of address, she thought de Vardes tiresomely obtuse. Yet she was uneasy; she had begun to feel afraid of him; and now, when she spoke to him of her brother's letters, it was only to ask his help in finding gold sealing-wax for Charles' ladies, or else some pretty little religious pictures for his wife to put in her prayer-book. To which de Vardes replied cryptically that he was too stupid to aid her, but not so stupid as she seemed to think him.

Then one day he brought her the news that de Guiche had been wounded in Poland; three fingers of one hand shot away, and his life saved only by the fact that the bullet, instead of killing him, had shattered the miniature of Madame, which he had carried next to his heart.

'And if it hadn't been that,' said de Vardes, 'it would have been his mother's prayer-book. Consistent fellow. Never misses his chance to be picturesque.'

But Minette did not hear his sarcasms. She was thinking of de Guiche, who had been wounded in a strange country, only that he might stay out of her way and save her trouble; who had done all she asked of him through the King, and never reproach her.

If he had been killed, it would indeed have been for her sake. As it was, he would never again be able to play the lute he loved so much. She remembered those long shapely fingers plucking out the wild tune of a *malaguena* from Spain – 'I shall have that beautiful thing with me until I die,' he said,

218

'and no one can take it from me.' And now she had taken it from him; he would never play it again. Tears filled her eyes; she never noticed them.

'I did not know I was so fond of him,' she said, and even then did not see de Vardes' face. She saw him swing round from her with clenched hand up across his forehead, and felt the nerves at the top of her head shrink as though they had but just missed a blow. He rushed out of the room; she sat stiff and cold, staring after him. If this were jealousy, it had scored a point, for she had quite ceased to think of de Guiche.

Olympe de Soissons was ill, a novelty for her. She refused at first to see Minette; then sent for her, talked in a forced, flippant fashion but never quite looked at her, was brusque, hard, almost as though she were angry with her friend for coming. Presently she sent away her woman, turned her head on the pillow so that Minette could scarcely see her face, and said in a harsh, mumbling voice, 'I am going to tell you something, but you must not be angry, you have a long life in front of you, and you will get over it, but I am going to die.'

'My dear, your voice is too strong for that – and too cross,' Minette added coaxingly, trying to make her laugh. But Olympe was not listening. She had at last turned her great eyes on her; her mouth was open, full and purple like a plum in her white face, which looked flabby in illness, yet still beautiful. A moribund splendour informed her large languid arm, stretched heavily on the silk sheet; she lay as if expecting death to come as a lover. But at this moment all consciousness of her beauty and her dread slid from her; she could think of nothing but what she had not yet said.

'You have been a fool with de Vardes,' she began. 'You have given him the power to ruin you, and now you make him angry. But it is easy to pretend, and it is not too hard to give one's body, even to a man whom one detests. You, who have had a child by your husband, must know that.'

Minette thought she was feverish; but Olympe went on impatiently, 'You do not yet understand. De Vardes has it in his power to betray you to the King – and now you have done your best to make him do so. How could you be so foolish as to show him you still love de Guiche?'

'But in what can he betray me?'

'Oh God, but you are simple! Think of those letters you showed him from your brother, the King of England? Worse still, the letters he sent for you by special messengers. He has traced copies of every one. Think further back — how you urged King Charles against the sale of Dunkirk.'

'I remember,' said Minette slowly, 'it was de Vardes who prompted me to write yet again about it here, in your house. But I did not give him the letter — I sealed it and sent it by one of your servants.'

'Yes, I know what you are thinking.'

Did she? Minette wondered, for she herself did not know. The room seemed to be dissolving round her, the face of her friend disintegrating before her eyes; now indeed the smell of death, of decay and corruption seemed to have penetrated the thick scented atmosphere. And there was Olympe's voice again, complaining, discordant, crumbling their friendship away.

'You are quite right. My servant took your letter to Ralph Montagu, but after he had opened it and traced a copy for de Vardes, and — oh yes, I was useful there — I had had your seal copied. A pretty pack of traitors, aren't we? But I would never betray a real friend — I had only made friends with you in order to use you. De Vardes and I were certain that you would oust La Vallière, and then if we could oust you I would reign again.

'But it has all gone askew, de Vardes has chosen to fall in love with you, and it is I who have been ousted, from him — left nowhere between you all — God, how I have hated you all! but now I am going to die, and I do not care what happens, and I think I would rather de Vardes were destroyed than you. But nothing will ever destroy him — you could stamp that man down into hell, and he would stroll in the next minute beside the seat of God.'

As Minette still did not speak nor move, Olympe began to sob out that she had been taught to betray from the beginning; her own sister had betrayed her, that devil Marie with her airs of superior purity (which only meant that she preferred hatred to any softer vice) had blackened her to Louis; and since then nothing had gone right, and now she was dying, dying, dying, she wailed.

With a restless movement Minette tore her thoughts away from her own problems, that had suddenly become so turgid.

'Don't go, Madame, don't leave me,' Olympe's soft hand

220

caught at Minette's and held it tight. 'I have been false and cruel to you, but I am dying—'

'If you say that again I shall pour a jug of cold water on your head. And I dare say it would be the very thing to cure you,' she added, laughing, and pressed the hand so that she might conquer her longing to snatch hers away.

'You don't hate me then?' said the sick woman. 'And I have done you such harm!'

Seeing that her friend was not going to reproach her, she could now permit herself to do it, but Minette interrupted her.

'You have not done me any real harm. De Vardes is not in love with me, I am certain of it; and you will get him back, and then you will get hold of those stupid letters and destroy them for me. That would be the best way out of it,' she added, forcing herself to think of the hateful business, for whenever she did so some fresh unguarded phrase of hers came into her mind and she pictured Louis reading it. Charles' indignation with Louis for her false position with regard to La Vallière – her own protestations to Charles over Dunkirk, the most serious affair of all – would not matter as much as little jokes on Louis' growing stateliness and love of precision, his heels and periwig getting higher and higher, his manner more godlike; and yet his continued fear whenever his mother put on her pea-hen voice and scolded him.

'Louis must not get those letters,' she said.

'Then you must get de Vardes to give them back to you. I tell you I have no influence. He does not know what love is, only pride. If you jar that he will conquer you, only to humiliate you. Give in to him utterly, oppose him in nothing, and you may get what you want from him.'

'I will see,' said Minette.

CHAPTER TWENTY-NINE

Was it her imagination that Louis had begun to grow cold to her again, stared at her when Charles was mentioned, talked aside with de Vardes more often than before? She remembered the first time she had noticed de Vardes lead him aside, at that ill-omened fête of Vaux when Fouquet, poor hunted squirrel, had climbed his highest before his capture and im-

221

prisonment in a remote dungeon. She remembered the sense of power that de Vardes had then given her, her certainty that whatever he said would deeply impress the King, her wonder if he too were among the hunters whose ruthless pursuit she had divined that evening. And now there was no doubt of it, he was the hunter and she the quarry, but, more humiliating than any pursuit, he kept still as a snake and left her to circle round him. He would grant her a brief interview in an antechamber of Olympe's salon, taking care to do so when everyone should see them retire there, and then talk idly of anything but that one subject on which she stammered, pleading with him, paying her court to him.

His feeling for her, she now began to see, was nothing but a cruel vanity. Lust itself was subordinated to this icy passion. Since the Queen was a nonentity, Madame was the first lady in the land by right not only of birth and position but of charm and character. De Vardes did not much care whether she became his mistress or not, but was determined that before this happened every person in the court should believe she was.

'Oh God, you make me sick,' screamed Olympe in one of those violent revulsions of feeling that had come on her since her recovery, 'why don't you finish off the poor little wretch and have done with it? You and your master – Gorgons and basilisks, that's all you are, turning everything to stone.'

And she found herself longing for the old gay free days when their uncle had been alive and allowed them unlimited pocket-money, and she had not begun to trouble about fascinating that dull boy Louis, but had romped in men's clothes with the queer clever eccentric outrageous runaway Queen of Sweden.

There had been a time when Minette could not sleep for thinking of all the people who liked her and all the charming ways they had of showing it. Now she dared not close her eyes because against her eyelids there would come all the scornful, speculative glances she had noticed during the day. She grew unreasonably grateful for kindness from 'respectable people', and showed it by a mixture of timidity and gush. She lost hold on herself, even on her manners, in which she had been trained from infancy. She was slipping in the mud, de Vardes was dragging her through the mud, she was drowning,

222

drowning, said her senses, as at last she fell asleep, drowned in mud.

Then in the sunlight she would determine to shake off this shameful obsession, smile and talk a great deal with her maids as she dressed, and try not to wonder what they had thought of de Vardes' last peremptory demand, without any warning to her, for admission. She had her hair done very elegantly and wore a new dress with yellow ribbons when she went with the rest of the family to see her sister-in-law, Queen Marie Thérèse, who had been brought to bed too soon of her next baby, a girl, and was dangerously ill. Her mother-in-law thought such appearance most unsuitable in a sick-room which might so soon become a death chamber.

'Does she want me to wear mourning already then?' cried Minette, when Mademoiselle told her of the old Queen's dis-approval.

'There can be moderation in all things,' said her cousin, pursing her lips, and Minette thought that she was referring to a great deal more than the yellow ribbons.

She went back to her room; she sat at her dressing-table; looked at her lack-lustre eyes and the mouth that had begun to grow weak, even flaccid. Through her depression came a sudden sick and giddy sensation that nearly made her fall from her chair. She had felt like this when she had first be-come enceinte with Marie Louise.

At one stroke, de Vardes, her reputation, the goodwill of her husband's family, of her friends, of Louis himself, be-came of secondary importance. She might now have to fight not merely for herself but for an unborn child. She would make one final attempt to get the letters; she would tell de Vardes the truth; and then, if that failed, she would leave matters to take their course. She would be safe at least until her child was born, and by that time anything might happen; she herself might be dead, or it might be a son, and Louis so well pleased (for his own heir was distressingly sickly) that he would forgive her anything. But if her attempt with de Vardes succeeded, she would be so happy and free that she would be certain to have the finest son that any baby could be, 'and I will tell him that,' she thought, still hopeful.

It was not so easy to tell him. She had to force occasions to get a few whispered words with him – 'I cannot talk in these conditions,' she protested. Then he made an appointment with her in the waiting-room at the Convent of Chaillot. It was a convenient place for private conferences; lovers who wished to talk quietly and make appointments would go there on the pretext of calling on one or other of the many fashionable women lodged at the convent. It was therefore the last place where Minette wished to be seen talking to de Vardes; she said so, and he shrugged his shoulders and told her, 'as she chose'. In this new-found strength of hers she smiled at him as she had not been able to do for months, confident, aloof; and said, 'Very well, I will not trouble you or myself any more.'

At once he explained, almost apologized. He would plague her no longer; he saw now there was no hope of her willing love. 'I'm no romantic hero. I tried to hurt you – if you had ever loved you would know why. But I believe you incapable of that passion. I give it up. I'll do what you want. But I can't give you the letters in a salon, nor can you carry them away out of an ante-chamber. Meet me at Chaillot and I'll hand them over to you then.'

She tried to think it was her fancy that he had spoken louder than was necessary when he made the appointment. She asked him not to be late, and he arranged that he should be there early in the afternoon, call on a lady to give a reason for his visit, and meet her casually, as by accident, on the way out through the gardens.

She went at the time appointed, walked slowly through the gardens, walked back again. Wondered if she were early; if he had not been able to get away from his visit; walked back again. Encountered some inquisitive looks from the girls on the scholars' side of the gardens; remembered how she had walked there with her cousin Louise years ago, up and down those grass paths, discussing, arguing, disputing, with nothing in the world to worry them; walked back again. Once they had had a great quarrel all about Charles – why had it mattered so what Louise had thought about Charles? Louise was away at Mauberge and did not care now, and Charles had never cared. She walked back again. 'Never care what people think, never, never care,' she repeated to herself as a nun came towards her, asking if she wished to see one of the pensionnaires, and could she take a message?

'No, oh no,' said Minette, 'I am walking here because I like to remember the old days.' And she walked back again.

But the nun walked with her, talking about her mother, so calm, so gentle, a true saint, talking of Mère Angélique now,

224

alas, dead. She must get rid of the nun before de Vardes came; so she did not walk back again, but into the waiting-room, though this was more public. She must have missed de Vardes, and would find him there. The waiting-room was unusually full. De Vardes was not there; but she thought there was a large proportion of his friends and, as in a nightmare, all those staring faces wore the same look, covert, sneering, satisfied.

She realized slowly that she had walked into a trap. De Vardes had let his friends know that he had made an engagement with Madame which he would not be troubled to keep. Some of them had come to verify this, and were now rewarded for their pains.

She would not snatch at the belated pretext of now asking for one of the pensionnaires. She went out to her coach before them all, and drove back down the long road to Paris.

CHAPTER THIRTY

De Vardes had kept instead a subsequent engagement with an insignificant young girl. He took care that Madame should hear of this.

She also heard that one of Monsieur's latest young men, the Chevalier de Lorraine, had been paying court to a maid of hers; that de Vardes had smiled when he heard it, and said, 'Why so modest? It would be easier to get the mistress than the maid.'

This Chevalier de Lorraine was a carefully dressed young man with an extremely handsome, rather wooden face, straight nose, and hard red mouth. Monsieur declared that he was pure Greek, to which Madame had retorted that she didn't know the Greeks were as pure as that. Monsieur thought this funny enough to repeat to his new pet, who was young, self-conscious, and took himself as seriously as any Puritan. He was furious that a mere woman should presume to make fun of him; he was delighted with de Vardes' remark at Madame's expense; he now took occasion to show insolence to her whenever possible. But she ignored both his insults and de Vardes', and was surprised to find how easy this became. Her condition soon gave her excuse to avoid Court functions; her physicians prescribed her a thorough rest and a diet of asses' milk; and

Charles contributed more than any of these causes to her peace of mind by giving her a present of a barge for her own private use.

It was conveyed up the river to Paris by a Thames waterman called Ben Huskins, and ten underlings who grinned and shuffled their feet and scratched their forelocks, while the pretty little French lady ran all over the barge, exclaiming in rapture at its blue and gold hangings, its velvet cushions, its adorable painted and gilded carvings of mermaids and tritons. She talked to all of them in turn in an English that sounded almost as foreign as the shrill chirpings of her equally pretty little husband.

Charles had tactfully sent Monsieur a present of some excellent English horses at the same time; Monsieur returned thanks in letters elegantly tied up with pink silk, and was delighted when the *Gazette* referred to the barge as a fitting present from the King of the Sea to his fair sister.

This present did more to reconcile the Queens to their daughter and sister-in-law than all Minette's new good behaviour. Marie Thérèse's girl baby had died very soon after its birth; and she was low-spirited, and deeply hurt with Louis. Olympe de Soissons, in her restless, dissatisfied state, had let the Queen know that it was La Vallière who had all this time kept the King unfaithful to her. This softened the two Queens' behaviour to Madame; the younger even made some sort of apology for her ill-founded suspicion of her. And the barge clinched the reconciliation in the happiest way, for Madame was delighted to lend it to them, more and more often as the summer grew hotter and dustier, and the English galley by far the pleasantest way of travelling.

Minette herself never tired of the gliding motion, the swift and dream-like passage of the green shores, the reflection of the sunlit ripples on the silken awning. She would take her sister-in-law for little voyages that had no object but these delights, and the music of violins and singers, that sounded so much more enchanting as it wandered across the water. But they did not suffice Marie Thérèse, who always wanted to play cards with her ladies. Her passion for gambling was profitable to others, for she invariably lost.

'It is sad for her to be so stupid,' thought Minette, looking at the pale dumpling face – there she was living in this wonderful age when the Court had never been so splendid nor people so wise and witty, and she might just as well have lived hundreds of years ago or hereafter – 'she is not here now at all.'

'Here' and 'now' were as acute to Minette as to a prisoner who does not know if he is awaiting sentence of death. Somewhere in the background there was still de Vardes. The insignificant girl, for whom he had broken his appointment with Madame, had found life unbearable because of him, and killed herself. People said de Vardes was really too bad, a shocking scoundrel. But all the more women wished to prove it.

'You are the true judge of this age,' said Madame to Molière, 'can you not pronounce sentence?'

He wrote *Don Juan*. Everyone went to see this masterly study of cruel profligacy, admired it, but also admired the profligate. What a fellow! Nothing could down him. Hell itself could only swallow him alive and still kicking; it could not subdue his spirit. Women gazed at de Vardes, recognizing the prototype, and whispered their delicious terror; men told a hundred new stories of his, disgraceful, delightful. 'De Vardes,' said Madame de Sévigné, 'is the gospel according to the day.'

But Madame for the moment was free of the congregation. She stepped into her blue and gold barge on a broiling June morning, and was rowed up the river with Monsieur to Saint Cloud to spend the day. A party of strangers from England had been permitted to see some of the famous gardens there; Monsieur and Madame happened to meet them, and insisted on doing the honours themselves. Madame showed her favourite fountain which seemed to touch the sky, cooling the air for a wide space round it by its misty exhalation; Monsieur showed the new painted ceiling in his room of Ganymede snatched up to Jove.

The guests were appreciative and witty, they spoke French perfectly, they had travelled everywhere, they even knew the East. Who were they? Some rich and cultered English lords, no doubt, and a quietly adventurous, rather plain lady, who thought nothing of having ridden on a camel and visited a harem. Monsieur had not noticed their names in the excitement of encounter, 'but let us have no names,' he said, 'let this be the creation of a day. I am the Prince Orondate, and this my wife is the Princess Statira, and you are foreign potentates come to visit us, and we will hold our court, like Charlemagne, under the boughs of a great tree.'

So they did, and supper was spread on the lawn, and then

at dusk the whole party went on board the Princess Statira's magic barque. She bade the rowers lay by their oars. They drifted with the stream down to Paris, while the stars came out one by one overhead; and Monsieur spoke of the Loves and Zephyrs who were wafting them from their enchanted shore to the world of living men.

Black against the pale water showed the first bridge of Paris. The plain lady murmured some words in English which Madame asked her to repeat to her.

'The cloud dissolves, the dream is gone,
And Saccharissa turns to Joan.'

'Who wrote that?'

'Nobody. It was not a poet, only a clever young clerk. Here we are at Paris.'

'Here we are,' thought Minette, 'here and now.' She turned to Monsieur, and took his soft fingers in hers under cover of the darkness; she said low to him, 'Thank you for this day, stolen from time.'

He returned the pressure of her hand. He felt that they above all people had mastered the art of living gracefully.

De Guiche had returned from Poland, and the King permitted him to appear at Court as long as he did not enter Madame's presence. But there was nothing to prevent his visiting his new English aunt, the Comtesse de Gramont, until that hardened gallant, the Chevalier, declared he was sick of the sight of his lovesick puppy of a nephew about the place. But never once, since the return of de Guiche, did Madame visit her new friend from England.

It happened that Monsieur persuaded Madame to attend a masked ball at a private house; they went in a hired coach to conceal who they were, and were completely disguised under their strange head-dresses and masks. They entered the hall with other masked guests. Monsieur gave his arm to one of the ladies, and a cloaked cavalier gave his to Madame. She noticed that he had kept on his left-hand glove, and that three of the glove fingers fell limply as though there were nothing inside them. They went up the stairs to the ballroom; she said to herself, 'De Guiche had three fingers shot away,' and then she noticed that her partner was also silent. For de Guiche had recognized the perfume of carnation she used on her hair.

228

'I know you,' he whispered, and she pressed his arm to show that she knew him. They drew back against the curtain by the doorway into the ballroom. Here, in the very thick of the throng, they could talk more unobserved than anywhere. He told her how he had gone every day to the Comtesse de Gramont in hopes of seeing her.

'I know, I know,' she said, in distressed tones, 'but I could not go, I must not meet you – nor stay with you now.'

'Is that only because of the King?'

'Indeed yes. Who else?'

'There is no one you – love? Not de Vardes?'

At mention of his name, though whispered, she turned in terror to make sure that no one could hear, caught her foot in the curtain, and fell down the stairway, or would have done so if he, standing just below her, had not caught her in his arms.

The thing that for more than a year he had not dared to dream of had happened. For an instant that would last his lifetime, with people crowding them, exclaiming, asking if anyone had fainted, his arms encircled her waist, the poor remainder of his hand rested on her breast, and her head lay against his shoulder.

It was over; she was speaking in a squeaky, assumed voice to the busy inquirers, assuring them that she was perfectly well, she had only slipped. She hurried up the stair; he saw she was anxious to enter the ballroom, terrified lest either of them should be recognized. He would give his life to serve her; and the only way he could do so was by going downstairs again and leaving the house.

She heard a strange variety of reports. De Guiche and de Vardes had quarrelled; de Guiche had accused de Vardes of the blackest treachery and challenged him to fight; the duel had been prevented (very fortunately for both, since Louis had made the laws against duelling appallingly severe), and the next thing she heard was that de Guiche and de Vardes were reconciled, they were bosom friends, they were seen everywhere together.

'It will be amusing,' she thought, 'if he succeeds in turning even de Guiche against me.'

Nothing was to be of importance except the birth of her child, which was now close upon her. She lay in bed at Fontainebleau and heard the wind rushing through the great trees of the forest, where once she had ridden all night with Louis. That too was of no importance now.

Her child was born, a boy, the Duc de Valois, as was settled as soon as the sex was known. Monsieur rushed out of the room to write the good news to Charles, to hope that the child would grow up worthy of his friendship, and ask him to bestow it on his son. Louis, who was present the whole time, together with both the Queens (Madame considerately had but an hour's labour), wrote the same day to assure his brother of England of the excellent health of both mother and child. The Queen-mother, who had never quite shaken off her coldness to Minette, was now delighted with her, and told her a hundred times how fine and healthy her boy was, compared with the poor puny Dauphin. The little princess Marie Louise came toddling up to see the new baby, and poked a finger into its tiny fist, her round eyes inquiring gravely as to what strange animal this was.

'Your baby brother,' Minette told her, and kissed her over the top of her infant's head. In the midst of Monsieur's joyful pride, the relief of the King, the Queen-mother, the whole nation, and her own triumphant sense of achievement her love for this first child underwent a strange release. Not in remorse but in playful perversity, she knew that she would always love her the best of her children, because the first words she had spoken of her had been, 'Throw her into the river.' She was growing every day prettier 'and more and more exactly like you,' she had written to Charles, who had protested against such very contrary statements, since he 'had never thought his face was even soe much as intended for a beauty.'

In the midst of her happiness came urgent messages from de Vardes, begging her to grant him an interview as soon as she should be well enough. His business, he said, was a matter of life and death. She wondered whose. Now that her son was safely born and she herself much stronger than had been expected, she could at last let herself discover the truth. Three weeks after the birth she had him admitted.

He advanced into the room with none of his old easy confidence of bearing; there was something strained and harsh in the way his blue eyes met hers, as though he had forced them to the encounter. He began abruptly, 'Madame, I am desperate. If you were to see de Guiche, he would tell you. I hate you both. But that is all changed. You might have died in child-

230

birth – Madame, if that had happened, I should have killed myself.'

She heard a voice say, small and clear, from nowhere, and recognized it as her own, 'Well, and why not?'

He started back in an astonishment no less great than her own.

'You would have liked me to kill myself for you, then?' he demanded.

'For me, no. But there was someone else who killed herself, for you. So that you owe God a life, sir.'

She did not know until she had spoken how deeply she hated him; nor, until he kneeled to her, how much she feared him.

'I will speak no more for myself,' he said, 'I have made myself lothesome to you – I must bear that. But speak to him who is my friend as well as yours, he will tell you the whole matter.'

She looked stupidly at his hand, which was holding out a sealed letter with the superscription of her name towards her.

'That is de Guiche's writing,' she said, 'I have promisèd never to receive another letter from him.'

'Madame, this man has been wounded for your sake, is lonely, desolate, almost distracted that he can never see you. Will you be so careful of your reputation that you will not even glance at these few words from him?'

'Why has he appointed you of all people to plead for him?'

'He knows now that he can trust me, Madame.'

It was simply though proudly spoken. De Vardes had risen and stood at his full height, looking down on her. So had he stood often in the old days when they had talked together in a delightful friendliness, heightened by the sense of contrast between them, she slight and childish in comparison with his overpowering strength, not merely of weight and muscle, but of his easy mastery over the minds of men. And now, as once again she stood looking up into that clear hard gaze, a new weakness beset her; she felt her senses swimming; she saw his face as the face of a beast, devouring, terrible; and within her something leaped in exultation to see it.

She could no longer meet his eyes, while his sought hers as directly as ever. Yet did she begin to feel something treacherous in the very directness of his gaze. Could he not have taught himself such stony defiance of the truth?

'I will not take the letter,' she cried sharply, and wished she had not spoken, for it was the cry of a frightened woman. He dropped the letter and caught at her hands.

'Do not be so afraid of me,' he said in a hurried, low voice, almost a whisper, caressing, tender – she had never heard such a voice from him before. 'Can you not see how I love you, how I have tried to conquer it, drown it in hate, *cannot* hate you? I ask nothing, nothing, but that you will trust me as once you did – it was pleasant, wasn't it, when you were my friend?' The soft torrent flowed on; she scarcely knew what he said, but the sound of his voice soothed her, drugged her; he kissed her fingers one by one, speaking all the time as he did so, foolish tender nothings as one speaks to a child.

And sliding to his knees once again, he pressed his head against her body, and his arms enclosed her. She stood locked in his grasp, looking down at the bent, leonine head. She could not move nor speak; all thought had ebbed from her. Her gaze slid from his head to his crouched back, the great shoulders, the gold embroidered skirts of his black coat, the low red heels of his shoes, now uppermost. Close beside them lay a square white patch of paper. As though she did not know what it was, her drowning sense now riveted itself on that, a white stain on the smooth floor, a spot, a tarnish.

'That,' she forced herself to recognize, 'is de Guiche's letter.'

If he had come on behalf of de Guiche, he was now a traitor to him. If he had come on his own behalf, why had he brought the letter? At last her voice struggled through her returning confusion of thoughts, so weak it could scarcely be heard.

'You will go now,' it said, 'and take that letter.'

It seemed as though a convulsion had seized his body; he shook violently and his hands clutched at her skirts. He cried out against her cruelty of unbelief, he swore by Christ's dying breath that he meant truly by her; he flung himself on the floor and kissed her foot and tried to place it on his head.

And in this paroxysm of abasements there was nothing that struck her as ridiculous, only as terrifying in its uncontrollable force. In a panic now herself, she began to call out for her maids, to cry that de Vardes had gone mad, as indeed she thought he had; but, before her strength had recovered to call loud enough for them to hear, there came the sound of men's footsteps down the corridor; two gentlemen appeared in the doorway, stood aside, and announced the King.

CHAPTER THIRTY-ONE

De Vardes had got up from the floor in time; so much she noticed, almost in surprise, for he had seemed too utterly lost to control to obey his senses. Nor did he commit any such trivial errors as a furtive brushing of the knees. He stood there with his wig awry, glaring before him; then, as the King appeared, he bowed very low, and must have pulled at the long curls in doing so, for it was straight when once again he stood erect. He followed the two gentlemen out of the room, and then Minette saw the letter still lying on the floor, between her and Louis.

She watched Louis stoop and pick it up, turn it over, and examine the superscription. A curious smile grew upon his face; deliberately, without turning to her for leave, he opened it, glanced at the contents, and then, for the first time since his entrance looked full at her.

'You had not opened this letter,' he said in statement, not in question.

'As you can see, Sire. There was no need for you to do so.'

'Oh, but I had seen it before.'

He was evidently waiting in some amusement for her expressions of astonishment. But she was too much stunned already to feel anything sharply. She put her hand before her eyes as a sort of protection; if Louis looked at her too closely, he would surely see everything that had happened in the last half-hour.

'I don't understand,' she said wearily, and suddenly the room turned black and misty, and she would have fallen had she not caught at a table. Through the icy obscurity she saw his alarmed face as he rushed forward. He caught her in his arms and half lifted her on to the couch. She felt his kindness and his concern, knew instinctively that she had been in great danger and was now safe. The relief was too much for her; perhaps indeed she was glad to let it be too much, to have the excuse to break down and sob out the agony of fear and bewilderment that she had suffered under such rigid self-control for more than a year.

'And even now I cannot make it out; but it does not matter, for you are not angry with me, Louis, tell me you are not

233

angry.' But he had begun to tell her, and would not interrupt himself, how de Vardes had already shown him that letter and must have sealed it up again and taken it to her merely that she might walk into the trap. Now de Vardes was himself caught in it. Louis had suspected him, and set his servants to discover when he should contrive an interview with her; it was not accident that he had paid his call at this time.

A guilty shudder ran through her. Her heart and mind felt nothing but loathing, but her flesh had played the traitress to them, and de Vardes had known it. Even now, with Louis' arm still supporting her shoulders, she could recall the exquisite suspense of that first instant when de Vardes' arms had imprisoned her.

'He is a devil,' she cried. 'He has made de Guiche believe in him, he can do it with anyone. No one can stand out against him.'

And then she suddenly remembered the worst reason for her fears. Had de Vardes ever shown him any of her letters?

'Yes,' he replied.

It was alarmingly non-committal. But he had not withdrawn his arm. She said, 'Was there ever such a fool as I, and I thought myself so clever, and all I can have done is to stir up trouble between you and my brother.'

'Console yourself. We are not yet at war.'

She stole a look at him and dared to laugh. 'A pretty ambassador!' she exclaimed.

'A very pretty one, my sister.'

It was a compliment, a caress, and a warning. Louis had changed since the headstrong days when he had wooed her in the forest; and she, as the mother of his brother's children, had also changed. Not again would he allow himself to forget that she was his sister. The fact gave her a security in his affection such as she had never before known. She marvelled at the power of de Vardes to give the lie to this – 'he made me believe you hated and distrusted me.'

'We were both his dupes, so do not call yourself a fool too loudly. He showed you to me as a dangerous intriguer, but I did not after all see any such very treasonable signs of this in your letters.'

'There was Dunkirk,' she breathed faintly.

'What of Dunkirk?'

'Well—' she hesitated, wishing she had not spoken. Perhaps after all he had not seen her letter about Dunkirk.

234

But he went on – 'Oh that! Yes, but I had always known your fiery patriotism about Dunkirk. It has made no difference – since I have got it.'

Confronted with Louis' dry, matter-of-fact mind, she began to feel that she had all this time been fighting a chimera in the dark. How much had de Vardes' terrorism depended on his power to impress himself on the imagination of his victims? 'Do not think about him any more,' said Louis. 'You can leave him to me.'

Louis was as good as his word, and committed de Vardes to the Bastille. He did not realize that the prisoner's peculiar qualities could defy lock and key as boldly as Don Juan's soared triumphant over hell. His furious energy found a real prison a relief from the perpetual concealed imprisonment of his most natural forces; in so conspicuous a position he was even more dangerous than when at large. With as many visitors as he wished, he held a small court in the Bastille; was very funny about the new criminal offence of 'having pleased the ladies'; and built up the account of his last interview with Madame, and the King's interruption, until some were shocked by his details, and some even suspected him to be lying; but none could doubt that it made a good story. So buoyant a rascal was better fun than any hero. He was the most popular man at Court, while de Guiche, once admired with such romantic fervour, had quite dropped out after his campaigns abroad. Nobody could be bothered to remember the outlandish names of the places he had fought in – and then his hand! It was all very well to be wounded, but merciful Heaven! the man had been so tactless as to return a monster.

The King, who grew every year less in touch with public opinion, was not aware that de Vardes' punishment had but published his calumnies. It was pointed out to him, and not only by Madame; but he had signified his displeasure with de Vardes, and that should be enough to crush him. He offered indeed to commit him to a dungeon, and at that Madame protested and pleaded for him. He could not be troubled with such subtleties.

She asked Charles if he could find any way of dropping his brother-in-law a tactful hint. 'The matter is so serious,' she wrote, 'that I fear I shall feel the effects of it all my life.'

Her pen hovered over the conventional cocks and peonies that a Chinese workman had painted so cunningly in dark red and pale green on the tiny writing-desk. Another princess of her race, daughter to the first of the Stuart kings (he too had been murdered by his subjects), had come to this country to be married to a French prince, and had died of a scandal. Little was known of that unlucky bride of the eleventh Louis; she had kissed the mouth of an ugly poet as he lay asleep in a garden, because it had uttered the fairest things in France. Was that her scandal? Minette wished that her own were of such feathery quality – but indeed she did not know much better what hers was; it grew in the dark, a fungoid monstrosity, of which she could only catch an occasional glimpse when reflected obscurely in the faces of others.

Charles answered her in high indignation, though he reflected comfortably that he would 'have by this a better opinion of my devotion, for I am of those bigotts who thinke that malice is a much greater sinn than a poore frailety of nature.' His letter to Louis was firm, but carefully genial; it had a momentary effect (Louis said he would act, but had not yet thought how) which might or might not have lasted, had not de Vardes overreached himself through his erratic and now hysterical agent, Olympe de Soissons. Before the time was ripe, she accused Madame of plotting to get Dunkirk for herself with the help of de Guiche, who had raised a regiment for the purpose. This fantastic lie, projected but not directed by de Vardes, was at once exposed. The King was furious, dismissed Olympe de Soissons from the Court and banished de Vardes to the desolate little town of Aigues Morte, where all his future plotting would have to be conducted among the blistered rocks and dusty fields of Provence.

And now, however long might last the effects of what he had done against her, long, long after she was dead, Minette knew herself safe from him for the rest of her life. The removal of her need for energy and control made her feel strangely tired. Her enemies were crushed, and she would go soon to Saint Cloud.

'I shall rest then,' she said to herself, and thought of her favourite seat at the foot of the cascade, as she looked out of her chair at the sunlight lying like a dusty veil across the courtyard of the Palais Royal. A solitary figure in the livery of one of La Vallière's footmen was standing there, his shadow making a dark stain across the whiteness. It was somehow familiar to her; then, as he walked over to her, she caught at the window-ledge of the chair and leaned forward.

236

'Shall I never be at rest?' she thought as she recognized de Guiche, and then saw how ill he looked.

In a long talk with the Maréchal de Gramont, the old man had told her frankly that his son was safer anywhere but where she was, and that though de Guiche was then ill of a fever, he was anxious for him to leave Paris as soon as possible for Holland, to join in the Dutch naval campaign against the English.

The disguised man had reached her; he explained that he had a message from his mistress, and the footmen put down her chair, standing a little aside. He opened the door. 'I had to see you once again,' he said, and his voice was so low and weak that she could scarcely hear it.

'You are ill, my friend,' she whispered.

'Yes, I have been ill. Madame—' his speech failed, his eyes seemed to cling to hers, clouded, bewildered; then suddenly his head fell forward, and he was lying at her feet in a dead faint. She sprang out of her chair, ordered her footmen to carry him into the shade ('the poor fellow has fainted from standing too long in the hot sun'), and bathed water herself on his head and hands. He opened his eyes on her, and they looked at each other.

She ordered a chair for him, to be driven to whatever address his ingenuity could muster. She herself had to go on to the Louvre. She left him with a pressure of her hand, 'to make sure that the pulse is now steady', got into her chair again, drove away.

That too was over. De Vardes had gone, de Guiche was going. She would not see either of them again. She was not yet quite twenty-one, but she knew that in parting from both these men she had said goodbye to love both as lust and as romance. She had suffered too much agony of spirit ever to wish to encounter such manifestations of it again. The love that she was safe and free to enjoy was that of the two men who, as she now realized, counted more to her than any lovers could do. 'Charles first and then Louis,' she said to herself as she went into the Louvre.

BOOK IV

SUNSET GLORY

CHAPTER THIRTY-TWO

Since all people of birth now went to Court, there was not enough room for them even in the rapidly expanding palaces. That would be remedied, said Louis, when Versailles was finished. His plans for it grew more grandiose every year. Peasants workd unpaid on the building of roads and the digging of lakes. Thirty thousand soldiers dug a canal to make all the fountains play at once. But it did not work; bigger schemes had to be tried. Thirty-six thousand men together hammered and knocked and tinkered and drummed at the palace.

Louis' dream of his father's peaceful haven, lying forgotten in the woods, had suffered a strange metamorphosis. The little house had swollen into a noisy monster; a bloodsucker at that. The marshland round it was unhealthy; so many workmen died in the draining of it that their corpses had to be carried away in carts. The cost of human life was as high as in a war. But it was plebeian life, and therefore nameless; there were no sudden deaths of the great to astound the country with a sense of its loss. So the deaths continued; and the draining; and the planting of hundreds of thousands of full-grown forest trees, which like the workmen were always dying and having to be replaced; and the continual expansion of the buildings, or alterations of those already expanded, so that the making of this palace was like one of those Gargantuan impossible tasks that the giants in the fairy-tales delight to set the heroes. Already it was the largest and finest in the world; and when it was finished ('*When* it is finished! – we shall all be dead before then,' said Madame flippantly, but she was right only in part) then there would be rooms in it for all the courtiers, and all their servants, instead of their lodging hugger-mugger in the village, as they always had to do at Saint Germain.

In the meantime this silken world of eager, adulatory faces

239

and supple backs had to be kept convinced that theirs was the most splendid life that anyone could lead in the modern world. Building, and dancing in ballets, were not King Louis' only methods of impressing himself on his public. He wanted war, and to make as fine a show in it as ever he did on the stage. So said his detractors, while his admirers, and they were the vast majority, talked of La Gloire and La Patrie. These words represented a new idea. Louvois, the new young Minister of War, had a red bloated face, looked gross and stupid, but noticed everything. He had seen Cromwell's Ironsides march to their victory at the Dunes, singing their stern hymns above the thunder of the guns, and noted that enthusiasm was a useful thing in warfare. Instead of religion he fostered patriotism, and the image, not of God, but of the young King, a splendid horseman, a born fighter, for whom any soldier would gladly die when led by him to war.

This idea helped him and Turenne to transform the French army. Hastily mustered regiments, three thousand strong, ragged, ill-disciplined, snatching what food they could from the countryside, were split into battalions and squadrons, to be fed by a commissariat staff from the base. Even the weapons were condensed; the new bayonets, hunting-knives from Bayonne, were stuck into the muskets so that there was no more need for separate pikemen, and the infantry could now fight in line. Inspired by Turenne and helped by Colonel Martinet, whose name was a byword for the precision of his drill, Louvois' army made so magnificent a show at the autumn manoeuvres (another of his innovations) that Louis swore he must lead it into war himself. It clamoured to be used, would be wasted, rusted, discontented if it were not used.

There was a naval war between England and Holland; but that was no good. Louis wanted to show off his army, not his navy, and was, moreover, allied to Holland. He had done his best to restore peace, and sent a pompous procession of special ambassadors to England; but as Charles remarked to Courtin, the chief of them:

'My fleet has already set sail, my people are in a rage; what more is to be said?'

No more, clearly, since it was supper-time; but Courtin contrived to find so much to say that Charles, catching sight of Lord Jermyn in the passage, called out to him, 'Do come here; here is a little man I can neither convince nor silence,' and so made his escape from the astonished ambassador.

240

The Dutch and English war once again put off Minette's constant hopes of a visit to Charles; and now for nearly two years letters between them had practically to cease. De Guiche's restless pursuit of adventure had led him on to a Dutch man-of-war, where he fought like a lion until she was blown up, and then only saved himself by swimming ashore. After this he surprisingly returned to his wife; and his only matrimonial infidelity now took the form of long letters with a platonic lady friend.

The naval war gave Minette far more anxiety on account of James than de Guiche. She had some terrifying moments for his safety, for he insisted on staying on deck through the hottest engagements: and once his ship also was blown up, which caused a false report of his death.

He had good sense too as well as courage. He fitted out an expedition to take New Amsterdam, on the American coast, thinking it of importance to trade. 'It did belong to England heretofore,' Charles wrote to Minette, 'but the Dutch by degrees drove our people out of it and built a very good towne, but we have got the better of it and 'tis now called New Yorke.'

The name was in James' honour. Yet it was curious how little honour he won on the whole. His successes never got the publicity they deserved, while his defeats were made unduly prominent. This was no doubt largely due to his wife's religion; for she had been a Catholic for some years, and it was rumoured that he was studying that doctrine under a tutor with his accustomed thoroughness.

Louis heard of this with approval. He was beginning to show signs of resemblance to his mother's family; the heavy Austrian lip had thickened; he was more rigid, more exacting. He was sometimes vaguely aware of this when Minette made him laugh unexpectedly, as she was still often able to do. It would strike him then that he was quite a young man, still in the twenties, and that he would like a change.

This need for change, for a new excitement, was in the air. The wars of the Fronde were long forgotten; the country had settled down; people had grown accustomed to Louis' fêtes and theatrical shows, each more marvellous than the other; they had become monotonous. This new restlessness rubbed against Louis' slowly maturing plans for the conquest of Spain through the Netherlands, and caught fire.

France's long war with Spain had helped Louvois to encourage her modern sense of nationality. It had become right and natural to be at war with Spain. Only a year after the Peace of the Pyrénées and Louis' wedding with the Spanish Infanta, the French and Spanish ambassadors and their retinues had an actual battle in the streets of London, because neither of their coaches would yield precedence to the other. It was good fun for the Cockney citizens, who rushed to their shop doors to cheer and back the respective foreigners; also for all the young men about King Louis, who had been deprived of their sport and country life, but had nearly all been trained for a couple of years in the ranks of a crack regiment, and welcomed any chance of war. But it was not good fun for King Philip IV of Spain, who was old, ill and weary; had thought that he had brought peace with his daughter's marriage to Louis, and now had his new young son-in-law thundering threats of war at him, unless he gave full apologies and reparations. He gave them; 'anything for a quiet life,' he said in some stately Spanish idiom.

But he did not have it long.

The man that Velasquez loved to paint among his monstrous dwarfs, as if in barbaric parody of his kingship, the man with the heavy inert face, the eyes of a hound, and the chin like a shoe-horn – dignified, helpless, tragic – was dying, slowly, as they did everything in Spain. He would leave a sickly backward baby called Charles as his heir. He did not expect that his son-in-law would help to protect his son's rights; or that his daughter, Marie Thérèse, would show any more emotion over them than she had over her husband's insult to her father. Family relationships were so much automata to her; she had always asked the Court Chamberlain for permission to embrace her father. There was something wrong with the Spanish royal family; it seemed to be moribund; perhaps Spain was too. The defeat of the Armada in the last century, of Rocroi in this, had broken her power on sea and land. Her glory was leaving her piecemeal. And with his face turned threatingly towards her, this new young sun of France was now in the ascendant.

King Philip died. His sister, Anne of Austria, Dowager Queen of France, whom he had seen at last after so many years at that wedding at Saint Jean de Luz, also died. Louis, who had been really fond of his mother, was overcome with grief. But it was an advantage that with her death departed

242

many of the old standards of behaviour, which had still lingered on in protest against the modern youth.

And with the death of King Philip, Spain went to the baby son of his second wife. Marie Thérèse was the child of his former marriage; and Louis considered, on the advice of his lawyers, that he could make a claim to Brabant through his wife. He did not think it necessary to make any declaration of war on Spain; he merely went north in the summer with Turenne, the marshal-general of France, and an army of eighty thousand men, to secure his wife's territory.

So that Madame de Sévigné, returning to Paris after a prolonged visit to her country estates, complained that there was not a young man to be seen anywhere in the streets; they had all gone off, all the courtiers, all the officers of the royal household, to follow the King to war. The women followed the men. Venus would accompany Mars, and the King lead his Queen through his new domain that he had conquered in her name. Enormous gilded coaches or rather wagons, containing the Queen and her ladies, went trundling along the road to Flanders, in the wake of that endless procession of warriors in waving plumes and burnished breastplates, whose chargers had already gone lumbering down those atrociously bad, long flat roads between the poplars. This was an army greater than any seen in Europe since the crusades; a heroic display of banners, feathers, embroidery and cloth of gold, painted chariots and mule carriages, as superbly harnessed as if they were taking part in a procession of the gods from high Olympus.

Flanders seemed too much astonished by it to make much resistance. There was a solid seige at Lille for about five weeks, when Louis had an opportunity to show his courage in the trenches; and Turenne a hard task to let him do so without much danger. But for the most part the army marched solemnly up to towns that at once surrendered; and impressed the simple Flemish inhabitants, not so much by the force of arms, as by the show of fireworks, and the masked or full-dress ball which the King gave in every conquered town. The principal ladies in the palace attended it; were invited to the King's table, where dinner was served as ceremoniously as at Versailles; and there presented with gifts of jewellery by His Majesty, whose gallantry frightened them worse than the sound of the guns had done. The conquest of the town thus completed, the King passed on to the next.

Splendid pictures were painted by Flemish artists of Louis,

six feet high at least, caracoling before the armies on a white horse, pointing a marshal's baton in the vague direction of a stormy sky and a distant group of tiny men, very busy about nothing. A more accurate representation would have shown the engineer Vauban fortifying Mons and Lille and Armentières and all the captured towns that would give France an impregnable frontier; while Louis sat inside one of the coaches, as large as a small room, where the ladies were joking together over their picnic lunch, in fits of laughter at Madame de Montespan's mimicry of the manners of the Flemish burghers' wives.

La Vallière had given birth to her second child, and stayed behind at Versailles. Just before he left her there, the King had created her a duchess. He would not have dared to do so while his mother was alive; it was a sign that the new age had come into its full power. But it was not a good sign for La Vallière, whose charm was in her modesty, in her desire for secrecy, in all that Louis had found so different from the rest of the Court. How could she keep her hold on him when thrust into open competition with what she most dreaded?

To Minette it was a sign that La Vallière had already lost her hold. She suspected Louis of an inclination to regularize his conquests of the heart as well as of his territory. His amours would not proceed with as orderly a precision as his regiments; when he reached the point of acknowledging his mistress and her children by him, of presenting her with a duchy, it would show that he was ready to march on to the next. It did.

The black-eyed, laughing Mademoiselle de Mortemart, whom the King had once discussed unfavourably with his sister-in-law as they glided down the river on a summer evening long ago, had since married the Marquis de Montespan. He was a grave, austere man; and 'I see,' observed Charles in comment on her, 'that wives doe not like devoute husbands.' A picture had been painted of her as Charity, with babies sprawling round her and suckling her breast; her beauty was rich as a ripe harvest. There was none of this benevolent abundance to be found in her expression; for all its voluptuous curves, her mouth was hard, and her brilliant eyes were calculating. She had determinedly made friends with La Vallière, with no other purpose, it was said, than to get the King from her. She was a creature of such forcible life that nothing could tire or frighten her; and unlike La Vallière, she was of one of the best families of France. Minette had watched her dance a *pas de deux* with Louis in the last ballet and thought, 'She will be the next, and back goes La Vallière into the wings, poor tousled angel.' Nor did she feel altogether easy on her own account.

When Montespan went to war with the rest of the Queen's ladies, rumours floated back to La Vallière of her popularity; then she heard that the King was working so hard at his plans for the campaign that the Queen was worried about his health, for he would often not come to bed with her until four in the morning; then, that the King invariably worked in the lodgings of Madame de Montausier, a most virtuous elderly lady left over from the last reign. She was in charge of the Queen's ladies, and her lodgings on this journey were always shared by Madame de Montespan.

This last report had an astonishing result. The wounded dove turned bold as an eagle, and flew to its aggressors.

The Queen and her ladies were making ready for their journey to meet the King at Amiens, when the news came that La Vallière was joining them. Mademoiselle met her in the Queen's antechamber, looking half dead with fatigue. 'Such a journey!' she kept repeating to the tall princess as she tried to avoid her stare, 'I did not get a wink of sleep all night.'

But that did not explain the anguish in her eyes. Mademoiselle passed on into the Queen's room. Marie Thérèse was crying, and excused herself by saying she was ill. Madame de Montausier, in her great indignation, was saying, 'You see how it is. Just look at the state Her Majesty is in!'

'I will not see her!' sobbed the Queen. 'How can she force herself on me like this!'

Madame de Montausier and the Princess de Bade proceeded to cover her with condolences. Madame de Montespan swept through the room in waves of wine-dark silk; her fresh vigour, her dazzling health, her evident enjoyment transformed the lachrymose scene into high comedy. 'Heaven defend me,' she cried, interrupting the comforters, 'from being mistress to the King! But if such a misfortune befell me I should certainly never have the incredible effrontery to present myself before the Queen!' And she assured her Majesty that it was certain the King had not ordered La Vallière to come.

'How should you be so certain?' inquired the Queen sulkily.

By Her Majesty's orders, the steward gave La Vallière none of the dishes to hand to the Queen at dinner that evening. All the other ladies served the Queen, while the new duchess, who now had the right of precedence above them all, was left standing against the wall, looking as though she were crucified to it. It was an occasion for many smiles and glances; and, as soon as there was a release from ceremony, for a furious outburst of discussion. In the Queen's coach nothing else was talked of for the whole journey, while they jogged and jolted and bumped up and down, some of them feeling quite sick from the uneasy motion. They rested the night at Guise. The Queen gave orders to the officers of her escort that no one was to start in the morning before her, as she wished to be the first to reach the King and tell him what had happened.

In the morning as she got into her coach, she saw a cloud of dust blown across the plain, and before it a chariot driving at top speed. It was the carriage of La Vallière, who had seen the army from the top of a little hill, and before that vast audience had driven headlong towards Louis. The Queen was hysterical with fury; she screamed orders to her coachman to race after her and intercept her. The Queen's coach was actually seen by all to pursue that of the royal mistress, until her ladies made it evident even to Marie Thérèse that she could not catch her up, and that it was better not to try.

Madame de Montespan, her impudent nose cocked in an amusement that she made no great effort to conceal, declared that the King, who set so high a store by correct behaviour, would only be disgusted by the boldness of La Vallière. To which the Queen, staring with red puffy eyes out of her pale face at the sumptuous beauty of her lady-in-waiting, replied unexpectantly in an aggrieved tone, 'I'm aware of more than you may suppose. I have both sense and penetration, and am the dupe of no one, though no doubt it is thought otherwise.'

A painful silence followed. Mademoiselle had not once spoken; she stared out of the coach windows at the solitary chariot that careered across the fields towards the army, and imagined the groups of soldiers watching it, their jeers, their coarse laughter. 'Heaven, what follies women will commit for love!' she said to herself; yet on her silent exclamation there followed a strange uneasiness, as though, involuntarily, she had challenged that strange and inscrutable power.

An image rose in her mind of the terrible little Comte de Lauzun, whom the King had just appointed Colonel-General of his Dragoons, in recognition of his great courage and ability at the seige of Lille. As small as Monsieur, but with an air not so much of majesty as of volcanic power, he seemed made to do

246

extraordinary things and to do them without thought or effort; as though what to others would be heroic, extravagant or absurd, in him were merely natural. 'There now would be a man worth loving,' she thought, dismissing her royal cousin with a contemptuous flick of her mind. And her thoughts as well as her words fell into a brooding silence.

Only a thin wreath of dust now clung above the plain. La Vallière's horses, sweating from their gallop, had reached the King's tent. Vallière, in dumb agony, had flung herself at the King's feet.

From that time on, her subjection was complete. Montespan was determinedly friendly; shared lodgings with her; made use of her in the most amiable fashion, even induced her, when separated from her servants, to do her hair for her; and laughed with the King, while La Vallière wept.

Madame did not follow the army. She had been ill more or less ever since the death of her son; and then she had a miscarriage which very nearly killed her.

A contemporary writer remarked that princes were particularly unlucky in their doctors, that if the Duc de Valois had been the son of a simple bourgeois, instead of Monsieur and Madame, he might not have died before he reached his third birthday. It was a terrible blow to the whole family, for the Dauphin, Louis Toussaint, was still the King's only son, very delicate and not very interesting; whereas the Duc de Valois was a remarkably intelligent and handsome little boy.

For nearly three years Minette had been engrossingly happy in him, troubled only by her intense anxiety lest Monsieur should spoil him by telling him so often how fine he looked and how important he was. And then, in a few days, all happiness and all anxiety were dead.

His governess, Madame de Saint Chaumont, an aunt of de Guiche, had nursed him devotedly; and for some time she was the only person that Minette could bear to have near her.

But there might be one good result of the tragedy. Monsieur's short but stormy grief at the loss of his heir had thrown him under the influence of his Grand Almoner, Cosnac, the sturdy and indefatigably hopeful Bishop of Valence. He believed that he could make a man of his master; while people were still laughing at the notion, the war gave unexpected aid to the Bishop.

Adroitly flattering Monsieur by reminders that he had never

yet had a chance to prove his military ability and courage to be as high as his brother's, Cosnac almost literally pushed him into the battle-line. Monsieur was easily excited, but as easily bored. At one moment he thought he would like to be a hero, at another he was distressed to see his hands were dirty. The sun was ruining his complexion, and there were not enough mirrors in his tent. He had just been induced to enter the trenches when he noticed how muddy they were, and remembered that he had not made his confession.

'That will be all right,' said the Bishop, and briskly absolved him without waiting to hear it.

Ugly, plebeian-looking, ambitious, but so hot-tempered and outspoken that he spoilt his chances of advancement again and again; loyal, affectionate and furiously energetic; Cosnac was the most unlikely person in the world to attach himself to Monsieur. It was probable that he did so because his heart was already attached to Madame. It was he who said of her dancing that even her toes showed wit. And once when he had flung away from Monsieur in a rage, swearing to leave his service, he had said to her, 'For God's sake, Madame, let me go out honestly by the door instead of waiting to be kicked out of the window.'

But she had begged him to stay, and he had stayed, very fortunately for her. A pamphlet had been printed on her in Holland which purported to give the true story of her love-affairs, particularly of that with de Guiche. It was not as libellous as might have been expected; its chief accusation was of coquetry and the desire to please. But it would undoubtedly give Monsieur a bad excuse to tease and annoy her; and it was for this reason that the King showed it to her when his attention had been called to it.

'Do not let my brother see this,' he said as he put the book into her hands, and did not explain that the contents were after all fairly harmless, until she had nearly fainted at the sight of the title, *Les Amours du Palais Royal.*

She showed it to the Bishop of Valence, and asked what he thought could be done. Cosnac did not answer her; he stood with his legs rather wide apart, turning over the pages, and chewing at his lip in an angry, impatient way; then he abruptly left her without remark, without even handing back the book.

She did not see him again until a few weeks later, when he entered her presence looking rather wider than usual, flung out his arms, and let a small shower of books fall from the folds of his cloak to the ground.

'There,' he said, 'that is the last of them. Take them and burn them yourself so that you can have the satisfaction of saying as you do so, "This is the last but five, last but four, but three, but two, but one," and then, "*This* is the last of all." '

He had bought up the whole edition of 1800 copies and prohibited any further publication in Holland. She rushed to him and caught his hands.

'Oh!' she cried, 'if I could but pull the hat down on your head at this moment!'

For Cosnac's great desire, frankly expressed, was to win a Cardinal's hat before he died.

The man who could make Monsieur take up arms certainly deserved the highest distinction. And presently his hopes were actually justified. When Monsieur was interested, he showed understanding and flashes of real ability. His courage was unquestioned. He remained in the trenches under fire; Cosnac stayed at his side, and was careful to provide the *Court Gazette* with picturesque details of his master's heroism and military genius. Monsieur read the reports, was enchanted, and when the King promised him that he should command an expedition to Catalonia, he assured Cosnac that he would now show himself equal to his grandfather, Henry of Navarre.

Then one day the Chevalier de Lorraine rode into the camp. He sat erect on his charger, and the sun blazed on his helmet, in which he had had the tact to place three black plumes as background to the chiselled marble of his profile.

Monsieur rushed towards him with cries of joy.

'How delicious to see you in armour! You might be Achilles himself. You shall be Achilles, and I will be your Patroclus. You shall command the troops and I shall watch you reviewing them. My dear, you must be tired to death in this heat. Come into my tent and cool yourself. Have you brought the mirrors? I have only two.' And then, as Lorraine dismounted, he exclaimed in a low voice, 'How extraordinary to see anyone so beautiful after the Bishop of Valence! There he is. What do you think of him?'

'*What*? *That*?' replied Lorraine in his bored tones. 'I took him for a fishmonger.'

And the two young men, Monsieur giggling excitedly, while Lorraine condescended to a brief, contemptuous smile, brushed past Cosnac and entered Monsieur's tent.

After that, military operations for Monsieur consisted of his admiring Lorraine at the head of his troops three times a day. 'We will go into battle side by side,' he said, and they went. A bullet grazed Lorraine's arm, and Monsieur, who had been as cool as his brother on his own account, swooned at the sight of blood on his hero's sleeve.

'It might have been your heart,' he said, 'a few inches more to the side, and higher up, and it would have been your heart!'

After that he lost all taste for warfare. The Chevalier must be removed to safety, and he would never be separated from him again. He told Cosnac that this was the one true love of his life; that he intended to share everything in future with the Chevalier de Lorraine, to give him the best rooms in the Palais Royal, and to have no secrets from him.

Cosnac told him his opinion of the one true love in gross and ugly expressions which shocked his master, who complained of his Grand Almoner's lack of delicacy, and dismissed him from his service. The King sent for Cosnac, who boldly explained his position, and met with very gracious treatment. As the Bishop left the royal presence he observed to one of the nobles in attendance, 'That is a great man. He has made me more than ever disgusted with the jack-a-dandy it has been my bad luck to serve.'

And so he left the Court, and Monsieur brought back Lorraine to the Palais Royal.

CHAPTER THIRTY-THREE

At Saint Cloud, in Monsieur's absence, Madame walked with her greatest friend, Madeleine de la Fayette, between rows of Canterbury bells, stocks and sweet-williams, down shallow grass steps into the sunk garden. They leaned over the lily pool and saw their reflections clear and dark. In the water, everything had a sharpness of outline that it lacked in the air, for the summer morning was veiled in a warm haze. There was no sunlight, and yet the sun showed in the water so pale that it was like the moon, fringed with dark clouds, which in the sky were only mist.

A tiny crackling sound came every now and then from the round leaves as the goldfish swam against them, causing them to stir together and sometimes make a splash so faint that it could scarcely be heard. The only other sound was the hum of flies. The day would be very hot. Later on, Madame would bathe in the river.

At that moment the sun swam out for an instant from the mist, and the pool winked and sparkled; a blue dragon-fly sunned itself on a lily leaf, a jewel gleaming on a polished surface of hot green leather. A pigeon, attracted by the sudden brightness, swooped across the pool, spread its tail feathers above the white and gold cups of the water-lilies, paused to curtsey three times at the brink, and then flew off again with a rustling like an opening fan.

'There goes a competent lady of the Court,' said Madame, as they seated themselves in a rose-covered arbour at the end of the pool, 'bustling, yet graceful, and so efficient. Who is she?'

They amused themselves by suggesting names. Through their idle gossip Madame recalled how the superintendent of the new buildings at Versailles, a pleasant young man called Monsieur Perrault, had lately compared them all with the heroines of the old nursery tales. Madame, he had said, was the Royal Cinderella; and Mademoiselle, the Sleeping Beauty of those northern tales where the princess lay in warrior's armour, surrounded by flames, until her true knight should dare burst through the fire to awaken her.

'And what am I?' Montespan had asked, sailing forward in all her splendour of superb flesh.

'The Princess with a Heart of Ice,' said one, but Monsieur Perrault ignored that.

'You, Madame,' he had said, 'are the boy who has not learnt how to shiver.'

'What did he mean by it?' Madame now asked her friend. 'Is it true, do you think, that Madame de Montespan has had dealings with the devil to help her win the King's love?'

It was known that Montespan consulted a sorceress for her cosmetics, also, it was believed, for love-potions, and, added the scandal-mongers, the demand for such potions is usually followed by one for poisons. The witch, a good convenient body of the neighbourly name of La Voisin, was patronized by the Chevalier de Lorraine, by Monsieur himself, indeed by half the Court it was said. Was the Black Mass really still performed in some out-of-the-way church in Paris?

And with delicious horror she reminded her friend that Montespan had left a ball just before midnight in some precipitation; and that a masked lady had been seen that same night, whose black cloak had revealed a glimpse of cloth of

251

gold as she stepped out of a hired coach in a back street in front of a little church that bore an ill reputation.

'I wish she were not such friends with Lorraine,' sighed Madame in conclusion.

'Why, what harm can that do? My dear, you must not be fanciful. This garden is our cloister. Let us forget there is anyone outside it.'

La Fayette entertained an anxious maternal adoration for her delicate princess. 'You will burn yourself out,' she was apt to say, imploring her mistress not to throw herself so ardently into all her fancies, fears and enthusiasms. Madame shed tears when Monsieur Racine read them his new tragedy, and then with one of her butterfly changes she laughed and gave him leave to make use of them in his dedication to her. And now she was eating her heart out because Cosnac was going back in disgrace to his diocese, kicked out of the window, just as he had said he would be. Ah, but Madeleine did not know all he had done for her. She told her about Cosnac and the libellous pamphlet.

'Such a silly insipid thing it was! I could have written it better myself,' and at that the too bright colour rushed into her face; and her eyes, which were inclined to look half-shut like those of all her family, opened wide and sparkling; she caught at her friend's hand and said, 'Why do you not write it? Dear Madeleine, do tell my story for me, my very own story.'

'But, Madame, what story?'

'Yes, that is it, what is my story? But there have been so many stories about princesses who never lived long ago, in countries that were never on the map, and you, an author, Madeleine, owe it to your trade to do something new and audacious. Take a real flesh-and-blood princess of the present day for your heroine this time, and tell the truth about her, put in all the faults, as Cromwell told the painter to put in the warts.'

If she could find some pattern, like the measure of a dance, some thread of meaning that should bring together the confused and crowded elements of her life into a whole, then she might not feel that she had lived so foolishly, untidily, so utterly in vain. But perhaps God alone could give this harmony.

From the roof of the arbour the surprised white face of a single rose leaned down on its long stem, and peered in at the two ladies who sat there in a swirl of silk, dimly glowing in

252

the green shadow. Minette stretched out her hand into the sunlight and picked the rose, held it to her face and then away again to look at it, handed it to her friend, and said, 'Do not these modern scientists as well as the priests tell us of an order in all things, from the inside of a flower to the uttermost star?'

And then in a sudden flash of amusement, 'At least you will find de Guiche's part in my story in admirable order, for he has always behaved like the hero.'

'Ah well, he is now living happily with his wife.'

'Dear Madeleine, you said that as though he were dead!'

A little scream of laughter came rippling out of the arbour; it startled a blackbird, perched on its roof, so that it flew scolding away; it struck a pleasant echo from her own youth in the ears of Queen Henrietta, who at that moment came stiffly down the grass steps in her black dress and widow's weeds, leading her little granddaughter Marie Louise by the hand.

The Queen had returned from England to settle in France again; her rheumatism was now a constant trouble, and she lived retired in Colombes or at Chaillot. She had grown much older; it gave Minette a queer pang to see how much gentler her mother had become, adoring Marie Louise and spoiling her in a way she would never have done with her own daughters. She had always some of her little dogs with her, and told long stories of their remarkable intelligence. It was odd how these were never the most dramatic stories she could have chosen. Once in the wars, when she had been escaping from a house that Cromwell's soldiers were attacking, she had run back under a rain of bullets to rescue her dog Mitte (and an ugly mongrel at that, so her old friend, Madame de Motteville, had declared), which she had left sleeping on the bed in her room. But Minette could never get her to tell the story to Marie Louise. The Queen could still be vivid on the wars of the Fronde, and how grossly her poor dear good sister-in-law, Queen Anne, had mismanaged them, but did not seem to remember much about the wars in England.

That tragedy should fade into such dim confusion (—'I always remember Lord Jermyn saying of our march on Oxford – no, now I come to think of it, it was not he, but your dear father—') seemed more pitiful to Minette than the tragedy itself. How could it be one's 'very own story' when one's own mind could not retain it? Even now to herself the outlines of her own absurd tragi-comic affairs with de Guiche and de

253

Vardes had already grown blurred; so much had happened since to blot them out, so many more people come crowding into her life; and the excitements that had once been so breathless, now cost her an effort to remember. Would she too one day grow old like that, forget if it were de Guiche or Louis who had stood beside her in the moonlit forest, telling her that he was above law and convention, and would defy the world for her sake?

'Oh, but how young we all were then!' she exclaimed; it did not seem to her that in all the sober ages to come, youth would ever be so young again.

'I shall go back to the very beginning for your story,' Madeleine was saying. What was the first thing Madame could remember? Was it (the gentle voice dropped on to a solemn note) the terrible news of her father's murder?

A vision rose in Minette's mind, not of her father's head, but of her mother's, grey and dishevelled, resting on a table.

'Ah no,' she replied, 'I was such a child then, more concerned with my doll than my unknown father. I remember crying because I had dropped it. . . .'

Her words trickled on, informed only by her conscious thoughts. But even as she spoke them, she saw a confused scene, dreadful and dark, with figures that dared not move; heard a voice speak words that never should be uttered; that not a soul there present, including herself, would ever bear to remember.

And as this spectre rose before her, she watched, through the leafy arch of the doorway, her mother playing with two puppies and Marie Louise.

CHAPTER THIRTY-FOUR

'I am sorry to finde that cucolds in France grow so troublesome. They have been inconvenient in all countries this last yeare.'

Charles' reference was to the Marquis de Montespan, whose behaviour, since his wife's return with Louis from the wars, had given as much pleasure as any husband in his position could be expected to provide. He had struck Madame de Montespan and driven her out of the house; he had put himself and his servants into as deep mourning as if he were a

254

widower; and he had had a pair of horns mounted on top of his coach.

The King was annoyed at this original behaviour, and told Molière he expected him to ridicule yet another Marquis; the play *Amphytrion* followed, to justify the loves of Jupiter. It was a flagrant scandal; it gave open offence, not only to the Marquis de Montespan, but to the Queen, to La Vallière, and above all to the unfortunately virtuous Madame de Montausier, who had never known till the first night of the play how her chaperonage had been abused during the campaign in Flanders when Venus had accompanied Mars all too closely.

Molière complained to Madame that now he had introduced the fashion for cuckoldry into plays, he would never be allowed to write of anything else. He was so sick of the subject of horns that if he did but hear the word he wished to scream. But he had obeyed orders, not only because he was the King's servant, but because the King was the only real support he had in the theatre – and even his approval had not been able to save *Tartuffe* when the anger of the clerical party had succeeded in banning it from the stage for a time. Madame had then invited him to give performances of it in her house, and they had seen a good deal of each other.

He told her that *Tartuffe* and the *Misanthrope* were worth all the rest of his plays put together, and therefore were just those that his dunderheaded public could not appreciate. He had grown in irritability; he got hardly any sleep; he never got rid of that cough. She tried to persuade him to see a doctor; but no, he had not the time. His wife did not look after him; on the contrary, she kept him in a restless agony with her love affairs, most of which were with his recognized enemies, 'the marquises' as the courtiers were now generically called. He spoke as bitterly of love as of life; what was it but a theatrical illusion?

'But, my friend, who are you to talk, who never escapes from the theatre?'

He admitted Madame's accusation. The bewildering rush, the excitements, the absurdities, the quarrels of theatrical life, they had caught him fast and he could not escape. He had quarrelled with Racine, and that helped to make him bitter, for he had helped Racine to a literary career; he had prompted him to write a poem on the occasion of the King's wedding which had won a prize; and he had sent him round the country to look for plays for him. Now Racine was writing plays him-

255

self, and though Madame de Sévigné did not think much of them (she said that Racine and this nasty bitter drink, coffee, would soon go out of fashion together) yet Madame herself was inclined to put him above even old Corneille.

'And you are right,' said Molière, 'I don't like the man, I don't like him – well, I quarrelled with him, so naturally I don't. But he is a poet, and there is an air of dignity and leisure about him which I don't get. He is more of a gentleman, in fact.'

'And what have *you* to complain of,' cried Madame, 'you who are life itself?' And she told him of their old English dramatist, Shakespeare, whose plays she tried to read because Charles often went to see them, though indeed they were longer than the old romances and more shapeless than whirlwinds – 'and yet one can see the life in his people that has made them last on into another generation, just as yours will do for many more.'

But Molière replied that the English playwright had not been an official of the King's bedchamber.

The world was against him, this hard jewelled world that seemed to be painted in flat colours like an early enamelled miniature with no shadows anywhere. He was, metaphorically as well as literally, always having his nose rubbed by somebody's diamond buttons. His *Misanthrope* (no misanthrope, but that more modern product, the man of feeling) defied the world, pitted himself against it, and lost. Madame read in it her lesson. She must keep her place in this world, for there was no other for her. She must not flag, she must not be too sensitive, above all she must not be ill. She must keep Louis' interest as well as his affection (which, when undiluted, was apt to became rather a dull and inert affair), or else she would have no protection at all against Monsieur and the Chevalier de Lorraine.

Since his return from the wars, the Chevalier's airs had been intolerable. Monsieur had installed him in the best rooms in the palace, and could talk of nobody else. Madame asked him about the campaign, flattering him with all she had heard of his prowess; Monsieur replied by showing her dispositions of the field with candlesticks and mirrors. 'And now what shall we have for the outposts? Achilles, give me your little ruby watch. It will make an adorable outpost. There, what do you think of that, Achilles? Haven't I arranged a pretty little battlefield?'

The Chevalier looked on, his lip curled in scorn. Monsieur loved him to look cold and proud. For that reason he painted his already thin mouth until it was like a tight scarlet thread drawn across his face; and above it his eyes looked out, rapacious, unwavering.

Monsieur seemed to have gone back to his childhood for the time being. For days he sulked and was apt to weep, and would tell nobody why. Then it turned out that he had discovered that Lorraine had a love-affair with one of Madame's maids-in-waiting. It was an affair of long and respectable standing, since he was really betrothed to her. Monsieur reproached him in a thousand hinted, hidden ways; at last spoke out his jealousy; wept with joy when Lorraine assured him that he no longer cared for the girl, and rushed to dismiss her from her mistress's service, without even letting Madame know. Her family was furious at her disgrace, and blamed Madame. It greatly assisted her reputation for being changeable, capricious; any new admirer was apt to be on guard against her, sure that she was not to be trusted.

She knew this, of course. The danger was that the King should know it. She could not be for ever complaining to him of his brother, and to do so would turn Monsieur irrevocably against her. Her only hope of real help was in the trust which Louis reposed in her in his dealings with England. When she went to England she would have Charles' advice and help; perhaps, if matters grew too bad for her here, she would have them always.

And in the meantime there were Charles' constant letters. He was always protesting how faulty he was in this matter, either for not having written before or for writing so shortly now. There were a hundred reasons for this. 'I have been all this afternoon playing the good husband, haveing been abroade with my wife, and 'tis now past twelve o'clock, and I am very sleepy.' Or else he is just going to a new play 'that I heare very much commended,' or but just come from the play and would be up at six to play tennis, so must now to bed; or but just returned from inspecting his new ships in so high a wind that his head is buzzing with it. At one time he is off to Newmarket, to ride his own horses as jockey in the races there; at another, he had 'gotten into such a vaine of hunting and the game lies so farr from this towne as I must spend one day intierly to kill one stag.' Or his messenger is already booted and seated on the saddle after losing his money at tennis until a quarter of

257

an hour ago, so that no one had any notion that he would be off today at all; or else Charles is 'just now called away by very good company to sup upon the watter so I will say no more but that I am intierly

Yours
C. R.'

Yet with all these excuses, and the one strong reason of 'the natural laziness I have towards writing,' he did write continually, so that she had a vivid sense of his 'very good company' through all these years of separation; ever since he had told her, just after she had left England to be married, 'I do intende to write to you very often in English that you may not quite forgett it.'

She did not forget it. She read all the new books she could get from England. She was eager to talk it; it was even worth while to hold long conversations with the tiresome touchy old puritan Lord Holles, the English ambassador. In consequence he could not think why anyone should consider her frivolous, and expressed his high opinion of her so strongly in his letters to his royal master that Charles jokingly warned Minette to beware of Lady Holles' jealous claws.

There were plently of other opportunities for practising her native tongue. Visitors were continually arriving with letters from Charles, asking her to do what she could for them. He introduced Lord Rochester with the assurance that she would 'find him not to want witt'; it might have been better fulfilled if he had not been partly drunk all the time he was in Paris.

Young James, who had been known as Mr Crofts, and was now, as Duke of Monmouth, openly recognized as Charles' son, also came, and was so handsome, engaging and popular that Queen Henrietta agreed with her daughter that it was the greatest pity Charles could not now acknowledge him as his lawful son and heir. His wife had not yet succeeded in bearing a child, and it began to look as though she never would.

The young Duke evidently looked on himself as the true heir to the throne. He believed that his mother, Lucy Walters, had really been married to King Charles, and was fond of showing how much he was one of the family by calling Madame his dear aunt. There was an added piquancy in this as he was only three or four years younger than herself, and admired her in such a boyishly ecstatic fashion that Monsieur suddenly showed himself as the jealous husband, and insisted on bearing off his wife to his remote country château at Villers Cotterets. This insult was as alarming as it was annoying. Such high-handed action was a new development; she was sure he would not have behaved so before his passion for Lorraine; it was so strong that it seemed to be transforming his character, making it far more violent.

But her hopes kept her happy. Louis had discussed with her his need for England's alliance against the Dutch. That 'nation of shopkeepers', as he bitterly called them, had interfered with his brilliant career of conquest in the Low Countries by forming a Triple Alliance with Sweden and England to enforce peace between France and Spain. Had Louis pursued his course regardless of this check, he feared to find the whole of Europe up in arms against him. But if Charles would detach himself from the Alliance and act in unity with himself, they would be strong enough together to ignore the rest of Europe; he would be guarded by Vauban's fortress line, and Charles by his command of the sea.

So he said to his sister-in-law on the new terrace at Versailles, and she listened to him with the colour glowing in her delicate cheeks.

But what, she asked, would England herself say to it? England, who was as nervous of finding a popish spy under a French hat, as an old maid of finding a man under her bed. Some way would have to be found to compensate the greedy new gentry for the loss of their Church lands.

In Louis' and Charles' plans for the future of their kingdoms she discovered a reason for her existence. Louis told her that there was no one he could entrust so well as herself with so delicate a mission; and that if any secret treaty were to be made, it could only be when she went on an apparently casual friendly visit to her brother.

This was the hope, now grown into a definite promise, that sent her away so gaily to Villers Cotterets that Monsieur's sulks were surprised into good humour. He actually had a little quarrel with Lorraine, who had prompted this severe action by his sneers at Madame's behaviour with her nephew. It was not much of a quarrel, and kept to the school-room tradition of:

'You said I said—'
'I never said you said—'

But quarrels were not consonant with Lorraine's dignity; he determined to teach Monsieur a lesson by paying a visit

259

elsewhere. Monsieur, however, did not at once learn his lesson. His fretful nerves had been jangled by too much excitement, and he was glad of rest. Madame was gay; the vast forests round Villers Cotterets were lovely in their late autumn colouring; and Monsieur thought it a miracle especially arranged for him that the birds sang in the mild evenings as though it were spring. Charles wrote, 'I am very glad that Monʳ begins to be ashamed of his ridiculous fancyes; you ought undoubtedly to over see what is past, so that, for the future, he will leave being of those fantasticall humours.'

She took his advice, realized as well as Monsieur that it was of the first importance to provide France with a supplementary heir, and became enceinte. This time, after her miscarriage, she would have to take the greatest care. They had returned to Paris and Saint Cloud, but she had to live very quietly. Monsieur quickly got bored; he sent for Lorraine, who had cleverly determined not to make the first move.

The Chevalier had left Monsieur as an equal; he returned as his superior. He was still sulking; it was necessary for Monsieur to cajole, fawn, flatter and laugh immoderately at all his thinly acid remarks before he would consent to make up their quarrel and forgive his pet for that brief lapse into fidelity to his wife. It was not long before Monsieur felt thoroughly ashamed of it; excusable as it was on the score of a State necessity. That could be allowed, but there should be no emotion with regard to a woman, other than a delicate aversion. Monsieur retaliated with Lorraine's maid of honour. That, said Lorraine, was different; he had been much younger then, and cruder. A puppy can gnaw even the toughest boots.

He had grown in strength and determination, also in a curious power to force his tastes and standards on his company, without a word to express them. There was something censorious in the way he walked, like a cat picking its precise, fastidious path over the unclean places of the earth. Minette never felt so plain as in his presence. The hearty references of Charles to her shape on a former occasion had never made her self-conscious as she was now. It was an unpleasant new experience for this 'sylph of the Court', criticized so far only in that she was not yet sufficiently a woman, to find herself a mere gross instrument for the blundering processes of nature.

She began to fear and resent Lorraine's influence on herself as well as on Monsieur. And if even she could allow herself to be impressed by him, what effect would he have on the

260

rest of her household? It had already begun to divide into two parties, one for Lorraine and one for herself, and every day she felt that those attached to her were fewer and weaker. It was no doubt a matter of self-interest, but it was discouraging that so many thought it better worth while to back Lorraine than herself. But she was in no state to struggle with this. She avoided both Monsieur and Lorraine as much as possible, and spent all the time she could with her mother at Colombes.

Queen Henrietta's company was the more soothing in that she did not grasp the full difficulties of her daughter's situation. She did not at all approve of Monsieur's behaviour; but he reminded her of 'poor Gaston', who had always been her favourite brother. Also she had a certain weakness for him on his own account, given by a knowledge of her good influence over him in the past, and an ignorance that it was in the past. She looked on his tiresomely silly friendship with Lorraine as a last prank of adolescence. 'He has always been much too young for his age, but then you must remember how he has been kept back; his mother treated him so unwisely.'

She even (and at this Minette felt a pitying tenderness towards the innocence of her mother's generation) sought to encourage her daughter by comparing the friendship with that of her husband, King Charles I, with the Duke of Buckingham's father. She had found it so very trying – it had been the cause of all their early quarrels – that Charles had been far more inclined to listen to the Duke of Buckingham than to herself.

'Oh, but, my dear little Mam, that was quite different,' began Minette, and stopped herself. She remembered the Comte de Guiche hoping that she would never come to know Monsieur as he really was; and she was not sure that she now wished her mother to know it.

She ran instead to call off her daughter, who was bullying the little Princess Anne. This was her brother James' little girl, who had been sent over for some special treatment in Paris for her eyes, and was staying with her grandmother. She was a large stolid child with square cheeks; there was not a trace of her father's family in her; 'she is all Hyde, and tough at that,' said Queen Henrietta, in a brief return to her earlier manner. It was depressing to think that she had a considerable chance of being one day Queen of England.

Marie Louise was much smaller than Anne, but a great deal more clever, lively and pretty. She gave herself airs with the little visitor, led her and ordered her about as though she were a rather clumsy dog; and in return the Princess Anne gave her a dog-like devotion. Her grandmother, shamelessly partisan as ever, said how good it was for the poor child to have so bright a companion.

'All the same, I cannot have her pulling Anne's hair to see why it does not curl,' protested Marie Louise's mother.

King Louis came often to Colombes to discuss his plans with her; and she wrote two or three times a week to England, to Charles and to one or two of his advisers, who were partly admitted into the secret of the intended treaty. It would now have to be deferred until her child was born. But there was much to be done in the meantime; precautions had to be taken, a cypher was decided on, numbers were chosen to represent names, and the actual questions to be settled required continual rearrangement.

Charles needed assurance that France did not intend to encroach on him at sea, for Colbert had shown an alarming energy in building French ships. But Louis did not care about the navy, nor about commerce – another point in which Charles was very firm that England should be supreme. Louis promised to leave trade to England if he could extend his military conquests in Europe.

Minette saw her wildest dreams take shape and certainty before her eyes. Charles was to be lord of the sea, and Louis of the land. Charles was to declare himself a Catholic if and when a suitable opportunity offered, and Louis was to give him a portion of his now vast wealth, so as to secure his position if his subjects should turn troublesome. Between them they would rule the world to its own benefit and the glory of God. No longer would England be soured by thousands of conceited little sects, each thinking that it alone knew God; no longer would the new gentry of Henry VIII's time sit in their ill-gotten abbeys; the Church would be restored, there would be peace and unity through the land; her family would be secure on the throne as it had never yet had a proper chance to be; it would be the dawn of a new age in England, as great and glorious as Louis' reign was proving itself.

And only she could bring it about. From the first Charles had insisted that he would treat directly with no one but his sister; that she must come to England before he would agree to any treaty.

It was for this as much as for herself or her infant that she was so anxious this year should not be the last of her life, as she knew it might well be after that miscarriage.

'Let me live till after then,' was her prayer, 'and I shall be happy, whatever happens after.'

'Then' was the apotheosis of her life, which should unite France with England, her father's land with her mother's faith, and herself with her brother.

CHAPTER THIRTY-FIVE

Her baby was born at the end of the summer, and it was a girl.

'That is the third time she has disappointed me,' said Monsieur. 'Two girls and a miscarriage. And when she has a son, it dies.'

It was the third time that made it final. He had been told so by his sorceress. He would never now have a son by Madame.

Within a fortnight of her baby's birth, Minette's mother died at Colombes. She had been ill for some time and could not sleep. Her doctor gave her some opium pills; with the result, Mademoiselle brightly observed, that she never woke again.

Two months after her death there was an impressive funeral service at Chaillot, where Queen Henrietta had wished to be buried, and had always hoped that she would die. At Madame's request the Abbé Bossuet, whom her mother had admired so greatly, gave the funeral oration. The convent church was packed tight with people who bore some of the greatest names in France and England. Only the King and Queen of France had enough room to turn round and see who was there; but they were naturally far too well behaved to take advantage of this. Minette, wedged at Monsieur's side, found herself loathing his scent and his dapper profile.

There was a new *Dies Irae*, which Lulli's orchestra performed with majestic effect. People wept a little, and Monsieur flourished his lace handkerchief. Then Bossuet mounted the pulpit, flung back the silvery straight hair that lay as fine as spun glass on his forehead, and looked round the church with that piercing glance that made him so like a white eagle. This would be the greatest sermon he had yet given; all knew that, from the moment he began. Never yet had he had such an occasion for tragic narrative, for passionately personal admiration and grief. 'La reine malheureuse' was dead. Her heroic courage had been worthy of the last child of Henry of Navarre. He told the sad story of her fortune, of the warfare in her husband's kingdom, her exile, her agony and desolation.

'This is Bossuet, the greatest preacher in the world,' Minette told herself, gazing at the splended, generous head, 'he is speaking of my mother, who was Queen Henrietta Maria of England, and now is dead.' For she must not miss a word of this great man's sermon on her mother. What did it matter if Monsieur fidgeted, if the stuffiness of the church and the smell of the incense were almost overpowering? She would have time to breathe afterwards, but *now* she must listen.

She heard Bossuet speak of the royal infant born in midst of a siege, taken from her mother's arms when she was only a few days old, and restored by her governess's faithful devotion to be her mother's consolation in her grief and ruin. 'He is speaking of me,' she thought, and still it seemed strange, as though all this must be about somebody else rather than herself and her dear little Mam, who used to laugh so gaily and tickle her under her chin.

Why could she not listen more attentively; why was it suddenly so necessary to think out the course of their two lives for herself, instead of following it in Bossuet's grandiloquent words?

'Be quiet,' she said to her restless mind, and at once it answered, 'That was what she could never be.'

Heresy! and when she had never wanted less to criticize her mother, whose death had left her at this moment so terrifyingly lonely. What was it that jerked her into this unhappy doubt, this sudden determination that she must find out what her mother had been, and what she was herself, before it was too late? Too late for what? She did not yet know, but her thoughts now were playing uneasily round the coming treaty with England. She wondered if it were not almost too well planned, too consistent, too hidebound.

It was for her an act of love, but could such acts be comprised in complicated treaties? Love was simple.

'Mayerne, for love of me, go to my wife.' She had never thought of that since she had first heard it, sitting on Morton's knee, and Morton crying for her father's death, and now suddenly there it was ringing in her ears.

'Oh wife and mother, oh Queen incomparable!' rolled out Bossuet's great voice from the pulpit.

This scheme for the glory of God and England was surely blessed. It had rejoiced her mother's last months on earth. They had talked of it so happily, so hopefully. It was an insane trick of fancy that made her imagine Charles' nonchalant voice saying, 'Leave it alone.'

Yet that obstinate whisper in her mind persisted; reminded her now, not of any of the things that Bossuet was telling of her mother, but of the moment that above all others she wished never to remember, when Harry ran out into the court-yard, and Mam stepped into the coach without looking at him, and drove away here to Chaillot. 'Never let me look upon your face again.' And she never did. Yet Mam had loved Harry; she had only sought to influence him for his good.

And she herself – true daughter of her mother, as Bossuet was even at this moment calling her – had, at her mother's instigation, put her arms round dear Morton's neck and begged her, 'Do be converted, *ma bonne dame*, and I will love you all the better.' That too she had forgotten till this moment.

Morton had told her never to bargain with religion. But the treaty was a bargain. She was working so hard – letters, cyphers, numbers, building up the whole apparatus of busy secrecy round her. Charles had once said the curse of women was their industry.

'Be quiet,' said the anxious whisper, and then, 'oh God, make me love wisely, and not too well.'

Monsieur was jerking forward. The congregation were rising to their feet. She realized that, unless Bossuet would consent to print his sermon, she would never know what he had been saying.

CHAPTER THIRTY-SIX

Since her grandmother's death, the Princess Anne had been taken into Madame's nursery to be with Marie Louise under the charge of her governess, Madame de Saint Chaumont. It was a strange household for the little girl to be in; had she been of a sensitive nature she would have found herself very unhappy in it. Fortunately her hide was as tough as her grand-mother had complained, and she noticed little but that Marie

265

Louise had grown very naughty. Her aunt and the governess were very kind to her, and Marie Louise's scorn of her increased at each fresh sign of their kindness.

'You must be very good, for them to be so nice to you. Don't you hate them? I do. Anyone of spirit hates mothers and governesses.'

'Whom do they like, then?' asked Anne.

'Men,' said Marie Louise simply.

She adored her uncle King Louis so much that she was quite uncomfortable in his presence, so shy, so afraid to speak, so certain that her curtsey was clumsy, her voice squeaky, her whole person utterly unworthy of his notice. He was very fond of her, but he showed her the deliberate courtesy that had now grown habitual to him from long practice; it was very alarming to a child, as indeed to many grown people. He was the only person this rebel of eight years old respected.

But she was fascinated by the Chevalier de Lorraine; he was so handsome, so strange; he would stand in beautiful attitudes against a crimson curtain, looking indescribably mysterious and wicked, hardly condescending to answer her father (and who could wonder? Papa was so silly), or notice how he frisked round him like a little dog, fawning for his notice. But he would speak to herself with charming affability, treating her as though she were grown up, telling her how pretty she had grown; that at her age her mother had taken part in the Court balls; that she would far outshine her mother when she did the same, and no doubt that was why she was not allowed to begin. He showed her too how unfair Madame de Saint Chaumont was in favouring the Pudding Princess, as he called poor Anne. She must favour her, or she would not make such a ridiculous fuss when Marie Louise teased her in a playful way.

Her mother and her governess anxiously discussed the Chevalier's effect on the little girl. High-spirited and impressionable, she was evidently being induced not merely to be as naughty as possible, but to turn against them both. Madame de Saint Chaumont tried to reassure her mistress; the child was certain to outgrow his influence very soon – 'I have noticed that little girls are often so tiresome and excitable with men at that age, and then grow more pleasantly childish again in three or four years.'

'I do not want to wait all that time for my daughter to love me,' said Minette.

266

'Dear Madame, she loves you all the time, though she does not know it. Why else should she wake, calling on your name, when she has had a nightmare and wanted comfort?'

'Did she have a nightmare? When? What was it? I hope she does not often.'

'Some nonsense about the devil,' said Madame de Saint Chaumont airily.

She was stout and cheerful, sound in judgement and decided in manner, with round red cheeks and white hair, although she was only in her forties – an apple touched by an early frost, Minette called her. She found her common sense very bracing; the governess seemed the only entirely sane person she had about her; and if she were not there, Minette would begin to doubt the chances of her own sanity.

For she did not think it was such nonsense to dream of the devil in this house. She had made the mistake of thinking that Lorraine, as a mere self-seeking adventurer, could never be as dangerous as de Vardes, because he had not a tenth part of his quality. De Vardes had the makings of greatness in him, cramped and spoiled by his petty environment, his lack of elbow-room or opportunity to use his vigour. He might have been a rebel, a buccaneer or an explorer. But it was impossible to think of Lorraine following any career but the parasitic. With the face and body of a young god, he had the soul of an old miser. He could not think in any terms but those of money, and the speed with which he extracted it from Monsieur showed an almost unconscious skill, amounting to genius.

It was not in any fantastic hope of gratitude that Monsieur showered jewels, lands, pensions and benefits on the young man; it had become a mere habit, a condition without which he could not exist, since, if it ceased, the Chevalier de Lorraine would certainly leave him.

'But why should I weep?' demanded Monsieur of young d'Effiat, a secondary attraction on whom he could depend to be kind to him when Lorraine was not (as at this moment, when Monsieur had been unable to secure more than four really excellent horses from England, so that the Chevalier was justly incensed by so meagre a gift). 'Since I value him more highly than anything in the world, why should I not pay to keep him?'

Monsieur's sentimentality had increased since the unwelcome discovery that he was growing fat. His features, legs and hands were as neat as ever; but his chin no longer emerged clean cut

267

from his cravat, there was a softness beneath it, a distinct cushion; and there was no doubt now that his stomach protruded. Fate was cruelly unjust in this; he did not eat one-quarter as much as Louis, whose appetite was enormous, and yet Louis showed no sign of getting really fat. This tragedy assisted Monsieur's liberality, since it helped him to believe that Lorraine would never love him for himself alone – a belief that Lorraine's behaviour to him ran no chance of contradicting.

But the Chevalier's single-minded concentration on gold did not in any way lessen his power over others, as Minette had hoped. Wheresoever the source of that power might be – in bribery, blackmail or black magic (and all three were freely suggested as his common activities) – there was no doubt that it was gradually extending. Madame had begun to find that she was no longer regarded as the mistress of the house; her servants obeyed the Chevalier and scarcely troubled to acknowledge her presence. Even her steward and the captain of the guard paid no attention to her orders, if they had been counteracted by the Chevalier; she doubted if there were a soul in this house that she could trust.

There was Madame de Saint Chaumont, but even she was uneasy now in her manner towards her, frightened, anxious to conceal something. Minette begged her to speak freely.

'Who could do that in this house?' replied her friend. Never till now would Madame de Saint Chaumont admit that 'this house' differed so evilly from other houses. It was as though Minette had reached her last defence. She tried to speak in the brisk matter-of-fact voice that the governess had lost.

'Then come into the gardens with me. One is always more free when one is by the water.'

She led her to her favourite seat at the foot of the cascade. It was too cold to sit. The water fell in sheets of transparent silver through the wintry twilight. The gardens were grey, the trees etched in black. Behind them spread the palace, a vast shape, white as a corpse against the dun-coloured sky. Music came from its windows. One after the other each window lit up, like an eye opening on the two ladies who walked to and fro with hurried, uncertain steps, huddling their cloaks round them.

Madame de Saint Chaumont spoke now, almost in a whisper.

'You cannot stay here, Madame. If the King will not act,

you must speak to your brother. You have not a single friend here to support you.'

'I have one, have I not?'

'For how long?'

'You would leave me?'

'Not unless I were forced to. There are many means of force here. The Chevalier has tried to make me your enemy and has failed. So that I do not expect now to be here very long.'

'Ah, my dear friend, do not be so mysterious. Tell me what it is you fear.'

Madame de Saint Chaumont did not answer directly. She said that the Chevalier had spoken openly of a divorce between Monsieur and Madame, of Monsieur's determination to make the King give him the province of Languedoc, where he could rule in a kingdom of his own, surrounded by his young men, in a palace empty of women.

'What could be better?' breathed Madame, on a wish almost as passionate as Monsieur's own.

She returned to the palace separately from Madame de Saint Chaumont, who seemed to think this advisable. As she entered the hall she instinctively drew back a step behind a pillar, for a strange couple were descending the stairs. A little fat painted woman in pink satin and fair false hair – 'she is really dark, and that is why she looks so unnaturally vulgar,' was the first thought that came into her head as she wondered what creature this could be.

And then, like a face seen in a nightmare, the falsely flaxen doll became familiar, though still for an instant her mind refused to recognize what her eyes had seen.

Monsieur, dressed as a woman, in a modern fashionable dress all hung with lace, and a blonde wig of flowing curls, his face as pink and white as though a porcelain veneer had been laid over his olive skin, was mincing and fluttering at the side of the Chevalier, hanging on to his arm and leaning towards him to pat his cheek with his fan, coaxing him, caressing him in a maudlin whine. The Chevalier, in black, his cloak lined with silver, was as impassive as his companion was uncontained. His eyes had been blackened with kohl till they showed like two dagger-points in deep pits of shadow. The face, long and narrow, was a livid white; the mouth a scar. He might have walked in solitude for all the attention he paid to the creature at his side.

Yet Minette became that instant aware that everything

about him, the stealthy quiet of his tread, his unswerving stare, his silence, scorn and inhumanity, were all most carefully aimed at this utter subjection of his master. Other young men had held a brief sway over Monsieur by their attractions; the Chevalier, more subtle, would rule the longer through fear.

They passed within a few feet of her, and Monsieur, with his eyes flickering over her, did not see her; the parakeet could see nothing but the snake that had fascinated him. But Lorraine, who had never glanced at her, had seen her, she knew that, and did not know why she had not moved away in time. She too was fascinated, rooted to the ground by horror.

Across the hall two black slave boys in white and scarlet, whom Monsieur had appointed for his footmen, opened the doors for the pair to pass in to dinner. The strains of a violin came through the door and an Italian voice singing a thin high air; then a burst of applause acclaimed the entering lovers. The slave boys followed them, closing the doors. Minette was alone in the white and gilded hall.

That night she locked herself into her room and wrote to Charles.

Next day Monsieur stood in his dressing-room and arranged his toilet (a masculine one this time) before departing to pay a call on the King at Saint Germain.

'Madame,' he chirruped through the open doors into her room, 'have you neglected to say goodbye to Madame de Saint Chaumont? That was not very kind of you.'

'But Madame is here,' she exclaimed.

He combed his hair for a moment, watching her, then he said: 'No, Madame, she has already left. You will not see her again.'

CHAPTER THIRTY-SEVEN

Somewhere inside the vast superstructure of Versailles was the delicate 'card castle' that Louis XIII had built for his retreat. And somewhere inside the Sun King, whose every movement and mouthful was a public function, every word an official statement, and every gesture monumental, was the impetuous boy who had first proved his royalty by refusing to go to bed till dawn. But neither could now be easily discovered.

La Vallière had once again fled to Chaillot; but this time it was not King Louis who pursued her. Never again would he defy opinion, break his engagements, forget his time-table and keep a Court preacher and congregation waiting, while he hurled himself on to his horse and galloped by himself with a cloak drawn across his face to look for his lost love.

This time it was Colbert who was sent with an officer of the guard to threaten arrest if she did not return. Louis had tired of her, but he had made her a duchess; Court etiquette had been adapted so as to fit her into the niche he had formed for her, and he did not see why he should have to alter it again. No one should flout his regulations, not even his mistress. He did not often show cruelty, but when he did it was generally to women. Perhaps he revenged himself for the superior power they had had to upset the gradually perfecting equilibrium of his life.

He was not indifferent to his sister-in-law's troubles; the difficulty was in making him grasp how serious they were, and how far Lorraine was worse than the scores of other young men who had always fluttered round Monsieur. He was growing slow to gauge the feelings of others, shut off as he was from all friendship or casual intimacy. An hour or two in the afternoon with a mistress, or possibly his wife, was the only privacy he now enjoyed. Every day three hundred courtiers were privileged to watch him dress, dine and sup at a solitary table, and go to bed.

A generation of young nobles had now grown up whose best chance to get on in the world was to catch the King's eye as he looked round the obsequious circle to decide who should carry the ceremonial candlestick to light him to his bed that evening. It did not really light him; the rooms had all been lit already. But that their service was purely symbolical gave them no more question than is given to a devout acolyte who lights the candles on the altar. To the nobles of France the King had begun to represent God. They were now completely separated from their estates and the people; Louis had achieved his object. But in doing so he had separated himself, not merely from 'the people' but from people altogether. When he spoke of France he thought of the Court, which he had made a town and a country in itself, an isolated world of courtiers.

Charles knew well enough what Louis was like. When Minette was sure of a trustworthy messenger her letters had continued to be wholeheartedly indiscreet, safe in his assurance

271

that 'all things which comes from you shall never go further than my own harte.' So that when she appealed for his help against the Chevalier de Lorraine he realized that probably more was needed to jerk Louis into action than a mere private letter from his brother-in-law. He spoke to the French ambassadors, thereby showing that he considered his sister's domestic troubles a matter of national importance. If King Louis did not act speedily, the much desired amity between France and England would be lost. He had been negotiating for his sister's visit ever since the birth of her baby, and now told Colbert flatly that he expected to see her in the spring.

His peremptory messages startled Louis at a moment when he had begun to think he would be able to count on the English King as a paid servant, ready to further any of his schemes. But here was Charles as a perturbed brother, and quite ready to be an angry one and to upset them all. Louis was willing to agree that something should be done about his sister, but it ought to have been left for him to decide when to move. It did not occur to him that in that case it might have been left a long time.

Yet again he spoke with Minette on the new terrace at Versailles, yet again the three hundred countries dropped a little way behind, and hundreds more watched from the park among the newly planted full-grown trees. But ceremony dropped from him as he asked her what she wanted, and his grumpy tone delighted her, for here was the old Louis once again instead of the icy politeness of the new Louis.

She detailed Monsieur's scheme of a kingdom of his own in Languedoc, free from women. He was shocked.

'A kingdom of Heliogabalus, here in modern France!'

'That is what Saint Cloud is already,' she said.

'But not openly, while you are there?'

'I shall not remain to cloak your brother's vices,' she replied.

She spoke so quietly that the sense of her words only penetrated his understanding some time after he had heard them.

'But what has happened to make you so obstinate?' he asked.

She told him that Madame de Saint Chaumont had been dismissed without reason, that the Chevalier boasted openly of his domination over her household, that she had not a person in it she could trust, that if she stayed there it would

272

not be for much longer, for she knew the Chevalier was quite capable of taking her life.

'But when he is removed—' said Louis.

She noticed that he said 'when', not 'if'. But she would promise no attempt at reconciliation with Monsieur. They must be divorced, she said. The Pope had shown himself easily terrorized by Louis. Something could be arranged. She had been thinking all this time of Marie Louise, and now asked him to take her into his household if she were divorced. The child already spent much of her time with the little Dauphin.

She could not explain the reasons for her obduracy. So many princes had perverse tastes, especially when they were brothers to a King, encouraged to remain in the background. Was she being finicky, exacting, tiresomely modern in her self-assertion? She did not know; she only knew that whereas she had not thought it wrong before to have children by Monsieur, she now knew it would be wrong. She tried to tell Louis of that evening when she had returned to the palace and had seen Monsieur, dressed as a woman, going in to dinner on the arm of the Chevalier.

Louis thought it rather funny. She had noticed that he never objected to details that made Monsieur ridiculous. He was fonder of his brother than of any other man; he liked to have him by him constantly, and was amused by his jokes; and there was a gay insouciance in his happier moods that Louis envied, though secretly, even to himself. But he liked him to be kept in subjection, and not merely because Gaston d'Orléans had proved in the last reign how dangerous a royal younger brother could be. The moment when Louis had least liked his brother was not now, when he heard of him as a little fat woman, capering about in pink satin, but when he had heard that he was in the trenches with Cosnac, giving every hope of proving as good a soldier as the King himself. It was noticed that the King did not again give his brother military command, though indeed he had good excuse in Monsieur's vagaries on the arrival of the Chevalier de Lorraine.

No, Philippe was to stay at Court, to admire and amuse him, as once he had planned long ago when he had thought out his ideal kingdom – all of which had come true, for here he was at Versailles, in a palace finer than any in Europe and still only half finished, and half of the furniture was covered with gold, and half with silver, and painted ceilings showed the world how he emulated one after the other the gods of old. It was inconceivable that anyone should wish to leave it. His first spontaneous anger against his brother now rushed on him when he realized that this was what Monsieur actually wished – to leave him and go to Languedoc. It was Lorraine who induced such treasonable independence in his obedient brother. He promised Minette to rid her of the rascal. She begged that it should be on some pretext apart from her, else Monsieur would make her life a burden to her. He thought her rather unreasonably fussy, but agreed.

Monsieur made things easy for them by asking the King for the revenues of two abbeys for Lorraine. The King replied caustically that he did not consider the Chevalier a good substitute for the Bishop whose death had left them vacant. Monsieur, impatient of any joking that delayed his expected answer, replied with a perfunctory smile, 'Yes, yes, we are not all bishops, but tell me—'

'I tell you, no,' said Louis, and his underlip shut upwards like a trap fastening.

'But I have promised them to him,' cried Monsieur, 'am I to be laughed at, disgraced, as a King's brother who has no influence at Court?'

'Let it cure you of babbling, then. What right had you to promise what only I have the power to grant? Does Lorraine boast that he is the master in my house as well as in yours?'

Monsieur only heard the words 'my house' and 'yours'.

'I wish I had a house two thousand miles from yours,' he screamed, 'and I would go there now, with Lorraine, and never see your face again.' His voice reminded Louis distressingly of their mother in one of her shrill hysterics.

'There has been too much of Lorraine,' he said, 'he is making you as intolerable as himself.'

And he ordered the arrest of the Chevalier by the royal guards.

Monsieur could not at first believe his ears. He stood quite still, he went a greenish-yellow under his paint; as the door closed behind Bontems, who went out with the order for arrest, he tottered forward, putting out his hand in a groping fashion, then fell in a faint at Louis' feet. People rushed in from the anteroom at the sound of the fall; they found the King lifting his brother on to a chair and calling for help unaware that Monsieur no longer needed it. His eyes were open, regarding with satisfaction the commotion he had caused. Now, surely,

274

Louis would grant him everything. When he was tired of having water dabbed on his forehead, his hands slapped, his cravat and his stays loosened, he asked in feeble tones for a private audience.

Unwillingly, the King dismissed the company and Monsieur proceeded to make his scene. Louis was to some extent in training for it, for Montespan's scenes had proved a rude contrast to La Vallière's tender reproaches. But they could be covered in his mind as the passion of a proud beauty in love, demanding proofs of it from him. No such flattering phrase could cloak the fact that his docile, even adoring little brother had turned against him. For when Monsieur had knelt to him, grovelled at his feet, wept, lamented and implored all in vain, he began to storm and stamp, he defied the King, cursed him, and actually shook his beringed fist in his face. If Louis let go his rigid self-control for an instant, Monsieur would hurl himself upon him, and three hundred courtiers would rush in at the noise to find them rolling on the floor together as in the old days of their pillow-fights.

In his rage Monsieur's face went so dark a red it looked nearly black. Since he had begun to grow fat, it was noticeable that his neck was very short. This had helped him to faint, and in a quarrel like this he was quite likely to choke himself and die of apoplexy. Louis' conscious mind did not record this danger until many years later, when it had actually happened, and he never forgave himself for having been the cause of his brother's death.

At this moment he would have welcomed it. He was given no breathing space in which to show his anger. Monsieur would not be dismissed; he continued to rave. Louis turned on his heel and left him.

Five minutes later, Monsieur burst like a tornado into his apartments in the palace of Saint Germain, accused Madame of witchcraft in league with the devil that had enabled her to poison Louis' mind against Lorraine, swore that he would not remain in this hateful place one moment longer, nor ever eat bread under the King's roof again, and ordered his servants to dismantle the rooms and pack up his belongings as fast as they could move.

Even his bloodshot eyes and loose, trembling mouth did not frighten her so much as did the disorder of his dress. He had not tied his cravat since it had been loosed, his embroidered under-linen made several unusual appearances, and his unfastened stays had given him an odd shape. Their rooms were lined with mirrors, yet he had not once glanced at his reflection. She began to think that he must indeed have gone mad.

Within half an hour she was hurried into her coach and borne off by him to Paris. It was then evening; the Palais Royal was not ready for them, and everything was in the dreary confusion of a half-empty, unswept, ice-cold house. It did not matter, said Monsieur, for next day they should start for Villers Cotterets, and never more return to Court. Minette stood and watched a fire of damp logs which refused to light, while she absent-mindedly signed her name in the dust on the table.

'Why do you do that? asked Monsieur in furious irritation.

'Because I cannot write my name in water. If there were any here, it would be frozen,' she replied.

The rooms were nearly dark. Outside the dirty windowpanes a cold dusk was gathering over Paris.

Through the black skeleton branches of the trees in the garden she saw the irregular outline of roofs against the sky, a pricking of little lights here and there in their darkness. It looked like the outline of a monstrous many-eyed beast, crouching to spring; and she thought of what Louis had once said of the people of Paris, of the horror it would bring should they ever learn to use their power.

The servants brought in candles and stuck them in the glass and silver sconces round the walls. There were not enough candles; someone would have to go out and buy them. Two footmen came running in again with the curtains, and proceeded to hang up yards upon yards of the new watered silk of a pale green colour. The windows, which so badly needed cleaning, were shut out and the wall seemed in the flickering candlelight to be spread with running water. But Minette wished they had not done this; she could no longer see the roofs where other people lived, and was now shut in with Monsieur.

A servant came in to say that Mademoiselle had already heard of their arrival and had come to call. Minette removed her finger from the table; for an instant she thought that she must have been standing there for several hours.

'You find the place filthy, my cousin,' she said as Mademoiselle entered, declaring her delight at their arrival, which had taken her completely by surprise.

276

'And us also,' said Minette, who saw no reason why she should trouble to explain, since Monsieur was present. He hurled himself into the gap, told Mademoiselle that he could never attempt to do anything but he was crossed, that his wife had turned his brother against him, that he was of all men the most ill-used and miserable, and God had never ceased to punish him for being so ill-advised as to forsake the elder of the two ladies present for the younger. If Mademoiselle were shocked at his unkindness to his wife, she was now disgusted at his bad taste with regard to herself.

'What is it, my cousin,' she asked, coolly regarding him, 'that appears to be protruding at your hip?'

He looked down at himself, his eyes grew wide in horror, he fled from the room. Madame put her arms down on the dusty table and her head down on her arms. Sobbing with laughter, she explained what had happened, and Mademoiselle was annoyed that she had committed such a solecism as to refer to Monsieur's stay-bone. 'On my honour,' she said, 'I thought it must be a dagger.'

She was fidgeting, ill at ease. She was scandalized by her cousins' quarrel, but not really interested in it. She began to walk up and down the room; her cheeks were flushed, her eyes bright and remote.

Minette sat back in her chair and watched her. She thought in a clear decisive way, as though something were speaking inside her, 'My cousin too is perturbed, and no doubt it is just as important for her.'

'If I had but a single true friend in whom I could confide—' began Mademoiselle, and then went on walking.

'We have never known each other as well as we should,' said Minette, 'I wish we could now begin. Do you think we could? I know that you have a good heart, and I don't think you would find mine a bad one.'

'I don't think so,' said Mademoiselle abstractedly, and it was not at all clear to what this was in answer.

Presently she asked if Monsieur were likely to return. Madame thought it most unlikely in view of the cause of his rout.

Mademoiselle drew a tapestried chair closer to her cousin, and began to talk of Monsieur de Lauzun.

The fire hissed and spluttered. The few candles blew in the draught. A cobweb swung in the corner by the fireplace, its threads gleaming out whenever the light of the thin ineffectual

277

flames leaped high enough to gild it. Madame, glad that she had not removed her cloak, rubbed her hands together inside her muff.

'He has all the pride of a Gascon. His family name is Puy-guilhem, I find something strange in it, almost barbaric, do you not too? I believe that even the King is a little afraid of him. So that it is not surprising, is it, that I should feel that too?'

'Ah, my dear cousin!' cried Madame, in so soft yet sad a tone that even the preoccupied lady noticed it.

'Why should you be sorry for me?' asked an offended voice.

'I do not know – I only know that I should like you to be happy. Is Monsieur de Lauzun likely to make any woman so?'

Mademoiselle was disconcerted that she had disclosed her secret so quickly. She parried the question; she did not know any completely happy woman except herself, for so she had been until just lately, but now, she did not know how it was, she had grown weary of places and people that had hitherto pleased her. She had lived long enough to see how unsatisfactory were marriages for State reasons – ('You are right, dear cousin.') – She now believed that the greatest chance of happiness would be to marry someone who would be a perfect companion, a man moreover of so much lesser fortune that he would always be grateful to her.

She never mentioned Corneille; she forgot that she had always condemned love and inclination as motives for marriage. At forty she had fallen in love for the first time, and with the cleverest and most experienced adventurer in the Court. So that Madame had some reason to feel anxious for her cousin, as she sat in the dim, chilly room, wondering between-whiles where she would be this time tomorrow evening.

CHAPTER THIRTY-EIGHT

At three o'clock next day, Madame wrote on the little Chinese desk (the paint on one of the cock's wings had been a trifle scratched on this last journey) a note to Turenne to tell him that 'unless the King detains us by much affection and a little force, we go today to Villers Cotterets, to return I know not when.'

Turenne read it, scowling. The note was dated 'Friday, 3

278

o'clock,' enough in itself to raise a frown. Why could not women put 'Feb. 1st, 1670', as all reasonable men would do? But the contents jerked him from his chair and sent him calling for his coach. Madame referred lightly enough to her approaching exile at Villers Cotterets, though she admitted 'the unpleasantness of Monsieur's company in his present mood.' She would miss her friends, she said, and the Maréchal Turenne would have still better reason to miss her, since she owed him a hundred pistoles from cards. She hoped the King would not forget her in her absence.

She feared that, in her absence from the Court, the scheme to use her as agent between France and England might once again be allowed to lapse. The King had sent her a messenger this morning to ask what she intended to do in this behaviour of Monsieur, and to entreat her to promote as far as possible the dignity of France. Louis would not consider it promoted by her seizing this moment to break openly with his brother. She was greatly tempted, for it was an excellent occasion, but this too might well endanger her chances of her English visit. How could she represent France if she had severed her connexion with it?

Turenne was one of the few admitted to the secret of the treaty; he could see all these perplexities and did not himself know what to advise. Nor, when he reached the Palais Royal, did he have any chance to advise anything, since Monsieur was just about to start on their journey, and stuck all the time with jealous closeness to his wife's side. He had been enraged with Louis for asking her what she intended to do, encouraging her to fail in her duty to him. Did the King consider himself so absolute a monarch that he could come between husband and wife? They would see if he could be flouted like this.

And he urged on their departure, and was ramping up and down the room when Turenne arrived. Madame sat very still; when Monsieur turned and attacked her for the vile way in which his friend had been treated, she replied that she was no friend of the Chevalier's, but 'I am sorry for him, and for you. This is not my doing.'

Turenne looked with loathing on the little man. He waited some time before he spoke. Then, since it would make matters worse to ask for an interview with Madame, he addressed himself to Monsieur.

'Your Highness will remember,' he said, 'that Madame is of

279

importance both to France and England, and that you have made both these countries watchful of your conduct to her.' He turned towards her. 'I can be of no use to you at this moment, so I will leave you, Madame. But do not fear, you will not be left friendless at Villers Cotterets.'

Monsieur was so frightened that he did not speak for nearly five minutes after his departure. Turenne was also a little frightened. He could not but think he had somewhat exceeded his duties as Maréchal-General of France; but he was still more startled by the discovery that if he had stayed a moment longer in Monsieur's presence he would not have been able to refrain from wringing that short, empurpled neck of his.

He had a long talk with Colbert, who as chief minister set out in pursuit of Monsieur on behalf of the King. Just before he left Paris, messengers arrived with letters to Monsieur from both King Charles and the Duke of York, asking for his leave that Madame should visit her brothers in England. It had been agreed that this would be the best way of flattering his sense of importance into granting the required permission. But now there could not be an unluckier moment to present the requests. Colbert consulted long with Louis; it was agreed that the Minister should take the letters with him to Villers Cotterets, but not give them unless he found Monsieur in a better mood, and could persuade him to return to Court. Boredom alone should convert Monsieur after a few days among the wintry woods.

Louis did not realize that Monsieur was playing two new rôles, which were likely to engage his interest for some time. The first, inculcated by the Chevalier, was that of the high-handed husband who would brook no interference with his wife, not if it were from the King his brother, nor a whole pack of her brothers in England.

The second was that of Orpheus, whose Eurydice has been snatched under the earth by Pluto, king of darkness. Every day he wrote poetic effusions to Lorraine, and insisted on imagining him in some deep dungeon hidden from the light of day. He wandered the woods, distraught with eneffable longings, plucking the snowdrops and primroses, and murmuring to them messages to his lost love. What was most strange and disturbing was that Monsieur should follow these vagaries alone, with only the bare trees to whisper as he passed, and the shy creatures of the forest, birds and rabbits, and once or twice a bright-eyed fox, to peep out at this peruked, bedizened thing

280

that tottered over the uneven ground on his high heels, the tears making furrows on his painted face.

'He is not yet mad,' said Minette to Colbert in that curious dispassionate way that had come on her of late, 'but if he goes on pretending so hard I think he may succeed in becoming so.' And then she added, 'but what is he to do if he does not pretend? He must want to see himself as someone.'

She watched the Minister drive away to confess his failure to his master, with her brothers' letters still in his pocket.

In retaliation Louis ordered the removal of the Chevalier de Lorraine to a far-away fortress at Marseilles, and forbade any communication between him and his friends. He even informed his ambassadors at foreign courts of the reason for his quarrel with his brother, for the newspapers everywhere were full of the scandal, and wildly differing reports were abroad.

At last Monsieur could feel that the whole of Europe was talking about him. But whatever copies he saw of the *Gazette* or other journals all showed plainly their sympathy for Madame. He had got his audience, only to find it hissing him. He had been accustomed to think of himself as a golden youth, made for love and fantastic pleasures. Now he saw his reflection in the eyes of others as a cruel and unreasonable husband who had imprisoned a dearly loved princess; his reflection in the glass added, 'and is getting fat'. The next adjective to that would be 'middle-aged'. Monsieur seriously hoped that he would die before he reached the age of thirty. In the meantime, since people persisted in misjudging him, he would act up – or down – to their idea of him. He would be a tyrant, he would show that he was to be feared just as much as Louis.

At Saint Germain, the ladies of the Court were to be seen with pens in their hands at all hours of the day, writing to Madame, hoping for her return, and 'with her the Graces who always follow in her train.' 'She alone can bring us back the springtime,' they said, and did their best to show that Monsieur's Eurydice was not the only one to be missed. The English envoy, Lord Falconbridge, was much impressed with the devotion of the Court to her.

He sent his secretary down to Villers Cotterets; later came himself; both were delighted with her, for 'she has something of particular in all she says or does that is very surprising.' The English visit was discussed, and Madame still did not despair of it. Louis thought it could be arranged when he took the Court through Flanders later in the spring. It was essential that Madame should now return to the Court. He sent down Colbert yet again, and this time with a quantity of presents for her, jewels, diamond garters, embroidered gloves, laces, perfumes, pretty leathered purses full of money, all of which he said he had won with the tickets he had drawn for her in her absence at the Court Carnival lottery.

Falconbridge was struck by this fresh evidence of Madame's influence with the King. Another person to be impressed by the gifts was Monsieur. Colbert had given him in the King's name a command for his return, and an assurance that the Chevalier de Lorraine had been set at liberty in Italy on condition that he remained out of France. Yet these royal commands scarcely had so much effect on Monsieur as the sight of so many pretty things, which, had he been present and had the luck, he might have won for himself. He had actually forgotten that he was missing the Court Carnival and the best lottery of the year. The great fair at Saint Germain would be the next excitement. He could not miss that.

So they all packed up and went back to Saint Germain together. There was a great welcome for Madame, and more royal presents. King Louis did all he could to make up for the unkindness of his brother. Nor was the Queen jealous now; she received Madame with real affection, and told her in one of their few moments of privacy that she should not look so sad nor so ill, for everyone loved her and thought Monsieur most unreasonable, and that odious Lorraine was to be exiled for ten years.

Yet in the extraordinary persistence of his hold on Monsieur, and on others, Minette began to feel she would not be surprised if at some corner of the passage she should see Lorraine standing, watching her, with that insolent smile just twisting his thin scarlet mouth. She tried not to let this dangerous fancy obsess her; but thought she was not the only one to have it. It was strange how none of Monsieur's other friends in his household, the chubby-faced little cherub, Marsan, the languidly affected Chevalier de Bevron, the rather stupid-looking and therefore, she hoped, more honest Marquis d'Effiat, ever semed to attempt to supplant Lorraine. What was it they could still so fear from him, now that his absence had been assured for so long? Did they know that he would soon manage to return?

Monsieur had already got wind of the plan of the English visit through a spy of Lorraine's, and was furious that he had not been consulted before. He knew well enough that there was still more that he did not know, and suffered agonies at being left out while the King talked over the business every afternoon with Madame. He told everyone that he detested his brother-in-law, King Charles, a man utterly untrustworthy; that he believed he had planned the expedition simply to oblige his friend the Duke of Buckingham by enabling him to carry on his long-interrupted intrigue with Monsieur's wife. Everything that he could dig up against Madame in the past he now aired abroad, telling people how she had made assignations with de Guiche in her private rooms, with de Vardes at Olympe de Soissons' house.

Mademoiselle told him acidly that since he had condoned these matters in the past he had no right to go back to them, and though 'condone' did not ring very pleasantly in Minette's ears she understood that in her stiff and angular fashion her cousin was standing up for her.

The friendship between the two women had not progressed as much as Minette had hoped. Mademoiselle was preoccupied with her new sensations; she wished yet feared to confess her ignorance and perplexity, her nervousness in Lauzun's presence and her boredom in his absence, her resolves to act towards him in one way, and her discoveries that she was acting precisely contrary, to the little cousin, fifteen years younger than herself, whom she had snubbed and patronized for so long.

It was said of Lauzun that other men were not permitted even to dream as he lived. Small, wiry and audacious as a terrier, he yet had more the air of a grand seigneur than anyone about the Court. Unlike most men of his type, he took no trouble with his dress; he wore his own hair, which was lank and untidy; and his red pointed nose, instead of being ridiculous, was somehow alarming in its acuteness and ferocity. There was nothing into which that nose would not dare to poke itself. There was nothing that would satisfy it. He spoke in character when he told Mademoiselle that he could never marry a woman who had ever had the least minute blemish on the perfect purity of her reputation.

Mademoiselle, swallowing the bait greedily, rejoiced in her virtue, which had lately caused her some rather troubled reflections.

Having been given command of the dragoons, Lauzun saw no reason why he should not have that of the artillery. The

King promised it to him on condition that he spoke of it to no one for the present. But Lauzun, hoping to secure it the more firmly, confided the precious secret to a man whose influence should help him. He, however, betrayed it to Louvois, who hated Lauzun, and remonstrated with the King. Louis was angry that Lauzun had chattered, and said no more of his promise. Lauzun waited, hung about the royal bedchamber, caught the royal eye and received a frigid stare; began to see that something had gone wrong.

Thorough in all things, his next step was to seduce a chamber-maid of Madame de Montespan's.

Montespan was a friend of his, and it was known that she could get anything she wished from the King by making one of her scenes. Petulant, rapacious, violently uncontrolled, it was a relief and a pleasure to her to show how capricious she was, how incapable of fearing him. She scoffed at Versailles – 'All this to-do about a palace a thousand times too large for anybody. Give me one of my own, on a human scale.' So the first Trianon was conceived, a delicate treasure, a toy palace of porcelain at the end of the great lake, that Louis might visit her by gondola as romantic lovers do in Venice. It was thus she secured buildings, money, jewels for herself or her family or friends, and arrogantly displayed the extent of her power.

Yet Lauzun did not quite trust her glib assurance that she would do her best for him 'this very afternoon'; there was something in the persevering way her brilliant eyes outfaced his that struck him with a suspicion of her mockery, possibly malice. He was determined to hear what she said to the King, and with the help of the terrified but adoring chambermaid he contrived to hide under her bed that afternoon on the occasion of the royal visit. There, where the least cough or movement would have betrayed and destroyed him, he lay and listened to her laughing at his pretensions as those of the most insufferably swollen-headed Gascon.

No sooner had she and the King departed than he dashed out, gave a tweak to his clothes as he passed a mirror, and waited in the corridor outside her room, where she was dressing to go to a rehearsal of a royal ballet. When she came out, he asked if he might attend her there, gave her his arm and asked what she had been able to do for him. She began to repeat a volume of speeches that she had never made. He led her on with false credulity to commit herself as deeply as possible; then told her in a low hissing voice that she was a liar, a cheat, a dirty drab, who did not know the meaning of the word honour, and proceeded to tell her, word for word, the conversation she had just had with the King. She tried to make her escape, but he held fast to her arm, occasionally pinching it, until he had repeated the last word she had said against him; then he permitted her to leave him. She rushed away to the rehearsal, could not do a word or movement correctly, and finally fainted. For once, Madame de Montespan had learned how to shiver; as she came to, she babbled incoherently of magic and the devil and a resolve never to trust in them again. Later, she told the King that Lauzun was in league with the devil, and knew every word that they had spoken together that afternoon.

The King was astounded, and found it very embarrassing when next he met the little man's angry eye fixed upon him. Lauzun had the right of the grand entries, he soon seized a chance of a private interview, and demanded why Louis had not kept his promise to him. Louis replied that Lauzun had not kept the secret.

In a fury of disappointment Lauzun turned sharply from him, drew his sword, and broke it under his foot, crying out that never again should it be used in the service of a prince who had broken his word. It was the second shock the King had had lately to his pride, that first his brother should defy him, and now Lauzun, for whom he had always felt that tenderness that a man will entertain for some wicked little dog that bites every hand but his. Now it had even bit his master. Louis raised his cane to strike, recovered himself just in time to see what he was doing, and turned instead to the window, flung it open, and threw out his cane.

'I should be sorry,' he said, 'to use it on a man of your quality,' and went out of the room.

Lauzun was once again committed to the Bastille, but only for a few days. The command of the artillery had by now been given to someone else, but the King sent Lauzun his offer of pardon and the post of Captain of the Guard. The sharp nose sniffed at the offer, and rejected it. The incredible happened; the King sent again to the Bastille; Lauzun was entreated to come out and accept the King's favour. He let himself be persuaded.

But Minette, who could guess at Montespan's nature better than Mademoiselle, could not feel easy when called on by her

285

cousin to rejoice at these fresh proofs that Lauzun was 'extraordinary in everything he did'. Montespan would not fail a second time to injure someone who had now gone out of his way to make her his enemy.

She had her own fears with regard to that lady. The close friendship which Louis now showed for herself, his complete confidence in her, his consideration and kindness, so much superior to that which he showed either to the Queen or his mistress, were certain to enrage and alarm Montespan. It had been enough (it was now too much) for La Vallière to be his mistress. But Montespan would be paramount in every particular; Louis might be allowed his lesser loves, but not a greater influence than hers over his mind. There were moments when she gathered her forces together in a dark and dreadful intensity, like a snake about to strike. Minette had once caught her so, when she was looking at herself.

But all her fears and hopes were concentrated on one thing only; the visit to England. If she achieved that, she would live or die happy. The doubts were gone that had beset her last November, while listening – or not listening – to her mother's funeral oration. It is a merciful law of nature that the brain cannot harbour too many worries at once; they tend to counteract each other. The warning ghosts of the late autumn had been dispelled by the threatening shadow of Lorraine. It had become necessary to her very existence that she should go to England.

CHAPTER THIRTY-NINE

Monsieur now said that he would permit his wife to go as far as Dover to visit her brother, on condition that he went too, 'so that she shall not carry off all the honours of the expedition as she wants to do.'

He had given up speaking to her; but conveyed what he wished by talking to other people in front of her. On this occasion he ran on into a brief lecture to Mademoiselle and other ladies round her on the regrettable tendency of the present day to separate husband and wife, and his determination to uphold the married state.

'And this is to be accomplished,' cried Minette to Louis that afternoon, 'by showing England a prince who will not speak to his wife, nor treat her better than a dog, until she begs for a young man to form a third in their union!'

She was trembling all over; she felt sick with cold; all her courage had given out at the thought of Monsieur accompanying her to England.

'I would rather not go at all,' she declared, and then at so desolate a possibility she began to cry; not stormily, but feebly, piteously, as though now that she had begun she would never be able to stop.

They were sitting at the table in the long room that had been given to her to work in at her business and correspondence every afternoon. This room was in the old part of the Palace of Saint Germain, while all the royal apartments and hers and Monsieur's were in the new. She had liked it for being remote from these, and for its view across the gardens of the road and river on their way to Paris.

At this moment the room was full of April sunshine; the windows glittered with blue sky; and from the distant road came the tinkling of a myriad little bells, telling that a shepherd or goatherd was passing with his flock. She lifted her head to listen; for an instant the opposite wall, the long table, and Louis' serious face, framed in its wig, disappeared; then as he spoke, they shut in on her again.

'He shall not go,' said Louis.

'But if he persists and you refuse, it will advertise to all the world that I have some secret mission, and that is the one thing Charles says is essential, that England must guess nothing.'

The necessity to talk sense had stopped her tears; she was twisting her lace handkerchief round her fingers. Would God allow all their great schemes for their respective nations to be destroyed, as well as her personal happiness, by this perverse and childishly tormenting creature?

Louis thought not. The best way, he said, was for Minette to appear perfectly amenable to her husband's wishes, but to say that she must naturally leave it to King Charles to decide who was to visit England, and to write and tell him of the suggestion. If he knew anything of King Charles, he would find excellent and courteous reasons for refusing the proffered honour.

In her weariness she did not see why she should take so much trouble to save Monsieur's daubed face. This passion to keep up appearances, to try and behave even now as though there were no quarrel between them, was tantamount to the

Spanish tradition which declared the Queen of Spain to have no legs.

But she obeyed Louis, wrote to Charles, and told Monsieur what she had done, whereupon he at once raised a flutter of further objections. If he went, he would not go to London. London had had the worst attack of plague in modern times, and that was only five years ago; and since then it had been destroyed by fire; it was a dangerous city; and since he would not go, she should not either. No doubt she fancied herself marching into London, and all the crowds huzzaing and everybody making a fuss over her as they had done the last time she was there; she had had it once, and why should she have it again?

Forgotten jealousies, resentments, terrors, doubts of himself, all that he had then suffered as an uneasy adolescent, now awoke to tease him once again with little stabs of memory, that mocked him for having ever hoped to love as other men could love.

His unhappiness was obvious. Some thought it was sending him out of his mind; others, that when it did, no one would notice any difference.

Louis had always bullied his brother, and yet he could not bear that he should be hurt. He gave Monsieur his permission to go to England, so as to put him in a better humour, and never realized how much the worse that would be for his consent when Charles' refusal arrived.

Minette found these tortuous courses of action bewildering. The difficulties she encountered all through her life were those of an ingenuous and simple nature in a set of people so closely knit together, so regulated and restricted by the artificial circumstances of their life, that they had become more complicated than any set of people before or after.

It had been said of her that to whomsoever she spoke she offered her heart. She could see no harm in this as long as it was a good heart; she did not realize that people look at hearts as at mirrors, to find the reflection of their own motives. It had often been as unwise for her to be truthful as if she had slandered herself. She saw the world through her own spectacles, of rose-colour generally, sometimes of smoke or fire, but never quite with the same eyes as other people. This it was that gave her her peculiar quality, that made ambassadors, bishops and memoir writers give up any description of her in despair, and fall back on the lame phrase, 'there is nobody like her.'

Now, more than ever before in her life, she felt the need of a quiet and single mind. The Abbé Bossuet was in Paris. She sent for him to thank him for his beautiful oration on her mother, but when she saw him, admitted on an impulse that she had scarcely heard a word of it. She would be grateful if he would lend it her to read – he had surely kept a copy? He had. He kept copies of all his sermons, and was not above hoping to see them published. But funeral orations were those that he least cared to do. It was not always easy to be sincere in them; they had too long been used as mere occasions to truckle to the worldly vanity of the families of the deceased, who looked on the publicity they afforded as of better value than notices in the *Gazette*. He had diminished that as much as possible, cut out all pedigrees and attention to illustrious relatives, and tried always to make his particular subject an occasion for the universal.

Unlike Cosnac, he never dreamed of the Cardinal's hat; had he been a shade more pushing, it would certainly have been his. He was Court preacher, yet only now was he awaiting the papal confirmation to his appointment at Bishop of Condom in Paris – and that was of the second rank of bishoprics. This unworldly strain in him at once found its counterpart in the princess, whom till now he had thought of only as the leader of pleasures in the King's Court.

She told him she was troubled; that her mind was often so restless and distracted that she could not sleep; that she wished, if it were not too late, she could begin to think of God and of her soul. His sympathy was as fiery as his eloquence. He lent her books whose weight and appearance at first discouraged her, for how could she attend to these long abstract inquiries into the nature of God and the Universe when, waking or sleeping, her head was buzzing with questions as to how Charles would contrive to fob off Monsieur (why had she not suggested this or that to him?) or what further obstacles Monsieur would manage to put in the way of her journey, and what means she could find to forestall him?

But she found that even when she did not understand or was not much interested in what she read, it yet helped to make her mind move in one piece, instead of a frightened scurry in all directions; above all, that it induced sleep.

This longing for sleep, forgetfulness, peace, what was it, she asked Bossuet, but the longing for death itself? Death was not an ending to life, but a necessary part of it, continuing through it. How could one live each day if one did not die each night, losing one's consciousness in the undiscoverable vast of eternity? Then the things that she most treasured were not after all subject to these capricious laws of chance and circumstance and human malice.

'Lay up for yourself treasure in heaven,' said Bossuet's urgent, persuasive voice, and she thought of her love and Charles', their hopes for England, her love for her little daughter, whom 'they' had succeeded in turning against her, but only for a time, not in eternity. These things were really safe; even Monsieur could not touch them.

She needed all her new security when Charles' letter arrived, refusing Monsieur's visit. The reasons were such as to go straight to Monsieur's heart, had it been any other occasion. The brother of the King of France could not, in any decent consideration of etiquette, visit England, unless the brother of the King of England were at the same moment to visit France; and as it was impossible for the Duke of York to go to Calais while Monsieur went to Dover, he deeply regretted that he was obliged to decline the proffered honour.

'Then she shan't go,' screamed Monsieur.

English envoys and ambassadors made the matter worse by assuring him that his wife would have greater honours in England than any royal visitor had ever had before; that she should take precedence of every lady (excepting of course the Queen), even of the Duchess of York; thus placing his rank higher than that of the heir to the English throne. But why should she enjoy such honours, which he had given her ('Where would she be but for me?' he fumed), without his being there to enjoy them?

When driven at last to consent, three days were all that he would allow her.

Three days after more than nine years' absence; one day for each three years; what allowance was that for two people who would have as much to say to each other as she and Charles? so Minette asked bitterly. The pattering little waves of time – seconds, minutes, hours, scurrying so fast upon her – had surged up once more, and drowned her brief vision of eternity.

It was now the end of April, and time to start on the expedition into Flanders. Louis summarily told Monsieur that he

290

had got to make up his quarrel with Madame, and bring her along too with a good grace. Monsieur said he would not do so unless she made the first advances. She was quite willing, and begged his pardon for everything he said she had said, whether she had said it or not.

'Never has anything been more wrangled over,' she wrote to Madame de Saint Chaumont, bidding her farewell, for she had not been able to reinstall her as governess. And she could scarcely believe it when on that very day she stepped up into the coach to start with the Court for Flanders.

It was raining. Monsieur was in his worst humour. But as they were driving in the same coach with the King and Queen and Madame de Montespan, now chief lady-in-waiting, he curbed it so far as to express it only about the weather. Minette minded nothing. She leaned back on the cushions and looked out of the window on the slithering yellow mud in the road, the thick drops that made miniature fountains in the puddles, the trees that surged out of the falling rain like green sea-monsters submerged fathoms deep.

'It always rains like this at the end of April,' said Montespan. 'When the month turns, it will change for the better.'

But it did not. It rained through France, it rained through Flanders, it rained all through May. They went through Senlis, Compiègne and Saint Quentin, where they met Lauzun, who had been appointed Lieutenant-General at the head of the troops, and continued through Arras, Douai and Courtrai.

Roads were flooded, bridges washed away, all the grand new uniforms were ruined, and the waving plumes looked like tails of wet string. Two or three times the royal party were cut off by the floods. On one occasion their coach was stuck fast in the muddy banks of a swollen river, and they all had to stay there twenty-four hours without food or drink.

On another, they had to sleep in a barn while a bridge was being repaired. Mattresses were spread on the floor for both the sexes. The Queen thought it would be unbecoming to lie down, even though they remained fully dressed. The King referred the question to Mademoiselle, whose head was spinning with fatigue. She said emphatically there could be no harm in it. There were none of their women with them, and Mademoiselle was in great anxiety lest her priceless family jewels, which had been left with her women, might have been washed away by the floods. The Queen would not touch the soup at

291

supper, and then was very cross afterwards that it had all been eaten, and she could have none the last thing at night.

'I am sure you must all know I am accustomed to take something hot last thing at night.'

There were no knives or forks; they had to pull the badly roasted chickens to pieces between them, 'like savages in a cave,' declared Montespan, her lovely face laughing through the rich gloom of the torchlit barn. It was as well, she said, they had no knives; for her part she was so hungry she might easily stab anyone who disputed her claim to this leg that she was tugging away from the carcase. She drank off the best part of a bottle of strong Italian wine and then called for brandy. Her unfailing health and high spirits were invaluable at times like these; the tantrums of the spoilt beauty were reserved for the hours of ease which did not suit her so well.

They all lay down to rest. There was a musty mingled smell of damp stray, wet leather, wet horses, mud and rats. In the next division of the barn were the chief officers of the army, who were continually passing and repassing for orders, to the great disturbance of the ladies. The Queen, still hurt about the soup, complained that she could not sleep a wink with this clatter of people coming in and out. The King suggested that a hole should be made in the wooden partition so that he could give orders through it and receive reports. There was a short burst of loud hammering and sawing while this was being done, and then comparative quiet.

The relentless rain could now be heard without a break; it swished down through the surrounding blackness; it sucked all other sounds into its vast wet maw; the subdued voices of the men and clanking movements of their swords and spurs on the other side of the partition; outside, the horses coughing and trampling in the squelching mud, shaking their uneasy manes, jingling and hauling their chains; canvas dripping; men calling hoarsely in the distance.

Minette lay listening to the rain that half-drowned all these noises; she cared for nothing, was anxious only lest her sore throat should make her cough as the others fell asleep. This nightmare progress through the conquered province was making her feel very ill; she was frequently not able to eat, and would go to bed immediately on arrival at any place, with only milk for supper. Yet she was more indifferent to her surroundings even than Mademoiselle, who cared only that she might catch an occasional glimpse of Lauzun at the head of

292

the troops, and therefore sat by the coach window with her head twisted perpetually sideways.

So much had always happened to prevent her going to Charles that Minette dared count on nothing. She was thankful that now there was nothing more she could do in the matter. When they got to Courtrai they would (if nothing happened to prevent them) find there envoys extraordinary from the King of England, with the request that his sister should come over for an impromptu visit to him at Dover. Everyone knew that a visit to England was planned; nearly all the ladies of the Court had clamoured for permission to accompany her, longing to display their attractions before such an appreciative audience as they had heard the King and Court of England provided. But they had no notion when this visit would take place. Nor had Monsieur. It would come as a complete surprise to everybody except the very few in the secret. Monsieur would do all he could to prevent it. He might succeed. It was better not to think of it.

'Cease to hope, cease to fear, cease to live,' said the steady rhythm of the rain outside. She watched the light of the torch, stuck at the side of the barn, flicker upwards over the rafters and the great beam that went across them. She saw a rat run across the beam and stop for an instant, the light gleaming green on its eyes like two sharp pin-points, as it stopped to peer down on the sleeping faces below. She raised herself on her elbow and also looked at them: the Queen, Louis, Monsieur, Mademoiselle, Montespan, all fast asleep. It seemed odd that she alone should be awake, looking at them, as though she alone of all that company were alive.

The torchlight grew paler, the shadows less clear-cut, the darkness colder and more grey. Someone came to the barn door and spoke to the guards there; they answered that His Majesty was fast asleep. Mademoiselle rolled over and opened her eyes. 'What is it?' she whispered to Madame.

'Louvois, I think, and Tréville. They are saying the bridge is now ready for us to go across and get lodging in the town.'

'Then for Heaven's sake let us do so. I have had a wretched night. I have scarcely slept at all.'

'But all the others are asleep. The guards are hesitating to disturb the King.'

But Mademoiselle never hesitated. She called out, loud enough to wake the King, that Monsieur de Lauvois wished to speak to him.

The King rolled over and cursed, then sat up, rubbing his eyes. 'What's that? Have they built up the bridge? Well, why not leave it till the morning?'

'Sire, it is already morning,' said Mademoiselle. The burly form of Louvois, the slender one of Tréville, showed dark for an instant against the pale raw light that entered with them through the open door. Beyond it the rain still fell like a grey curtain.

Louvois went up to the King, and Mademoiselle listened eagerly to him for any word respecting Lauzun. Tréville stopped to kneel down beside Minette's mattress, holding out a locket.

'I stepped on this trinket, Madame, in the mud and thought I had seen you wear it.'

She took it, thanking him.

'You should not be here, Madame,' he said in a low and anxious tone. 'You are ill. I beg of you, stay and rest in the town and do not go on with us.'

It was an odd request for an accomplished courtier. Tréville was the most promising young man at Court, the best Greek scholar and most brilliant talker. He was a great friend of Bossuet, and had edited Pascal's letters. The King thought so highly of him that he had asked Monsieur to make him captain of the musketeers, of his household. Madame had therefore seen a good deal of him, but though he looked at her continually he seldom spoke to her; indeed it was noticeable that he talked far less, and less wittily, whenever she was present.

She saw his concern for her with a little wonder, a little impatience. She knew that at this moment in this wan and cruel light she must be looking ghastly. She did not see that it was in this moment that Tréville found it impossible to keep out of his eyes the love for her that he would always forbear to speak.

'Do not trouble for me,' she said, 'I shall be able to rest soon.'

Louvois had finished speaking with the King. The company were heaving themselves off the floor, yawning and groaning, complaining of their cramped bones and the deadly chill of the four o'clock air. The King put his mouth to the hole in the wall and shouted through to somebody on the other side, where a great stirring and stamping and clanking at once began.

'Mercifully,' remarked Mademoiselle to no one in particular, 'I am seldom as much in need of rouge as others.'

But it was Montespan who looked the least impaired by their adventure.

Louis insisted on riding on with Louvois to look at the bridge before they crossed, so that Monsieur was alone with the women. As they settled themselves in the coach he remarked, smiling, that in spite of his hard couch he had had a pleasant dream, prompted by the last occasion when he had had his fortune told. 'La Voisin assured me,' he said, 'that I would be married three times. To judge by Madame's looks this morning, I think it extremely likely.'

The Queen turned her head away in disgust. Neither she nor Mademoiselle remonstrated, from the knowledge that anything they said would only recoil on Madame. But she herself seemed not to hear him.

CHAPTER FORTY

Only Mademoiselle's chambermaids had arrived at their lodgings in Landrecies; no one else's and none of the ladies-in-waiting. There were furious complaints of this, and worse jealousies when it was rumoured that Lauzun had prevented their progress and even halted the troops so as to let through these chambermaids first. The ladies, when at last they arrived, were naturally the most indignant of all.

'But I think he was quite right, and extremely kind,' said Mademoiselle, 'he knew my chambermaids were the persons I most needed to help me to bed. I shall make a point of thanking him myself.'

The ladies revenged themselves by secret giggling together over that, for Mademoiselle made a point of speaking to Lauzun whenever possible (and he seldom made it possible); of getting up at five in the morning and going out on the balcony in the rain to see him muster the troops; and there, if she could not catch his eye, she would call to anyone inside the room so loudly that even he could not fail to hear and look up at her – 'and then how happy I feel!' she wrote in her diary after so describing her actions.

In return for her thanks he told her that she had annoyed him as much as he had pleased her, by her uncontrolled complaints in front of the King of the length of the route and the badness of the weather.

'But it is not you I complain of,' she said in a piteous voice, like a child who has been unfairly scolded. 'Monsieur de Louvois arranged the route, not you.'

'Do you think I want preferential treatment?' he barked at her. 'On the contrary I detest it. Every time you ask the King to tell me to put on my hat when I am talking to him uncovered in the rain, you make me feel I want to go under the earth. The very reason I have always remained unmarried is that I could never bear to have a woman fussing over me.'

Her lip trembled. She felt her knees turn to water. If she did not speak at once she would burst into tears.

'Will – do you wish always to remain unmarried?' she asked humbly.

They pursued the question, which had become frequent with them, for a couple of hours. Two or three times he tried to make his escape, but on the whole he let himself be wooed in the ambiguous fashion which was all he allowed her. She told him that she had overcome every objection to matrimony that he had previously pointed out to her, had decided on the man she wished to marry, and that it only remained to inform this man and have his approbation. He replied that she must not be in a hurry, that indeed if she were to wait a whole century before coming to a decision it would hardly be too prudent.

'As I have already reached the age of forty,' she said rather sharply, 'I cannot agree with you there.'

It was the first moment in which she found herself talking to him with that authority of manner she used with everyone else. She took courage to add that she had made up her mind to speak to the King at the first opportunity, and that she intended to be married before she left Flanders.

He looked startled. Did he think she meant to marry anyone else? She hastened to reassure him by indirect allusions to himself. But without waiting to unravel them, or even listen to what she was saying, he abruptly left her.

For a little time she was in despair, but when they reached Arras, Lauzun was better dressed than on the march; she took pleasure in his noble air; she tried to behave as he would wish and not think of her own comfort as the most important thing in the world. When the bugles annoyed her by waking her too early she remembered that while she lay in her bed at ease Lauzun was out at the head of his men in the rain, weary, wet and uncomfortable. On hearing these reflections he remarked dryly that no doubt it gave satisfaction to think thus

296

of others; then told her that it was not becoming in her to attend to anything that was not practical and important.

It was impossible to know how he would respond to anything. At Tournay, wishing to speak to him, she asked him to help her from the coach; and he walked away, leaving her with one foot in the air, so that she nearly fell to the ground. Yet all his rudeness and scolding and all the ways in which he ignored and shunned her seemed to her in some inexplicable fashion as proofs of his love; as though his pride could only be satisfied by chaining her, the greatest unmarried lady in France, as an abject slave to his chariot wheel.

Even his deliberate cruelty could subtly flatter her. On the sudden death of a robust and popular young man of the Court, he reminded her at every meeting of her 'mortal and uncertain state'; and that because, as he knew, she feared the thought of death exceedingly. And now whenever she saw him approaching her, her face lit up with pleasure at so unexpected an event, but would fall into lines of woeful disappointment when she discovered that it was merely to tell her in a macabre whisper to 'Think of death! Think of it!' or 'Remember you must die.'

But at last her aspirations, if not her desires, had been satisfied, for she had found someone who was capable of acting consistently in a manner quite beyond that of anyone else.

On their way to Courtrai they were told that messengers had there arrived from the King of England. On hearing this, Minette at first flushed and then went very white; she avoided Monsieur's eyes, for she did not dare see how he took the news. But oddly enough he was not looking at her, nor did he appear to take the intelligence to himself at all. He was full of some mystery which seemed to concern Mademoiselle, for he goggled his eyes at her, nodded, winked, and at last, incapable of further restraint, observed portentously, 'I know something, but I am not going to tell you what it is.'

They all stared at him as if he were a speaking doll and worthy of as much notice. The King rebuked him for mentioning a mere flimsy rumour.

'But I haven't.'

'No, but you will,' replied Louis, 'so I had best do it,' and he explained that there was news of a Divorce Bill to be put before the English Parliament. This probably meant that King Charles intended to divorce his childless wife.

And the messengers from England,' cried Montespan, with a flourish of white hands, a flash of rings, a flutter of curls and laces, 'are then for the hand of Mademoiselle! It is well known King Charles has always been desperately in love with her. What could be more charming? She is so literary and writes so well – she will send him letters and a thousand little tokens, and all will end happily after all, as it does in a fairy tale!'

Montespan's eyes sparkled with malice as she spoke. Another's agony of mind was apt to give her an added zest and vigour of life. Watching the stricken face of the elder woman, whose red cheeks had turned an unbecoming purple, she drew in her breath with a little sharp sigh as though tasting strong wine.

For Mademoiselle, terrified of hearing any news lest it might bear unfavourably on the one project of her life, was overcome at this possibility and at once translated it into achieved fact – King Charles was already divorced, determined to marry her, and King Louis would never let her lose a match so advantageous to himself. She burst into tears.

The Queen patted her arm soothingly and said, 'Indeed I am with you, my dear cousin. It is quite shocking to think of any man, king or peasant, having two wives. I am sure that even if the King wished it, you would not consent to such a thing.'

Monsieur remarked, 'After all, it is a great opportunity for her, and I am sure it is high time for her to consider something of the sort.'

The King asked her what serious objection she could offer to the match.

'It is the thought of leaving you, Sire, that overcomes me,' she replied, dabbing her eyes.

The only person to sit quite silent was Minette, who felt as sick with apprehension as Mademoiselle, but for another reason. Was it possible that some such errand was the cause of the envoy's visit to Courtrai, and that something had prevented Charles from asking her to come to Dover? She could not believe it, and yet it really seemed as though Louis believed this rumour, and certainly Monsieur, so quick to catch what was in the air, showed no apprehension on her account. If only she could catch Louis' eye or whisper one word to him! But probably he knew as yet no more than herself. They must both of them wait a few hours longer till they reached Courtrai.

These past weeks of fatigue, bleak discomfort and illness

had passed in a dream-like condition that was almost peace, for she had been content to accept whatever happened, since it was nothing to do with the one thing she wished to happen. They seemed to have passed more quickly than these few hours were passing, now that once again she had been stung into life by the tortures of hope and fear.

They reached Courtrai and found the English envoys waiting for them with the news that King Charles was at Dover, and had begged Madame to seize this occasion for a visit. The English fleet under Lord Sandwich was even now awaiting her orders in the port of Dunkirk. Nothing was said concerning the rumour that had so disturbed Mademoiselle.

Monsieur had decided to believe in it as the sole reason for the envoy's visit, and was the more furious when he heard the true one. He swore that it was all a plot to cheat him, to take his wife away from him, that nothing would induce him to let her go. The King told him sternly to stop making that noise, for the journey was to be conducted in his interests and at his command.

At that, Monsieur saw he would have to give in; saw also that his brother had chosen his wife as his agent, and left him entirely out of his counsel. He complained bitterly to Montespan that his wife had come between him and everything in life that he held dear – she had turned his brother and his brother's wife against him – ('You see how the Queen treats me, as though it were not worth the trouble to answer my remarks!') she had driven away the Chevalier de Lorraine.

'I had a letter from him just lately,' said Montespan, 'he asks if you are getting more reconciled with your wife.'

'Tell him I will never be, never, that I wish I were rid of her more than anything in the world.'

'Yes, I will tell him that,' said Montespan.

Monsieur fell silent, brooding on a plan to assert himself as someone who had cut a figure in the world, for all that his own brother ignored him. Through the rest of the towns in Flanders where they had still to pass, the towns that he had helped to conquer, he would ride at the head of his regiment, sword in hand. If only it would not go on raining. He had seen Lauzun looking quite frightful with his greasy hair all uncurled by the wet.

And so Minette was spared her husband's company in the coach through Lille to Dunkirk, whither they all accompanied her. She was transfigured. A radiance of expectation shone

299

from her; she sat a little forward in the coach as if to urge it onward, looking out of the windows at the scene that passed so slowly; yet every yard or two there was something, a tree, a heap of stones, a church tower in front of them, then left behind, to show that it had changed, that they were coming nearer and nearer to Dunkirk, and the ships that would take her to Charles. Once again she was the Minette who walked down the gallery at Saint Cloud, holding out her hands to all that life had to give her.

Mademoiselle, seeing her thus, longed yet again to break the habit of reserve that the years had built up between them, to pour out all her hopes and fears to her and refresh them in that tide of eager and receptive life. But they reached Dunkirk, and still she had made no move.

They saw Madame go on board with a splendid retinue that the King had himself chosen for her – a suite of two hundred and thirty-seven persons, including a marshal and a bishop and such high names as that determined Anglophile, the Comte de Gramont, and his English wife and brother-in-law, Anthony Hamilton. There were five maids of honour, one of them quite new to her service, with an outlandish Breton name, harsh as the cry of a seagull, but there was nothing like a seagull in little Mademoiselle de Kerouälle and her soft, suave, babyishly pretty face.

Madame's relatives and friends went on board with her, embraced her with many wishes for a happy visit and renewed health as its consequence. All but Monsieur, who contrived to say so many spiteful things (though he chiefly reiterated, 'Only three days now – if you stay more than three days you will repent of it—'), that at the last moment, in the midst of all her joy, she was reduced to weeping.

Mademoiselle ran forward and took her hands. 'Do not cry,' she said, 'we all wish you well. You must know it.'

Minette embraced her cousin. 'I do,' she said, 'and indeed I wish you well.'

She half whispered this and so tenderly that Mademoiselle was more than ever annoyed with herself that she had not before now spoken out to her. And now they were weighing anchor, the ship was starting and could not be delayed even for half an hour, not even to let her talk to her cousin as she had never talked before.

The great sails were hauled up, flapping and filling with the

300

salt breeze, making vast white curves against the stormy evening sky. For once it was not raining.

Mademoiselle followed the royal party into the rowing-boat that took them ashore. There they turned and waved a last farewell to the *Royal Charles* that had borne the English King after years of exile to his kingdom, and was now taking his sister home to him. The sunset clouds had cast their glory across the water. Mademoiselle saw the huge ship, majestic and slow, sail out towards that unreal land in the west, the floating islands and great shapes that filled the sky with sails and wings of fire and flying mist. She was seized with a fancy that her cousin was sailing away, never to return, and that now she would never have the chance to speak to her as she had wished.

The other ships followed the *Royal Charles*. Like the towering clouds above them, they spread their sails to the wind, careening before it, dipping and curtseying, a gallant sight as they sped out to sea.

But it filled Mademoiselle's heart with an irrational sense of loss. Regretful, fearful, she knew not of what, she looked round her at the little company on the shore. All their splendid colours had gone black in the glowing light. Against that huge and evanescent scene they looked like pygmies.

She saw Monsieur going from one to the other to complain of his wrongs, until they each in turn managed to shake him off; and he stood there disconsolately picking up shells and turning them over in his hand.

She saw Lauzun standing for an instant by himself. She said to herself, 'Shall I go to him? (No, you had better not.) Shall I look hard at him until he sees I am speaking to no one, and will come over to me? (He will not come.) But this is foolish. I am a great princess and he a mere gentleman, it is for me to show he may advance. (You have shown it, you have shown it – do not go to him.)' But she went.

She told him how she had wept when she had heard the rumour of the English King's intention to marry her. Now surely he would see how much she loved him.

He replied that he had heard of her conduct, and that the only reason for it he could think of was that which she had given the King; that she could not bear to leave His Majesty. In every other way it was a perfect match, peculiarly well-fitted to her, 'since you always like to do extraordinary things.'

He said this in so wounding a manner that she turned from

301

him to hide her tears, and walked on along the shore without seeing that he did not follow her. Before her, with her back now turned to the sunset, the darker clouds were carved in the shape of a castle.

Once again she was in the centre courtyard at Chambord, with the castle soaring above her; once again she was a child, and there, at the top of the famous double staircase that Francis I had built, stood her father. She ran up the steps to him, and he ran down to her; but when she reached the top he was at the bottom, and yet they had not met; for that was the peculiarity of the staircase, people could ascend and descend without meeting each other. Down she ran again and up he came to her, and there they were again; she at the bottom this time and he at the top. How they laughed as they chased each other!

'The staircase is enchanted,' he cried, 'and we shall never meet.'

So it had always been with her and her father; and so now with her and all those whom she loved – that she went out heart and soul to meet them, and perhaps they also went some way towards her, and yet – was it because of the sad tangle of existence, common to all who lived and loved? or was it because of some rigid, impassible quality in herself? – they never really met.

CHAPTER FORTY-ONE

Minette sailed towards the sunset, towards her own month of June, and into midsummer weather, as the sailors told her it had been in England this week past. Once again the weather was important, as it had not been for nine long summers. A miracle (for so it seemed after the rain and mud of Flanders) had arranged that she and Charles would have nothing to mar their enjoyment. She went to bed almost as soon as they had started, for she was determined to be quite well by tomorrow.

She woke to see a dawn of pearl and amethyst filling her porthole. An instant later Mademoiselle de la Kerouälle came into her cabin and told her that they were nearing England. She hurried into some clothes and went up on deck. The sun was already up but very pale. The sky was turning to a milky turquoise, the sea much smoother than yesterday evening, a

302

glimmering white. The air tasted wet and salt and sharp. The ship moved slowly within a circle of sparkling mist. There came a steady rhythmic sound, growing louder, the sound of oars in their rowlocks. The haze thickened into the shape of a long rowing-boat, skimming swiftly towards them. She ran to the gunwale, and now she could see that three men sat in the boat beside the rowers; they stood up and waved to her, and she waved back, and soon she was calling out to them, little cries so full of naked joy that they could find no words in which to clothe themselves.

Louise de la Kerouälle, coming out of the state-room, saw three tall men come up on deck, and her new mistress caught up and enfolded among them.

'Who is that? and which is that one?' she demanded eagerly of one of her colleagues.

'The dark one is King Charles, and the others are his brother, the Duke of York, and his cousin, Prince Rupert, who must be the older one, the tallest of all.'

'Indeed,' said Mademoiselle de la Kerouälle, determined not to show herself too much impressed, but secretly congratulating herself on her good fortune in thus seeing the world at the very outset of her career at Court.

'Charles! Charles!' said Minette, looking up into the face that had grown considerably more than nine years older. She heard his deep voice say the words she had seen written so often, 'My dearest Minette.'

'I have all your letters with me,' she said; and then she laughed and turned to James, putting her hands round his. He too looked much older, she could now see, and yet her first feeling had been that neither of them had changed in the least, that the last nine years had suddenly slid out of their lives, and they would all go on talking exactly where they had left off.

'Your little Anne is very well,' she said to James, 'I think her eyes are really cured. She is so sweet and patient with my little horror of a daughter. Charles, do you know what I said when she was born? I said, "Throw her into the river," and she has determined to justify it ever since – so you see, in her way, she is a dutiful daughter. Is it true you have had this lovely weather all the time in England? It only rains in France. Oh, our journey was so funny! I shall die with laughter whenever I think of it. Imagine – we all slept together in a barn one night, it was so amusing, a real adventure.'

303

'She is just the same as ever,' said James to Charles. Prince Rupert had not yet spoken; it was difficult for him to do so as the others talked so much.

The cliffs of Dover were now plainly to be seen through the pearl-coloured mist. In the sunrise they looked like the vast walls of that cloud city to which she had been sailing overnight. Her breath caught in her throat at sight of their beauty. There was her own country waiting for her after all these years; she pointed to it, calling to the others to look too.

'Look, I am coming home,' she cried, and they saw that through her laughter there were tears in her eyes; that the colour that had flooded her cheeks was now confined to two bright patches, and round them her skin was transparently white.

Her looks made Charles anxious; so did her obvious shrinking from his question when he asked her what was this nonsense of her staying only three days.

'Oh,' she said, shrugging her slight shoulders under the unreasonable burden, 'what does it matter? I am *here now.*' She emphasized the words to herself rather than to him. 'I am so happy,' she said, 'that if I stayed three years they would pass like three days – just as on the other side three days have often seemed to last three years.'

And she even for a moment tried to dissuade him when he remarked that her philosophy was very fine, but he would keep it for visitors whose company was worse than hers, and sent back one of the ships with messages to King Louis, now at Calais, that no business could possibly be concluded in so short a time.

She remembered Monsieur's last words to her, and felt a momentary fear; 'but what worse can he do to me than he has already done?' she asked herself, 'except indeed to kill me, and is that so much worse?'

Now at last she could pour out the whole story of his behaviour to Charles, who showed such black fury that she found herself checking and modifying the details. 'You must not mind so much,' she said, 'for here I am with you, and who could be happier?' Indeed it seemed that she had never been parted from him.

He remarked that with Lorraine out of the way she could at least have nothing to fear, since his rivals were unlikely to plot for his return.

'But no,' she said, 'though it is so strange, I think they do.

304

He must indeed be the devil, for he makes them do all he wishes, even though it be against themselves.'

He thought her fanciful and overwrought; he saw that it frightened and worried her to make plans; even the suspense of waiting for King Louis' answer was telling on her. But when it came, and the French King gave his brother's permission to his wife to stay ten or twelve days longer in order to conclude any necessary business, she danced with happiness, she hugged Charles and laughed her agreement to his comment that ten or twelve was as much as to say twelve or fifteen, a day or two made no odds, and they would contrive to spin her visit out to nearly three weeks in all.

No fearful apprehension now visited her at such boldness. Three weeks wa~ ~~ ~~ ~nity of bliss – who cared what might happen at the end of it?

She walked a~~ ~~~ over the downs with Charles, cruised along the shore in his beautiful ships. Her health confirmed her spirits in the assurance that she had been away for several months.

And why not for ever? Charles could now discuss it with her rationally. She could not of course snatch at this occasion to run away from her husband and never return from England. That would discredit the whole procedure of her visit and destroy the amity between the two countries. But a separation had been talked of; Monsieur himself had declared frequently how much he wished it; the Divorce Bill was even now being discussed by Parliament, and Minette was an English princess who should (or might at a pinch, said Charles) have full claim to the protection of the English law.

She found that he had no intention of divorce for himself. The Duke of Buckingham had obligingly thought of abducting the Queen in order to give his master good occasion for it; but Charles had discovered and put a stop to the plot. He would not have the poor woman abused, he told Minette; she had enough to put up with from him as it was.

'Is it possible people have told her things against you? How incredible! How do such stories get about?' she mocked him.

Queen Catherine had been sent for, and the Duchess of York; the whole English Court came hurrying down to greet her on this impromptu visit that had been so planned and thought out and longed for during the last few years. Dover was crammed to overflowing; the two hundred and thirty-seven distinguished French visitors had to find what lodging

they could in the village, but after the discomforts of the bad
weather in Flanders they thought this a glorified picnic: it was
such perfect summer weather that some hardy spirits suggested there was nothing to prevent their rigging up tents out
of old sails and sleeping on the sands or the downs.

'Ah yes, let us all do that!' cried Queen Catherine, clapping
her hands and looking like an eager little girl. She was very
small, rather plain, with large brown wistful eyes that followed
her husband everywhere. She was instantly friendly with
Minette, talking as artlessly to her as though she had always
known her, 'and so indeed I have – all the things Charles has
told me of you, and the presents you have sent me – those
pretty pictures of the saints I have now in my bedroom, I think
of you every time I pray to them, and Charles says I have
made you into one of them, a Saint Minette.'

She spoke of him with the greatest tenderness; it was he, she
said, who had saved her life when she was so ill, and her
attendants had kept up a determined caterwauling round her
bed, moaning and shrieking that she was dying, and entreating
her to make her will, until Charles got so furious that he very
courageously drove them all out.

But she had been very happy while she was ill; for two days
she thought she had borne him a fine boy and had already
presented him with a family of three boys and two girls. If
she could bear him an heir she would not mind how unfaithful
he was to her, indeed she did not mind so very much even
now. At first it had been terrible; she had shut herself up in
her room all day to cry alone. Then she had thought how silly
it was to be so miserable, and had tried to be as gay as the
rest of the Court; had set her chaplains to dance country
dances in her bedroom, and gone jaunting to a fair in disguise,
was recognized, nearly mobbed, and thankful to be rescued
and taken home on the pillion of an elderly knight; and when
they reached Whitehall there was Charles with the Duke of
Buckingham standing out on the steps and laughing at her
escapade.

Now she was content to be herself, to adore her husband,
and accept without demand or question the self-reproachful
affection he could accord her.

Minette's other sister-in-law, James' wife, was a great contrast to this little convent-bred foreigner. She too was a new
friend to Minette, who had seen very little of her during that
visit nearly ten years ago, when poor Anne Hyde's marriage to

the Duke of York was still being hotly wrangled over. Now she had grown in stoutness and self-confidence, increasingly plain, but full of sound good sense, and laid down the law in a manner that was growing very like that of her father, the Earl of Clarendon. As she complained to Minette of his treatment of her, it was odd to see how exactly that bright conceited eye, that plump determined chin resembled his. 'My father had grown really impossible with everybody,' she said apropos of the old man's late disgrace. He had quarrelled with everybody at Court and in Parliament, he had made himself thoroughly unpopular with the country; they had cried everywhere that Hyde must go, and so Hyde went.

Though a convert, she was no bigot. She thought it might be a good plan to marry the young Protestant Prince William of Orange to her eldest daughter Mary. It was evident why James, who set such value by spoken opinion, had found refuge in her directness, her argumentative and logical mind. He liked his wife, and his mistresses to, to tell him what to think.

'That is interesting, I must think it over.'

These were, said Charles, the usual early stages in the courtships of James, who was as great a libertine as himself, 'but not likely to have as bad a reputation, since he gets the less pleasure from it.'

'You think that, do you?'

'Yes, I had considered that before.'

But as morality is mainly a matter of comparison, it is not surprising that Minette found the atmosphere of King Charles' Court refreshingly pure.

Neither fear nor formula oppressed the air. If men were bad, it was because they were so by nature, not because their souls had been imprisoned, crippled, tortured out of shape by conforming to a meaningless pattern of existence. Charles was far more promiscuous than Louis, but there was no spectacle at his Court such as that of La Vallière, vanquished, but forbidden to retire from the arena, dragged in the mud too long to care what further humiliations were in store for her.

'Love and let love' was here the order of the Court. Charles bore no resentment for his treatment by Frances Stuart, who had encouraged him to the last point, then, to escape him, secretly married the Duke of Richmond. Charles had been deeply hurt at the time, but went to see poor Frances when she had the smallpox, and forgave her.

307

Nor was such a fate as Vatel's possible in this easier air, Vatel who had been steward to the Prince de Condé ever since the downfall of Fouquet. When King Louis came to stay, he fell on his sword and died because he thought the fish had not arrived in time for the fish course.

'And after all it had arrived,' said Minette.

'He sounds a poor fish – and even so it could not have helped to feed the company.'

Charles showed an amused horror of his brother-in-law's regime of ceremonial, particularly that of the bedchamber, and the three hundred gentlemen who were privileged to see Louis put on his breeches. 'Does he go through all that when he's drunk?'

Louis drunk! Louis lose command of that icy consciousness that kept him always watchfully aware of himself and his surroundings – always – ever since that summer nine years ago!

'He has never been drunk. It would not be possible for him. He would feel it so – untidy.'

That was the word for England. Even the disorder of all the different little religious sects could not help striking her as amusing and a little touching, as well as exasperating. Guilty of spiritual pride as they were, was it not rather a magnificent pride to insist that each individual was free to save or lose his soul by himself? They certainly made everything a great muddle, yet perhaps that suited England.

The Court was haphazard, amazingly free. When women were jealous they showed it openly. The King's latest addition to his more or less permanent mistresses was a Cockney actress, who had carried the manners of the Drury Lane market into the Court, and proved them not amiss there. Barbara Palmer, Countess of Castlemaine, Duchess of Cleveland, did not need the new Mrs Gwynn to teach her the language of Billingsgate. A rough good-humour, a coarse vigour in the enjoyment of abuse and practical jokes made their quarrels ridiculous, not deadly.

There were no whispers here, as in France, of the Black Mass performed on the naked body of the King's most brilliant and high-born mistress; nor yet of a sorceress, employed by half the Court, who could supply anxious heirs with a *poudre de succession* for the removal of tardy relatives, and was believed to sacrifice unwanted bastard babies to Satan, to furnish ingredients for her infallible recipes.

Charles could scarcely believe his sister that an educated people should still take such things seriously. Since his institution of the Royal Society in pursuit of science at the beginning of his reign, there had been but two instances in England of doing a witch to death, compared with the many hundreds of the few previous years. This Society was his favourite hobby, to which he devoted more of his spare time than to his women or even his horses; but not as much as did his cousin.

Prince Rupert would shut himself up in his private laboratory the whole day for days at a time, and if the King, on a visit to 'the alchemist's hell', happened to interrupt some particularly interesting experiment, he would coolly throw some nauseous-smelling chemical on to the furnace to smoke him out.

He had invented new firearms, and improved gunpowder to such an extent that it would probably alter the whole course of warfare in the future. He had also made a drop of cooled glass, with a long tail, which could be hammered without breaking, but if the tail were touched with a pin the whole exploded in infinitesimal fragments into thin air.

'A brittle triumph,' said Minette, but Charles told her that Prince Rupert's drops had formed the basis of a new principle in chemistry. 'To increase the Powers of all Mankind', she read in his book of the annals of the Royal Society, 'is greater Glory that to enlarge Empire, or to put Chains on the necks of Conquer'd Nations.'

'Shall I show this to Louis?' she cried. 'It would be very good for him.'

She turned over the fat calf-bound volume in her hands, observed at the end of it that men will 'not only injoy the cold contentment of Learning, but that which is far greater, of *Discovering*'; became hopeful of a picture in a folded page in the middle, but was disappointed that it was only a diagram of some mathematical instruments, and, next door to it, fell on the most remarkable passage in the book: 'The rest of the Queries are not answered because the time is short since I received them, and especially because I cannot meet with anyone that can satisfie me, and being unsatisfied myself, I cannot nor will obtrude anything upon you which may hereafter prove fabulous; but shall still serve you with the truth.'

'To this man,' she said, 'science is as holy as religion.'

Her own words struck a strange chord in her mind. In echo

to it rose a memory from a hot misty morning at Saint Cloud with her dear La Fayette, when she had longed to discover a harmony in the irreconcilable twists and vagaries of the mind. 'What is my story?' What was her mother's? Not theirs after all then, but God's.

They said the world was very old, just coming to an end; but here in England it was perhaps beginning all over again, and God might yet come to reveal Himself in new ways. How then could there be any lasting authority over the mind, when that mind itself might be changing – growing – 'Then even the Church—?' she cried, and dared not finish her question.

But Charles reassured her that the authority of any body of living men was preferable to the imbecile tyranny of the dead words of the Hebrew prophets that he had suffered under in Scotland. Undoubtedly it was a tragedy for mankind that the Church had split off the Protestants; for if it could have swallowed the new learning it would have swallowed anything, and 'the Powers of all Mankind' would have increased with its aid and not in its defiance.

And so they might yet do here in England, she urged. Charles had said that the Church in England must be free of the Pope; only in this independent, contradictory island was such a thing possible; and so then would a faith be possible that would impose no fetters on 'this Learned and Inquisitive Age' (she could not stop dipping into the book) but would seek truth for truth's sake alone, 'as this Thomas Spratt does, and you, and our cousin Rupert.'

With such apostles of the new Church, she built up a very happy future for England with him all that summer afternoon.

It was a relief that some disturbance had called James back to London, so that he was not able to stay and discuss the treaty. Logically and argumentatively he had become convinced that the Catholic religion was the one consistently true Church; his zeal as a convert was proving uncompromisingly rigid, and he would have had no patience with either Minette's fancies or Charles' provisos.

The business was all concluded in the first week of the visit, only the day after they had all gone over to Canterbury to commemorate the anniversary of the Restoration and Charles' fortieth birthday. Minette saw a very witty improper new play there; she danced with half the Court round a giant maypole; they wandered in and out of a maze of little rambling old

310

streets; they stayed till after dark to see the leaping bonfires lit all round the town, and then drove home on the brief blue darkness. She was in a light flying chariot with Charles; she fell asleep with her head against his sleeve, and woke to see the sun rise over the pale downs. It seemed she had always lived with him in this castle on the cliffs by the sea.

Charles signed the treaty that day, the first day of her month of June. She was so sleepy after being up all night that she yawned all through the final conclave that achieved her hopes of the past years. No doubts now disturbed her joy, as she saw his dark hand sign the paper that was to set England against him and his family for ever.

CHAPTER FORTY-TWO

'You are glad you have done it? Dear Charles, you are truly glad?'

In the nervous and irritable condition of his country, he suspected the wisdom of any too decided stroke of policy. England was like a hysterical woman who had never got over a series of shocks – the civil wars, religious mania, plot scares, plague and the Great Fire. He had kept her soothed as far as possible, meeting the continual attacks on his royal power with the apparently yielding resistance of a feather-bed, which gradually blunts any weapon turned upon it. Now for once he had committed himself to an arbitrary and energetic course, and felt rather as though he had poured a new and heady wine into some shaky old bottles.

Eight years ago Minette had passionately and ignorantly opposed his sale of Dunkirk, which he had not wanted, since he had no wish to meddle on the Continent, and had found it an enormous expense to keep up. But her young instinct might well prove to be right (she had a way of being right without reason), that the English would use the sale of Dunkirk as a handle against him, even as they would certainly use this treaty if they had the chance. Then they must not have it. Opinion was all a matter of success or failure.

He said to his sister, 'If my successors should lose the throne again, you may be sure that everything they do, and we also, will be found to be wrong. It is failure that is the unpardonable sin. Let us pray that we may be kept innocent of it.'

311

And he was careful to communicate none of his doubts to her; assured her that it was the best possible way they could have commemorated his restoration ten years ago, better even than when he had lately instituted the Newmarket Plate, a race to be run always in honour of that event. Last year he had himself carried off the prize as his own jockey on his topping horse, Blue Cap.

They would have nothing to do but enjoy themselves for nearly a fortnight now the business was safely over. Nobody had any understanding of its true nature; the Dutch spies assured their masters that nothing was thought of in that village down by the sea but dancing and sailing and jollification.

Even Buckingham, who imagined that he was conducting the whole treaty, knew nothing about the religious side. He had fallen headlong in love with Minette all over again; he had not notion that the last ten years, which had transformed her from a pretty child into a delicately lovely young woman in the middle twenties, had dealt far less kindly with himself. Two or three years younger than Charles, he was tall, fair, superb, and still floridly handsome; but his mouth and the skin round his eyes had sagged, with the effect of curtains drawn back to disclose the emptiness of the stage there set. For there was nothing in his bold eyes to match the steady strength of those in his master's almost equally dissipated face. But he had his value, for he was the best mimic to be found anywhere.

The young Duke of Monmouth suddenly discovered that he hated 'that old satyr', and could not understand how his adorable little aunt could be so civil to him. He raved over Minette like a schoolboy; he was very lively and charming, with the beauty of a petulant cherub, and so full of life and spirit that he must always be dancing, laughing, springing out of his seat in his excitement over something or nothing. There was a story against him that some fair lady had let him out of her window in a clothes-basket, had been interrupted, and had to leave the rope fastened on the window-sill, and the Duke suspended in mid-air above St James' Park for a couple of hours – 'surely the longest time young James has ever kept still,' said his father indulgently.

Never was there such a fortnight for falling in love. It was the weather that did it, Minette assured her brother, when he scolded her for the disturbance she was causing in his Court. 'No one could possibly have fallen in love with me in Flanders'

312

– and suddenly she saw young Tréville's eyes in that damp barn, as he begged her to remain and rest at Landrecies. She shook herself free from the reminder of France. All that was a thousand miles, a hundred years away. She was here, now, a child again, whose summer day is as long as a lifetime, for she had lost all sense of the hurrying hours; as secure in her present happiness as if it had always been hers, and would be so for ever.

Like her nephew, she could not keep still. She ran along the edge of the cliff, the edge of the deck, looking down into the sparkling water; her French attendants were startled by her daring, and turned compliments on her fitness to be the sea-king's sister. She could not have felt afraid on that visit. She seemed to be on a voyage through halcyon seas, from which she would never have to return. Adventure opened before her. There were endless possibilities now in her life. She might – she certainly would at first – come back here to live in England. And then, there were countries, other seas.

It was Prince Rupert who spoke of them, the greatest adventurer of his age. He was now nearly fifty, lean and tired; he often suffered from the shot wound he had got in his head while fighting with France against Spain; and his magnificent physique had ben exhausted by the hardships and privations he had endured in his buccaneering days with his brother Maurice in charge of the Royalist 'fleet', a few rotten treacherous ships, never more than seven in number, and often only three. He had always been a keen sailor, and had studied ship-building ever since he was sixteen, when he had enlisted the help of his uncle Charles I in a wild plan to found a colony in Madagascar with himself as organizer and ruler.

Marston Moor had first taught him in midst of his young triumph that he could fail; his pride and confidence had never recovered that blow. But the sea took dearer things than these from him.

There was a storm off the West Indies which his leaky ship fought for three days, his men pumping continually; then at three o'clock on the third morning she sprang a plank, and they trod down all the raw meat on board between the timbers, and nailed planks over them. Still the sea rushed in; the sails were torn away; the men who tried to go on baling were drowned in the hold. They threw the guns overboard to lighten the ship, but she was doomed, with all the gains of the past

313

year on board, and sixty of Rupert's best men. Prince Maurice swore he would save his brother or perish with him. He fought his own mates to make them bring his ship alongside, to her own great danger. But it proved impossible to run across her bowsprit to save anyone on board. Rupert tried to shout his last direction to his brother, 'but,' said one who was there, 'the hideous noise of the seas and winds over-noised their voices.' He wished to go down with his men, but they, finding him obstinate, seized him by force and thrust him into a small boat with two or three others, to be rescued, miraculously it seemed in that storm, by Maurice's ship.

Now Rupert was as frantic in his efforts to save the rest of his men as Maurice had been to save him. But all proved vain; the boat sank on her second journey; and slowly, after some hours, the ship sank too, with all on board. It was now nine o'clock at night; the sea was calmer; two fire-pikes flared up in the darkness in farewell to Rupert as the ship went down. For the time, he was broken; he left all direction of the fleet to Maurice.

Then came a hurricane off the Virgin Islands; for two days the wind was so strong the men could not stand at their work, and the weather so thick that they could only see a few yards ahead. At the third day the hurricane abated, but Maurice and his ship had disappeared. This time Rupert could not let himself be broken. There was no Maurice to take his place, even for a few hours. From this time on he was alone.

Through the years of ill-health that followed, there came rumours and reports that Maurice was not drowned; the most circumstantial was that he had been taken by a pirate of Algiers and was now a slave in Africa. Rupert, whose oppressed senses had known before it was discovered that Maurice had been swirled into the sea in that hurricane, let his conscious mind be tortured with a mockery of hope. In vain he stirred up half the countries in Europe to appeal to the Great Turk. Maurice was never found.

Rupert never spoke of him, nor told the story of those two wrecks till now, fifteen years later, when he walked up and down the deck of the *Royal Charles* on a dazzling June morning with Minette. Tomorrow she would return to France. For a last picnic they were making an expedition to the Isle of Wight, whose shores round Yarmouth now shimmered golden with reedy marshland that stretched out into the sea. It had seemed one of the far tropic islands of which he had spoken before he plunged without warning into his story. The island before her became a mirage, the sea a glittering lure; 'cruel, cruel, cruel,' whispered the little waves against the ship's side; they had taken from this man beside her everything that he most valued, Maurice, and his magnificent strength. Yet, above all men she had met, he was to be envied; more than all others he was free.

As she looked up at that lined and hardened face, the face of a man tested to the last inch of his endurance, and still indomitable, there flashed across her inward vision a profile, seen in church, of a sharp intelligent nose breaking a puffy outline – the fluttering motion of plump little hands, the short fingers spread outwards like a starfish in eager, grasping movements – the hands of a sensual woman, of a greedy child.

And to Rupert, with no word in answer to his story, she cried, 'I cannot go back to him. You forbade it once. Can you not help me to escape?'

Soberly, as though it were the most natural and practical of his schemes, he discussed with her the possibilities (if Monsieur should after all turn round and refuse a separation) of following her to France and carrying her off in a ship to this new England that was springing up on the other side of the world.

The other side of the world – James' city, ' 'tis now called New Yorke,' which he had not yet seen – continents still unexplored – surely there would be room enough there for her to live away from Monsieur. Rupert was saying casually that he had for some time intended to go there and see if one could not discover a north-west passage through the great lakes of Canada.

'Do they lead then to sea on the further side?'

'No one yet knows. They appear to be seas themselves, yet they are of fresh water. If not sea, then vast tracts of land are waiting to be discovered. A traveller has made friends with the strange red men who roam there and hunt in packs like wolves, he has gone further west than any other man. And he swears that on a clear evening he saw mountains higher than any others in the world, rising in a rocky barrier across the sunset.'

They had reached the island. She gave him her hand and they went on shore.

315

CHAPTER FORTY-THREE

The next morning she woke very early; and she had been up late the night before, but that did not matter. There would be time enough to sleep later, for ever, if she might. A sentence in a romantic English play had clung to her these last hours:

> *'If it were now to die,*
> *'Twere now to be most happy.'*

A week in May, twelve days in June, they would be all eternity if she could die now. She looked from her window and saw the depth of the drop to the ground. A cowardly escape. Rupert had not taken it when he had been left with less to live for than she.

She could see one of the ships that were to escort her that day to France, the signs of life and business on board, little men like ants running up the rigging. She must take this voyage first, and then there would be another for her – to England again, or perhaps to an undiscovered country. Again she saw the mountains in the west of the world, of which Rupert had spoken yesterday.

Early as she was dressed, Charles was earlier. They walked along the shore. They had discussed her plans so often, there was no more to say of them now. It was not easy to find anything to say. Charles strode faster and faster; she had to break into a run every now and then to keep up with him; and the sand filled her shoes.

He was going to escort her for part of the voyage. So was James, who had returned from London for the purpose. Queen Catherine would not come too, for the sea always made her sick. She cried as she kissed her sister-in-law goodbye; 'You must come back,' she told her again and again, 'indeed you must come back very soon.' The Duchess of York also showed her a warm but brisker affection; she sent a great many instructions to her little daughter Anne, and begged Minette to be careful of her diet. She was sending some English ale for her to drink at breakfast, it was more strengthening than the French wines.

316

The sailors were singing a chanty as they hauled up the anchor; Minette asked what the words were, and heard that the refrain was:

> *'Only one more day for Johnny,*
> *One more day,*
> *Oh take and roll me over,*
> *Only one more day.'*

She laughed immoderately at that, and Charles, delighted at the effect on her spirits, suggested more songs. She sent for her guitar, and they picked out old tunes and words together as they sat on the deck, and the ship swam out to sea.

'Do you remember at Colombes,' she said, 'Bablon in her yellow dress playing the harpsichord for you? You were so much in love with her.'

'And yet she went and married a German duke.'

'On condition she should spend as much time in Paris as she wished. I shall find her there now, and will give her messages from you, I suppose, just as I used to do.'

Others were made to join the music circle, and the courtiers who could not sing stood round it, listening. The white sails towered above them across the blue sky; the white gulls swooped and cried; the white walls of England slipped further and further away. Now they could see France, but Minette did not look towards either country, but out to where the Channel became the open sea.

Someone sang a song that Charles had liked in a play for the rude simplicity of its words, but now he would have stopped it lest it should make Minette sad. But she too had heard and liked it, and must have it this once more. There was nothing sad in that song, it was all happiness and peace.

> *'Fear no more the heat o' the sun,*
> *Nor the furious winter's rages;*
> *Thou thy worldly task hast done,*
> *Home art gone and ta'en thy wages:*
> *Golden lads and girls all must,*
> *As chimney-sweepers, come to dust.'*

' "Wages!" ' exclaimed the Duke of Buckingham – ' "ta'en thy wages"! How exquisitely low!'

Charles defended it as the line he liked best, 'and let us pray the taskmaster is not so hard that he will not throw in a little extra for charity, else some of us will be badly off indeed.'

He had been right. The song had made Minette cry. She sprang up and called for a country dance, 'Your favourite tune, Charles, "Cuckolds all awry".'

The sinking sun had spread purple shadows of the sails across the sea. The company stepped up and down the glistening deck to the music of the fiddles; their satins and jewels now glowed with a fierly splendour in the evning light. The sailors watched. The second mate, a Puritan, observed to his nearest companion, as King Charles took his sister's hand, 'Man is a thing of naught; his time passeth away like a shadow.'

The fiddles were silent, the dancers still. And then, since Charles had given her a thousand presents – magnificent jewels, money to cover the cost of the expedition for her whole suite, the cost of a chapel at Chaillot in memory of their mother – Minette sent one of her maids-in-waiting for her jewel-casket, and said Charles must choose something from it for her parting gift to him.

Little Mademoiselle de Kerouälle stood holding the open casket, her eyes downcast, their long lashes dark against her cheek. The sunlight struck lustre from the jewels on to her hands; close beside her stood the Negro boy that Prince Rupert had rescued as a baby from a burning village of savages; his eyes fixed on her in admiration, his black shining skin in ebony contrast to her fairness.

'You should be painted so,' said Charles, smiling at her, 'and the little nigger too.' And taking her hand, he turned to Minette and said, 'Here is the jewel I wish you would leave behind you. Let her stay as one of the Queen's ladies.'

Not an eyelash fluttered on Louise de Kerouälle's smooth cheek; she glanced neither at her mistress nor at the tall man who stood over her with his hand on her wrist; she kept quite motionless while the colour flooded slowly up into her fair face. It was a pity that Lely, when he came to paint her long afterwards, complete with adoring Negro page and jewel-casket, could never see her so.

'She is not my jewel,' said Minette, 'she is her parents', and I have promised to bring her safely back to France.'

There was a little joking and laughter, the subject was dropped, and so was de Kerouälle's hand. Charles chose his present from the casket.

He had now to return. They stood round her to say goodbye,

three tall men as she had seen them come on deck, two, three weeks, a hundred years ago. Charles kissed her goodbye, again and again, then James. To Charles she clung for herself; for James, as always, she had an odd fear, an unreasoning sense of pity. So rational, persistent, and yet defenceless, he would never be able to yield to life, to make it fit him as his brother had done.

Now Rupert, who had spoken no word of love to her, came forward and took her hands. He held his rugged cheek against hers, an embrace officially accounted cousinly, and said low to her, 'If you do not come back, I will come for you.'

He followed his cousins to the ship's side, but Charles had turned and was hurrying back.

'I forgot to say,' he began, but forgot what he had forgot to say. He caught her into his arms and repeated again and again, 'How can I let you go? Minette, dear heart, don't cry.' He was crying himself. He went away, and then returned again. At last he went; he turned on his heel and strode off with very long steps, not looking back.

She went to the bulwark. She saw his ship careening before the wind, speeding away from her. She held fast to the rail, seeing nothing more for her tears. The water flew past beneath the ship, wine-dark in its deep shadow, the seagulls swirled and cried. People came and spoke to her; she did not notice what they said.

The coast of France grew clear before her, white walls of cliffs as at Dover, a grey-green line of downs in the dimming light. Thunder pealed out from the approaching shore; the great guns were welcoming her return. Smoke and flashing fire, crash after crash, volley after volley, a battle-line to greet her home-coming.

'Look, Madame!' cried little Mademoiselle de Kerouälle, her self-confidence, surprisingly increased since this morning, 'it is the full royal salute!' And she added insinuatingly, 'Will not Madame arrange her face a little before going on shore?'

There were royal honours all the way, an escort of the King's guards at Abbeville; the English ambassador, now Ralph Montagu, at Beauvais; there would have been the King himself there too, to conduct her to Saint Germain. But there was a hitch, it was most regrettable, a host of explanations followed. Minette gathered that the hitch was that Monsieur had flatly refused to accompany his brother; so that Louis had

319

had to forgo a courtesy which would make Monsieur's conduct to his wife the more marked.

'So it begins again,' she said to herself.

Her leisurely progress through France had taken five days. Her twenty-sixth birthday, on the 16th of June, took place in the middle of it. Neither those she loved nor those she hated were with her for it. This journey was an impersonal interlude which gave her time to collect herself.

Like the ship that had borne her brothers and her cousin from her, England receded fast into the distance; the sea flowed round it; it had become an island again, remote, inaccessible, yet growing steadily clearer in her mind now she was no longer in it. In that delirious dream she could be conscious of little but her joy. But now, while she spoke and smiled and curtseyed and replied to speeches, among admiring faces that she had never seen before and would most likely never see again, faces as ephemeral for her as the mayflies that danced for a day above the wayside ponds on her dusty journey, now she could through all this withdraw into herself, and live over again in delicious memory all that had been said and done in the last three weeks.

So she came to Saint Germain; and when still a few miles from it she saw the royal party coming towards her, that being the utmost distance that Monsieur could be induced to go to meet his wife. The King and Queen greeted her with delight, Mademoiselle with a hug rather than a courtly embrace.

'I have a thousand things to tell you,' she whispered.

'How well she looks and how pretty!' exclaimed Marie Thérèse.

Louis said, 'Well done,' in the tone that his courtiers dreamed day and night that he would one day address to them, even as mad hermits in the desert dream of heaven.

Monsieur put his cheek against hers, and bit her ear. She cried out in astonishment more than pain, for it was not more than a nip. Everyone asked her what was the matter, and she said, 'Oh, I thought I had trod on a snake.'

She got into the royal coach with the rest of the family, and avoided looking at her husband. But his unusually silent presence brooded over that gay party.

Saint Germain was as much a triumphal progress as her journey home had been. Ambassadors had come out from Paris to pay their court to her; the King showed her the highest honours, showered presents on her, insisted on paying for the whole of the expedition and told her she could keep the money Charles had given her for that purpose for herself Everyone here guessed that her apparently impromptu visit had cloaked some important displomatic mission that only she could be trusted to undertake.

'At Versailles we can talk of it in peace,' said Louis to her in the midst of the visits, the receptions, the compliments, the introductions. As usual, he was in a hurry to be off, next day if possible. He never cared for Saint Germain, he had always a sensation of chill, desolation and apprehension on entering the palace, but was now far too mature to connect this with the icy dawn of that January morning when two frightened, cold and hungry little boys had arrived from Paris without any proper clothes or food or baggage. He would not even have thought that he remembered it on this day of burning June, when he walked down the steps of the palace, mopping his brow under his heavy wig, and set off for Versailles.

Another hitch occurred; Monsieur would not come to Versailles, nor give Madame his permission to go without him. To all persuasions and arguments he replied, 'You can take me by force as your prisoner if you wish. Otherwise, I shall go to Saint Cloud.'

The coaches were ready, the wagons packed, the horses were champing their harness, tossing and swerving their uneasy heads under the cloud of flies. The road burned in the sunlight, the dust was choking. No one had the strength to dispute any longer.

'Goodbye then for the present, my dear sister,' said Louis, embracing her, 'I shall send for you very shortly, you will see.'

They drove to Versailles, and Madame with Monsieur to Saint Cloud. There the storm broke on her. Since she could do anything she chose in Europe, gadding about from country to country as though she were an ambassador or a high foreign potentate or anything you please, why did she take such care to do nothing for her own husband?

What was she to do?

Why, recall Lorraine to his home with Monsieur – make the King confide his secrets to his brother, and treat him with that honour and confidence that he now obstinately persisted in giving only to his brother's wife – see to it that ambassadors came out from Paris to do him honour and not her – arrange a visit in which he should have a chance to prove himself as powerful and popular as ever she had been.

Madame went and had a bathe in the river.

CHAPTER FORTY-FOUR

A continual stream of visitors broke the continuity of the storms. Bossuet and Turenne and Madame de la Fayette drove out from Paris several times during that week. La Rochefoucauld paid a visit, a most unusual act for him, and told her suddenly, apropos of nothing, that he had once been unkind to her and she had taken it very well. Tréville forgot his shyness of her when she talked of England, and told her his curiosity and admiration for its odd, inconsistent and forcible race.

Ralph Montagu brought over two young English noblemen, Sir Thomas Armstrong and Lord Poulett, who were on a visit to Paris, and they all sat for hours in the garden, discussing English poetry and the Royal Society and a little scandal about Lady Castlemaine and one of the new English playwrights, a coarse young man called Wycherley. All the new young writers in England were coarse, especially the women, they thought they could not be clever without it. But then how dull the old school were, the Court poets with their compliments! She could not resist showing them the farewell ode that Waller had placed in her hands as she embarked for France, the same poem to all intents as that which he had written more than twenty years ago on the occasion of her escape to France with her governess.

—'*The kind nymph, changing her faultless shape,*
Becomes unhandsome, handsomely to 'scape—'

Was that really the best way of telling one how lady Morton had disguised herself with a hump made out of a bundle of old rags?

'Too consummately absurd!' crowed young Chicken, as the other men called Lord Poulett and Monsieur, moodily pacing a sidewalk, heard shouts of laughter from the little group of men round Madame's favourite seat at the foot of the cascade. How superbly tall and strong these Englishmen were! Lorraine himself was not more arrogant than they in their un-

322

conscious power; and there they all were clustered round a poisonous, mischief-making woman; and if they saw him, they turned their eyes away as at something unclean.

He peeped at them through the hedge of jasmine, and heard the youngest looking, with the fresh ruddy face and fair hair, talking in that silly yaw-haw jargon. What was he saying to her? Something against her husband, he would swear to it. That sneering down-dropped eyelid, that cool, curt tone that yet had an odd note of diffidence (young English nobles always affected shyness) – what could he be saying but something against his host.

'Laugh! Laugh!' whispered Monsieur on the other side of the hedge. 'I will give you something to laugh for one day.'

He raised himself with a start as a servant came down the grass walk towards him, and handed him a letter. Monsieur recognized the royal seal. Louis had kept his word. He had sent so peremptory a command to Monsieur to bring his wife to Versailles that he dared not refuse. But he still insisted that they should not stay the night. They went over only for the afternoon and evening.

'How long is this to go on, I wonder,' Louis exclaimed impatiently to her; she thought of Charles and Rupert, and replied, 'Not very long.'

He had not yet had his talk with her about the treaty. They went into a room that looked on to one of the inner courtyards, where they would at last be undisturbed. Louis plunged into questions, congratulations. It was wonderful what she had effected in so short a time. He had scarcely believed his eyes when he had actually seen the paper, ratified by his name and Charles'.

'You have it there, the paper?'

'Certainly. You would like to see it again? You have good reason to gloat over your work.'

From his inner pocket he produced the treaty, which he had intended to go over with her, point by point. She sat with it in her hands. 'Supposing I were to tear it up,' something said inside her, but not aloud. She looked up at Louis.

'I think I know better now than I did,' she said, 'what a terrible thing it would be for my brother if this treaty were known of in England. Promise me you will never use it against him.'

'Do you take me for a blackmailer?' asked Louis haughtily.

'No. But the best of us do some very odd things.'

323

It must be the heat, she thought. She could not believe she had really just said that. And she was not surprised when Louis suddenly lunged forward and seized the paper, though not till the next instant did she see the reason for it, that the door was slowly opening. Monsieur put his head round it.

'Charming,' he said, 'I did not know your Majesty was here. Now we can have a pleasant little family talk. Was Madame telling of her visit to England? I shall be delighted to hear of it, for I can only do so when she speaks to others. She tells me nothing.'

'We are speaking of my private business,' said Louis.

'Is it well to have private business with another man's wife?'

'You know well enough that my business is political.'

'And why can I not be trusted to know of it as well as she?' He was now inside the door.

'If you come in here,' said Louis, 'I shall not say another word.'

With small deliberate paces, as if he were counting them, Monsieur stepped up to the table and seated himself at it.

The silence beat down on the three of them, as did the sun on the white stone outside. The thud of hammers throbbed through the air, only a little louder than the pulse of each one in that room. Thirty thousand workmen were building up the palace, and in the heart of it sat the three most important people in it, silent, frozen with anger and fear.

Louis got up and walked out of the room. Madame quickly followed him. Monsieur followed his wife.

There was a great banquet that evening in honour of Madame. Monsieur suddenly exerted himself to talk again as was his wont, to show an amiable interest in her visit by asking questions.

'And so you saw that eccentric Prince Rupert, he who once wished to be King of Madagascar, ha, ha! How childish, how touching! All these big men are of an infantile vanity.'

How was it she had never noticed how *foreign* these people were, their neat little idioms, their chattering formulas? The echo of a slower, more casual rhythm rolled in her mind; in this country where she had lived all her life, she was now desperately homesick.

Even Louis' rather complacent questions jarred on her; he only asked what Charles was building because he knew that he could do nothing like Versailles. But was it not a greater work

324

to build a new London, a whole town of simple but dignified red brick houses, and spacious gardens for ordinary people, than any number of such palaces?

She told them that a beautiful brass statue of her father on horseback had just been recovered by Charles for the price of £1600 and set up at Charing Cross. Forty years ago the sculptor of it had been paid £600, 'so you see an artist is worth more than twice the money when he is dead. Indeed, it has been a very golden goose of a statue, for it was believed to have been broken in pieces years ago by Cromwell's orders, and so a clever brazier sold quantities of brass thimbles, spoons and patty-pans, pretending they had been made from the pieces. For years good loyalists have been treasuring them as relics, and now see the statue itself stuck up before them, where it can lay no more such eggs.'

She looked round for laughter, and saw that everyone was shocked. Louis hoped gravely that the impious brazier had been punished with suitable tortures for his deception.

'Well – no. It is he who has been paid the £1600.'

'The English are not merely mad,' said Monsieur, 'they are exasperating.'

It was clearly the opinion of everybody present, and moreover that she and Charles, who had enjoyed the tale of the ingenious brazier, were guilty of gross and callous impiety. She was out of her element here; already, in so short a time, England had done that to her.

A young man called Monsieur de Tonnay-Charente, a connexion of Madame de Montespan's, had been at Dover during Madame's visit, and thought to please by describing her triumphs there. He could not have chosen an unluckier theme. Madame de Montespan certainly showed sympathetic interest, particularly when he described the raptures of the English gallants, who would drink no toast but to the little lady from over the water. The Duke of Buckingham had sworn to raise a troop of her admirers to follow her to France, fight only in her service and be known always as the regiment of Madame. But it was the Duke of Monmouth who—

'I find the English names terribly difficult to digest,' said Louis, looking at his brother, whom they appeared to have choked.

'To pronounce them properly one needs to mutter, croak and then spit,' said Madame de Montespan. She gave an encouraging glance at her young cousin and added, 'Now, "Monmouth" – there is no definite sound in that at all.'

'His sentiments on the other hand are entirely definite,' said the eager youth. 'If you had heard what he said in praise of Madame! He said that of all women, and mankind too—'

'The Duke of Monmouth is a great hope of the Protestant party in England, I believe,' said the King; 'I am told too the Duke of Buckingham counts himself an Anabaptist, which sounds an odd thing for a duke to be. Perhaps Monsieur de Tonnay-Charente will explain to us the mysteries of these religious sects.'

But Monsieur de Tonnay-Charente was quite impervious to these hints and headings off. He summed up the religious sects in a half-sentence, which he broke off in the middle to revert to the Duke of Monmouth's lyrical bursts of admiration for Madame.

The King rose from the table, remarking in a weary tone to his sister-in-law that the young man must have come from Madagascar.

Monsieur's efforts to rise to the festive occasion had collapsed. He insisted that they must return to Saint Cloud immediately. There might be a storm. The evening was heavy with heat, the sky dull. They went out on to the terrace, where it was still daylight, to see the fountains playing in Madame's honour.

At last the hammering and knocking was over. The air was so still one could even hear a bird now and then on a thin, long, questing note, as though incredulous of the silence. The artificial lakes below lay like sheets of lead, the huge trees were nearly black, without form or depth, like bunches of wool. The fountains shot up against them in spears and needles of moonlight. There was no colour, no substance, no shadow anywhere, only an unreal flat scene like one of Prince Rupert's mysterious mezzotints, with all the light concentrated in those fantastic shapes of water. 'Listen, my cousin,' said Mademoiselle hastily. 'You have been back a whole week now, and yet I have had no chance to have a word with you, and you have no idea of all that has happened with me since you left—'

Her breath failed at the depths of Madame's ignorance. But there was no chance to continue. The King and Queen had joined them. Monsieur was on tiptoe to be off, prancing, fussing, stinging.

326

'You must come back soon to Versailles, my sister,' said Louis.

'Yes, come back soon,' repeated Marie Thérèse in her monotonous fashion.

'Come back! Come back!' called the long note of the bird across the lake.

She looked round her on the grey and silver scene. Every detail impressed itself on her. It was as though she had never seen it before, or would never – a paroxysm of terror seized her.

'Must I leave you?' she said. 'But what will happen to me if I leave you?' She was crying.

They thought she was hysterical. 'It is the heat,' they said, 'certainly the heat today has been excessive. You must not stand about here any longer.'

So they saw her into the coach with Monsieur, and Queen Marie Thérèse said, 'You do not look as well as you did. You must not lose your English roses so quickly'; and Mademoiselle said, 'I must drive over to Saint Cloud, for I must certainly have a talk with you'; and Monsieur said, 'Are we to keep the horses fidgeting until they bolt?' and they drove on, they drove on and on; the trees slipped past them, they got blacker and blacker; the sky shut down on the trees, and nothing could be seen outside the coach window.

CHAPTER FORTY-FIVE

There was the house again all round her, watching her, whispering. Not a soul in it but was Monsieur's servant, and might be Lorraine's. How should she ever escape when the time came for her to do so, since there was no one here that she could trust? She did not think now that Monsieur would agree to a separation. He hated her too singly to agree to anything that would make for her happiness. She had begun to see that he had endured a real agony of envy rather than jealousy all the time that she was in England, free from him, enjoying honours and popularity such as he had never known. He would never consent that she should continue in such freedom. Out of his longing for Lorraine had grown his loathing for her, and now it was the stronger of the two.

For Lorraine had now been absent from him for six months,

327

a long time for even his fascination to last unrefreshed. Lorraine no doubt had realized that, and was revolving plans far away in Italy. Minette looked at the faces of his friends that surrounded her, and wondered what they had last heard from him, what they were even now writing to him. Madame de Montespan, she knew, kept in touch with him; and Madame de Montespan was far from pleased with the glory that Madame's English visit had won for her, placing her, as far as any real intrinsic importance was concerned, in the position of the first lady in Europe, which is as much as to say in the world.

And here personal jealousy as well as envy was involved, for Montespan nearly burst a blood-vessel in her rage after seeing King Louis' reception of Madame, the high honour in which he held her, the respect as well as the warm affection that he now showed her. Madame knew this through Mademoiselle de Kerouälle, who had a great friend in the service of Madame de Montespan, and thought to please Madame by telling her with discreetly sly amusement how Montespan had wrecked her bedroom in her fury because nobody could speak of anything but of Madame, Madame, Madame.

'And she threw a hand-mirror at the children's governess, the widow Scarron, and it broke, and so she screamed that it would mean her death and that Madame had done it by causing this storm; and that evening off she whirled in a hired coach, all by herself, no one knows where, and did not come back till very late.'

This account made Madame very uneasy. With all the friends she had in this country, Louis was the only one who could protect her, and his support was a continual source of fresh dangers. She had tried to make him give that support with a tact that would not disturb others so fiercely, but it was proving impossible to make Louis tactful with women.

'The King does not know how to make people happy, even when he wishes them well,' she had said to Charles, and told him how his mistresses, even Montespan, of whom he was distinctly afraid, had to suffer continual rebuffs from him.

Montespan's jealousy, Monsieur's spiteful envy, Lorraine's distant but powerful determination to re-establish his ruthless clutch on Monsieur's whole being, all these influences were closing round her once again, threatening to choke out of her life everything that she most cared for.

Her little daughter had run towards her at the first instance,
328

then remembered the rôle she had been taught, cocked her nose in the air with the icy aloofness of eight and a half years, and said in her mother's hearing to the Princess Anne: '*You* can go and hear about England, it is your horrid old country. *I* don't want to hear about it.' Her former governess, Madame de Saint Chaumont, had written her a letter, but Monsieur had sent it back without letting the child see it. Everyone in the house had told her what an unpleasant, deceitful woman Madame de Saint Chaumont was, and how blindly her mother had trusted in her. And it was her mother who had told lies to the King had made him send away the poor Chevalier de Lorraine. 'You remember the Chevalier de Lorraine? Look, he has sent you this pretty puppet theatre all the way from Italy, so you see how he remembers you.'

All of them were working secretly for Lorraine and against herself, Minette knew it. Little Marsan's chubby face outstared hers with the insolence of a cherub who has decided to follow Satan and the fallen angels; the Marquis d'Effiat, whom she had always thought the most honest, did not seem able to meet her eyes.

The ambassador, Ralph Montagu, rode over on Friday, the day after their visit to Versailles, for a private talk about the political side of her visit to England; but someone must have informed Monsieur, for no sooner had they begun than he at once bore down upon them and interrupted the conference. He had made up his mind to force or pry his way into the secret that concerned herself and the two kings. Montagu had only an opportunity to ask her very low if she were certain of the safety of King Charles' letters to her. 'Letters are safest burnt,' he added hurriedly.

When he had left, Monsieur declared that it was too hot to do anything that afternoon but go to sleep in a darkened room, 'like an Eastern queen.'

Minette went into her rooms, and drew out the casket of buhl and mother-of-pearl that contained all Charles' letters. She was about to call for a lighted candle to be brought her, when it struck her that this might cause speculation and that Monsieur would plague her to know what papers she had been burning. She must destroy them in some other way. If she returned to Charles, she would need no written record of his companionship through all these years. If she did not – but whatever happened, or did not happen, she would not stay here.

She took up the last letter she had received and tore it across with some difficulty, then the next to it and the next. The stiff paper curled up and crackled in her fingers. These of the last year all concerned her prospective visit and the treaty to be then arranged between France and England, and were the most dangerous for Monsieur to discover. But when she had gone back as far as just a year ago, she paused with a letter dated the 24th of June, 1669, in her hand. Both it and the one before it were so full of numbers (in disguise for important names) that they looked like sums in arithmetic. She began to dip among the others. Here was something that would certainly infuriate Monsieur worse than any politics, for it referred to the Duke of Monmouth.

'James intends to put on a perriwig againe when he comes to Paris, but I believe you will thinke him better farr, as I do, with his short haire, and so I am intierly yours

C. R.'

'That shall stay,' she laughed to herself and put it back. Other endings less abrupt caught her eye—
'And so, my dearest sister, good night, for 'tis late—'
'You have my hart and I cannot give you more.'
Not another word would she destroy. She thrust all the remaining letters back into the casket, locked it, and hung the key round her neck. She swept up the torn pieces into a little silk bag, then went to the window. The sun had shone out again now, and the rich light of the late afternoon lay upon the gardens. She went out to bathe, and met Dr Esprit, the household physician, who told her she must do nothing of the sort.

'Where can the harm be? It is so hot, even the water is lukewarm.'

'Only this morning, Madame, you told me you had a pain in your side.'

'Oh, that. But I often feel that. It is nothing, it goes off again quite quickly. I don't feel it now.'

She would not listen to his expostulations. She had begun to think with the Palatine family that doctors were no use and the soundest thing was to follow one's own instinct. Rupert had had no trouble with that poisoned arrow in his arm which he had cut out himself with the surrounding flesh, when he was among the savages, but the shot wound in his head had continually irked him ever since it was treated by the doctors. She told Esprit that she was so craving for the cool touch of water against her skin that it would be against nature for it to harm her.

He said to a colleague later, 'Madame imposes her own feelings on nature as she does on mankind. She will not believe that they can harm her.'

His humane opinion, like his medical, was behind the times. For Madame had certainly begun to believe that mankind could harm her, and it was because of this that, at Saint Cloud, she felt her only escape from the struggle was into another element.

All her life she had felt herself to belong to this other element – to the fountains in her childhood, where rainbows were caught in the falling spray, and the water-lily leaves were islands that adventurous elves might discover in the uncharted ocean of the pond; to the river where she had drifted in Charles' 'magic barque'; to the glittering seas that had surrounded England all this last month; even to the storm-swept ocean of Rupert's tragic story, where human strength and courage endured its uttermost, but where disaster came swift and clean and terrible, not sneaking round a corner with averted eyes.

And one other water there was that ran, pale and shining, through a dark country, but she could not remember what that was; if she had seen or heard of it, or only dreamed of it; but it had always been there somewhere in her mind.

Now once again the river was all round her, cool and clean. She had left her Court self on the bank, together with the stiff apparatus of her clothes. The voices of her ladies chattering there reached her only as an echo from some strange world, such as the world of humans might appear to a fish. Whatever they were saying, whatever others in the palace were saying, doing, plotting, it could not affect her here and now.

Her free body gleamed opalescent white beneath the water; she had snatched at a willow branch and let herself swing in the current downstream; then leaned back and looked up at the reflections that ran higher and higher into the overhanging branches from the ripples made by her movements – ring after ring of silvery light, scintillating, evanescent, creating a new intangible world of light and shadow, where all the fevered anxiety of the 'real' world was lost, forgotten; and her highest ambition was to see a kingfisher.

But one thing this time she carried from that world, a silk bag full of torn paper and in it a heavy stone. She had had to

331

be very careful that none of her ladies should see her take it with her into the water; now, safely beyond their view, she let go of it and it sank, leaving a few bubbles which swam for an instant downstream.

Her little dog Mimi was racing up and down through the rushes on the bank with yaps of excitement over a suspected water-rat. The glowing colours of forget-me-not and willow herb, and the huge leaves of some tall weed made this part of the river seem to her like a tropic pool, such as Rupert must often have come on in his travels. She had bathed in this place hundreds of times, and yet this evening she felt all the excitement of discovery. The world was new again, and she at the beginning of her life. She struck out downstream.

In a deep patch of shade under the huge beech trees the water was very cold. A little band of foxgloves standing close together in the green darkness had a startled ghostly look; their purple showed but dimly. A blue-black butterfly came straggling up the stream. A white wet arm flashed upwards out of the dark water towards it.

Then she turned and swam back, more and more slowly. It was an effort to reach the little landing-stage. Her ladies exclaimed as they dressed her and saw how pale she was; her breath too seemed to be coming with difficulty. 'I have got a stitch in my side,' she said. It might have been from that cold place under the beech trees where the sun never reaches the water, but she did not think so, for she did not feel cold. But she did not feel at all well. She was glad to go to bed. She might have got a slight chill, said the doctors. She was undoubtedly suffering from fatigue, the effects of too much excitement and rush all the time she was in England.

'Yes, that is certain,' said Monsieur, 'I knew England would make her ill. I said so, and no one would listen to me. Now you see.'

She vowed to herself that she would never see a doctor again if she could help it, and next day insisted on getting up, and declared she felt much better, only a little tired. She promised she would not bathe again just yet, and sent for Madame de la Fayette to come out that evening and spend the Sunday with her.

La Fayette did not arrive till after ten o'clock, but Madame had not gone to bed, for she declared that she was now quite recovered. She led her friend out into the gardens, where the long dusk was trembling to a colder light as the moon rose

332

behind the trees. They sat in the seat at the foot of the cascade, and the moon came out and shone clear upon it.

'This is my stairway into heaven,' said Minette, and fell silent, forgetting all that she had meant to talk of to her friend. But presently she spoke of England and her brother and of Monsieur de la Rochefoucauld and how glad she had been that he had come to see her. She did not want to return to the house; it was perfect here; she felt better than she had done all day. But at last she rose and went back over the grey lawn towards the lighted house, with her arm in her friend's; she turned her thin, pointed face up to the sky, saying, 'Look, there are the Children in the Moon again. The last time I saw them was at Canterbury when we danced round the maypole. To think that was the last full moon, only a month ago!'

'It will not be full moon till tomorrow night,' said the accurate Madeleine.

They found it was after twelve o'clock when they entered the palace.

And the next day was Sunday.

Madame had had a good night, she said, but then she had a long talk with Monsieur. She had thought he seemed calmer, more rational, and therefore chose this moment to ask what he thought of the question of their separation. Monsieur replied that he was not thinking just now. After that he would say only, 'No.' When she asked for his reasons he said they were unnecessary. He had said 'No,' and 'No' was enough for her.

He had shut down into one of his long sulks. The last time he had done this he had refused to speak to her for several weeks; it seemed likely that this would recur.

She left him, and when she met Madame de la Fayette told her that she was feeling out of humour. 'You will find me a very bad companion to go with to Mass,' she said, but so sweetly that Madeleine only laughed at her supposed ill-temper.

After Mass they went to see little Marie Louise, whose portrait was being painted by an English artist. She was full of importance as a subject for a picture; but this was her third sitting and she was beginning to be very tired of keeping still. Her mother, pretending to talk to the painter, but really speaking to her daughter, told stories about a country on the other side of the world, so far west that a chain of mountains had been seen in the very heart of the sunset; that no one knew what was on the other side of the mountains, if indeed they

333

were really there, and not a vision of mountains in the sky that guard the gates of heaven; that the people in that country were red as though made of copper, and wore only blankets and feathers. Marie Louise sat without moving till the end of her sitting.

Madame seemed much happier after this. 'The child will be her natural self again,' she told La Fayette. 'They are forcing her to hate me, but they are mistaken in that, for she is one who will always resent coercion.'

They went to see the baby Mademoiselle de Valois, now ten months old, who was crawling about very happily on the nursery floor under the faithful charge of the little Princess Anne. She had transferred all her adoration of Marie Louise to this fascinatingly helpless creature, carried her about, showed her all her toys in turn, and talked baby talk to her by the hour together.

They all talked baby talk for a time, and then La Fayette told her friend of an odd accident that had happened to her just lately. A piece of the marble chimney-piece in her house in Paris had fallen down on her head when she was sitting just beneath it. She said that she was now none the worse for it, but that the blow had only missed the most dangerous part of the skull. Minette made her take her hair down and looked at the wound, when she exclaimed at its depth.

'Indeed you might have died!' she said, and then grew thoughtful and added, 'Would you have been afraid? I do not think I should be afraid to die.'

They dined with Monsieur in his rooms and with some of Madame's ladies. He was happy among so many women, most of whom made a business of admiring him; he talked about his new portrait which the English artist was also painting, and discussed all the different positions in which he might have been painted, and why he had chosen the one he had.

After dinner Minette lay down on some cushions on the floor, leaning her head against La Fayette's chair. She was fond of sitting on the floor, it was far comfier than a chair, she said. For an instant she was able to speak low to her friend, and told her that she would not be so stupid and cross if only she could talk to her by herself, but that she was so tired of all the people round her – 'so tired, so tired,' she repeated, as they clustered near to her again, and suddenly retreated from them by falling asleep.

334

It seemed as though it must be a pretence, but no, she really slept.

'How happy to be able to fall off so quickly,' thought La Fayette, 'like a child or a dog.' And yet it disturbed her; it did not seem quite natural, as though Madame had indeed fallen off a secure perch in life, into a sudden abyss. She looked at her from time to time in wonder, noticing how quickly her face could change. It must be, after all, her intelligence and vivacity that made it lovely, for now she did not look so. And yet she had never thought this before when she had seen her asleep; Madame had looked as charming then as when awake; it was only now that this change had come over her face, making it like the face of someone else, and suddenly La Fayette thought of Madame's father, and wondered how that delicate, tapering face had looked on the way to execution.

It was the strangest fancy; she wished she had not had it; she looked down into Madame's face and wished she would wake up. As if in answer to a call from her, those long eyelids lifted a little way and then sank again, as though unequal to the effort; the pale lips parted; Madame's face opened into consciousness once more.

'Oh,' she said, 'I have been—' She stopped and looked round her, bewildered for an instant, then finished, 'I don't know where – somewhere very far away.'

'She looks very ill,' said Monsieur, 'do you not think she looks remarkably ill?'

He asked everyone in turn, then recommended a little rouge. He avoided speaking to her direct, nor did he seem to hear her when she spoke to him. She might have been a doll whose bad appearance he was discussing.

He was setting off to drive into Paris for an afternoon visit. On the stairs he met Madame de Mecklenburgh, once Madame de Châtillon, now married to a German count whom she had left in his country while she returned to Paris. Monsieur brought her back to see Madame, conversing gaily with her, for 'Bablon' was one of the people who could make everyone feel well with himself. Minette ran out into the passage to greet her, into her arms.

'Dear Bablon, you were almost the last person we talked of, my brother and I.'

A flood of talk followed. The ladies interrupted each other happily. In her animation Minette looked quite well again, but La Fayette noticed that she held her hand to her side now and then. She offered her visitors refreshment. They had dined early, and it was now five o'clock. She herself sent for some iced chicory water which she preferred to coffee in this heat. It was brought her from the cupboard at the end of the passage. No sooner had she drunk it than she cried out, and put the cup hastily down on the saucer again, catching at her side with both hands. The two ladies rushed towards her, asking what was the matter. Her face had flushed and then turned grey with pain; her eyes sought theirs in terrible entreaty, as if to beseech denial.

'I must be poisoned!' she said.

CHAPTER FORTY-SIX

At Versailles Mademoiselle walked with the Queen beside the ornamental waters. She was in an extremely nervous state, for she had at last informed Lauzun of her intentions towards him. All her efforts to do so directly had failed, for he had always sheered off at the last moment just as she had reached the point of telling him the name of the man she loved. On the day after Madame had come over with Monsieur from Saint Cloud, she said she would write the name on a scrap of paper and give it to him to read, and then he could write his opinion of her choice at the foot of the paper. She wrote '*C'est vous*', folded the paper and handed it to him – then she remembered that it was Friday, her unlucky day, and besought Lauzun not to unfold the paper nor glance at it until the Saturday.

This he promised; he would sleep with it under his pillow, he said, and open it when he woke the next morning. In consequence, Mademoiselle did not sleep at all that night. But next morning she did not see Lauzun about, and after many roundabout inquiries she found that he had gone to Paris. Nor was he back for Sunday Mass the next day. By the afternoon, Mademoiselle felt that if she did not confide in someone she would go mad.

So she went to see his sister, Madame de Nogent, to whom she had often repeated that she was not happy, with all her wealth, and that she wished to change her condition. As she had then always led the conversation round to Lauzun and kept it there as long as possible, she concluded that Madame de Nogent could hardly have failed to discover her intentions.

Today she plunged straightway into the subject:

'You would be surprised to see me married shortly, would you not? But tomorrow I shall ask the permission of the King. My affair will be decided in the next twenty-four hours.'

She then asked her friend to guess the name of the man she would marry, adding that she would be glad if she guessed right.

'It is no doubt Monsieur de Longueville,' replied Madame de Nogent.

'No, indeed! It is someone very superior to him, of infinite merit.'

'Does the gentleman himself know of your intentions?'

'It has long been my anxious study that he should understand them – but respect has prevented him from admitting that he has discovered them.'

But it was tiresome that his sister's respect should do the same. She could have cried at that 'Monsieur de Longueville'; it was somehow a bad omen.

Madame de Nogent coyly guessed name after name, which began to amuse Mademoiselle. 'You can look out of the window,' she said, 'and name all the gentlemen of the Court, and when you come to the right one I will stop you.'

And it struck her what an enchanting good omen it would be if Monsieur de Lauzun were to come marching round the corner of the terrace, returned from Paris just in time to supply the right name. She leaned out of the window. 'Take care or you will fall,' said Madame de Nogent.

Together they stared down on all the rich coats, the sombre and sparkling colours, the curling wigs like enormous overblown chrysanthemums. The courtiers walked below, their long shadows sprawling behind them, some coming up to the palace and some away from it, but all keeping in the shade as much as they could. For an hour the two ladies pointed and named and giggled over various absurd guesses; then even Mademoiselle grew weary of the idle game and impatient of her friend's failure to sympathize with her.

'You are wasting your time,' she said suddenly, 'he is gone to Paris, and will not return till the evening.'

She ran out of the room and went to join the Queen for her evening walk by the canal. She felt exasperated with her own behaviour, it had surely been more suitable to an untried schoolgirl than to a great lady. The worst of it was that

Madame de Nogent probably thought so too, and would say so to Lauzun; and now she came to think of it, she had already played the same childish game with him, when she had tried to make him guess his good fortune, and he had persisted in thinking it was the Comte d'Ayen who was so happy as to be honoured by her.

And there was the Comte d'Ayen – was that an unlucky omen? – hurrying towards the palace with a grave, urgent face.

As he went past her he said, 'Madame is dying. Go and make the Queen hurry if you wish to see her alive. The King has told me to find Doctor Vallot and take him at once to Saint Cloud.'

She scarcely heard the last words as he went on up the great staircase, two or three steps at a time.

Whenever now she heard any news, her first thought was always, 'How can this affect myself and Lauzun?'

It was a habit she resented, for it made her feel like a slave, chained always to the same post; an ignoble attitude of mind.

But she could not resist it, and now as she hurried to the Queen she said to herself, 'I knew it. I should not have given him that paper on a Friday. Now Madame will die, and Monsieur will want to marry me for my fortune, and the King will be angry at my refusing, and will not let me marry Lauzun.'

The Queen was in the centre of a group of ladies, all talking in hushed, shocked voices. She turned as Mademoiselle came up to them, and said eagerly, 'Did I not say so, Mademoiselle? Do you not remember how when Madame left us only last Thursday, I said that she had death written on her face?'

The Queen was rather fond of seeing death written on people's faces. Illness had now been added to food, cards and Louis in her list of subjects for conversation.

'She certainly wept very much, as though she had some foreboding,' said Mademoiselle, 'but we thought that was because of Monsieur's treatment of her.'

The Queen seized her hand and led her a little aside from the group of ladies. 'Yes, indeed,' she said, 'and do you know what they are saying? – the most terrible thing of all, that she has been poisoned!'

Mademoiselle gave a hurried glance at the scene round her. The ladies' bell-shaped satin dresses shone in the evening light; they looked like inverted tulips. The ornamental waters made stripes and squares of burnished gold through the grounds; the unfinished palace towered above them like a sunset cloud.

338

Two, or was it three evenings ago, Madame had looked at this scene with her; and now she was dying. Had Monsieur hated her so much that he had poisoned her – and would she herself have to marry Monsieur?

Her thoughts went wandering after Lauzun again: what had he thought when he had opened that paper yesterday morning, and saw the two words that told him her love for him? Had he been so much overcome with joyful astonishment and awe that he had fled to Paris in order to recover himself before he saw her again?

Ashamed of her obsession, she shook her attention sharply back to the present scene; the gilded canal; the gleaming figure of the solemn Queen beside her. She said jerkily, without waiting to choose her words, 'What is it all about? I have heard nothing except that she is ill.'

A messenger came towards them, and said that it had all been a false report. Madame had a slight attack of the colic, that was all, caused by the heat and fatigue; the doctors were in no way anxious about her, and Monsieur Vallot, the King's doctor, would be returning himself very shortly and would thoroughly reassure them.

So they walked on up and down the canal, and the hot light grew cool and dim. Monsieur Vallot came back from Saint Cloud and gave the same report as the other doctors. It was nothing but a colic, it would pass off quite soon.

But at the same time the King came out of the palace, where he had stayed indoors all day, being somewhat indisposed from the heat, and said abruptly to them, 'My coach is waiting. Come at once.'

'But Madame is better. She is in no danger. Surely there is no need to go at this time in the evening,' said the Queen.

'I have had a message from Madame which contradicts the doctors,' he said, 'and I am going to her with all speed.'

His voice came curtly through tight lips. His face was like a mask, except for angry watchful eyes that yet looked at nothing near them. He seemed to be staring at something far away or long ago.

They got into the coach with him and drove to Saint Cloud. The Queen mentioned the rumour of poison, but the King cut her short.

CHAPTER FORTY-SEVEN

It was close on eleven o'clock when they arrived at Saint Cloud. The full moon hung over the gardens, transforming them into an alien world. The palace gave no impression of its size in this vast and shadowy whiteness. Its four-square solidity had vanished, become grey, thin, almost transparent.

But as they went up the steps, it loomed over them, massive, customary. In the patch of yellow light that issued from its doorway, some figures were scurrying importantly in and out in black silhouette; seen from below, they were strangely small and top-heavy, with the candlelight striking through their spindle legs as though it were splitting them in two.

They went into the palace and up the stairs. Thousands of candles were burning, making the crowded passages unbearably hot. There was a smell of melting wax and thick clothes and strong scents; the light glistened on little beads of sweat on the perturbed faces clustered together. More than once in the buzz of low, excited voices, Mademoiselle caught the word, 'poison'. Here was this horror once again in their midst; no man knew if the neighbour to whom he spoke were in the plot, or suspected himself of being in it. Who would be the next to be struck down by a sudden and nameless disease? Therefore the faces looked on each other and looked away, ill at ease in this small bright society that made their whole world, and had suddenly grown menacing.

The arrival of the King took them by surprise, for such a thing never happened that he should walk through a crowd that was unprepared for him. All the questioning, scandal-whispering groups were stricken into silence, their awed faces turned on him in consternation. But Louis perceived nothing; he hurried with set, stern face to Madame's room.

It was Mademoiselle, following in his wake, who thought that so might death himself go stalking through this crowd of anxious chatterers frozen into immobility as they saw who passed. In the thick heat of the corridor she shivered.

A group of young men were talking in a corner in high lisping voices, and from them even came a shrill laugh, striking discordantly on the strained air; then they too saw the King, and their rough, solemn faces stared like frightened dolls.

The doctors Yvelin and Esprit were conferring by the door of Madame's room, and Vallot, who had returned at the King's command, had just joined them. The King paused to ask if Madame were any better, and they all three assured him there could be no danger.

At that instant the Prince de Condé came out of the bed-chamber and, bowing to the King, said abruptly, 'Go at once to her, Sire. She is asking for you and she has not long to live.'

The doctors drew themselves up, rustling a little, and turned offended glances on each other.

'I would answer for her life with my own,' said Doctor Esprit.

'So you said of my son, and he is dead,' cried an agitated, squeaky voice. Monsieur had fluttered up behind them, and was horrified to see his brother. 'Nobody warned me of your Majesty's arrival. We are all at sixes and sevens. A thousand apologies – no one to receive your Majesty—' his voice faded aimlessly away under Louis' heavy stare. A bewildered, futile figure, more astonished than distressed, Monsieur plainly did not know what he should do next in this unrehearsed scene.

The King paid no attention to his apologies. He seemed to be collecting himself together to speak to his brother, but finally thought better of it, turned sharply on his heel, and went straight through into Madame's room. His wife and brother followed him, and Mademoiselle more slowly, her heart heavy with dread.

Her eyes sought distraction by fastening on the Prince de Condé, who stood there like some gaunt bird of prey that has moulted and got out of condition, mewed up in peace time. She could not believe that for years she had wished his wife would die so that she might marry him herself, that for his sake she had fired away her chances of marriage with King Louis. Had Louis ever quite forgiven her for that affair? It had made her very uneasy all today when she had resolved to speak to him within the next twenty-four hours, to ask for his permission to marry Lauzun. But now who knew what might happen before the twenty-four hours were over? She entered Madame's room.

Madame was lying at the further end of it, on a little bed that had been made up in a corner by the window. The room was darkened, compared with those outside, but there was light enough to see her face, and it was that of a dying woman. Her hair lay dishevelled on her shoulders, for her incessant pain

341

had been too great to allow her women to arrange it for the night; her chemise was unfastened at the neck and arms. This disorder was due to her suffering, for till now she had not been able to keep still, but tossed herself to and fro. Now her exhaustion was too great to move; she lay back upon the pillows; her eyes sought theirs, one after the other. There was agony in those shadowed, questing eyes; something else was there that was incommunicable; already she was removed from them, and saw them only from a distance; their world no longer concerned her.

The King had gone straight up to her and dropped on his knees by the couch, putting his arms round her, and his cheek against hers. 'You must not leave me,' he whispered, 'the doctors say you are better.'

He put his head down on her shoulder that she might not see his tears.

'They are wrong,' she said faintly. 'You will hear of my death by the morning.'

He sprang up, brushing his hand across his eyes, and strode back to the doctors.

'Surely,' he said, 'you will not let a woman die without trying to save her?'

They looked at each other helplessly. In a low, furious voice he began to suggest about a dozen different remedies.

Madame had embraced the Queen tenderly; now she held out a hand to Mademoiselle, who stood at the foot of the bed, not daring to advance. 'I was beginning to know and love you,' she said.

Mademoiselle was crying too much to answer her. She knelt at the foot of the bed and laid her head against it, sobbing. Presently Madame de la Fayette led her out of the room.

'Surely something should be done,' said Mademoiselle.

'The doctors ordered her a cup of soup,' said Madame de la Fayette, 'and that increased her pains terribly. It was only Madame de Gamaches who thought of feeling her pulse. She cried out that Madame had no pulse, and that her hands and feet were growing numb. But the doctors say that these are but ordinary symptoms of colic.'

They talked in hurried, nervous whispers. One or two other ladies joined them, and then 'Bablon', who had sent a messenger for the English ambassador at Madame's request. From the first, they told Mademoiselle, Madame had known that she was dying; and she had cried out at first that she was poisoned, but she had not said that lately, nor seemed to mind whether they gave her antidotes or not.

They drew closer together as they whispered. Madame de la Fayette admitted that when the question of poison was discussed she had looked hard at Monsieur. But he had worn the same stunned, perplexed air throughout the evening. The maid who had mixed the chicory water had drunk of it herself, and some was given to a dog. But was it the same as that which Madame had drunk? Or was there poison on the cup, some deadly Italian poison? No one needed to add that Lorraine was in Italy; they fell silent.

Then one said that a valet had that afternoon seen the Marquis d'Effiat coming out of the cupboard at the end of the passage, where the chicory water was put ready for Madame; that when he saw he was observed, he explained that he had come in dying of thirst after playing tennis in the heat, and had gone into the cupboard for a drink of water. But why had the valet said nothing of this before? Why had the chicory water not been examined before Madame drank of it?

'These things are not thought of at the time,' said Madame de la Fayette; but the others thought them clear indications of a horrible plot. Only Madame had shown no fear at the thought of it; not once, they said, had she cried to the doctors to save her, nor expressed self-pity that she should be cut off thus in the flower of her youth and the hour of her greatest triumph.

'Not a fortnight since her twenty-sixth birthday,' said 'Bablon', gazing sadly at a mirror on the wall; it was many years since she had had hers.

'And June, her month, is not yet out,' said another. 'We called her the midsummer princess, you remember—'

'Nine years ago,' said Madame de la Fayette.

Mademoiselle cut across their sad head-shakings with a sudden violent gesture. 'In the name of God,' she said, 'what are the doctors about?'

It was agreed that the doctors had lost their heads; that they had made light of her illness at the beginning, and now felt they had got to hold to their opinion in self-defence – or – (and once again that horror crept upon them) – was their obstinacy due to a fear of what they might discover? Would the King himself be grateful to the man who might prove cause for a charge of murder against his brother?

'In any case, she must have a confessor,' said Mademoiselle, 'it will be a disgrace to everyone present if she does not have a confessor.'

She was told that Madame had asked for hers and he had been sent for, but as he was not at home the Curé of Saint Cloud had come instead, who did not know her at all well and had conducted a very perfunctory confession in about five minutes.

'Then someone more suitable must be sent for,' said Mademoiselle.

She felt once more as she had done when she had rushed to the Bastille; she alone was capable of handling the situation and doing what was required for her cousin. She strode across Monsieur's path as he drifted by, and demanded that a proper confessor should be summoned.

'Yes, yes,' said Monsieur, his eyes wandering unhappily from one to the other of the group of ladies, 'who shall we have? Whose name would look best in the *Gazette*?'

Madame de la Fayette said that Madame had been speaking of the new Bishop of Condom only that afternoon.

'The Abbé Bossuet, admirable. I will send a messenger to Paris for him at once.'

Mademoiselle stood over him as he gave the order. The others had moved away. The messenger went.

'You think she is dying?' said Monsieur.

'I am certain of it.'

She stared at the bedizened little creature in front of her. 'If there were a plot against Madame,' she thought, 'they would not have taken that rubbish into it. He could not have kept the secret for a day.'

'Then,' he said, 'I might come to marry you after all. That would be odd, wouldn't it? You are not likely to have children now, I suppose, and in that case you should have no objection to settling your fortune upon my daughter. She is certain to marry the Dauphin, so it will be in a good cause.'

'You do me great honour,' said Mademoiselle in a parched voice, that could only just issue from her lips. In a sickening revulsion of memory, that she tried in vain to check or to deny, she recalled how she had once wished that the Princess Henriette would go into a convent, would lose her beauty in the smallpox, would – yes, it was true – would die – so that she, Mademoiselle, might not be prevented from her rights in marrying the King's brother. How was it she had only thought of Monsieur as the King's brother, and now saw him as he was?

The King went back to Madame's bedside. He too had thought of the possibility of a terrible reason for the doctors' inaction; and had urged his wishes on them even to the point of himself mentioning the suspicion of poison. But he was forced to the conclusion that sheer stupid bewilderment was at the root of their behaviour, and that they were beginning to feel an uneasiness that they would not yet admit.

He stood looking down on that small, grey-white face against the pillow, the hair dark with the sweat of agony, pushed back from the forehead. A moth's wing of a face, he had once thought of it, and so now it seemed in the dim light; a shadow, almost transparent – was it indeed to fade so quickly from his sight, for ever?

'It is no use,' he said, 'I have suggested at least thirty things to those blockheads, and they say only that it is not yet time to try them.'

'One must even die according to the proper formula, I suppose,' said Madame, smiling at him. Her voice was much weaker than her words; her smile tried to ignore the anguish that caught and twisted her lips, just as she had led him back into their old shared intimacy. He flung himself down beside her couch, and put his forehead against her hand.

'Ah, Sire, do not cry so,' she said, 'or you will make me cry.'

She begged him to say goodbye to her now, and leave her while yet she was conscious. 'You are losing a good friend to you,' she said.

She kissed the Queen goodbye, and Louis went away with her not caring who saw the tears that poured down his face.

La Vallière had arrived with Montespan and he went past them without seeing them. Once La Vallière had seen him cry as he was now doing, when he had quarrelled with her over Madame and her secrets, but then he had been shamefaced of his tears, and hidden himself for a long while that no one should see he had been weeping.

A passionate envy of Madame swept over La Vallière. Was it so sad to die young? For one who had tasted the joys and hopes and fresh beginnings of life, what need was there to wait for the dregs, and find them stale?

'He too is thinking of that first summer,' she said to herself, and knew that it was not of herself that he was thinking.

345

Of that summer with Madame at Fontainbleau – before his life settled down, hardened, grew in time unalterably fixed in the mould that he himself had prepared for it; an iron régime in manners, religion, dress; that habit of obedience in thought as well as deed, which he had planned for others, never thinking that it must inevitably ensnare himself; the slow crystallizing of etiquette into a time-table as terrible as the prison régime of a later day; the rigid shapes of his recognized amours taking precedence of each other according to the formula. Of that summer, before he had condemned himself for ever to love by formula – live by formula – die by formula.

Yes, he too was thinking of that summer, the first of his reign since Mazarin's death, as the ten years following it had been the best and happiest. The reign of Madame was the true age of Louis XIV; but he could not know that; he knew only that something lovely and precious had left his life. 'I shall never care to dance in a ballet again,' he said to himself, and he never did.

His shadow went bobbing and swaying down the wide steps before him, projecting its tiny stripe of blackness into the moon-washed spaces of the night.

Lauzun was at the foot of the steps. He had ridden out from Paris, and his sharp face shone red where the light of the lamps from the royal coach struck on it. Mademoiselle drew near him, but dared not ask if he had looked at the two words on her paper. But she knew that he had done so when he said in a low voice, 'I believe this will put an end to your projects.'

She had no time to answer; she had to follow the Queen into the coach, where she could weep openly for Madame while she cried to herself, 'Why does everything conspire against me, even Madame's tragic fate?' And she, who had all her life set such store by her noble birth, wished with her whole heart that she was the meanest peasant girl, and free of the obligations of her rank.

Monsieur was crying in short uncontrolled bursts of loud sobbing, like a frightened child. Madame had said goodbye to him; she had told him she was very sorry he had been so unhappy. 'But I never wronged you,' she said.

He left the room and looked for his brother; but the King had gone. Gone without bidding him good night. And Louis had stared at him so heavily, cruelly. He flitted uneasily down the stairs, out into the garden, all his gay colours turned grey in the moonlight, the rouge on his face a ghastly shade of dark green. He moved here and there, not daring to return into the house, where lurked the terror of approaching death.

Everywhere in that house unkind, furtive glances pursued him, then turned quickly away; all those hundreds of eyes were watching him with an especial hideous interest to see how he took this and that, until he had become so nervous that he hardly knew what he was saying. Thank Heaven he had burst out crying; a man would hardly cry like that if he had arranged the death of his wife. But then he had kept it up a little after it had really stopped – had anyone noticed that? And he began to cry again from terror and self-pity.

'Why should all this happen to me?' he asked, and felt how cruel it was, since his nerves were not strong enough to bear it. If only it were this time yesterday, if only it were this morning – nothing had happened then.

'Let it not happen now,' he prayed, 'let her live, and I will be kinder to her.'

But it was still himself he was sorry for; she was dying while she was still so young, and people all still thinking her beautiful and charming, and making such an absurd fuss over her.

But he had to live on and catch their ugly glances, and see himself in the glass grow fat and old, and know that next year he would be thirty. The tragedy of his kind bore down on him. One cannot stay young for ever; and for him it was essential to do so. All the perpetually young men about his Court obeyed the law of their nature; for they could not be pretty boys, with high voices lisping childish impertinences, when they were forty, or even thirty.

Let time roll back, stay still, and Madame would not die, nor the world say it was because of his cruelty; and he would not grow old.

So praying, rambling, uncertain and distracted, feeling the night wind on his face, for by now there was a soft wind that tore the clouds into thin strips and sent them scurrying across the sinking moon, he came to the grass path between high hedges of jasmine where he had walked last week, and heard Madame talking and laughing with her three tall Englishmen in her seat at the foot of the cascade.

There she had sat for nearly two hours with Madame de la Fayette only last night. Why did she not sit there now? If time would only roll back, stand still. Once again he peeped through the jasmine hedge. Yes, she sat there, in her favourite seat, her head bent a little sideways, looking up at the staircase of water that climbed above the trees. He drew back, then looked again, but she was still there.

For an instant he let go of his reason; he thought, 'It has all been a dream – she is not dying – no one believes I have poisoned her – I have run out from the palace to escape a nightmare, and all the time she is safe and well.'

He stood between the walls of jasmine, his shadow long and black at his feet, and suddenly, strangely still. The madness that he had been beckoning towards him all this time, playing with it to create an effect, to win pity or fear or at least some sort of notice, was now close within his reach. He had only to accept it, and then everything could be as he wished. Time would have no more hold on him; he would be just nineteen again, and never grow any older; when he looked in the glass he would see the face and figure of Adonis. That was what he truly was, a golden youth belonging to the time when all the world was young; it was only this harsh age, to which he was unfitted, that had made him into a cruel husband, accused of murder. But that too was untrue, for Madame would not die; was not dying; she sat in her favourite seat at the foot of the cascade, and would sit so for ever.

And he approached that thin gap in the hedge to look at her there again, but suddenly drew back and began to tremble; and now his long shadow wavered and moved perkily up and down once again; for Monsieur, instead of encouraging his approaching madness, had at last begun to fight it. The contest gave him agony and terror, drove him back finally to the house from which he had fled. He knew now it was her ghost that sat there; this place was haunted by her, and she would remain always.

As he ran under the small scudding clouds that stretched after him like a pack of pursuing hounds, he felt that that still wraith was more real, more permanent than he; and himself nothing but a hunted spectre, the mere shadow of a creature, that had never succeeded in being a man.

At a side door into the palace he stood still a moment, panting, and stroking down the disorder of his wig and dress.

'I must pull myself together,' he thought, and was only dimly aware that he had already done so, that he had made a choice which involved more effort and courage than any he had yet

348

undertaken. Henceforth he must find his refuge and his *raison d'être* in formula and etiquette. Never again would his emotions shake him beyond the reach of reason. He would settle down, find his place in the world, and keep it.

A grain of shrewd wit that still lived somewhere inside him and occasionally made startling appearances, told him 'And you will be happier next time with a plain wife, who will not cut you out.'

He was going up a back stair that he might not cause fresh surmise by appearing wild and dishevelled among the company. From a passage above, he heard bursts of laughter and shrill childish voices. He entered it, and saw by the light of a hanging oil lamp his daughter and the English Princess Anne trailing up and down with blankets tied round their shoulders and feathers, plucked from their riding-hats, stuck in their hair.

Shocked by this mummery at such a time, he demanded what they were about. Marie Louise told him that they had been woken up by people going past, and it was too hot to go to sleep again, so they had got up and played at being the Red Indians of which she had heard this morning – or was it yesterday?

He said it was disgraceful, heartless, unfeeling, but forgot to say why, before he was carried away by a fresh idea.

'Tomorrow,' he said, 'you shall wear, not blankets, but a mantle of violet velvet that will trail five yards upon the floor, and all the Court will come and kiss your hand and offer you condolences.'

'Will Anne have a violet velvet mantle too?'

'Yes, certainly, as my niece she will have one.'

'And the baby?' asked Marie Louise, giggling pertly, but her father did not notice that, and replied gravely, 'She is not old enough to support it, but all the Court will go and kiss her hand in the cradle.'

'How silly he is,' said Marie Louise as Monsieur went away.

'Shall we really wear violet velvet mantles?' asked her cousin.

'I expect so. It will be very hot. But we can go on pretending we are savage chieftains in blankets on the other side of the world.'

'That will not make them any the less hot,' said the Princess Anne.

Madame de la Fayette had asked Madame if she would not

349

see her little daughter, but she had refused. She would not have the child frightened, made unhappy hereafter by thoughts of her in this state. Nor did her late coldness and bad behaviour now trouble her. Love, like death, was not a matter of these changes and chances – was not of time but of eternity. In years to come, when she had been long dead, perhaps even forgotten, yet she and her daughter might then be closer together than they could be now.

'I would rather she remembered me as I saw her this morning,' she said, and then she wondered if it were now next morning.

'What time is it?' she asked, and they told her midnight was past. It was now the morning of the thirtieth and last day of June.

For over seven hours she had been in continuous torture, and still she was kept from the relief of unconsciousness or even delirium. The doctors had at last begun to contradict all that they had said two hours previously; the cold numbness of her hands and feet were not the ordinary symptoms of colic after all, but of gangrene reaching the heart; there was no hope for her. Another doctor with a new and brilliant reputation had been summoned by the King. He ordered her to be bled in the foot, and she told him that if they wished to do it, it must be done quickly, for her head was growing confused. Yet she never betrayed any sign of confusion, nor even of apprehension, which was largely the reason why the doctors had not believed her to be dying.

But they now said she ought certainly to receive the Sacrament as quickly as possible, and it would be better not to wait for the Bishop of Condom. A Jansenist canon called Feuillet, famous for his severe piety, confessed her, and in accordance with his reputation told her that she had spent her life in selfish and frivolous luxury, had never known God, had been sinning against Him for twenty-six years and only now had begun to do penance in these last six hours. She listened, agreed, accepted. His rough words buffeted her as the doctors had been doing, but she was beyond any sense of personal injustice or injury. She had her business to do, and that was to die as best she could. She managed to make a general confession and then asked to be allowed to receive Jesus Christ. The simple language of her confession surprised the priest. He did not think it that of the ordinary woman of the world, even

350

when on her death-bed. He was still speaking when Ralph Montagu arrived.

Madame turned eagerly towards him. Feuillet did not move away. He stood there, his neck stiffened in offence at the interruption. But Minette did not see him, she was speaking low, in English, of Charles.

'I wish I were not leaving him,' she said, 'that is the only regret I feel. Do not forget to tell him that – I have no regrets except for him, so he must not grieve too much when he hears I am dead.'

She paused from weakness, Montagu thought, but she was overcome by all the things that she must wish to say to Charles – so many things – so short a time in which to say them. For this once more, time had flooded up, hurrying her, worrying her, just as she had begun to sail into eternity. But all that she wished to say to Charles was safe there, and soon he too would know it.

The chief work of her life had been done, only just in time. The treaty – but why was it she had once felt doubtful, apprehensive of that treaty? She tried to collect her thoughts more clearly but the pain seemed to be deadening them, driving them down. She said: 'You remember what we began to talk of two days ago. Tell my brother that I only urged him to this course because I was convinced that it was to his honour and advantage. Tell him that.'

But Charles would know that. What need was there of words? She could say nothing that would lessen his sorrow when she was dead.

'He is losing the person who loves him best in the world,' she said, and then – 'Thank him for all his kindness and care of me.'

'Madame,' said Ralph Montagu, low, 'do you believe that you have been poisoned?'

The word being the same as in French, Feuillet understood it and interrupted them, telling Madame to accuse no one but to offer up her life as a sacrifice to God.

The ambassador stared haughtily at the priest, then turned, and again asked Madame the same question. With the faintest movement she shrank up her shoulders on the pillow; then she whispered to him with an urgency that astonished him in her weak condition, 'If it is true, my brother must never know of it. He must be spared that grief. Above all, do not let him think of revenge on the King here, for he at least is not guilty.

351

If the friendship between them be lost through me, then all that I have lived to do is useless.'

She took a ring from her finger and told him to give it to Charles with those her last and most important words to him.

She then sent messages of love to James; thanked Montagu for the zeal and affection he had shown in her service; told him to ask her maid for the casket containing her brother's letters, and to accept for himself the present of money that Charles had given her for her English journey, which Louis' generosity had made unnecessary. This he refused, but promised to distribute the money among those of her servants whose names she now told him, one by one, without faltering. As he wrote them down he thought of the letter he must write his master on the morrow. 'What can I say? It is the saddest story in the world.'

He retreated to the side of the room, and there saw a young man kneeling in prayer, his face distraught with grief. It was Tréville, and standing by him was Turenne. Looking on both the young soldier and the elderly. Montagu saw that Madame had true friends here. But they could avail her nothing; and she, who also saw their sorrow, could do nothing but bid them goodbye before she drifted away from them.

She was drifting fast; faster at the moment that Feuillet could advance to administer extreme unction; for an instant she lost sight of him and recognition of what he was doing. The room had grown much darker, the further wall was indistinguishable, the succeeding waves of pain were dulled and strangely distant. She saw the corners of the furniture transformed into rocks and castle towers, and somewhere between her and the furthest darkness, where the carefully shaded light glimmered on the polished floor, there now flowed a river of pale and shining water. It was there she had to go. She had always known it; she had forgotten it for many years, but now she knew that the hour had come for her to embark on that wan water, to float on it out through the walls of her room, which had melted away into nothingness, out of the palace, out of France, to an undiscovered country.

The room hushed back, and the faces round her bed, but they had suddenly grown unfamiliar, since among them she could not discern the face of her governess.

She would have cried out, but her lonely fear was answered before it was uttered.

'Hope, Madame, hope, hope!' cried a great and loving voice.

352

Bossuet had entered and flung himself on his knees beside her, placing the crucifix between her hands, holding it there with his warm strong hands round hers. Her face was living once again, lit up with joy as it turned towards him. With all the glory of his vigour and tenderness, he prayed for the soul that was now passing from them. The waves of pain flowed back, engulfed her. He told her to offer them to God, in union with those of Jesus Christ on the cross.

'That is what I am trying to do,' she said faintly.

He withdrew for a few minutes to let her rest, for as the pain dulled again, a drowsiness came over her. But she fought against it, for there was something else she had to do. To one of her maids she whispered in English, to spare his delicacy, 'Give him – Monsieur de Condom – the emerald ring I had made for him – when I am dead.'

A few minutes later she said, 'It is all over. Call back Monsieur de Condom.'

Bossuet came back and saw that her face had changed. He said, 'Madame, you believe in God, you hope in God, you love God?'

'With all my heart,' she said, low but clear; as the crucifix dropped from her hands, they saw that she was dead.

HOUSE OF STUART

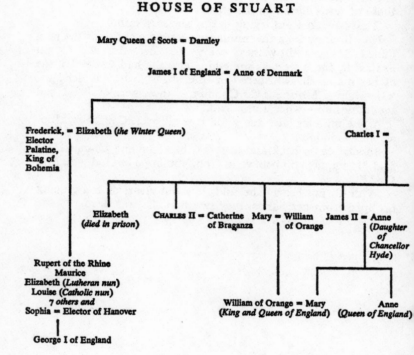

HOUSES OF FRANCE AND SPAIN

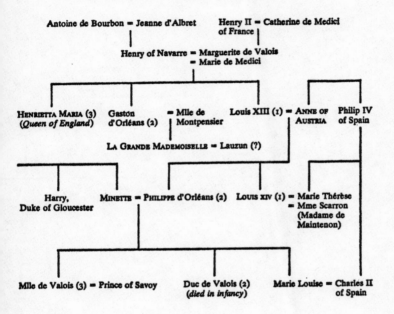